To Margaret "n
Harris, enjoy
journey through the pages
of this novel

Murder Pure and Simple

Wishing you good
reading. best wishes
from the author
CARL T JACKSON

SUNDAY
1st September
2019

Murder Pure and Simple

Carl T. Jackson

Copyright © 2015 Carl T. Jackson

The moral right of the author has been asserted.

Apart from any fair dealing for the purposes of research or private study,
or criticism or review, as permitted under the Copyright, Designs and Patents
Act 1988, this publication may only be reproduced, stored or transmitted, in
any form or by any means, with the prior permission in writing of the
publishers, or in the case of reprographic reproduction in accordance with
the terms of licences issued by the Copyright Licensing Agency. Enquiries
concerning reproduction outside those terms should be sent to the publishers.

This is a work of fiction. Names, characters, businesses, places, events
and incidents are either the products of the author's imagination
or used in a fictitious manner. Any resemblance to actual persons,
living or dead, or actual events is purely coincidental.

Matador
9 Priory Business Park,
Wistow Road, Kibworth Beauchamp,
Leicestershire. LE8 0RX
Tel: 0116 279 2299
Email: books@troubador.co.uk
Web: www.troubador.co.uk/matador
Twitter: @matadorbooks

ISBN 978 1784625 023

British Library Cataloguing in Publication Data.
A catalogue record for this book is available from the British Library.

Printed and bound in the UK by TJ International, Padstow, Cornwall
Typeset in 12pt Garamond by Troubador Publishing Ltd, Leicester, UK

Matador is an imprint of Troubador Publishing Ltd

I dedicate this book to my shipmates, friends and colleagues with whom I served in the Royal Navy and laboured alongside, underground, at Pleasley Colliery and those devoted, often undervalued Nottinghamshire police officers wallowing in life's detritus fighting crime on the all too frequent meanstreets.

The list would not be complete without reference to my wife Margaret, daughter Lynne and son Ivan who have put up with me for so long. Thanks gang. And last but certainly not least I dedicate this novel to those of my friends and colleagues who served with me in one or more of the tough jobs I have mentioned above, and who in naval parlance 'have crossed the bar'. To them when the sun is over the yardarm I raise a tot and toast "Absent Friends". I pray they have all found safe anchorage. CTJ.

PART ONE

Nineteen Forty-Three

ONE

Big John Oakley, still in his pit muck, strode through Langwith colliery yard on his way home. Hanging from a leather strap slung over his broad shoulders a Dudley water bottle and snap tin clattered together. They created a rhythmic metallic beat to be picked up by his heavy segged boots sparking the well trod cobblestones of Pit Lane.

To John it was no different to any other working day except his stride was that much longer, his pace that much faster. Without checking his step he gave a well practised tug on the Albert looped across the front of his waistcoat, flipping the attached time piece from the pocket into a huge hand.

"Half two," he muttered, "Should just about make it. I've made good time sin' checkin' in me lamp."

Reassured, John brushed his heavy moustache with coal begrimed fingers and with a twist of his strong wrist and the dexterity of a music hall conjuror popped the watch back into its pocket. As he headed home John's mind was pre-occupied with thoughts of the task currently concerning him.

"If I finish this bit o' business today it'll mean gerrin' up a bit earlier in mornin's but it'll be worth it int' long run."

Reaching the main street of the village he passed the Co-op general store and picture house. On either side of the road rows of terraced pit houses stood bleak and mean. Over the clinker and ash yards he could see lines of family washing blowing in the

3

breeze. The houses were blackened with years of grime and muck from the colliery and railway. They contrasted with the freshly swilled pavement and still-wet green and white tiles sparkling on the walls of the butcher's shop on the corner of Church Street. A heavy pall of smoke hung above the grey slate roofs. The ever-present filth abused his nostrils and throat with its scraping stench. But like most of the miners and their families he'd got used to it. John acknowledged friends and neighbours hurrying about their business, now and then respectfully touching the peak of the cloth cap set firmly upon his shock of greying hair.

At the railway crossing a sparrow of a man Freddy Price fell into step with him.

"Ayup John. Just finished?"

Without breaking step or looking at his companion John replied, "Yes Freddy, can't stop. I've got a bit of business to attend to."

It didn't have the desired effect. Freddy was still trotting alongside him and asked, "They're at 'ome tomorra then?"

John was comfortable with the question. After all Freddy Price was asking after one of the loves of his life, his football team.

He answered confidently, "They are lad, playing agen' Shirebrook Red Roses, next tut top of Spartan League. We'll have to be on our mettle to beat 'em.

"Are yer lads playing?"

"That they are Freddy. It's an important match. We can't afford to lose this one. We'll need my lads t' gerra result."

"What about Tom? In't he faightin' on Sat'day naight?"

"Our Tom'll be playin' and he'll be at Institute faightin' Bembridge."

"I don't know how he does it John. He must be fit as a fiddle and strong as a bull."

John's huge chest swelled with pride. "Aye our Tom's a good 'un alraight but they're all good lads every one on 'em. An' they're not just brothers you know they're best of pals."

Freddy nodded. "You're raight there John. There's no doubt about that."

The two men reached the bottom of the road.

"I'll bid ya good day John and I'll see thaigh at rec for the match an' I'll be at 'stute for Tom's faight. If I'm there fost I'll save thaigh a seat 'afore I do a bit o' business. I'll be making book. There'll be a few as'll want to wager a couple a bob on Tom and I can't miss out on a chance like this. I've got a living to make same as next man."

"Good day to you Freddy. If I'm there fost I'll keep a seat warm for thaigh. But tha'll get nowt from my pocket I can promise ya. And you'll not find my name in your book."

To the clatter of heavy studded boots the two men went their different ways. John crossed Portland Road, and made his way down the alley between more ugly terraced pit houses squeezed together in crowded rows. As he walked, his mind went back to the time all those years ago when he was courting. He remembered how he'd been called to the pit top estates office to collect the keys for a company house. They didn't become available too often. It was generally dead men's boots. He'd been very lucky, though the previous occupant hadn't. He died with his boots on and the place was left vacant. It was mucky and wanted some fettling. But after plenty of elbow grease, carbolic soap and lashings of whitewash they'd made it decent. He wed within the month. It was their first and only house and where their five children had been born and raised.

With a smug sense of satisfaction he said to himself, "Aye and under this roof Polly and me have made it into a happy family home all these years. We've got a lot to be thankful for."

As he neared his house he could see the green painted wood and glass porch standing out from the back door setting it off from the rest of the row. He'd built it some years ago with the help of his oldest boy Jack. Polly liked to sit there in her chair and watch the world go by and see the flowers and look across the fields to Scarcliffe woods in the distance. John stopped outside the porch taking in his wife's view across the fields. He could see the distant hazy blue horizon and the rambling rose scrambling over the trellis around the door. It had a delicate scent but though it tried hard it struggled to compete with the smoke and fumes from the pit. Even then he thought it still looked beautiful. The lace curtains in the windows were down to Edith, the woman's touch. She always liked things to look nice.

From the back door John cast a contented eye over the seasonal vegetables and flowers growing in the long back garden. The plot sloped down to the red brick coal house and privy that backed onto the ash lane. It led to his smallholding, stable and allotment. He kept his pigs and rabbits there and grew more garden produce. John loved his garden. Along with the family and football team it was his passion, and during these uncertain times it helped keep his family's bellies filled.

The porch door was open and he took off his cap as he went in. Sitting down on the wooden stool just inside John undid the laces of his heavy pit boots and pulled them off. Reaching over he removed a dead flower from the large plant growing in the fancy copper jardinière. At that moment a feeling of sadness drifted over him and Polly again came into his mind. He looked at the beautiful red and yellow blooms thrusting out from beneath their large green leaves. Admiring their colour, strength and vigorous vitality he recalled how Polly had been like them afore she took ill, a beautiful flower to be nurtured and cared for.

John put on a pair of worn carpet slippers retrieved from beneath the stool. Pulling the shoulder strap over his head, he tossed the Dudley and snap tin into a corner producing a clattering finale. They would be seen to later. This afternoon he had business to attend to.

"Is that you Dad?"

John brushed aside his gloomy thoughts and smiled at the young woman standing at the living room door wiping her hands on a neat pinafore. He took in the bobbed auburn hair, ruddy complexion and erect stance of his daughter. She was an Oakley alright. She even wore wire-rimmed glasses like her Mam.

"Don't leave your boots where somebody'll fall over 'em. Put 'em in the corner."

Patriarch John did as he was told without argument and said, "Alraight Edith I'll bring the bath. You can fill it for me, I've got a bit o' business tonaight."

Going outside into the small yard adjacent to the porch, John removed the galvanised tin bath from its hook on the wall. On his way through the living room to the scullery he glanced at the empty rocking chair standing next to the open coal fire. Reflected flames flickered and danced in the polished surfaces of the black leaded fireplace.

"Is your Mam upstairs?" he called to his daughter.

"Yes Dad. She was feeling poorly. All aches and pains and a nasty headache. I've put her to bed with a hot shelf out the oven. She was asleep when I last looked. Don't go and disturb her now, the rest'll do her good."

7

John nodded and said forlornly, "Your Mam's been badly now for nigh on three year and there don't seem an end to it. Doctors don't seem to know what's up wi' her. They gi' her pills and take me money but she gets no better. She's still an invalid."

Concerned, Edith hugged him and said, "Don't upset yourself Dad. She'll get better one day. You see. The Lord'll watch over her."

"You're raight lass," John said with conviction in his voice. "If He can't help nobody can. I'll keep sayin' prayers for my Polly and rely on the Lord's good grace."

Big John set the tin bath down on the stone scullery floor. Edith continued kneading bread dough in the large earthenware panchion settled on the scrubbed wooden kitchen table.

John said, "Fill me bath lass and I'll get me Sunday suit and leather shoes out."

As she continued to work the dough Edith cocked her head to one side and in an exaggerated questioning voice she enquired, "Your Sunday suit and shoes? Where are you off to then John Oakley?"

Tapping the side of his nose with a coal blackened finger he smiled and said, "Them as asks no questions gets told no lies. But the sooner you draw my bath me gel the sooner I can get about my business and the sooner you'll know the answer to your question."

Edith grinned. She wiped the flour from her arms with her pinafore, picked up the panchion of dough and carried it through to the living room. She placed the large mixing bowl on the pegged rug in front of the fire before covering it over with a piece of muslin.

She said, "I'll leave it there to rise Dad."

John nodded. "You're a good girl Edith. I don't know

what we'd do wi' out ya'." He kissed her gently on the top of her head.

"You soppy ha'porth Dad. Mind you don't get any of that pit muck on my hair."

She brushed a hand over the top of her head before turning to ladle hot water from the fireplace boiler into a bucket.

Big John stopped her. "Nay lass thaigh's done enough a'ready I'll see ta that."

He took the ladle from her and continued to fill the bucket which he carried back into the scullery and poured into the tin bath.

Edith returned to her baking. "Dad's up to something," she muttered.

TWO

The half-yearly visit of the Divisional Inspector was underway at Langwith rural police station. Sergeant Jack Smithurst and his Constables Rod Jarvis and Charlie Underwood had been hard at it to ensure all was spick and span. Jack smiled inwardly, knowing that, much to the Inspecting Officer's disappointment, his white gloved hand had not found one speck of dust to gloat over. Moreover, all the official books, ledgers, accounts and files were up to date. So there he and his constables stood in their best number one uniforms. All creases and bulled-up boots, under the scrutiny of their superior officer. Jack didn't like parading in his own cubbyhole of an office. Not enough room to swing the proverbial cat. He felt ill at ease. Always did on these occasions. This was his patch, his domain, not the narrow-shouldered, weasel-faced Inspector's seated before him. He'd seen it all before from these Headquarters heroes. Still he didn't like to see whoever it was sitting in his chair, at his desk, on his cushion, made for him by his dear wife, without even a "by your leave."

Jack thought on. "What ever the outcome it's not going to alter the way I run my section. I'll have to put up with him for a while longer. Just let him have his say. Make him feel important for a few minutes. He'll soon be on his way back to the ivory tower and the waitress service at Headquarters. China tea cups, saucers and digestive biscuits."

After brushing his neatly trimmed dark moustache with the side of a finger the Inspector spoke.

"His Lordship is very concerned about the increase in night poaching on the Wembourne estate."

Peering over his gold pince-nez, he observed the officers' reactions. Satisfied he had driven his point home the Inspector continued, "Private shooting parties, guests of his Lordship, provide additional revenue to the estate. Help maintain it and keep staff in employment. Poachers, especially the Durnley gang, blight that scenario. They steal and kill, yes gentlemen, steal and kill game reared and nurtured for the shoot at great expense to his Lordship. And they are not averse to using excessive violence to prevent their arrest. It is therefore up to us to apprehend these thieves and put an end to their activities."

At this point the Senior Officer removed his glasses, making great play of cleaning them with a snow white handkerchief removed with a flourish from an inside tunic pocket. Satisfied, he settled the gold-rimmed spectacles upon his aquiline nose before haughtily re-addressing his subordinates.

"Pompous Headquarters stuffed shirt," thought Jack.

The pompous one droned on. "To continue, gentlemen, I expect increased night patrols in the locations infested by these parasites that locals see as romantic figures. A legacy of their feudal past; the weak and poor against the strong, wicked, landowners." Again, he stopped for effect.

Sergeant Jack shuffled uneasily and glanced down at the threadbare carpet before touching his forehead respectfully with an extended forefinger.

He said, "With respect Sir, all poachers aren't parasites. As a lad I was handy with a net and ferret and I know Bade Durnley and his pals well."

The District Inspector glared at Sergeant Smithurst.

Jack returned his leader's scathing look. He knew that the Senior Officer was all bluff and bluster and was seen by the rural officers as a "Townie" who spent his time at Headquarters and didn't know tripe about country matters.

Sergeant Jack got his word in before the Inspector had recovered his composure. "Rudyard Kipling doesn't agree either Sir."

"Kipling Sergeant, what an earth has Kipling to do with poaching on the Wembourne estate?"

Sergeant Jack was not about to lose the initiative.

He said, "Begging your pardon Sir and with apologies to Mister Kipling, if you'll permit me." With thumbs hooked into his tunic breast pockets he broke into verse, 'They'll drink every hour of the daylight and poach every hour of the dark. It's the sport, not the rabbits they're after, and we've plenty of game in the park. Don't hang them or cut off their fingers. That's wasteful as well as unkind. For a hard-bitten South country-poacher makes the best man-at-arms you can find."

After the delivery, the officer thrust his left foot forward crashing it onto the carpet, giving added effect to the eloquent oration.

The Constables looked first at one another then at the great orator and finally the Inspector who sat open mouthed with pince-nez in hand. Quickly regaining his composure he responded.

"We are not here to discuss sport or the quantities of game on his Lordship's property, or whether poachers should be treated leniently as reward for taking up arms. We are here, Sergeant Smithurst, I remind you, to decide on a plan of action to trap these thieves. I will overlook your inane ramblings on this occasion but do not let it happen again."

Jack was not about to let go. "Begging your pardon Sir, Kipling was explaining, in his poem 'The Norman and the Saxon' that English poachers are the salt of the earth. When the call came they rallied to the defence of England against the invader and oppressor. That's all I was saying Sir."

Constables Rod Jarvis and Charlie Underwood showed their appreciation of the Sergeant's performance, breaking into a spontaneous bout of enthusiastic clapping. The Inspector's glare cut them short.

"Quite so Jack, quite so. You make your point well with your surprising literary knowledge. We'll leave it at that, but remember, Mr. Kipling spent a great deal of his time in India and other distant parts of the Empire. He didn't have to wrestle with the problems of real poachers at Langwith. You and your Constables do. I expect to be reporting to his Lordship at the next Hunt Ball that we are on course to resolve the problem of, er, the local salts of the earth. Alright? Thank you for your attendance. Dismiss."

The three officers came to attention, turned right and smartly left the room before returning to their constabulary duties.

*

Edith glanced at the pendulum wall clock. Her Dad was later than she had anticipated and there were still tasks to be completed. So tonight she would take it upon herself to do the job he did every evening without fail.

Tucking the blanket around her mother, sitting quietly in the chair by the fire, she said, "I'm just going to make sure the pigs are settled in for the night and everything is locked up. Rita won't be long, she'll be home from work soon. You'll be alright won't you?"

Polly gripped her daughter's strong young hand. In that reedy, singsong voice that had developed since her illness, she pleaded, "Don't be too long then love. It's not like Dad to be gone all this time. I hope he's alright, he didn't say where he was going did he?"

"No Mam, it's just a bit of business, he shouldn't be long."

A final adjustment to the blanket and Edith left, closing the door behind her. Buttoning up her cardigan, she hurried down the long garden path passing the outside lavatory and coalhouse. Opening the back gate, she stepped out onto the ash lane. No one was about. An eerie silence settled over that narrow alleyway. It was here, in the darkness, the night soil men collected waste from the lavatories. Through small cast iron doors in the rear wall of each lavatory block the stinking cargo was loaded into special carts, drawn by large black horses. Edith shivered and looked nervously over her shoulder. Stories told by her mother dashed about in her head. She remembered tales of the fearful shadowy 'ten o'clock hosses' that spirited naughty children away. To disappear forever amidst the muck and mire in the creaking, groaning carts. It was getting darker. Edith was uneasy and again looked over her shoulder. She quickened her step. As a distraction from fearful black horses, she thought on other things.

"I wonder where our Rita is. She knows how Dad is about us girls being out late. And our Tom's as bad."

She knew their big brother would hear nothing said about them. Not that it was, mind. And at the pit canteen where Rita worked, she was adored. With hands on hips, and a defiant toss of that raven black hair, Rita seemed like an exotic Spanish gypsy, a good looker all right thought Edith. For a brief moment, she felt envious. She was the plain Jane of the two, no glamour, just a skivvy. The young woman spoke aloud as she neared the door set in the wall leading to the smallholding.

"Yes that's me, just a skivvy. Like Cinderella, except I don't get to the ball and I haven't met a handsome prince or even a good-looking frog."

Edith stopped suddenly. She could see that the door in the perimeter wall of the smallholding was ajar. Nervously, she slowly pushed it open praying that it would squeak loudly and scare off anyone on the plot. However, all she heard as she entered were pigs and chickens. That was normal. Except for sounds coming from the stable. It sounded like a pig.

She thought, "Oh! Just my luck. I hope a porker hasn't got out and gone into the stable. I'll never get it back on my own."

So as not to disturb the rogue animal she could hear grunting and squealing she tiptoed to the stable door. The noises were louder now. She strained to listen.

"That doesn't sound like our pigs," she muttered.

Bobbing down the young woman peered through the gap between door and jamb. She was alarmed at what she saw. With eyes widened and glasses nearly falling from her nose, she forced a hand across her mouth to prevent any sound from revealing her presence. It wasn't pigs. Though there was grunting and squealing a-plenty. The naked, muscular buttocks of the man standing there thrust backwards and forwards with an easy sensual rhythm. The long shapely legs in stockings and suspenders held him close, drawing his moving body into the figure lying on the bales of hay. It was from here that the grunts and moans emanated. Edith watched, spellbound. She had never witnessed such a thing before. Never having kissed a boy and never having seen the sexual act performed Edith was strangely excited. The blood rose to her cheeks, her whole body shook. She touched herself as she watched, unashamedly enjoying the closeness of the two engrossed in their sexual activity. Suddenly the woman on the hay raised her head, arching her body in what seemed a final surrender to pleasure. The raven black tresses fell across her shoulders as she gave a last uncontrollable sigh. Edith gasped. It was Rita. Recognition caused her to press both hands over her mouth to prevent a cry bursting out.

Forcing herself away from the stable door, she dashed back to the lane and raced down the ash path. She stopped, breathless, at her own garden gate and struggled with her confused thoughts before going into the house.

John arrived home later, a pleased look upon his rugged face. He twisted his moustache with both hands and looked at Edith. Though he detected something not quite right with her he was eager to tell about his business.

Speaking quietly he said to his daughter, "Is your Mam in bed?"

Edith nodded.

"Where's our Rita?" he asked.

Before Edith could answer, the door opened. Rita flounced in.

"Just been to the lav, Dad. Are you alright?"

She went over to her father and planted a kiss on his cheek. Edith stared in disbelief at her sister's outrageous performance.

Still speaking in an excited whisper, John said, "I don't want your Mam to hear." He paused to listen for any movement upstairs. All seemed well. He continued, "I've finished my bit of business. Got a good bargain. A bit of haggling but we finally spit on it and shook hands. It's a beauty. I think everybody'll like it."

Rita, ever the one to drive the conversation, asked inquisitively, "What is it then Dad? Where've you put it, what ever it is?"

She giggled and looked at her sister. There was no response. Edith just stared at her. Rita shrugged and returned to her father.

"Well Dad?"

"Keep it down, I don't want it broadcasting all over the village. They'll know soon enough."

"Come on then Dad tell us about it," pleaded Rita.

With all the enthusiasm of an excited schoolboy the big man sat down. Leaning forward with hands on knees he confided to his daughters, "A pony and trap. I've bought us a pony and trap."

John sat back. He awaited the response. A smug look lit up his face.

"Oh Dad that's lovely. Mam'll be able to get out a bit now. It'll do her a world of good." Rita went to her father, threw her arms about his neck and planted a sloppy kiss on his forehead.

Edith's response was different, if not unexpected.

"A pony Dad? Who's going to look after it? It'll need a lot of looking after. Grooming, exercising, mucking out, then there's shoeing and feed and Vet's bills."

"Don't you worry lass. I'll be up extra early to see to it. Everybody will have to take their turn. It's for your mother after all."

Rita spun round, skirt swirling, showing her shapely legs. She was excited.

"And for us Dad," she insisted. "We can ride in it as well.

Just imagine what the neighbours will say. I can sit there in my best frock, with long lace gloves and a parasol. A real lady. All the girls in the village will be jealous, won't they Edith?"

Edith retorted, "Will we see you up at the stables then, mucking out?" She watched her sister for a response.

"I don't mind going to the stables." She spun round again. "It might be very good fun." She laughed and struck her gypsy pose, hands on hips.

"Come on girls, don't fall out about it," John implored.

As he spoke, his three sons tumbled in through the back door. Their usual boisterous good-humoured banter stopped abruptly as Tom called out, "Ayup Dad. You're looking all posh, dressed up tut nines in your Sunday suit and tie."

Throwing his sports bag onto the floor drew an instant rebuke from Edith.

"You can pick that up our Tom and take it to the outhouse. I'm not here slaving away, keeping the house spick and span for you to muck up with your sweaty boxing kit."

Tom smiled at his sister. Brushing back his auburn hair with a strong hand, he went to her, picked her up like a rag doll and threw her into the air. She screamed, more in surprise than fear. As he caught her, Tom planted a kiss on her cheek. Edith beat a tattoo upon his solid chest as he held her around her slender waist.

"If I take my kit down outhouse, it'll mean more work for you sis. You'll have to bring it all back tut scullery to boil int' copper."

"Oh! Alright – you always win in the end our Tom."

"I hope he does tomorrow. Seaman Bembridge is a tough faighter," declared Ted.

"Oh you're a misery our Ted," Rita scolded. "You know he never loses."

She spoke with some authority, having seen all her brother's fights, every one a victory. The live wire added, "You can beat Bembridge tomorrow for the pony and trap."

"Pony and trap? What's beating Bembridge got to do wi' a pony and trap?"

It was clear Tom had no idea what Rita was talking about.

"Trust you and your big mouth to blab out the surprise before Dad. You're so selfish at times. I don't know whether you do it on purpose or not." The glare Edith gave her sister rivalled the Medusa.

With another quick spin and a toss of those raven locks, Rita laughed.

"It was because I was feeling so happy about everything. The surprise, our Tom's fight, just everything. It just slipped out."

Edith muttered, "Mmm. That's not my recollection."

"Nothin' to worry about Rita," soothed John. "It don't matter who tells who. It's a family surprise."

"What is?" asked the dour Jack.

"I've bought a pony and trap for your Mam, a Hackney with a lovely high stepping trot. It's a good English breed used to pulling light traps."

"What sort of trap is it Dad?" asked the stocky, auburn -haired Ted.

"It's a beauty lad. Coachbuilt, two wheeler, carry two comfortable, four at a push. Finished in high polished green with gold inlays. Your Mam'll be proud as a Queen when we're out in it."

Rita, still in a state of excitement, asked, "Can we see it Dad?"

"It's too late now Rita. The pony'll be well set fort' naight. He'll be feeling a little strange in our stable so we won't disturb him. See him tomorrow. You can feed him his breakfast before you gu to work."A mischievous glint twinkled in John's eye.

"Oh, I suppose I can wait till I get home. He's not going to run away."

"I thought the idea of getting up early and work wouldn't go down too well with you my lady."

"Oh fiddlesticks to you Edith." Behind a hand she stuck out her tongue to her sister and added, "I'm going upstairs."

After all the excitement of the day, the Oakley household returned to some semblance of normality. With the rest of his family abed, John sat quietly in his high-backed wooden chair, pondered on his good fortune as a father and husband and prayed silently for the return of Polly's health and success for Tom in his pending fight.

THREE

From the servery of the Langwith colliery canteen Rita Oakley watched Calver Wilson come into the dining room. Miners off night shift were gathering for a welcome breakfast and a smoke. From beneath the peak of a battered ratting cap Wilson's restless eyes scanned the room. He was wearing a heavy overcoat that had seen better days, and fingered the neckerchief knotted about his throat. The newcomer scuffed his muddied boots onto the back of the knee-length gaiters he wore over brown corduroy trousers. Rita guessed by the state of him that he'd been out all night. His clothing was mud-stained and unkempt but she knew it wasn't from working down the pit. A sneer distorted his thin lips. With an air of menace the man slowly and deliberately intertwined his strong fingers and cracked his knuckles. The sickening sound reverberated through the room like a pistol shot. His wild eyes took in the miners' mixed reaction to the demonstration as he sauntered up to the counter where Rita Oakley was serving. She continued to watch as he walked, slowly swinging his shoulders in an exaggerated swagger. He openly displayed his arrogance as comfortably as the well worn heavy over-jacket he sported. But she could see he remained focussed and alert. At the counter he removed his cap, shoving it deep into an overcoat pocket.

One or two of the younger men off the night shift

gave a cursory nod in response to his glance but the majority of miners ignored him. At least they avoided his eyes showing more interest in their breakfast than the likes of him. He ran dirty fingers through his tangle of dark hair and grinned mischievously at Rita. Even in her uniform, apron and cap she looked a stunner.

"Ayup Reet. I'll 'ay egg, bacon, black puddin' and chips an' a big mug a tea. Three sugar me duck. I've had a long naight an' am half starved, so don't be stingy wit' chips."

Rita fluttered her eyelashes and said provocatively, loud enough for all in the canteen to hear, "When have I ever been stingy with anything Cal Wilson?"

The suggestive comment caused Wilson to momentarily lose his composure and shuffle his feet uneasily. He looked around the canteen taking in the knowing grins and sly nudges.

Instinctively he attacked. His words rattled out like a machine gun.

"Any body who 'as owt ta say come and say it to me. Don't sit there sniggerin'. Be a man and come over 'ere'. Look me in eyes. Tell me to me face. Then I'll gi' 'im a beltin'."

No one took up his challenge. Wilson hadn't expected them to. He stood with arms folded; his thin lips curled in a sneer, untouchable. They all knew he was part of Bade Durnley's gang and the dark lanes and gas lit streets of Langwith weren't safe places to be if you were on their hit list.

Durnley's lieutenant turned his back contemptuously on the silent miners.

He was faced across the serving counter by Rita, her dark eyes blazing.

"You can get outside if you're going to start throwing

your weight about Cal Wilson. Anyhow you're not entitled to eat here. You don't work at this pit." She added sarcastically, "In fact you don't work anywhere, you're just a waster like that lot you knock around with."

The youth towered above her as he stretched to his full height, grinned and held up his hands in mock surrender.

"Okay Reet you win. I know when I'm beat." But as a warning to all present he added, "It's a good job I think so much on yer lass else you'd have had a good beltin' for openin' yer mouth like that."

It was a determined woman that came from behind the counter to stand face to face with Wilson.

With hands on her hips she declared, "Neither you nor any other man will give me a belting. Unless I want him to. Because we've walked out a couple of times doesn't make me your property. Just bear that in mind."

She turned away and with head held high, heels clacking upon the tiled floor, strutted back behind the counter. Wilson watched her go with more than a hint of admiration. He could almost hear the castanets and the gypsy violins.

"You'll not begrudge me a mug a tea then will ya Reet?"

"That's all you're going to get from me Mister Wilson."

She poured him a large mug of tea before getting on with her work. He threw down a few coppers in payment before sprawling out his rangy frame in a chair at an empty table nearby.

*

Outside, Constable Rod Jarvis leaned his bicycle against the wall. He often called at the canteen – it was on his beat and a regular tea stop. It gave him the opportunity to keep an

23

eye on things, let the locals know the law was on the job. Making sure the machine was secure he made his way into the canteen. On entering his eyes immediately set upon the sprawled-out figure of Wilson. He appeared to be dozing at a table next to the servery. From the state of the man's clothing and boots Constable Jarvis suspected that he had been out all night with his gun and dogs. From experience he knew that it was pointless at this time boning Wilson about his suspicions. The firearm would be well stashed with the night's booty and the dogs kennelled with any of a dozen fellow gang members. For the moment he satisfied himself with the knowledge that he had come across the poacher at this early hour of the morning in the pit canteen and had noted the condition he was in. He would enter details in his note book and the station intelligence register. It may prove of value later.

The sight of Constable Jarvis walking into her canteen brought about a flurry of activity from Rita. Shaking back those dark tresses the manageress performed a quick shimmy, hands smoothing down her smart uniform, accentuating a shapely figure. The policeman walked slowly and deliberately to the serving point acknowledging miners as they looked up from their meal to greet him.

"Good morning Mister Jarvis. Is there something you particularly like that I can serve up for your breakfast?"

The officer never had the opportunity to reply. Rita's *double entendre* struck home but not at its intended target.

Wilson sat bolt upright in his chair. Though appearing to sleep he had observed Constable Jarvis walk in and heard the comment from Rita. Now, with narrowed eyes and taut jaw he glowered at her and then Jarvis.

The policeman could see that Wilson was burning a

short fuse. Rita had made him look a fool. He wouldn't like that. Better be prepared for trouble.

Wilson stood up quickly knocking over his chair and sending it clattering to the floor. Constable Jarvis braced himself.

The angry poacher turned to the men in the canteen who were watching the action expectantly. He wagged a finger toward them and sneered, "There's not a man good enough among the lot on yer. None on yers got the balls."

Point made he headed for the door. As he strode past PC Jarvis he growled, "An' that gus for you an all copper."

Undeterred, PC Jarvis ordered, "Before you go Wilson pick up the chair. I'm sure you wouldn't want to offend Miss Oakley now would you?"

The poacher hesitated. The officer looked him in the eyes. He could see the hatred blazing there. Wilson glanced over to where Rita stood arms folded, eyes glowering, lips a thin harsh line. He snatched up the chair and set it straight before heading for the door.

Rod Jarvis called to him, "About the balls mister. I'll no doubt come across you again and then we'll see if you've got any."

The impish grin from Rita said it all as she watched her young suitor stride out of the building and slam the door behind him.

"Oh men! They're so predictable."

"Was that your intention Rita, to upset the lad?"

"Mister Jarvis, I'm not that sort of girl. These local boys take things too seriously. I'm not a one-man woman and I don't intend to be shacked up with a poacher or a collier for the rest of my life." She gave the officer a hard stare and said suggestively, "I'm sure you realise that I'm not like the rest of the girls in the village."

25

The officer looked at the attractive woman before him and nodded.

"You're certainly different Rita; you can fetch the birds down off the trees but don't go playing with men's emotions and making enemies. The consequences can be dire."

As she poured the Constable his regular mug of tea Rita whispered, "For them Mister Jarvis, not me."

Slender fingers brushed against his hand.

FOUR

Having spoken to the groundsman preparing the football pitch at the local stadium John Oakley was satisfied it would be in good order for the Spartan League game between his team, Langwith Imperials, and Shirebrook Red Roses. Next stop the Miners' Institute, where a noisy crowd was already gathering. The local Derby between Langwith and Shirebrook always attracted a large crowd.

Today John found himself involved in discussions not only about the game but also the evening fight between the tough battler Seaman Bembridge and his son Tom.

Freddy Price was already making book and came over to John.

"There's one or two here John lad. A lot of brass is flyin' about. Ridgeway's takin' lion's share but I don't mind I'm happy with me lot."

"How's it lookin' then Freddy?" John asked.

After quickly consulting his book he replied, "Odds is in favour of Imps John and there's a lotta money being laid on your Tom. A lotta money. If I'm not careful I'll end up wi' no roof over me head and int' workhouse." The little man chuckled. John smiled.

Freddy asked, "Are thaigh aying a bet then John? Could make a bob or two ya know."

"No thanks Freddy, you know me. I've signed pledge like

you have but I keep Covenant I've made wit' Lord. But that's your business between you and Him."

"I'll have to face that problem when time comes John but I don't think Lord will look too unkind on me. I alus put a goodly sum ont' plate on a Sunday and say me prayers regular."

"I'm prayin' that my lad'll come out on top with none too many problems Freddy. But whoever wins tonaight they're both warriors. That ring is loneliest place in world. It takes a special kind of man to slip between them ropes and battle toe to toe wi' an able opponent. Wi' nowt but a big heart and two fists."

"Aye ya raight there John. Sooner them than me. Any road I'm off ta make a few more bob to gi' a special plate on Sunday. An' I know you're worried about your lad but remember he's won all his faights and not got a mark to show for it. He's the best round 'ere by a long chalk. I'll see thee later."

John took some comfort from Freddy Price's well-intended words and pondered over them. Catching sight of his eldest boy Jack across the room he beckoned him over.

"Ayup Dad. Looks like bein' a good turn out at match and for our Tom tonaight." He put his strong young arm about his father's shoulders. "I know you frown on it but I've done a double wi' Freddy and all bein' well I might make enough to buy in some better stock to improve me pigeons."

"Aye lad there's goin' to be some as go home happy and some as won't. I hope as we go home happy. And as for layin' a wager son that's your choice. You've sweated and grafted for your money down pit and you use it as you will.

It's yourn to do as ya please. I'll none criticise thaigh. You're a good lad to me and your mam same as your brothers and sisters and I love all on ya."

Jack responded with genuine affection. "Thanks Dad. We all feel the same. And me and our Ted'll be in Tom's corner tonaight like allus. We've made sure he's up to scratch with his training and prep so you've no need to worry. I'll see tha later wi' me winnings."

As he watched his first born walk away John's thoughts turned to Tom. He hadn't wanted him to become apprenticed to the Kelly brothers. True, they were known to be first class tradesmen in the building game but they were hard drinkers and bar room brawlers. Not what he wanted for his son. But on reflection it was better than a life "down't pit", and apart from his boxing he was now a time-served plasterer. In the building trade he was seen as their man, their own Jack Dempsey. Tom fought from a crouch like the former world champion "The Manassa Mauler" and like Dempsey would fight anyone put before him. And that wasn't always in the ring. He'd talked to his son about that and Tom had promised not to get involved in unpaid fights. But he worried that every local street fighter and bar room brawler wanted a piece of Tommy Oakley, wanted their share of his glory. So far he had come through his encounters unscathed and no amount of talking would make Tom run away from a fight. He was an Oakley.

Across the room John could see Tom's manager, the bookie, Albert Ridgeway. He didn't like the man. With black trilby and long black overcoat hanging from his tall scrawny frame he reminded him of a vulture. He was making book, stuffing money from eager punters into his satchel. Tom trained at Ridgeway's gym in Mansfield. John wasn't happy about that. He knew Ridgeway had a murky past and moved in shadowy circles. He only invested in his boy because he was a good earner. Tom was popular with the fight fans but there were the others, including the poacher Durnley and his gang.

"Talk of the devil," muttered John as Bade Durnley joined Ridgeway.

They were talking behind their hands, making sure nobody could hear. Just like conspirators thought John.

His lad hadn't yet won a title but he'd won an enviable fighting reputation. He was recognised wherever he went and John knew he enjoyed his popularity. Even though it was his boy he had to admit that sat astride his Norton motorcycle he was a dashing figure. With auburn hair that gleamed like gold in the sunlight, his beaming smile and Clarke Gable style moustache he turned many female heads and hearts. Tom didn't court popularity or success. He didn't have to. Simply being Our Tom drew them to him. That worried Big John.

*

Up at the football ground John joined the rest of the spectators in a hearty cheer as the referee started the game with a blast on his whistle. Within a few minutes it was working overtime. Short, sharp at first then more frantic and prolonged as players in the heat of battle ignored the referee's signal. At his usual spot at the front of the stand John took it all in. His large face beamed as the crunching tackles went in from the warriors on both sides. He looked for Freddy Price who had been seated alongside him but the little man was mingling with the crowd taking bets on the outcome of the game. The tackles were still going in hard. If Leonidas the Spartan had been watching he would have cringed as studs crunched against flesh and bone. Ted Oakley on a breakaway run down the centre was upended by the opposing right back.

John bellowed to the referee, "Did ya see that ref? Shocking tackle. Should'a' been sent off. Get a grip on things else you'll lose control. Show 'em who's gaffer. Play up the Imps."

But Big John's outburst wasn't intended to be personal. He knew that the man in the middle was a tough referee, a man who wouldn't stand too much nonsense, who could dish it out as well as take it. The village bobby, Police Constable Rodney Jarvis, was well tried and tested as a former soldier and active sportsman. He had earned the respect of John and his family since he'd been posted to the village and he was up to the job, on or off the pitch. But today John wore a different hat and Rod Jarvis was simply a target for him on which to vent his spleen, especially if things went against his team.

He yelled, "Play up the Imps."

*

It was also a special day for the women folk. In the kitchen of the freshly painted pavilion, spirits were high as they chatted and gossiped. Edith and Rita were supporting their Dad's team. Edith adjusted the large stainless steel tea urn standing on the kitchen draining board then cast an expert eye over the spread of sandwiches and homemade cakes. They made a fine display arrayed upon a collection of miscellaneous plates and dishes, set out on a trestle table covered by a spotless white tablecloth.

With arms folded she said, "That's a lovely do so far. It won't be bettered."

Edith bent to the task in hand, prim and proper in her blue print frock and smart white apron with the small daisy motif. Her headscarf tied turban-like, neat and tight, hid her bobbed auburn hair. Holding the freshly baked bread to her chest she quickly sawed off thick slices. Rita casually buttered them as they fell into the wicker breadbasket standing on the trestle table.

"Come on Rita you're getting behind, you'll have to move faster than that."

Rita gave her sister a "so what?" look and deliberately reduced her already slow rate of production.

Tossing back her shock of black curls she retorted, "I didn't come here to work my fingers to the bone. I came to see the match."

"Work your fingers to the bone? You're only buttering bread, that's not hard work. I don't know what you do in that pit canteen but it can't be very much."

Rita snapped back, "For your information Miss prim and proper I'm the supervisor. I tell the others what to do. When you've got dogs you don't bark yourself."

Edith stopped half-way through cutting, peering at her sister over the top of her metal-rimmed glasses.

"Mighten you do sister but you should be thinking about working not barking. Work's there to be done and it's for us to do it and everybody has to do their fair share."

Rita was not amused.

She retorted, "I do my share. But I'm not going to be a misery and end up an old maid like you. I'm going to enjoy myself while I'm young and find myself a rich young fella to look after me. So there."

With arms folded across her breasts she challenged her sister defiantly.

Edith did not take up the challenge but busied herself cutting the bread. She had said what she had wanted to say and though her sister's peevish response had upset her she didn't dwell upon it too much.

Three sharp blasts of a whistle signalled half time and the end of the sisters' fiery exchange.

A lusty cheer followed by an array of chants and confrontational banter indicated that the crowd were enjoying the intense rivalry of the occasion. Constable Jarvis clattered into the pavilion kitchen.

"Hello Edith, hello Rita, do you mind if I get a drink and a quick rinse before I restart the game?"

"No Mister Jarvis by all means help yourself. There's soap on the draining board and a towel on the nail in the corner."

"Thanks Edith I'll try not to get in your way. You look very busy."

"Would you like a cup of tea Mister Jarvis?"

Even such a simple question from Rita sounded like a siren's call.

PC Jarvis stuttered, "Er, thank you Rita. That would do nicely."

The way Rita cast her eyes appreciatively over the police officer didn't go unnoticed by Edith. But she had to admit to herself that he was a fine figure of a man what with those broad shoulders, narrow waist and sturdy legs. He looked as masculine in referee's kit as he did in uniform. Rita gave a sigh before pouring a large mug of hot tea.

As she handed it to the constable, she said to her sister, "Have you brought your camera?"

Without looking up from her work Edith answered curtly, "You know very well I have. You told me to bring it."

Ignoring the tone of her sister's response, in her coquettish way Rita hooked arms with Constable Jarvis, pulling the surprised officer to her, almost upsetting his mug of tea.

The siren took it from him and said, "We'll put that out of the way and have our photo taken."

Edith put down the bread knife and half cut loaf. Fumbling in her shopping bag beneath the table she took out the little box Brownie. It was her pride and joy. Though she appeared reluctant she really delighted in displaying her skill at photography. It was one thing she had over Rita.

Through the small aperture on top she could see her subjects. She took charge.

"Mister Jarvis move a little closer. You as well Rita. That's it. A big smile. Cheeese."

The little box camera clicked and rattled. Edith wound on the film.

Rita hung onto the constable's arm, turned to him and said, "Thank you Mister Jarvis; I'll have something to remember you by now." She planted a wet kiss on his cheek.

"Hello Rod – thought I'd find you here."

Edith watched the attractive fair-haired woman walking into the kitchen. She didn't like Mrs. Jarvis but then not too many did. The officer's wife smiled at PC. Jarvis, put a hand on his shoulder and with her hankie wiped Rita's lipstick from his cheek before giving him a routine peck on the other.

In Edith's eyes Police Constable 589 Rodney Jarvis had momentarily become the little boy caught with his hand in the candy jar.

Even she smiled as he blurted out, "Hello Brenda. I'm, er, just snatching a cup of tea before I go out again. Everything alright then?"

Brenda Jarvis looked coldly at the two sisters before replying derisively to her wounded spouse.

"Why you should ask I can't imagine. In the circumstances everything seems alright for you. Obviously being seen to, getting everything you want."

Edith ignored the spiteful comment, turning her back to the woman. But she did feel sorry for PC. Jarvis. He was obviously embarrassed by his wife's undisguised insinuations and smiled weakly at the sisters. Women nearby sniggered at the predicament of their village bobby.

As if he had an asbestos throat the referee gulped down his mug of hot tea before making play of consulting his watch. Forcing a smile he looked about him. The coven was in full session, the harridans enjoying every minute of his discomfort. He adjusted his football stockings and checked his bootlaces. The referee was aware his attempt to regain some composure and authority within that weak smile wasn't too convincing.

He managed to stutter, "Er, thank you ladies. Just look at the time. Must get the game re-started," before clattering out of the kitchen and its pressurised atmosphere into the more welcoming heat of the local Derby.

Rita smiled and executed one of her leg-revealing twirls. Mrs Jarvis was not amused.

Edith shook her head at what she saw as her sister's provocative act and thought, "She's tempting providence."

FIVE

ig John was bursting with pride. His team had won
the traditional soccer Derby and his boys had been
in the middle of the action.

Freddy Price, wearing his business hat, said, "If Tom
wins tonaight it'll be a good double. We might all make a
bob or two."

John glowered at Freddy who recognised the look
immediately.

"I mean *when* Tommy wins tonaight John. It goes wi'out
sayin'. Let me get ya a bottle in."

"No need for that Freddy, I'm not a drinking man as you
well know. This ginger ale'll do me fine thank you very much
but, like I always say, when beer's in, brains is out. How long
to go now?"

For the third time in as many minutes the big man gently
shook his pocket watch alongside his ear before tapping the
glass with a horny finger. He noted that the second sweep
still stuttered around the ornate face whilst the minute hand
seemed frozen in time.

Looking up at the large clock at the back of the hall
Freddy announced, "It should be startin' in five minutes."

For the third time in as many minutes Big John returned
the watch to his waistcoat pocket and wiped his sweating
brow with a large blue and white spotted handkerchief.

The Miners' Institute was full to capacity and buzzing.

Fight fans were still coming in and that meant standing room only at the back. Behind the bar in the club John could see Amos Jimson, portly landlord of the Net and Ferret. He seemed hard pressed to serve the crush of thirsty drinkers. Streams of perspiration oozed from every overworked pore in Jimson's bloated body whilst a constant smile played upon his heavy florid face. It lit up his whole countenance as he watched his staff pulling the pints non-stop and feeding the insatiable appetite of the constantly ringing till.

"If Sergeant Jack sees this lot he'll about close it down, could be a crowd problem and we don't want to see anybody hurt."

The concern in John's voice did not go unnoticed. Bade Durnley from a ringside seat spoke.

"A fine sentiment John but it's a sell out 'cos crowd want to see somebody hurt. There's a lotta brass flying about on this faight and my friend Sergeant Jack wants to see it as well as next man. He'll not stop it, mark my words."

Durnley leaned over to John and from behind a hand he said quietly, "I suppose ya know John, Tom fixed me and Cal up wi' these ringside seats. I didn't get 'em for nowt tho'. Int' morning don't be surprised when ya find a couple a brace a fine birds in Polly's outside larder. And tell Tom we've settled. OK?"

John nodded. He didn't care for Durnley the poacher. A "likeable Rogue" Tom called him, and he had been known to accompany the gang on their illegal activities. But John was a realist. Tom had dealt the hand and it was his play.

The noise in the large hall was deafening. Suddenly the lights dimmed. A hush descended upon the excited crowd. The overhead flood lights burst into life illuminating the ring. A sporadic outbreak of cheering from the back of the hall indicated the challenger was entering the arena. Appreciative clapping greeted Seaman Bembridge as he clambered through the ropes.

"He's a big 'un John. Looks tough."

"Bigger they are, harder they fall Freddy. And byt' look of his face he don't know that faightin' is supposed to be the gentle art of self defence."

"Ya rait there John. He's stopped a few haymakers wi' that nose."

"An' them ears is better than any caulis I can grow."

The subject of their comments jumped up and down centre ring, arms aloft, punching the air with bandaged hands to acknowledge the shouts and cheers of his supporters and jeers of his dissenters. He sported a navy blue silk dressing gown with the motif "Seaman Bembridge" emblazoned across the back.

John wasn't impressed. For anyone within ear shot he declared, "He's goin' ta need more than a fancy dressin' gown tonaight."

Durnley heard and uttered what sounded to John very much like a gypsy warning.

"Bembridge aint goin' ta hit Tom with his fancy clobber John. It's them brine and vinegar hardened fists that Tom'll ay ta look out for. He's a big hard man and knows his way around. He can dish it out and take it. He'll gi' Tommy a run for his money, mark my words."

John Oakley didn't comment. He hadn't liked what he heard. He looked at his watch again and licked his dry lips.

Suddenly spectators leapt from their seats, shouting and cheering. Even John was affected. He jumped to his feet clapping his big hands in support of his son who was making his way to the ring. Bembridge seemed unconcerned.

John thought, "He's a cool 'un alraight. But it's no good him trying to ignore this ear bashin.' He might as well try to stop a runaway coal wagon."

It rolled and swelled thundering against the ear drums. John was pumped up. He joined in the chorus of support and shouted, "If Bembridge thinks that were an ear thumper he's in for a shock."

He was right. As his boy sprang into the ring the noise reached its crescendo. It was Tommy's turn now to parade and strut in his green dressing gown, its message in scarlet emblazoned across the back "Tommy Kelly Oakley Langwith White Hope." Proud father John watched his son shadow boxing, bobbing and weaving, loosening up, easing the tension in his finely tuned muscles. The young athlete never spared a glance for Bembridge who was limbering up in the other corner. The commotion peaked and subsided as the sharp clatter of the bell announced the presence of the compere centre ring. Both fighters, surrounded by their handlers, moved easily in their corners as the white shirted referee supervised the individual fitting of their gloves and checked they were using gum shields and groin protectors.

"Ladieees and Gentlemennn!

As the compere introduced the two fighters John spotted Ridgeway deep in conversation with Durnley at the back of the hall. He saw a large wad of what appeared to be banknotes change hands. But then that was the bookmaker's business and John did not intend to allow such matters to distract him from the more serious business at hand.

However, the transaction held a greater significance to another watcher. Whilst others attended to their particular business Police Constable Jarvis was about his, aiming at all times to be a constant thorn in the side of Durnley and his gang.

Rod Jarvis spoke quietly to John. "They are up to no good John that's for certain. Money's changed hands. There's some skulduggery afoot. I'll bet a pound to a penny, but not with Ridgeway, it's to do with the main event."

"Ay I spotted that and I 'ope you're wrong in your assumption mester Jarvis." He paused and offered an alternative viewpoint. "Maybe it's your job. Ya takin' things too serious. Ridgeway's a bookie after all an' the gypsy's money is as good as the next man's."

"Maybe so, maybe so. We'll leave it at that John and enjoy the evening."

But the officer wasn't convinced.

Tommy stripped off his dressing gown. Gasps of admiration rippled around the hall as the magnificent physique of their local hero was revealed. The fair hair on his arms and chest glinted gold under the glare of the arc lights suspended high above the ring. Rugged good looks topped with a shock of wavy auburn locks and Clark Gable moustache were a promoter's dream.

"Fit as a fiddle and strong as a bull." John remembered the words of Freddy Price and spoke them aloud with pride.

"Aye you're right John, he's a magnificent looking specimen. I'm glad it's not me that's facing him. With that mean glint in his eye, nobody'll stop him." Constable Jarvis spoke with genuine admiration for the local fighter whom he valued as a friend.

Rita, sitting next to her father, leaned over to speak to the officer.

"A Greek God. The physique of a Greek God. What Goddess could resist it Mister Jarvis?"

Looking a little nonplussed the policeman muttered, "With a physique like that I don't suppose any Goddess could."

From behind her hand she whispered, "I'm not talking about my brother Mister Jarvis."

Constable Rod Jarvis gulped and turned a hot flushed face towards the ring. John did not appear to have heard his daughter's flirting words. But Wilson had.

The compere was still speaking. Durnley took his seat at ringside, a satisfied look on his swarthy, hawkish face.

"...for the area title. Presenting the two contenders. On my left in the red shorts, from Mansfield, that well known battler Seaman Bembridge." A measure of sporting applause greeted the introduction with a smattering of solid support from an area towards the back of the hall.

"And from Langwith ..."

What followed was drowned in an avalanche of frenzied cheering, stamping and chanting. John was in the thick of it, carried along by the raw energy exploding about him. He soaked up the atmosphere and revelled in the unadulterated excitement created by the presence of his son, his own boy. He felt so proud. When Tom raised his gloved hands and saluted each section of the hall, the compere gave up. It seemed to John as though he could not compete with the overwhelming sound crashing about the rafters and walls. It continued as the referee brought both fighters to the centre of the ring. In anticipation of the next chapter in the saga, the noise eased. Even then the referee was obliged to shout his pre-fight instructions through cupped hands, giving him an unexpected close-up of Bembridge's cauliflower ear. After the formalities he wished them luck and sent both men back to their corners with the final direction that they come out fighting.

To John's mind he need not have wasted his breath. Both men were up for it. They had come to fight and fight they did. It was noticeable that the styles of the fighters were in direct contrast. The Seaman stood upright in the tradition of the old English bare-knuckle pugilists, leading with his left from a wide stance, left foot advanced. Tom fought from a crouch, American style, bobbing and weaving from the waist; he was a south-paw. Unlike Bembridge he led with his right, with right foot advanced, often a confusing style until the opponent could fathom it out, but against Tom there often wasn't enough time. Two long, crisp left jabs from the Mansfield man were slipped cleverly by Tom, who quickly went under the jabbing arm to deliver two ferocious hooks to the unprotected body of his opponent. The growl of pain from Bembridge could be heard in the ringside seats.

John through cupped hands yelled excitedly, "Ooogh! Great shots son. You've hurt 'im. Go for his body. Undert' short rib. Aim for his ribs and solar plexus. As good as a punch tut point o' jaw. They'll slow 'im down. Gu for 'is body an' 'is head'll fall."

But it wasn't all going Tom's way. An unexpected hard right hook to the head staggered him. It was his turn to be hurt. John could see that and was on his feet in an instant shouting encouragement.

"Hang in there son, hang in. Take a breather."

From experience he knew his son would be feeling as though his head and legs were disconnected, his arms leaden and his brain puddled. Until his head cleared no amount of advice would help; the yells and shouts would be distant echoes at the end of that long, cobwebbed tunnel.

Tommy was still on his feet. He'd been hit hard many times before, and knew what to do to gain those few precious seconds needed to recover his senses. He hung on to Bembridge, smothering his attempts to deliver another telling blow to the rapidly clearing head. The frantic clanging of the bell brought added relief to the Langwith White Hope who quickly regained his composure thumping his gloves together in frustration and anticipation as he walked to his stool. John wiped the sweat from his own face and slumped down in his seat. He felt as though he'd just gone through that round blow for blow.

Ted threw water over his brother's tousled hair and rubbed down his sweating body.

"What are you doin' fallin' for a punch like that?" Jack leaned toward his brother, fanning him with a towel. "You'd just give him two nice hits to the body and he caught you admiring your work. Hit and out, hit and out, don't stay around and get caught. This man's no slouch so keep your wits about you. There's a long way to go so don't get careless."

"Seconds out."

Tom was up and half way across the ring as his opponent was rising. He clearly intended to make amends and punish Bembridge for that wicked shot. Like a vengeful tornado he hurled aside Bembridge's piston jabs before crashing knuckle-jarring blows to his body. The Seaman, obviously hurt, but still very strong, retaliated by hooking and uppercutting Tom.

"Oooh! It's a grueller. They're takin' no prisoners tonaight John."

John did not respond to Freddy Price's succinct assessment of the fight.

The furious clatter of the bell brought the bloodied gladiators' exertions to a temporary halt and they made their way back to their corners.

"Not much between them at this stage John." Constable

Jarvis tactfully played down the truth of the matter for Rita's sake.

John licked his lips and unconsciously preened his moustache. He was worried about his boy.

In the ringside seats Calver Wilson clenched and unclenched his fists, bobbing and weaving in his seat, eyes alight with excitement. The sight and smell of blood and the pain inflicted to the combatants seemed to stir the hunting, killing streak within him.

"A good faight hey Bade? Lotsa blood."

"Alraight so far but I'd sooner it were his."

Durnley's nod toward Police Constable Jarvis received silent support from Wilson who glowered as Rita leaned over Big John to voice her concerns to the officer.

The fourth round followed the pattern of the others.

"Oh! It's like a butcher's shop up there," declared a shocked Rita. "I don't like it, there's too much blood. Just look at our Tom's face. I've never seen him like this before.".

In an attempt to alleviate her concern Rod Jarvis offered a more balanced view of the fight.

"Tom's not losing Rita. He's in front on points. He's more aggressive. They're both bleeding a bit but they're not serious cuts to a fighter. The ref can see that and he won't step in unless their eyesight is affected or the cuts are too dangerous. So don't worry on that score. Tom won't be bothered about cuts and bruises. That's his game and he's good at it."

Rita wiped her eyes and nodded.

Rod Jarvis added, "Tom's a lot stronger than Bembridge and hits harder. You'll see Tom's not sitting down between rounds. Bembridge is. He's getting tired. Tom knows that and will go all out to end the fight. You mark my words."

In the meantime PC. Jarvis watched the close-headed mutterings between Durnley and Wilson. Something passed between them. Wilson palmed it. During the next interval, whilst the seconds saw to their fighters, Jarvis watched Wilson make his way to Bembridge's corner. He leaned on the ring apron and entered into conversation with Chick Bembridge, the fighter's older brother and chief second. That wasn't unusual, many passing spectators engaged in friendly banter. Wilson reached through the ropes and shook Chick's hand before moving off. Constable Jarvis knew what was happening when the chief second appeared to be wiping down his man's gloves. The officer was powerless to intervene as the bell sounded.

Bembridge knew what to expect from his younger opponent. His strength was waning whilst Tom's was unaffected, it was all or nothing this round and he'd received his instructions from Chick. He met Tom centre ring, head on. Tom thrashed away at the red blotched body drawing gasps of pain with each crashing blow, the fight and the title was his.

From his corner a cry of, "Watch him Tom, watch him," came too late.

The thumb rammed into his right eye. Tom knew the moment it struck he was in trouble. His eye seemed to explode. Loss of vision and the searing, burning pain that bored into his brain was the worst he had ever experienced. It wasn't the first time he'd been gouged but this was different. The pain didn't subside, it grew worse. His head seemed to have become a huge balloon that Bembridge was able to punch at will; and he did. Tom clinched and hung onto his opponent. But the vision didn't return. What made it worse was the impaired vision to his other eye. The shouts of desperation from his corner and the extra attention from the referee told Tommy it really was serious.

A barely discernable nod passed between Ridgeway and Durnley. As the poacher eased himself back into his seat a look of smug satisfaction registered upon his weathered face.

Wilson, eyes and veins in his neck bulging, shouted and screamed, encouraging the Seaman to "Kill the blind bastard."

Durnley dug his elbow into Wilson's ribs bringing a gasp of pain, at the same time breaking the grip of the blood lust momentarily consuming him.

"Shut yer trap! You'll give show away and have Jarvis and Tommy's pals on our backs."

The piercing eyes drilled into Wilson causing him to start and mutter, "Right Bade."

Constable Jarvis took it all in.

John could see his lad was suffering. He knew what had happened and could do nothing about it.

Tommy could get no relief from the blinding pain his tortured eyes were suffering. Streams of salt tears mingling with the sweat on his face; and Bembridge didn't let up. Punch after punch found their mark and Tommy, unable to see his attacker, threw wild, swinging punches. They were brushed aside as the Seaman saw his moment of glory amidst the blood and gore of the once feared Tommy "Kelly" Oakley.

There were cries of concern from the Oakley entourage as they watched the tragedy being played out before them.

It was clear that under the unanswerable onslaught it was inevitable Tom would succumb. He went down on his knees as if in supplication. Then his head sagged upon his chest, too heavy to hold upright, too painful to feel, too bludgeoned to care. The hall was in uproar. His brothers were in uproar.

From his brother's corner Jack Oakley yelled, "Oh no! Our Tom's down. He's takin' some stick. Summat's wrong. He can't see where the punches are coming from. He'll get killed. I'm stoppin' it."

He scrambled to the ring apron and threw in a towel. The referee picked it up and quickly tossed it back into the corner. Jack knew the ref wouldn't be influenced by the towel being thrown in. It was only a desperate gesture and carried no official standing. Jack, like everyone else in the hall, understood the ref was the sole arbiter of the outcome of the fight.

The official knelt alongside the stricken figure of Tom Oakley and picking up the count from the time keeper shouted it to him, at the same time thrusting his fingers in front of the fighter's face.

With all fingers extended he yelled to the helpless fighter, "Ten and out."

Powerless now and confused Tom, still on his knees, rubbed his eyes frantically with gloved hands. Bembridge's helpers were in uproar. The crowd were in uproar. Big John sat in silence, his eyes closed as he prayed for his boy. Ted and Jack helped the shadow of their hero back to his corner where he slumped onto the stool pawing at his eyes with bloodied gloves. His seconds pulled them off .

After quickly examining the red and swollen eyes Jack snarled, "The bastards have doped him."

It took Ted and Rod Jarvis to keep Jack from crashing into the Bembridge corner to extract vengeance.

"What about this ref? Check Bembridge's gloves." PC. Jarvis joined in the chorus of dissenters eager to see a wrong righted and the cheating Bembridge camp disqualified and punished.

At the back of the hall Durnley boasted to Ridgeway, "An old Romany potion Albert. Undetectable. It'll have worn off in a few minutes."

He laughed as Ridgeway slapped him on the back and slipped a wad of notes into his jacket pocket.

Big John joined his sons in the ring where knots of men in passionate discourse unashamedly showed their individual loyalties with intimidating stares and physical gestures directed towards their perceived enemies.

Anonymous voices shouted from ringside, "Them Bembridge bastards as done Tommy Oakley. They put summat on their man's gloves an' blinded him."

"Ay. Let's 'ay 'em. They couldna beat Tommy fair and square they've had to fix the fuckin' faight."

"Whose goin' ta settle up wi us? I've lost all me week's wages on this fixed faight. Somebody'll ay' to pay else I'll teck it out their 'ide."

"I know where them cheatin' bastards live. If'n I don't get a fair crack I'll pay a visit and burn 'em out of house and 'ome. Believe me mester."

John was worried. The potential for bloody recriminations hung heavy in the air. He could sense the seething anger, smell it in the atmosphere of the place amidst the stale sweat and resin. Thick and clinging, it waited to be released in a rush of violence from drink-fuelled avengers.

He voiced his concern to Constable Jarvis, on his feet next to him, "I don't like this officer. Our Tom's like a primed powder keg. Ready to go off moment fuse is lit."

"You're right John. And I think he'll light his own fuse. And nobody will stop him once his fighting dander's up."

Suddenly, as if responding to the prophecy, the fuse was lit. Both PC. Jarvis and Big John were taken by surprise. The Tommy Oakley powder keg exploded. The boxer's savage fighting instincts were unbridled. No one could stop him, not even Big John.

Tom, bare knuckled now, felled Seaman Bembridge in his own corner with one mighty blow to the jaw. Crashing to the boards, his head struck the canvas with a bone-splintering crunch. Next, Chick Bembridge, attempting to spar up to Tommy was swept aside by a whirlwind of heavy blows that left him unconscious alongside his brother. Through the scarlet mists of the volcano erupting inside his head, the enraged fighter saw only those who had conspired to bring about his downfall. Vague outlines, distorted blood red figures flitted within his clouded vision to be dispatched by avenging fists.

But as suddenly as it had materialised the crimson blurring vanished.

With vision returned, Tom gloated over the battered Bembridge brothers. As he watched the Seaman being taken away on a stretcher he called out triumphantly, "Who's last man standin' now Bembridge? It int you nor your brother. Nor them other bastards you've brung wi' you. No it's Tommy Kelly Oakley. I'm the best man and' I'll gi' ya a rematch any time. If 'n you're fit enough."

Tommy turned back to the ring. What he saw caused him to yell, "God almighty!"

He hurriedly joined the group of men centre ring tending a prostrate figure lying on the canvas. The man was obviously hurt. Tom knew he was responsible for the injuries to his battered face.

"Let me get through. I want to see 'ow he is. I din't mean

to punch 'im. It weren't his fault. He were only doin' his job. It were nowt to do wit' referee. I'm so sorry mester. I'm so sorry."

The triumphalism had left him. Crestfallen now he watched the official stretchered away.

John Oakley, who had witnessed the whole bloody confrontation, felt gutted. But at the moment his main concern was his son. Together with his other boys and loyal supporters he escorted the despondent Tom to his changing room. He knew in his heart Tommy Kelly Oakley would never fight again and he feared for his future. It didn't take long for the newspapers to blaze out the headline.

LOCAL FIGHTER STRIPPED OF HIS LICENCE AFTER FIGHT FRACAS.

"Tommy 'Kelly' Oakley, victor of numerous bloody battles, finally KO'd by cigar smoking Mandarins at their London HQ. Whilst sympathising with the local fighter, hero to many in and around his home town, the British Board of Boxing Control unanimously voted to take away his licence to fight professionally, in the greater interest of the sport. The fact that he had been allegedly doped by gambling interests would be left to the police to investigate, but the violent assault upon an impartial Boxing Board official could not be ignored and must attract the ultimate sanction under the Board's rules."

As he read the gut-wrenching headlines Rod Jarvis felt for his friend and the rest of the Oakley family. He contemplated those terse, clinical sentences which he knew had knocked Tom Oakley onto his arse as surely as the mystic potion used by his enemies. They both put him down for the count, but he knew the revocation had rolled him over, into the gutter where he didn't have to work too hard to remain. The policeman thought how the once proud athlete, having been hauled from the pedestal of youthful adulation through skullduggery, was left shattered like a fallen china teapot. What made it worse from his professional point of view was that no one was indicted for the crime against him.

He watched, unable to help as his friend spun out of control, outwards to the ragged fringes of society, where he wrapped himself in a cloak of drunken despair and violence. Rod Jarvis pondered on where destiny's helter-skelter would deposit his friend.

SIX

Big John dozed in his favourite chair in front of a comforting fire. On the pegged hearth rug Rita lolled at her Dad's feet, her head resting on his knees.

She suddenly asked, "When's this war going to end Dad?"

Stroking his daughter's luxurious black tresses, he was a tired old man.

John sighed and said sadly, "I don't know my girl. The world's gone mad. It's like a runaway pit cage hurtling down't shaft out of control and heading for a mighty smash."

He sat back, eyes closed, and recalled the day in 'thirty-nine that Prime Minister Neville Chamberlain confirmed the worst and England was at war. He'd been thankful his boys Jack and Ted were in reserved occupations working down the pit and weren't called up. But in 'forty-three after Tom lost his boxing licence, his brothers joined up. His youngest, Ted, joined the Royal Navy, Jack the Army. Then in 'forty-four the telegram came. John swallowed hard recollecting the directness of its message .

Sir, It is my painful duty to inform you that a report has been received from the Admiralty notifying the death of Able Seaman, Oakley E. Royal Navy, on active service, which occurred at sea on the 3rd December 1944.

The accompanying message of sympathy from their Gracious Majesties the King and Queen and the Lords of the Admiralty at the sailor's death in his Country's service did nothing to alleviate the pain of their loss. Then there was Jack, serving with a commando unit. They never knew where he was. And every day there were reports of fatalities and casualties amongst the volunteers who had left the village to "kick the Nazi arse." But Herr Schicklgruber had proved tougher opposition than expected. The telegram boy on his red bicycle was no longer a welcome friend. He was the harbinger of dread news. The buff-coloured envelopes were becoming more frequent now and drawn front room curtains confirmed the sacrifice of another local hero.

And then there was his lad Tom. Following his brothers' example he went to enlist. By that time the bottle had become his constant companion. At the recruiting station, set up at the colliery, he collapsed in a drunken heap and had to be taken to the pit ambulance station for first aid treatment. His Medical Board assessment was "grade three" the lowest. He couldn't even get into the armed forces to fight for his country. What a come down for a once uncrowned King. Now a clown prince and laughing stock of the village. That hurt John. He was aware that his son still raced about on his Norton motorcycle, in drink or not, and the latter wasn't very often. His son seemed to have a death wish. He'd had words with him but it had no effect. PC. Jarvis spoke to him as a friend. His advice was ignored. Tom would sooner listen to Bade Durnley and his clique, wouldn't accept that they were responsible for his problems. But John knew they had no real interest in him since he had lost his boxer's licence and celebrity status. They only used him when it suited their criminal purpose. Meanwhile his son drifted in and out of drunken stupors.

And Polly got no better, though she enjoyed her outings in the pony and trap. At the moment John wasn't a happy man. Life had taken a dramatic turn for the worst. What with Ted's death and Tom's troubles coming on top of the other family problems that he was living with. And then there was this uncertainty that he was experiencing. He couldn't put his finger on it but something was worrying him, pulling at his gut and clumping about in his head. Was it a premonition of some sort, a warning of worse to come? He hoped not.

Come Sunday morning the disturbing sensations hadn't left him. Those unexplained feelings of anxiety and unease walked with him step for step. When John and his family attended the usual service at the Methodist chapel the overall discomfort persisted. They became more pronounced as they went to take their regular seats. John saw the way the congregation gave tight-lipped smiles and cast their eyes down, avoiding direct contact with him and his family. John knew Methodists are traditionally seen to be dour and dull, and Primitive Methodists more so, but today he felt it was more than that. There was a definite coldness from the chapel-goers. Freddy Price, though he tipped his cap to Polly as John pushed her up the drive in her wheelchair, didn't stop to pass the time of day, hurrying with his wife into the rapidly filling chapel.

The preacher's sermon added to the discomfort. It highlighted family values, the need for parents to exercise stricter control over their children, especially their daughters, warning of hell fire's curse and eternal damnation for those who played fast and loose with the pleasures of the flesh. John stared hard at the minister during his delivery, seeking to find some reason for the sense of isolation he was experiencing. All he found was the hard look returned, leaving him with a suspicion that the sermon was directed

54

specifically towards himself and his family. The big man intended to get to the bottom of it after the service.

As the sombre congregation filed out of the place of worship John handed the care of Polly to Tom and ordered, "Take your mother straight home. I'll see thaigh there shortly."

Tom was sober today, though the athletic posture was missing, but he was still a strong, powerful young man and he used his strength to do as his father directed. He leaned into the wheelchair, driving it homewards as if it were a toy.

Big John hurried after Freddy Price who was quickly making his way down the path towards the road.

"Freddy! Freddy Price, hang on a minute I want a word."

The little fellow stopped in his tracks as if grabbed by the collar from behind.

Straight into the heart of the problem, not wasting words on formalities or niceties John boomed, "What's going off? Is there something I should know?"

Freddy shuffled from one thin leg to the other, taking off his cap, twisting it in his hands, putting it on again only to take it straight off. He couldn't find words to answer. John snatched the cap out of Freddy's nervous hand and thrust his face up to the little man's, almost nose to nose.

He would have an answer. In a frenzy of indignation he cried out, "I've asked ya once what's goin' off. I shan't be askin' so nicely next time."

Freddy had never seen him in this frame of mind in all the years that he had known him. He pleaded with the big man, "Ask somebody else John, every body knows about it, don't put it on me."

He cringed as John took him by the front of his best Sunday suit hauling him to his toes.

"I'm askin' *YOU* Freddy Price. To your face and I want an answer *NOW*."

Freddy knew he was beaten. He sagged, an empty potato sack in John's firm grip. His resolve had gone.

He whined, "All I can say John, is ask Rita."

John still confused yelled back, "Ask Rita what?" He shook the little fellow until his dentures rattled.

Screwing up his eyes and licking his parched lips in anticipation of the blow that he felt would surely follow, the little man blurted out from that dried prune of a face, "Just ask her. Ask her what she's been up to."

A few stragglers from the congregation averted their eyes and hurried past on the other side. John didn't wait to hear any more. Depositing Freddy in a crumpled heap on the pavement outside the chapel, together with his screwed-up cap, the confused man strode off towards his home, face flushed and jaw tensed.

John burst into the living room, a bull out of control. Blood vessels stood out from his neck; face the colour of a guardsman's tunic.

He bellowed to Edith who was tending her mother, "Where is she? I want to know what's going off."

Edith had never seen her Dad in such a state. Polly just sat there in the rocking chair, and rocked.

"Just calm down Dad. I've got the kettle on we'll have a cuppa tea when it's mashed."

"Calm down? Calm down?" The words were spat out in a fury. "I've just been humiliated in my own chapel, in the House of God, before the people who I've worked and slaved all my life to help. I want to know what's what. Fetch her down before I do."

"She's down at lav dad. I'll go and tell her you want her."

Without waiting to hear Big John's response Edith fled from the house.

The distraught young woman dashed down the garden path to the outside lavatory where she banged on the green painted ledged and braced door.

She shouted, "Rita! Rita! Dad wants to see you. You'd better hurry, he's in a foul temper. I've never seen him so."

From behind the door the calm, even voice of Rita replied, "I'll come up when I'm ready and not before."

"Don't make things worse our Rita. Dad's wild as a bull dog that's sat in a bed a nettles."

"Don't you wait for me. I'll sort things out in my own way. He'll either like it or lump it."

Edith hurried back to the house.

John was pacing up and down in front of the newly stoked fire when Rita deigned to make her entrance. She met his glaring eyes with defiance.

"Sit on the sofa miss I've some questions to ask."

In a measured voice she asked, "What about, Dad?"

This was one of the most difficult times in his life. As difficult as the time when Doctor Wilson told him Polly was ill or the news of the loss of Ted. He had negotiated with autocratic owners over the running of the pit, stood his ground on matters of principle and working conditions for the men and always been his own man. Today in front of this defiant young woman, the daughter he loved with all his heart and soul, he walked a path to hell fire.

With jacket off, sleeves rolled up and silvered Albert swinging at the front of his waistcoat, John Oakley leaned on the table almost head to head with Rita. He glared at her.

Then suddenly straightening up he turned to Edith and ordered, "Ask your sister what she's been up to."

Edith, taken by surprise and still being swept along by the rapidly developing situation, blurted out, "Rita. Me Dad wants to know…"

She was cut short by her sister. "I heard what me Dad says our Edith. Tell him if he can't speak to me direct then he's not to bother speaking."

John was taken aback by the defiance but gathering his composure he said, "Tell your sister I'll not have her speak to me like that. She was brought up to respect her elders and have good manners. I'll be obliged if she remembers that."

With arms folded Rita declared, "If he won't speak to me I'll speak to him. I do respect and love my elders, my Mam and Dad, my brothers and sister but I won't be treated like a Victorian servant girl. This is the 1940's not the 1840's and unpalatable things can't be hidden beneath women's bustles and men's top hats any longer."

At that moment John did not appreciate his daughter's directness, he wanted the truth out in the open though he feared meeting it full on when it came. That he was head of the family and master of the house was not in dispute, as a product of strict Victorian values he demanded respect from her. He was aware that those values in modern times were called to question but not under his roof.

John hesitated for a moment, brushing his moustache with a gnarled forefinger. Standing with back to the fire the big man searched his daughter's face. That face, that child he loved so much. The twisting, tingling nausea in his gut told him that very soon she was to cause him immeasurable pain.

"I'll ask thee straight miss and I'll expect a truthful reply." He braced himself to ask the impossible question, the answer to which he dreaded. "Are you int' family way lass?"

Big John involuntarily flinched as he asked his child that

demanding question. The reply struck him like a body punch from Tom.

"I am Dad. Nearly two months gone."

Having bared her soul Rita burst into a bout of uncontrollable sobbing.

John was rooted to the spot, unable to speak, unable to react to the devastating truth sitting before him.

Polly silent all this time, from her chair shrieked in that sickly, reedy voice, "The shame of it. A bastard child. I'm not having it here. It's not living under this roof. You'll have to get rid on it."

Edith was in tears. She had removed her glasses to rub her red and tearful eyes.

Tom, returning from putting the wheelchair away in the outhouse, caught the dramatic revelation and mother's frenzied outburst as he entered the room. The young man stared at his sister.

Rita, leaning on the arm of the sofa, sobbed. The whole scene was one of utter despair and uncontrolled misery. John, slumped in his chair, elbows on knees, head in hands, spoke to Edith.

"Daughter, you've got summat else to add to your list. Mam, Tom, Ted and now this. All it wants now is for't telegram lad to bring us bad news about our Jack. Hard as that might be it wouldna be worse un this."

Edith yelled, "Dad!"

"At least I'd know my son had died like his brother, honourably, fighting for a just cause. Not like your sister, a trollop, dropping her clouts to any Tom, Dick or Harry. And everybody but me knowing about it."

Rita unable to contain herself, jumped up, making her way to the stairs.

John, thoroughly dejected but still head of the family, said sharply, "Sit down madam! We've not finished this business yet."

Rita instinctively obeyed and returned to her seat. Wiping her reddened eyes she sat upright, arms folded.

John hurled out the next question. No, it was more than that, it was a demand.

"Whose is it?"

All eyes were on Rita. Names running through heads. Edith saw those thrusting buttocks and muscular thighs. Who was it that had taken Rita?

The whispered reply from a defiant Rita didn't help, "I'm not saying Dad."

"You young hussy," wailed Polly.

John, having got over the initial shock, was calmer now but insistent that his position and authority should be respected.

"You will if I have to take my belt buckle to you."

Tom stepped into the room, his protective instinct aroused, rallying to his sister whilst not wishing to be disrespectful to his father.

"There's no need for that Dad, she's not a collier to be belted. Our Rita's not fost and she won't be last to be babbed. We've got to stand by her, not chuck her out like swill for pigs."

John, with a pained expression, looked at his rebellious son, wiped his eyes and without another word walked over to the sour-faced Polly. Picking her up like a child he carried her upstairs.

Tom wanted to take his father and mother in his arms and hug them. Tell them that he loved them, that everything would be alright. But he knew it was useless. His Dad wanted to be with his Mam. They could grieve together and shed their tears in the solitude of their lonely bedroom and wonder where it all went wrong and where it would end.

Tom joined Rita on the sofa, putting a huge arm around her shoulders. The girl rested her head on his chest and sobbed. Edith cuddled her from the other side, stroking her long hair.

Tom spoke. "Whoever it is sis, is he doin't right thing by you?"

The sobbing eased. "He doesn't know."

Tom didn't respond immediately. After a few moments in thought he said, "There ya are then. It's not as bad as it looks. There's plenty of time to make it raight."

Rita looked at her big brother through wet and reddened eyes. "I'm not going to tell him. It'll only make things worse. I'll go away like Mam says and take me shame with me."

Stifling a sob Edith pleaded, "You can't go away Rita. We all love you and want you to stay. Gi' the babby away. Nobody'll ever know. It'll soon blow over you see."

Rita responded with a shake of her head saying, "No. I'm responsible for it. God willing I'll bring it up. But I'll not give it up."

Tom knew his sister's mind was made up. Now he wanted the man responsible. He wanted his pound of flesh. No not just the flesh but blood and pain too. The big man's insides tingled. His teeth ached as he ground them in time to the flexing of his huge fists.

He asked coldly, "Who is he then Rita? Do I know him? Is he at pit?"

Rita looked at her brother and sighed. After all he had gone through he was still concerned about her. She hugged him and planted a kiss on his cheek.

"Don't keep on at me Our Tom, please. I've made up me mind. I'll pack tonight and go to Nottingham in the morning. I can catch the seven o'clock bus to Mansfield and then change. I'll be alright you see. I'm a big girl now you know."

She gave a strained laugh.

Edith sobbed. If salt tears could have helped the war effort she cried enough to float off a grounded battleship.

Tom hugged Rita and held her tight. But his eyes, staring past her into the changing images within the fire, reflected the angry flickering flames. They mirrored the dark thoughts in his mind. He struggled to identify the one responsible for his sister's predicament. The three sat in the firelight's glow until the last glowing embers turned to ash.

*

Tom and Edith waved Rita off on the seven o'clock bus. It was on time, it usually was. Tom had lifted her suitcase onto the platform of the double decker and settled it securely in the luggage compartment under the stairs. It didn't seem much, though she assured him it was and she had sufficient money in her purse and some in her Co-op savings account. He slipped two large white five pound notes into her coat pocket without her knowing. She wouldn't have accepted them otherwise. Edith wiped her eyes on a soggy handkerchief then hugged her sister. She gave her a brown paper bag with sandwiches and cakes to keep her fortified on the journey.

"I'll keep in touch and let you know what's happening, so don't worry too much about me. Tell Mam and Dad, and our Jack when he comes home, that I love them and I'm sorry for any shame that's touched them through my dark shadow."

Final hugs and kisses were brought to an end. Edith

and Tom bade their sad farewells to Rita and stood on the pavement as the bus burst into life. They waved and watched as slowly at first it made its way down the main street past the Co-op, the picture house and rows of dreary pit houses. The vehicle gathered speed and passed the front door and neat garden of the home where Rita had been born and raised. She tried not to look but from the corner of her eye saw the dainty lace curtain in the window move and the large unhappy face peering out. She turned away as a large rough hand wiped away a large wet tear before tugging at a large greying moustache. Then the face was gone.

The sinister figure in the war poster at the front of the bus pointed an accusing finger towards Rita. Bold words printed in scarlet, resembling dripping blood, declared *"Careless acts cost lives."* She was intimidated, and with tears in her eyes quickly looked away.

The seven o'clock turned the corner at the end of the lane passing out of sight. It headed for the stop opposite the Net and Ferret Inn carrying Rita away from the village into a wider world, and God only knows what.

*

It was the talk of the village. At every street corner cloth-capped men gathered and guffawed behind heavy hands. Outside the rows of grimy little pit houses their womenfolk pumiced and scrubbed door steps and window sills. Today they did it with more relish than usual as they gossiped and giggled amid the soap suds about the "carryings on" of Rita Oakley.

"All airs and graces. Thought she was better'n anybody else."

"Young Calver Wilson'l have to watch out for Tommy Oakley now."

"Do ya think it's him then?"

"Who knows. He's latest. Could be anybody int' village. Owt in trousers were fair game."

"If Tommy loses his rag Bobby Jarvis'll have his hands full trying to sort mess out."

And so it went on. The fallen angel had flown the place of her shame, giving licence to the village harpies to tear and rend her memory and cast the net of aspersion around the village at any man falling victim to their bile; a candidate for their crucible.

SEVEN

Calver Wilson sank his second pint in as many minutes. Through half-closed eyes Bade Durnley watched him across the table.

"What's problem Cal? Brewery been bombed?"

"Ya know what's problem. She's just upped and gone."

"Only thing she could've done int' circumstances. What else were there for her to do?"

"She could've stayed and I'd have looked after her and kid."

Durnley looked around the room as furtive as if on a night expedition and leaned across the table to Wilson.

"Be careful what you say lad. If Tommy hears you talking like that you'll end up like a butchered rabbit on a spit."

Rita's young admirer reacted by sweeping the empty pint pot off the table. It smashed against the hearth of the open fireplace.

"Tommy Oakley? I'm not afraid of Tommy Oakley. Langwith's white dope. I'll fait him drunk or sober. " He paused and giggled, "It'll have to be drunk cos' he's never sober."

The Poachers' Bar began to empty.

*

The telephone in the public call box outside the Net and Ferret rang. Constable Jarvis, making his two o'clock point, answered it.

"Right I'll attend immediately. Book me straight up." The officer checked his handcuffs and service truncheon before entering the premises. At the main entrance the landlord Amos Jimson met him. He was as usual sweating heavily, wringing his hands and constantly wiping them on the tea towel tucked into his belt straining beneath his heaving beer belly.

In his shrill voice he whined, "Thanks for coming Mister Jarvis but I don't want no trouble. Just talk to 'em, nice like, and get Calver to pay fort' damage. I'll be happy with that."

The local bobby pushed open the door of The Poachers' Bar. Apart from Durnley and Wilson, who were seated at their usual table near the fire place, the room was empty. He saw the shattered glass in the hearth.

The two men appeared to ignore him as he approached.

"You responsible for this Wilson?" PC. Jarvis nodded towards the broken glass.

With a fresh pint in his hand the man stood up and stared at the officer. He then deliberately sank his drink in one huge swig, wiping the residue from around his mouth on his jacket sleeve. He belched. With a grin on his now florid, sweating face and fuelled by alcohol he hurled the empty beer glass at the fireplace. Amidst a myriad of flying splinters it shattered at Constable Jarvis's feet. The officer calmly took in the damage, brushing a few pieces away from him with the toe of a boot.

Wilson smugly surveyed his handiwork before responding to the officer's question.

"Aye I'm responsible. And for that one an all Constable."

He indicated the other smashed glass and sneering said, "What ya goin' ta do about it?"

The Constable showed him. Reacting quickly he gripped

Wilson's left arm with his right hand and said, "I'm arresting you for being drunk and disorderly on licensed premises and causing malicious damage."

Before he could say anything further Wilson swung a clenched right fist towards the officer's head. Jarvis was prepared. He avoided the intended blow and got in first. Having released the grip on his prisoner he struck him forcefully with a crunching right cross. It smashed into Wilson's jaw. He was out before he hit the floor. The poacher lay bundled in the hearth bleeding among the broken glass. The officer stood over him.

A feeling of satisfaction coursed through his lean frame as he said, "You can add assault on police to your charges Wilson. That'll see you down the line for a good stretch."

As he bent to 'cuff his prisoner he said, "When we last met mister you were ranting on about having balls. You'll recall I said we'd meet again? Well I can tell you from experience that big mouths aren't fighters. And to have balls you need brains, fast hands and a good chin. You lose on all counts Wilson. As teacher no doubt used to tell you 'must try harder'."

Durnley, on his feet now, glared at the policeman. Burning hatred consumed him, radiating out towards PC. Jarvis, so intense that the officer could almost feel its heat, smell its canker.

The gang leader spat out at the officer, "There were no need for that. He's only a young lad, wouldn't hurt a fly."

The Constable, busy handcuffing the prone figure in the hearth, replied, "If he can't hold it Durnley he shouldn't drink it." As he hauled the prisoner to his feet Constable Jarvis added, "and don't think the matter of doping Tommy has been forgotten Durnley. You may be seeing the inside of Lincoln Jail yet."

Bade Durnley gripped his empty pint pot and made a step towards the police Constable. The officer stopped and turned to face him. Durnley hesitated before thumping the pot down on the table. Picking up his trilby hat edged with fishing fly he stormed off, nearly knocking over the landlord who had come from behind the bar.

The poacher stopped at the door. He turned and pointed a finger towards Constable Jarvis, now in control of his prisoner.

In a menacing voice he warned, "You'd better watch your back from now on mester."

PC. Jarvis ignored the threat. Durnley ducked under the low oak beam and hurried from the inn.

In an authoritative voice the officer said to the quivering landlord, "Amos, ring the station. Tell Sergeant Jack to get the cell ready and send the van. I'm bringing Calver Wilson in for drunk and disorderly and assault on police."

Wilson, conscious now and realising his predicament, blurted out, "I'll swing for you yer bastard. Mark my words I'll swing for you yet."

The officer hauled on the handcuffs forcing a yell of pain from the prisoner as he swung him towards the door and wryly commented, "My turn first mister, my turn first."

As they left the public house Amos Jimson at his cringing best pleaded, "Don't forget the damaged glasses Mister Jarvis."

*

Big John opened the door of the conservatory. Constable Jarvis noted the listlessness in the once keen eyes and the broad shoulders now stooped as if bearing a heavy weight. His friend looked old, exuding an air of sadness shrouded in melancholia.

"Good day John, thought I'd pop round and have a chat."

Even in despair John's propriety did not leave him. "Come in Constable Jarvis, you're most welcome, but I'm afraid my company and conversation won't be up to much today."

"I've really come to offer my condolences for all that's happened recently and see if there's anything I can do to help."

"Thank you for your concern, but there's really nowt you can do in the circumstances. Nothing can bring Ted back and Tom's got to face up to things like he did int' ring. Won't be long aforet' war's ended and my other lad'll be home. He won't want to come to a house full of miseries after what he's been through."

The policeman looked down towards his heavy black boots shuffling uncomfortably on the large pegged rug.

Edith broke the silence, "Before you both get down to all that men's talk, here's a cuppa tea."

PC Jarvis took the cup and saucer as he thanked the young woman, smart and spruce in her white apron with the daisy motif. He looked hard at her bespectacled face and short auburn hair. Suddenly he was staring at Rita, mischievous and teasing. Alarmed, he shook his head and the apparition disappeared, leaving a bemused Edith to question, "Are you alright Mr. Jarvis?"

"Er …yes Edith. Thanks. I er was wondering about Rita. Is there anything my wife and I can do to help?"

John interjected. "We no longer mention that name in this house Constable Jarvis. She's made her bed and now she must lie in it. There's nowt to come from this family as far as she's concerned."

As he spoke, a thump to the door was followed by Tom staggering into the room, almost falling over the large dining table. As he fell the big man grabbed at the brown plush tablecloth with its tasselled fringe. Edith managed to hang onto it, preventing it from following her brother to the floor.

John was up in an instant.

"You great useless lump! Lolloping all over in ale. Where's your self-respect. Hav'na we got enough trouble wi'out you adding to our shame. Get on your feet and get upstairs."

As the drunken man rolled about attempting to regain his feet, Rod Jarvis grasped him beneath the armpits pulling him upright. Lifting and carrying he helped his friend up the steep stairs to his room. John, with head in hands, rocked in Polly's empty chair, declaring his humiliation to the village Constable and the world.

Police Constable Rodney Jarvis left the house with a heavy heart, pushing his bicycle down John's garden path, out onto the ash lane, past the allotment gate, to continue his rounds.

EIGHT

Calver Wilson and the rest of the Durnley gang huddled around tables pushed together in the corner of the taproom of the Net and Ferret. They were deep in animated conversation but apart from the occasional banging of a fist on the table or a foul mouthed expletive they kept their voices low. It was clear that their business was their business and no one else's.

"So his Lordship's set on some more keepers. They've never bothered us 'afore. Why all the worry now?"

The heavily built, dark haired man with the bruiser's nose and twisted mouth glowered at his companions, demanding an answer.

The calm, measured voice of Bade Durnley responded with authority. "'Cos the law is being brought in an all Jess Fallows. That puts a different shine on things. You sort out a keeper and that's bad enough. Beatin' one of the constabulary 'll get ya fourteen year hard labour on a rock pile. OK? Owt else to say Jess?"

Fallows wasn't about to cross Durnley. He said, "OK Bade. You're the boss."

The gang muttered amongst themselves but fell silent as Durnley, after taking a swig of beer, continued.

"Constable Jarvis knows us all and Cal's facing hard labour a'ready 'cos of that rozzer. If he's captured out on bail it'll be all the worse. If Jarvis is out there with his pals then it makes life difficult. We'll have our collars felt before you can say Jack Robinson," he paused and looked hard at the previous speaker, "or for that matter Jess Fallows."

Calver Wilson spoke out. "So what do we do Bade? It's the right time now. Plenty a good shooting about. Quality game, that's what customers want, not just bloody rabbits. It's likely I'll be drawin' quite a stretch at next Sessions so I'll ay to build up me stash before I gu' down."

In that cold measured way he had Durnley cautioned, "Hold steady Cal. Hold steady. Ya can do a bit o' bird standin' on yer 'ead but there's no need to panic. It might not come to that. We'll give punters what they want. We'll have to box clever that's all. See if we can't minimise the opposition."

Jess Fallows ran a hand through his thatch of shaggy hair and with a bewildered look said, "I don't understand a word you're talkin' about Bade. Milim, Minitim, bloody 'ell man what are you talkin' about?"

Picking up his battered, sweat-stained trilby hat, hooked about with fishing fly, Bade set it at a rakish angle upon his head. Dark locks curled out beneath the well handled brim. A toothy grin creased his weathered face as he knowingly tapped the side of his nose.

"Get rid o' the problem, that's what I'm sayin'; get rid o' the problem."

Still not sure of what was being said, the big man asked, "How do we do that then Bade?"

With more than a hint of intrigue in his voice he answered, "That's my worry Jess, that's my worry."

With that final dismissive declaration Bade Durnley picked up his pint pot, drained the remaining contents, tipped the brim of his hat to his poacher gang and left the smoke room of the Net and Ferret.

*

8ᵗʰ May 1945

Edith Oakley rushed into the front room of her home shouting excitedly, "Dad! Dad! It's over. The war's over. Hitler's killed himsen and't Gerries have surrendered!"

Her father asked incredulously, "Are thaigh sure lass. Where've ya got that from?"

"It's right Dad. It's been on the wireless. Constable Jarvis has had a message from his headquarters and he's on the street telling everybody. There's a van going round later with a loudspeaker. Oh Dad! It's over. Our Jack'll be coming home soon. They say there's going to be big street parties and the King is going to broadcast to the nation. Oh! I'm so happy Dad."

Edith threw her arms about her father's neck and planted a big kiss on his forehead before hugging her mother and tucking her up in her chair.

"Well I'll be dashed!" declared John Oakley. "What about that then Polly? I bet you never thought we'd see this day did ya?"

He gently hugged his wife as she sat in her rocking chair and, kissing her pale cheeks, said tenderly, "Is that a smile I see lass? Dang my eyes it is. Now that really makes my day."

The big man fussed around and after checking the wet batteries were sufficiently charged to power the wireless he declared, "I'll switch it on and we can all sit down and listen to what's gone off."

All eyes were on the receiver settled upon a shelf alongside the chimney breast. From within its well polished wooden casing the valves flickered and the unmistakeable

73

sound of Prime Minister Winston Churchill's voice came to them over the air waves.

"It's Winnie," declared John. "We've missed a bit. It's started a'ready."

In awed silence they huddled around the set listening to the stirring oratory of the man who had inspired the nation from the outbreak of war, through terrible times to ultimate victory. The Prime Minister's final emotional words to the people "God bless you all" echoed the sentiments of the Oakley family.

John was beside himself, overjoyed by the realisation that the black cloud of war had been lifted and a new dawn beckoned.

Turning to his daughter he said, "Come on Edith – gi' me a hand wi' yer Mam. We'll go out int' street and join in wit' celebrations. It's about time we had some good news to cheer us up."

Edith wrapped a blanket around her mother and John lifted his dear Polly into her wheelchair. He was a little concerned that Tom wasn't with them. But he soon brushed those thoughts aside as the happy band of Oakleys made their way onto the street, joining the other villagers dancing and singing, ecstatic at the news.

John Oakley led his family in the celebrations. There was back slapping and hugging aplenty. Patriotic songs filled the air, becoming more energised and raucous as the beer and potent home made hedgerow brews began to flow. Edith and the other villagers set about trimming up the village. Attics, cubbies, cluttered glory holes, sheds and outhouses were rummaged and pilfered. Anything and everything able to bring a vestige of brightness and colour to the usually dirty, drab pit village was seized. Red white and blue bunting,

Union and St. George's flags, streamers, even Christmas trimmings were strung across the narrow communal streets and yards. The result was a veritable renaissance. A kaleidoscope brightening up the dark alley ways and jennels. The village, a microcosm of the nation, decked out with the symbols of national pride and a great sense of joy, after six long painful and costly years of war.

And so the war was finally over. It was the moment everyone had been waiting for and now it had finally arrived. Peace! The men were coming back home, or at least those that had survived would be coming home. From bomb-torn cities to depleted hamlets the nation celebrated. Langwith celebrated. Very quickly street parties were organised. The Oakley clan played their part. Everyone mucked in to help. Spotless white bed sheets ponched and boiled in dozens of scullery boilers were prepared, in order to be spread across rows of tables that would be set up in the streets. They would show off the delights on offer conjured up from the secret corners of war time larders and American food parcels. Dried egg, raisins, currents, jellies and blancmange and home made ice cream. The children especially would love it. John would butcher one of his pigs up at the allotment. He would use the congealed blood with barley and oatmeal filler, seasoned with fresh grown herbs to make scrumptious black pudding; and he wouldn't report it to the Ministry. It would be the highlight of the villagers' celebrations and they would all share in the hog roast. Later as the returning service personel arrived home many children would be seeing Dad for the first time. In some households that no doubt created its own problems.

Jack Oakley returned a decorated hero. His joy turned to sadness when he learned of the events at home. Having fought

75

his war and lost many friends and comrades he found that added to the list of casualties were a brother killed, another a shell of his former self and a shamed sister. But the soldier had become hardened by death towards death. He took the family tragedies in his stride, paid homage to his absent siblings and set about preparing for his new life in Civvy Street.

But Edith saw no change in Tom. He continued to carry bitterness deep within his soul where it seemed to eat away like a canker. Drink, instead of lessening the black hatred, appeared to make things worse. He became more vocal and aggressive. Her big brother had become a man to be pitied or ignored, and all too often in his cups, feared.

The changing circumstances didn't interfere with Edith's trips to Nottingham on the seven o'clock bus. She never told her Dad but confided in Tom during one of his sober moments.

"I've been to see our Rita in Nottingham like I promised," she said.

For a moment Edith thought she saw a reaction in her brother's eyes at the mention of his sister's name. She hoped so as for so long they only mirrored his inner desolation.

Tom asked expectantly, "How is she Edi? Is everythin' alraight?"

"She sends her love to you Tom and doesn't want you to worry about her. Everything'll be alright, you'll see."

"Everythin'll be alraight? What's that mean, is summat wrong then? If there is I want ta know," he demanded.

"She's alright." Edith was trying to choose her words carefully. "She said you'd start to worry. But there's no need. She's being looked after. There's been a bit of a problem with the pregnancy but it's not as bad as they thought."

Voicing his concern Tom asked anxiously, "What problems. Is she goin' to lose the babby. Rita's alraight in't she?"

Edith thought for a moment before responding and took her brothers huge hands in hers. She looked into his sad still handsome face. She could see the worry in those once vibrant eyes now dulled through drink and hopelessness.

She said quietly, "I'm not going to keep anything from you our Tom. She's your sister as well as mine. And I know you love her just as much as me."

"Go on then," her brother said irritably.

"She's in hospital. Not very well. At moment baby's fine but there are problems and she could lose it. "

In a voice aquiver with concern he asked, "What about Reet, She's not goin' to die is she?"

Edith could take no more. Here was her big brother with all the troubles of his shattered life to contend with, showing such love and compassion for his young sister's predicament. She threw her arms about his neck and resting her head on his shoulder, cried.

Tom put his arms about her and said softly as if he was comforting a baby, "There, there. Dunna cry lass. Shhhh. Shhhh."

Regaining her composure the young woman said, "It's fifty, fifty with her. We could lose her and the baby. The next twenty four hours are critical. Oh Tom! What shall we do if she dies?"

Tom held her tightly to him. "We shan't look ont' dark side sis. Let's pray for our Reet and her little 'un. Whilst there's life there's hope. The good Lord'll see to her. Never you fear."

Edith gained control of herself and said, "You're right

our Tom it's in the good Lord's hands now. We can only pray and hope that he answers our prayers." She added with a note of caution, "Don't tell me Dad about it. I'll tell him in due course and I'll keep you up-to-date so stop worryin'. It'll all work out right in the end."

Tom nodded. Both he and Edith knew there was nothing more they could do to help their sister at this difficult time. The fate of Rita and her unborn child was in the hands of a higher authority.

NINE

Sergeant Jack and his two constables had rendezvoused at the footpath leading into Scarcliffe Park. In the distance St. Luke's church clock struck twelve. As the last fading chimes floated across the darkening countryside and wooded acres, the sergeant consulted his watch and confirmed, "Midnight."

He cast a sharp eye over his men, Constables Rod Jarvis and Charlie Underwood, ensuring that they were properly kitted out for night duty.

"Fine,"he said approvingly. "Night uniforms and capes. No shiny buttons or badges. All black non-reflective. You'll blend better in the shadders . And you'll be thankful for that cape. It's going to be a cold 'un out in them woods tonight." As an afterthought he advised, "Shove your truncheon in your waist belt that'll give you quicker access to it. Not so much chance of it snagging. Could be the difference between life and death. Now produce your appointments."

Both officers produced their lamp, staff and handcuffs for the Sergeant's inspection and checked that their whistle and pocket book were available if needed.

Satisfied they were ready for duty the supervisory officer said wryly, "I don't know about them poachers if they're out there but you're a fearsome-looking duo and you'd scare the living daylights outta Lucifer himself." He continued, "Right you know the plan. Rod you make your way down to the

Spinney. Wait there until six o'clock. Take your snap but keep it quiet. If they don't know we're out here tonight, they soon will. We're on their territory and they know it inside out. Charlie, over to the Old Mill end, same thing. Stay till six o'clock. I'm going down to the lake. We'll rendezvous at Spinney. Wait till the last man arrives. Any problems three blasts on the whistle. Any questions?"

Both officers shook their heads.

"Good. Be careful now. Don't take unnecessary risks. I don't expect any problems but if there are, three long blasts for help and we'll get there in double quick time. OK?"

With that final piece of advice he watched his two men make off into the darkness, pushing their service pedal cycles. When they were lost to view he made his way along the narrow footpath through the wood that would take him to the lake.

*

Rod Jarvis had been out like this many times before but it didn't make things easier. In darkness the woods seemed to encircle him, attempting to intimidate with cold, nocturnal fear. Nature's odour of death, that special earthy stench, damp and musty, of rotting vegetation, drifted on the night air heightened by the stillness and dark. The gloom played tricks with his eyes. Twisted tree stumps took on the form of stooping, furtive figures, flitting between the hazy outline of the massed tree trunks. Swaying branches and dark foliage added to the confusion of thought and imagery which embraced him. Disorientation became accentuated by sounds unheard in a daylight world. A nightjar's churring call and owls hooting mingled with the high-pitched bark of a fox and grunt of a badger. Currents of air gusting in the overhead canopy created an uncontrollable rolling rush, intending to roar like an angry ocean crashing onto a rocky shore; only to fade with a whimper amidst the rattle of a million leaves. Movement in the darkened undergrowth, exaggerated in the blackness, caused the Constable to stop and look back along the dark path. He saw only the dark and heard only the sounds of the night.

Suddenly an alien sound, a sharp crack from the spinney floor over to his right caused him to stop once more. Was some prowling nocturnal creature foraging out there in the shadows? Or something more sinister? Poachers after quarry? For all that Sergeant Jack romanticised them, he knew they were not the salt of the earth, but dangerous thieves, not averse to using firearms if it prevented their being taken. Peering into the darkness, head to one side, he strained to identify the sound. He didn't hear it again. Cautiously he moved on.

Down at the Spinney, his allocated post for the night, Police Constable Jarvis pushed his cycle out of sight into the bracken and took up a position near to the footpath that intruders would undoubtedly use.

Beneath his cape he gripped the truncheon and said to himself, "They'll have to be good 'uns to take on me and you my lad." As an after thought he said, "and I thank the Chief Constable for my cape. Warm and protective, it's worth its weight in anything you care to mention."

Snap time, all being well, about three o'clock. He always had his old miners' snap tin on such tours of duty. Tonight he had a pack up of cheese and tomato. He could smell it in the bag at the back of his bike. It was something to look forward to on such a cold night.

PC Jarvis's thoughts were interrupted by the sound of a motor vehicle approaching in the distance. The officer crouched in the darkness peering towards the sound. It had come from the road the other side of the wood. Then the engine suddenly cut out. A good distance from his position but he knew poachers could move quickly and silently through such areas. They knew every inch of the terrain. Not like the old days, he recollected, when motor vehicles were the playthings of the rich. Now all sorts of people had access to them, including poachers. The big gangs all used vehicles. They could travel greater distances and take away more booty. In these depressed times the demand for their services was even greater. The poorer classes wanted rabbits, the richer the stylish game. Quality restaurants paid big money for prime birds and venison.

Police Constable Jarvis, alone with his thoughts, was taken by surprise. The dark figure emerged like a phantom from the wood to confront him. His mind raced. He could not tell how many there were. In the dark he had heard and seen nothing. The officer cursed the cape preventing him from quickly bringing his staff into operation.

*

Dawn broke across the lake. Geese, varieties of ducks and drakes, dabchicks and water hens gave vent to their feelings as they glided or scurried across the mirrored surface. The pale light of morning increased its intensity. Streams of glittering colour rose and fell in the wake of cruising waterfowl, jewels sparkling in the splashed pools of waders.

"All very pretty," muttered Sergeant Smithurst from his hide in the wood as he shivered in the cold morning air.

"Nearly six o'clock, nothing's going to happen now. Give it a few more minutes and I'll call it a day."

Having resisted the temptation all night, like the good professional he was, Sergeant Jack took out a packet of Wills Woodbine and lit up a cigarette. He sucked the warm smoke into his lungs

"Ah! Wonderful, worth waiting for," he purred.

That was before the coughing fit reduced him to a floundering jelly, for minutes of no use to man or beast. Recovering his bicycle from the undergrowth, giving a final cough and spit, he rode off to the rendezvous, cigarette hanging limply from his lips.

From the direction of the Old Mill, Police Constable Underwood pedalled towards the meeting place. Nothing had happened of interest all night. The only thing, apart from scavenging wild animals and birds, had been the motor vehicle in the distance but it had been too far away to concern him, more in Rod's direction. He looked up at the morning sky.

"It's going to be a nice one today. A couple of hours a bed and I'll go to Carburton lakes for a bit of fishing."

As he reached the junction with the foot path leading into the Spinney he saw Sergeant Smithurst approaching, pedalling at his usual steady pace, bicycle clipped trousers legs slowly rising and falling.

"Mornin' Sarge. Nothin' to report. All correct."

"Thanks Charlie, same my end. Silent as the grave." He looked at his watch.

"Book me at ten past six. Alright?"

Charlie nodded and said, "Right Sarge. Wonder how Rod's got on?"

The answer to his question became apparent almost

83

immediately. He could see a pair of legs clad in service trousers and heavy duty boots thrusting out of the undergrowth into the dirt path.

"Christ Sarge! It's Rod! He's down!"

Leaping from his cycle he let it crash into the grass verge where it fell onto its side with rear wheel spinning. Charlie rushed to the prone figure. With heart thumping he approached his friend, not knowing what to expect. Dropping to his knees he reached into the undergrowth. He felt Rod's neck. It was cold. There was no pulse. Sergeant Smithurst pedalling furiously rode up to join him and despite his bulk alighted quickly from his bicycle which he thrust unceremoniously into the undergrowth. He knelt down alongside Charlie Underwood who was crouched over the prone figure of his other man.

Not too sure of the situation but fearing the worst he enquired, "Well Charlie?"

"He's dead Sarge. Been dead three or four hours. Maybe more. Rigor mortis has set in."

"What's happened? Has he been shot?"

"Don't know Sarge but his face is a right mess and whoever's done it is long gone."

After a cursory examination of Constable Jarvis's battered face Sergeant Smithurst reached over and placed two fingers upon his fallen officer's neck. He removed his helmet and pressed his head against Rod's chest. After a few moments he stood up and replaced the headgear. With a grim expression upon his usually cheerful face he ordered, "Right Charlie. You wait here. I'll go and get some help. Protect the scene and make a sketch and written record of everything. I'll be back as soon as I can."

Charlie Underwood watched the portly Sergeant, bent

over the handlebars of his heavy service bicycle, pedalling like a fury down the narrow track. With cape fluttering, bike-clipped legs rising and falling like pistons on the pit winding gear he was soon lost to sight. Charlie took out his pocket book and started writing.

*

PC. Underwood was relieved to see the group of uniformed and plain clothes officers hurrying up the narrow footpath towards him.

"They've made good time," he muttered, "only an hour or so since Sgt. Jack left."

He'd not liked being there, alone with Rod. Somehow it didn't seem right. Him lying there, bloodied and battered, half hidden by the bracken, insects crawling over him, biting and laying eggs. After all it was Police Constable 589 Rodney Jarvis stretched out there. On a number of occasions he'd half expected him to get up and say, "Fooled you Charlie and Sergeant Jack. Made you gulp a couple of times. Are we going fishing later on?"

But it didn't happen, couldn't happen. Rod was dead. Charlie even found himself talking to his lifeless friend, couldn't help it. It was so surreal.

"Come on Rod, you've had your bit of fussy now let's get you brushed down and think of what we're going to tell Sergeant Jack. He'll have your guts for garters. You see."

But Rod still lay there. Lay awaiting the formalities of identification and official declaration of death. Charlie Underwood grimaced as he thought of the indignity his friend's body would undergo as the Police Surgeon thrust the thermometer up his back passage. And the emotion as

85

his battered body was stretchered in deathly silence, along that narrow uneven path, to a vehicle waiting to transport him to the mortuary for post mortem.

As he moved to meet the approaching group the rural bobby muttered, "Chief Constable and Head of CID! Bloody hell Rod they've turned out in force for you lad. Must have smelled your cheese and tomato pack up."

Some yards away from the body Charlie Underwood held up his right arm, as if he were on traffic duty at the miners' gala. The advancing party stopped. Charlie walked a few more paces, came to attention in front of the tall, military looking figure of the silver haired Chief Constable and saluted. The Chief returned his salute with a practised flourish.

Charlie reported. "Police Constable 492 Underwood sir. I must ask you and your party to advance with care from this point on. Rod, er, Constable Jarvis is lying just there." He turned and pointed to the partially hidden body. Heads turned and eyes focused in the direction he indicated.

"The scene should be preserved as much as possible to enable a proper examination to be carried out by scenes of crime officers under the command of Detective Chief Superintendent Rawlings. Sir." Constable Underwood saluted.

The Chief Constable responded and nodded in agreement. "We shall certainly respect your wishes, PC Underwood, and the dignity of Constable Jarvis."

Alongside him, Detective Chief Superintendent Rawlings, a tall, heavily built man with a rugged face and drooping moustache, wearing civilian clothes beneath a heavy overcoat, spoke.

"Thank you Charlie, you've done a good job, is there anything else I should be aware of?"

The Constable had known Frank "The Fox" Rawlings all his service; joined up together but their careers had taken different paths.

"Yes sir. There's something I can't fathom. Last night it was cold and we all wore capes. I wore mine all night and I think Sergeant Jack ...er... Sergeant Smithurst did as well." All eyes turned to the portly supervisory officer who nodded in agreement. "But if you look at Rod, you'll see he isn't wearing his."

The group stood an acceptable distance from the body as the doctor knelt to certify death and briefly examine the obvious head injuries. Charlie turned away as the police surgeon took out his thermometer. The Chief and his party averted their eyes and listened intently to Constable Underwood.

"For some strange reason sir his cape's neatly folded on the path with his helmet, lamp, handcuffs and staff atop." Everyone turned, looking toward the neatly piled objects as Charlie wrestled to understand the implication of his find. "Why Sir?" he asked. "I just don't know. That's about all Sir. Oh! Except there was a vehicle about last night after midnight, I heard it in the distance, more towards Rod's position than mine. That's all Sir."

The Head of CID replied, "Thank you Charlie that's a good report. I know you'll want to stick with the enquiry but you've been up all night and you'll be better after a good rest. Get off home and we'll see you later."

Charlie didn't want to go but he needed to be alone with his thoughts. He cycled slowly home. "I'll go fishing, won't sleep anyway."

*

The scene didn't tell DCS Rawlings too much. Apart from the mystery of the piled up equipment there were obvious signs of scuffling on the footpath and a definite track through the bracken in the wood to the road at the other side. But there were no distinct footprints visible and no discernible tyre tracks on the road. The body yielded no immediate clues and it was clear nothing had been taken from the dead officer.

*

Whilst scene of crime officers sanitised and processed the area around the body Sergeant Jack spoke to Detective Chief Superintendent Rawlings.

"Rod's whistle is still in his tunic pocket sir. He's never attempted to use it."

The Chief Superintendent didn't answer immediately then invited the sergeant to expand his observation. "What's the significance of that Jack?"

The sergeant took off his helmet and scratched his head. "It appears to me sir that Rod knew his attacker."

Sergeant Smithurst had Rawlings attention. "Go on Sarge."

"Well Sir, like I was saying, he's not used his whistle. It was part of his brief to use it in the event of trouble, and he didn't." He paused. "So I reckon he knew his killer but didn't see him as a threat."

Rawlings was interested in Sergeant Smithurst's theory and pressed him further, acting as devil's advocate. "But what if he had been taken by surprise? He wouldn't have had time to use the whistle."

Sergeant Jack had the answer. "But he couldn't have been taken by surprise sir, 'cos he had time to take off his helmet and cape and remove his staff and handcuffs and lay them neatly on the path."

Superintendent Rawlings thought for a moment. "Right Jack. But whose to say he took them off whilst the killer was present and not before?"

Sergeant Jack had no definite answer to that poser but he responded with common sense. "With respect Sir, I can't imagine PC Jarvis intending to spend most of the night, which was very cold, without his helmet and cape. I suspect he knew who ever were confronting him."

"If we go along with your theory Sarge it raises a number of important questions. Firstly, even if he knew the offender, why remove those items? Secondly, it's likely that the vehicle heard during the night transported the killer or killers. Thirdly, who then did PC Jarvis know who held a murderous grudge against him and had access to a motor vehicle? Fourthly, who knew where he was posted? And finally, was the fatal encounter accidental or preconceived? If we can answer those questions we'll progress the investigation."

Sergeant Smithurst nodded and replaced his helmet. There were a number of matters he wanted to sort out in his head before he responded to those propositions.

"Leave that with me sir. I'll make a few enquiries and get back to you at Head Quarters."

As he assisted in carrying the stretcher bearing his dead colleague's battered body down the footpath, Sergeant Jack turned his mind to recent incidents involving Bade Durnley and Calver Wilson. He vowed that the death of Rod Jarvis would be avenged and knew what he had to do.

TEN

Sergeant Smithurst and his team, hiding in the woods near Creswell Crags, watched and waited in silence. Dawn was breaking. The first light of the new day filtered through the trees. Now Sergeant Jack could see their target more clearly. The cabin under surveillance was well placed. It blended naturally with its wooded surroundings but Jack didn't find it too inspiring. All in all it was wretched, dark and uninviting; and the cold night air didn't help.

Detective Chief Superintendent Rawlings, wrapped in his greatcoat, spoke in hushed tones to the Sergeant. "Sarge, quietly pass the word to stand by and wait for my signal."

Jack nodded. The order was relayed to the watchers. Rawlings slowly raised his right arm then brought it down sharply.

Sergeant Jack shouted, "Right lads, Go!"

The response was immediate. The roughly hewn timbered door of Baden Durnley's dwelling crashed open. Torn from its hinges by the heavy shoulder charge of two burly Police Constables. Durnley was taken by surprise and dragged unceremoniously from the matrimonial bed. Wide awake now the naked man resisted violently.

In the unlit room Megan Durnley sat up in bed, holding a baby protectively to her uncovered breasts. The black haired Romany uttered not a word. Her flashing ebony eyes spoke for her. Three young children, awakened from sleep, cowered alongside their mother.

Sergeant Smithurst struck a match and lit the oil lamp on the table. The diffused light, reflected through the lamp's smoky glass chimney, pushed aside the darkness, opening the room to life in the warm golden glow. Jack held up the lamp and followed its mellow gleam as he looked around the cluttered room. He was unprepared for what the dancing flame revealed and declared, "It's a poacher's den alright."

Fastened to the grimy walls the head of a fox and a badger stared down. Their beaded eyes set him, whilst fanged jaws appeared to gnash and snarl in the moving shadows and flickering light. Piled in various corners were traps, snares, nets and badger tongs. The open fireplace was clogged with cold grey wood ash from the previous night's fire. Leaning against the wall stood the poacher's twelve bore shot gun. In his skilful hands through its twin barrels, topped by gaping nostrils, the beast in action breathed out flame and death to unsuspecting victims.

Sergeant Jack's troubled mind suddenly saw the half-hidden corpse of an unsuspecting victim – Rod Jarvis – an illusion created by the lamp's unsteady flame and his distorted reason. He quickly turned to the struggling Durnley, arms held behind his back, resisting the handcuffs.

The officer, disturbed by recent events, exacerbated now by the gypsy's violent resistance, struck the prisoner a backhanded blow across the mouth. Blood flowed and Durnley dropped to his knees. The manacles were screwed into place.

A worn army blanket was pulled from the bed. With little thought for the dignity or comfort of the occupants it was thrown over the bloodied, naked prisoner. He was dragged to his feet and bundled before the senior detective silhouetted in the doorway.

Rawlings, grim faced, took hold of the gang leader and said coldly, "Baden Durnely, I am arresting you on suspicion of the murder of Police Constable 589 Rodney Jarvis. You are not obliged to say anything unless you wish to do so but what you say may be put into writing and given in evidence."

Durnley wrapped the blanket about him, spat out blood and replied defiantly, "Jarvis? Had it coming to him. He won't be missed. Have you lifted Cal Wilson?"

It took two of his colleagues and a forceful glare from Rawlings to stop Sergeant Jack from striking the prisoner again. Durnley grinned and spat out more blood. As he was bustled to the police vehicle secreted in the nearby lane Smithurst noted the prisoner's reply and said, "Your partner in crime Wilson? He'll be banged up by now together with Fallows and the rest of the murderous scum. The writing's on the wall Durnley, it's the end of the road for the lot of you."

Rawlings ordered that the prisonrs be kept apart, isolated in separate cells in police stations scattered around the County. He knew they'd quickly realise the seriousness of their position. Murder of a Constable was high on the Calendar. And in truth there is no loyalty amongst thieves. Experience had taught him that to poachers taking his Lordship's game was one thing, but this, oh no! They didn't intend facing the hangman at Lincoln jail for someone else's murderous felony. The rules of the game were changing. He would see to that.

Fallows cracked first. Quickly distancing himself from his cronies, blurting out anything he thought Rawlings and Smithurst might want to hear.

"We know'd the law was out after us. And Bade said Constable Jarvis would lift us quicker'n you could say Jack

Robinson. But not to worry he'd sort him out. Get rid of the opposition he said."

It was exactly what Rawlings wanted to hear.

Later Amos Jimson recalled the recent incident in the Net and Ferret. "Constable Jarvis had to defend himself against Calver Wilson. After he'd been knocked down and 'cuffed Wilson swore to swing for the officer. You could see by his eyes that he meant it."

"What about Durnley?"

"He didn't have a go. Didn't fancy his chances against Mister Jarvis then. But his threat was clear enough. Warned him to watch his back in future."

Sergeant Jack recorded the words of Fallows and Jimson in his notebook. These two would be important witnesses in the future trial of PC Jarvis's killers.

*

Rawlings and Smithurst visited John Oakley. Sergeant Jack saw that the big man was shocked to hear of the death of the popular local Constable, a friend as well as a policeman.

He sounded like a blood and thunder revivalist preacher as he declared, "I've been saying it all along, there's no sense nor reason for all that's going off lately. The world's gone mad plunging out of control. Believe me it'll lead to its ultimate destruction."

Rawlings was not interested in Big John's prophesy of doom, he was more concerned in the activities resulting in destruction on big fight night.

"What did Constable Jarvis make of it Mr. Oakley?"

John, slower in his delivery of late, thought for a moment and said, "He was certain Durnley and Wilson had doped

93

our Tom and meant to prove it. He reckoned Wilson had slipped something to Chick Bembridge between rounds and doctored his man's gloves. When my lad couldn't see and he were taking some fist off The Seaman, Wilson were screaming for him to 'kill the blind bastard.' He'd fixed Tom alright. Wilson's got a violent streak wouldn't put anything past him."

Rawlings asked, "What about the relationship between Wilson and your daughter Rita?"

John sat upright in the chair and closed his eyes. He said, "I don't have a daughter of that name. The one I had brought shame on this house and no longer belongs to us."

Rawlings couldn't do with these outdated Victorian attitudes but knew he would get nowhere in confrontation with John. He came at him from a different angle.

"Was Wilson jealous of the attention she paid to Constable Jarvis?"

With no elaboration Big John simply said, "Yes."

*

An examination of the tyres on Durnley's pickup truck revealed soil comparable to that in the lay-by on the road opposite the scene of the killing. And debris in his boot soles matched that in the wood. But then he was a poacher and the woods were his hunting grounds. Material on the base plate of the shotgun stock was identified as blood but could not be categorised.

At the subsequent Assize court trial the jury listened intently to the evidence. Rawlings was sure he had a case, albeit circumstantial, that would put the noose around the necks of the police killers Durnley and Wilson. The senior investigator even put forward an explanation for the neatly folded cape and the other items found at the scene.

"My Lord, Durnley and Wilson drove up to the lay by knowing that PC Jarvis was in that part of the wood. They surprised him at his post. Then, to humiliate their enemy and prevent him from defending himself, he was ordered at gun point to remove his cape, helmet, handcuffs and staff. Unarmed and disadvantaged, the officer was then subjected to a brutal battering to the head and body with fists, boots and the butt of the shotgun. The defenceless officer died at the hands of the two merciless killers brought before you today."

The jury seemed impressed.

The senior detective also told the court that blood had been found on the clothing and boots of both accused. It was damning evidence. However, under cross examination he was forced to concede that, as with the blood found on the butt of the shot gun it could not be categorised. But the implication was clear. The damage was done.

Jess Fallows was produced as a witness for the prosecution.

During his evidence in chief the Crown prosecutor asked the poacher, "Were you with Durnley and Wilson on the night of the murder of Constable Jarvis?"

Fallows replied forcibly, "No. Definitely not."

"Did you see the accused that night?"

"No Sir."

"Where were you?"

"Well I weren't with them two killin' a bobby."

"I asked where you were Mr. Fallows. Please answer the question."

"I were rabbitin' on Wembourne estate. On me own. And I didn't ketch a deal either."

95

"Are you certain Mr. Fallows that Durnley and Wilson were not with you that night?"

Fallows addressed the Judge, "Me Lord I'm speakin' the truth." He made great show in crossing himself and said, "God's honour."

His Lordship removed his spectacles and glared at the witness. He said, "Quite so Mr. Fallows, quite so."

The prosecuting barrister said, "Thank you Mr. Fallows. Wait there, defence counsel will ask you some questions."

Fallows shuffled uneasily and gripped the front of the witness box. He watched the defence counsel adjust his wig and take hold of the front of his gown with both hands before standing up to confront him.

The brief stared at the witness for a moment then went at him like a fighting dog.

"Fallows, you're a poacher aren't you?"

He replied confidently, "You know the answer wi' out askin me. You got me sent down a couple a year ago."

"Answer the question Fallows. You are a poacher aren't you?"

"Yeah."

"And on the occasion that you have just drawn to the attention of the court who were you convicted with?"

"Does it matter? That's got nowt to do with this case. This is the murder of a local bobby. Not a few rabbits from park"

"Again Fallows answer the question."

"For what it's worth it were Bade. Bade Durnley in't dock there." He nodded towards the accused who tipped his forelock with an outstretched finger and gave a mock bow.

"And I put it to you Fallows that Mr Durnley is regularly out at night with you taking conies. Isn't that so?"

"We call 'em rabbits mester. Not them fancy foreign names. Who's goin' to buy them off yer? Nobody. Punters want to know what they're gerrin. They want good English rabbits. Nowt else. "

From the bench his Lordship, seemingly intent on moving the case forward, said to the witness, "Mr. Fallows answer the defence counsel's question. It is quite straightforward. Does the accused Durnley accompany you on your night incursions onto the Wembourne estate to poach rabbits? And was he or Wilson with you on the night Constable Jarvis was killed? Is that clear?"

Fallows gave an exaggerated bow to the judge and in an almost reverent voice said, "It is M'Lord. Clear as day. And with a clear conscience I can swear on a stack o'Bibles that though we go out together a'nights with dogs and things Bade Durnley weren't with me that night and neither were Calver Wilson. And that's God's honest gospel truth." He added with another bow to the judge, "M'Lord."

Turning to the defence counsel the Judge directed, "I think that matter has been taken as far as it can go. The witness has answered your question. He is clearly not intending to change his evidence. If you have no more questions of him we will move on. Alright?"

There was noticeable consternation on the defence benches and the accused were not too happy either.

Detective Chief Superintendent Rawlings on the other hand seemed delighted with Fallows's evidence. The gallows tree loomed large.

It was at this point that Durnley's controversial reply to the charge of murder realised its significance. From the witness box Sergeant Jack Smithurst played to his audience, his best performance ever. Kipling would have been proud of him.

He set the scene of Durnley's arrest and the contempt in the gang leader's voice as he spat out, "Jarvis? Had it coming to him. He won't be missed. Have you lifted Cal Wilson?"

That heartless reply, uttered so soon after the police officer's brutal slaying, did nothing for the defence. Though both men continued to deny the charges against them Durnley and Wilson were doomed. But then they had been from the outset of the investigation. The police and public knew who the cowardly killers were and the evidence proved it. Justice had triumphed. Their appointment with the hangman was written in blood. Rawlings and Smithurst celebrated.

*

The bedraggled woman wrapped in a heavy shawl stood before the great studded doors of Her Majesty's Prison Lincoln. Rain sheeted down determined to wash away that unwelcome morning. But it only heightened her awareness of that cold depression which seeped into everything. Through the rattling spray bouncing ankle high off the cobbled drive she scarce saw her feet or those of the three children clinging to her long skirts. Beneath the shawl she shielded the baby clasped to her. Alone, they stood as one, as rivulets of rainwater scurried across the uneven forecourt, cascading over the kerbstone edge, before rushing along the streaming gutters to bubble and gurgle down cast iron drains. The woman stared upwards, never once flinching in the downpour. She stared at the clock in the tower above the prison gate. She stared at its black finger progressing unerringly, minute to minute; jerk and stop, jerk and stop. She willed it to stop forever. The rain teemed down. She watched the long black finger move the measured distance to the hour.

"It's such a short distance," she bemoaned, "such a tiny measurement, such a little mark, the moment between life and death."

The clock struck nine, the moment of destiny. The woman finally lowered her head. Rain ran down the lank tresses. She gathered her brood about her, adjusted the position of the baby and with head held high made off on foot towards the town.

A prison officer opened the wicket gate, set in a corner of the main prison door. He peered after the departing figures, almost hidden in the rain, but didn't venture out. He shrugged and with a quick glance at the paper in his hand intended for Megan, pinned it to the notice board inside reception. It read:

WE THE UNDERSIGNED HEREBY DECLARE THAT JUDGEMENT OF DEATH WAS THIS DAY EXECUTED ON BADEN POWELL DURNLEY AND CALVER WILSON IN HIS MAJESTY'S PRISON LINCOLN IN OUR PRESENCE AT 0900 HOURS.

SIGNED. PRISON GOVERNOR. DOCTOR AND CHAPLAIN.

*

Megan Durnley stood on the bridge spanning the River Witham and looked out across the swirling waters. For the first time her stoicism faltered. Her head, crowned with hair black as polished ebony in the rain, dropped to her chest. She hustled her children to the low parapet, gathering them beneath her wide skirts in a futile attempt to keep the insistent downpour from them. A sob wracked her slender frame. Salt tears mingled with the rain running down her cheeks. She could taste their bitterness on her lips and feel the suffocating blackness hanging heavily about her.

Over the wide expanse of moving water she called out, "Where are you love? We need you, come back to us. Don't leave us."

The children, silent in their innocence, clung to their mother. The dark floodwaters rushing beneath the bridge called back to her offering a gleam of hope. Amid the smothering gloom of those twin deceivers, darkness and despair, Megan saw the solution to her desperate plight.

*

The alarm was raised when a baby, wrapped in a soaking shawl, was found on the bridge.

It was some time before the others were located. Megan Durnley and her three children were snagged among the tree stumps and debris trapped at the weir. The bodies of the mother and her children, like large rag dolls, rose and fell as the waters tugged and pulled, determined to drag them over the edge of the weir into the boiling water below.

The bodies of Megan Durnley and her children were pulled from the weir and taken to the General Hospital mortuary.

PART TWO

PART TWO

ELEVEN

8TH AUGUST 1982
SUNDAY NIGHT

He was uneasy, something wasn't right. Though his mind was bludgeoned by alcohol the big man sensed it. Pulling his shabby raincoat about him, he steered an unsteady course between pavement and road. Stopping once again in the dimly lit street he peered over his shoulder. There was nothing to be seen but the dull glow of the streetlights fading into the dark distance. He shook his head attempting to clear the confusion in his mind. It didn't help. Those mists were always there, often a place of refuge, a place to hide from realities of a life that for years had been spiralling downwards into grim nothingness. He could no longer hear footsteps behind him, only the rush and rhythmic clatter of a train in the near distance. Reassured, he stumbled on, bobbing and weaving, throwing drunken punches at imaginary opponents. Now and then with fists clenched in victorious salute he staggered, acknowledging crowds of wavering shadows, inhabitants of his dark mind, drifting out onto the silent street. Reeling across the road to the far pavement he stopped just before the railway bridge. He fumbled with his flies, intending to relieve himself in the hedge that ran alongside. But there it was again, that uneasy feeling, echoing footsteps, quickening, closer. Something wasn't right.

9th AUGUST 1982
MONDAY MORNING

It was another miserable day. Condensation building up
on the window in my office didn't make it feel any better.
I rubbed a hole in the grey, dribbling stuff. Shouldn't have
bothered, didn't improve anything, just released the foul, wet
stink of somebody's stale cigarette smoke. I got close up to
the window, but not too close, and peered out. It confirmed
what I already knew. It was belting down. I could make out
the railway station on the far side of the car park and figures
hurrying back to work after the weekend, sheltering beneath
umbrellas and turned up raincoat collars. Many would be
cursing the rain as they strove against its relentless battering,
cursing work and cursing employers, cursing life itself.

It was the same here at Mansfield Police Station. Except
that hard nosed detectives don't curse life, they're too familiar
with death for that. Instead they curse the red whistle on a
dented kettle that I could hear screeching away in the kitchen
down the corridor. It was always the same. The kettle screamed
but nobody gave a toss. I continued staring out of the window.
Not really looking through the steamed up glass just waiting to
see how long the tortured scream would go on.

After two very long minutes somebody yelled, "Can't you
hear that bloody kettle McLean? Or have you got your head
up your arse?"

Now this was getting interesting, a damn sight better than
watching rain running down a window. I sat back at my desk
and flicked through the mounds of paperwork piling up in
my IN tray and waited for "Mouthy's" reply. That's what the
regulars in CID call Constable Andy McLean, "that mouthy

southerner." He came from down south somewhere, joined the job later in life than most and now I'd got him from uniform on a CID attachment. I'll give him his due, he's learned quickly to mix it with his northern counterparts and give as good as he gets. With his mouth at any rate. I didn't have long to wait, he was soon amongst it.

McLean yelled back, "Can't hear you mate, got my head up my arse and that's not easy when you're on the blower. And what's wrong with that bleedin' kettle? Can't you hear it or are you deaf or somethin'?"

Somebody switched off the bleedin' kettle but it wasn't McLean because the tall smartly dressed CID aide was standing at my open door.

"Just taken a message from control. There's been a flier at the railway sidings, they're asking for you to be notified."

Now I'm not a fussy guy, been about a bit, but that arrogant, disrespectful way he's got when he speaks gets up my back. It's immature, bordering on offensive. I continued shuffling paper.

Without looking up I asked him, "Is that it then Constable?"

"It is for him. He's come off the bridge and been hit by a train."

I pushed my paperwork to one side and looked at him. His dark eyes took me on but he must have thought better of it and lowered his head slightly and appeared to be staring at my twisted nose.

I said, "Are you speaking to me Constable McLean."

He replied, "Yeh."

There, he's done it again. I gave him a scorcher, stared right through him. I pointed to the door. "Just go out and tell me what it says on that name plate outside."

105

He didn't react, no verbal, just turned, walked slowly from the office looked at the name plate came back and stood in front of my desk.

"Well Mister McLean?"

"It reads Detective Inspector James Stirling Mansfield CID. Sir."

He emphasised the last word. He was learning. Slowly, but he was learning.

"Now what was it you were saying earlier Constable?"

"There's been a flier at the railway sidings Sir, they're asking for you to be notified."

"No more detail than that?"

"It appears to be one of the winos who sleeps rough in the railway carriages sir. Jumped off the bridge got hit by a train."

"If it's a straight up suicide what do they want me for?"

"Don't know Guv, probably uniform wanting a belt and braces job. Let CID make the decisions. Covers the duty Inspector."

There he goes again. Can't make this guy out. I gave him some free advice. "Be careful what you say Andy, you never know who's listening. If you don't make the grade on this attachment you're back in the blue serge suit, pointed helmet and big boots."

I knew it couldn't last. That cockiness was bursting to get out.

"I'll make it Guv. Need the overtime to pay for the whistle." He flicked an imaginary speck from the lapel of his jacket.

I had to smile. Maybe it's me. Maybe I've got him all wrong. He's still got a lot to learn, clearly intelligent and keen to get onto CID. He left a career in the bank to come on this job. We'll see, he might even surprise us all and make the grade.

"Right Andy tell control I'm on my way. If there is anything suspicious it's mine anyway."

*

Twenty minutes later with raincoat collar turned up, hands deep in my pockets, I navigated a path among the masses of railway lines at the sidings. It was wet and cold. I shivered.

"Have I killed a robin or something? It's hammering down. I'm miles from anywhere looking for a mangled corpse on a railway line. I could be back at the nick in a warm office with a nice hot cuppa, laced with Pusser's rum. You'd have thought I'd have learned by now."

I'm talking to myself again. Suppose it's my way of preparing for the unpleasant tasks ahead. Now I haven't got Angie to confide in I haven't got anyone to act as a safety valve. No release from the stress and pent up emotion of the job. That doesn't sit easily with me. Maybe it was my fault. The worst part is I'll never know. It's only eighteen months but it seems a lifetime. And I still miss her. I've got to stop thinking about it. Push it to the back of my mind. Get on with the job.

I never enjoy this part of it though. You'd think that after twelve years of it and having dealt with almost every type of violent, unnatural death that the first encounter with the corpse would be routine. Not for me. I've never got used to it. It's a psyching up job every time, a gulping affair and trying to look unconcerned. It's not a nice experience but you've got to pull it off. Can't give coppers wolfing down their subsidised pre-frozen spaghetti bolognese in the police canteen, the satisfaction of revelling in the Detective Inspector's embarrassment if he bottled it. But it hasn't happened and it won't. I've been at the sharp end for too long. Any qualms I keep under wraps. Save them for home. Behind closed doors I can be my own counsellor. See off a tot and talk to myself and the cat. In a couple of days it'll be history. Report papers filed away, until the next one.

The rain chattered down, rattling the gravel bedding the sleepers and bouncing off the criss-cross network of railway lines; glinting ribbons of wet steel disappearing into the distance. The rain slashed into my face and for a moment I was back on the fo'castle of a destroyer in a storm. Keeping a weather eye on the anchor chains and cables secured to the pitching bow during a middle watch. But the biting rain drove away the distant memories. Through the downpour I could see railway carriages in the sidings. Near to the bridge where they were shunted each night. Further over, dark and silent, a line of National Coal Board wagons straddled the rails. Big and heavy, they awaited the engine that would draw them clanking and creaking back to life. To be hauled to some colliery or power station in the Trent Valley. It felt like being in a bloody B-type movie. All it wanted was a body.

But before I could add it to my wish list there it was, or part of it, angled across a sleeper between the lines. A human leg, obscene and stunted, severed above the knee, still covered in the remains of a trouser leg and well-worn boot.

"Poor bastard!" I said.

Stooping in the downpour I examined the gruesome find and stroked my twisted nose. The leg had been cut off clean as a whistle. And even taking the rain into account I noted that there wasn't much blood.

My deliberations were interrupted by a shout, "Over here Inspector."

Chief Inspector Wooton beckoned to me through the partly opened window of the first railway carriage. I raised an arm in acknowledgement. Shook my head in a flurry of displaced water and hurried through the puddles towards the carriage and the rapidly shut window.

I could see why they wanted CID, didn't fancy getting their nice smart uniforms wet. Not too happy, I got my head down against that torrent of stair rods and pushed on. Next thing I'm arse over tit. Lost my footing on a wet sleeper and nose-dived full length. I was heading for a bath in the oily pools that were springing up all about me in the gravel. Luckily I piled up on top of this bundle of old tarpaulin, saving me a bigger dry cleaning bill. I didn't have much time to ponder upon my good fortune because I realised quickly I was sharing my bed. A lifeless face with a shattered skull lolled close to my cheek. Given a choice I would have preferred the scummy water. Scrambling to my feet I peered at the once handsome face, crowned now by a bloodied tangle of hair, bone and brain. Staring at the remains I could see that he hadn't simply experienced life, he'd clearly confronted it, taken it on and suffered. Even in death the waxen face streaked with blood couldn't disguise the ravages of time and the excesses of life that had now deserted it.

I drew the tarp over the silent form and muttered, "Poor sod. No one deserves to end up like this."

I sloshed into the carriage shaking myself like a shaggy dog. Chief Inspector Nigel Wooton and two other uniformed officers present were bone dry, I noted. By their expressions I could see that they were trying hard not to show that only moments before they had been laughing at my predicament. I rubbed my hands through wet untidy locks. I wasn't in the mood for humour.

"Funny was it? Well, you two get outside, cover the body properly and arrange for Scenes of Crime to attend with a tent to protect the scene."

The two Constables no longer seemed amused.

In a voice dripping with concern one of them said, "It's chucking it down Sir."

Responding with mock surprise I said, "Is it? I hadn't noticed." Turning to the Chief Inspector I asked, "Had *you* Sir?"

Wooton, a young Chief Inspector, is one of the new breed of Bramshill Police College fast trackers. He mumbled something unintelligible and then churned out, "Er ... yes Scenes of Crime with a tent."

I could see he'd lost it. His thin veneer of authority had been severely tested. I soon stripped that away.

"And get a cover over that severed leg up the line." Before Wooton could reply I snapped, "Thought it would all have been done by now Chief Inspector."

Wooton didn't respond. Instead, turning up his raincoat collar he followed the two Constables out of the carriage. I suspect he was seeking solace within the curtain of driving rain.

It was wrong I know but I couldn't resist shouting after him, "You'll find you won't melt Chief Inspector. It's only rain and you are waterproof."

I'd made my point and felt better so I stretched out on the plush First Class carriage seat. Steam was rising from my wet clothing. Through endless rivulets of rainwater tracking down the steamed up windows I watched the vague, distorted silhouettes of Wooton and his officers struggling in the downpour.

With just a hint of devilish sarcasm I muttered, "Mmm! Might be wrong. Could well melt in this lot."

*

Later, under the protective covering of the SOCO tent, I looked more closely at the deceased. The Police Surgeon, taking into account body temperature and prevailing conditions, had estimated, give or take half an hour, death occurring about midnight. Initial examination suggested multiple injuries caused by falling off the bridge into the path of a train. SOCO had taken the photographs and samples I'd wanted and left the crime scene with me.

I was kneeling besides the body giving it a bit more attention, running things through my mind when the tent flap opened and Constable McLean came in.

"Hello Guv," he said, "Thought I'd come down to see if I could help."

"Thanks Andy. I was going to call you. It's a good opportunity to get some practical experience of investigating a violent death. Nothing like the real thing. Have a look. What do you think?"

McLean squatted alongside me. He seemed pleased being invited to assist in the investigation.

After a few moments of deliberation he spoke. "I'd say he's had a belly full, fed up with life, he's jumped off the bridge and caught the midnight flier. Suicide straight up and down boss."

"OK. That was my first thought, and the police surgeon's. Why the midnight train?"

"Er. Just a guess really, a figure of speech. You know the midnight special?"

Midnight special? I think he's got to get real. First time he's been involved in a homicide investigation and he's down the Grand Old Opree with Lonnie Donegan or somebody.

111

"Come on get it together Andy. You disappoint me. I thought you'd used logic to come up with something, not Top of the Pops."

He didn't like that but if I don't say something he'll never learn. And it's no good him glowering. He won't catch villains throwing mardy tantrums.

"Just take a moment or two and think about your theory. Look at the position of the body, examine the clothing and footwear, go outside and look around, when you're satisfied check the bridge."

I don't know if it was done for my benefit but McLean's eyes narrowed momentarily and he flexed his jaw. This is the side of him I don't like to see. Not to dwell on it I moved things on.

I said sharply, "Well?"

McLean in a cold precise manner recited his observations.

"It's a white male, early sixties some twenty yards from the bridge, lying on his back very close to the main line. The skull appears to have received impact damage, probably when coming into contact with the railway line or gravel bed. The left leg is severed at the upper thigh, consistent with being run over by a train. I still support suicide Guv."

"OK, now the bridge."

I think he'd still got it on him when he left. Not used to being told what to do, but he'll learn.

The rain had stopped and from outside the tent I watched McLean picking his way over the spread of railway lines before making his way onto the stone bridge. He seemed to be having difficulty seeing over the parapet. That was significant.

I shouted up to him, "Think about your theory now. Had a belly full didn't you say?" McLean must have heard me because his head quickly disappeared from view.

At the left hand side of the bridge something took my interest. A piece of broken fence had left an untidy gap in the hawthorn hedge that separated the road from the railway banking. A muddy track led down to where I stood. It wasn't too difficult to scramble up the iron rungs set into the stonework of the bridge and reach the road. I took a closer look at the fence butted up to the bridge. It confirmed my initial suspicion. The break in the timber was recent. On the mud and further down the grassy bank small splintered pieces had been pushed into the soil. Something heavy had done that. Perhaps the dead weight of a body dragged over them? What appeared to be fibres were snagged on a broken upright. I carefully took possession of them as possible exhibits. I always had a couple of SOCO envelopes with me and again they came in handy. On my haunches I looked at the bridge parapet. Sheltered by the overlap of a coping stone I could see tiny pear-shaped dark brown splashes. It could be blood, could be paint, could be anything. But my gut reaction was blood. On hands and knees I grovelled about on the pavement looking for something that didn't fit naturally into the location. The rain hadn't helped. It needed Forensic up here. I felt this was an important part of the crime scene that wanted a thorough going over. There wasn't much more I could do so I clambered down the rungs. McLean met me at the tent. He seemed pleased with himself.

"Cracked it?" I asked.

It was a confident reply, "Yeah Guv. I still go with suicide."

"Okay. Let's look at a couple of points. Belly full of beer. What brings you to that conclusion?"

"He's a dosser, an alcoholic, so he always had a belly full."

113

"Good. Now from where I stood, the bridge parapet seemed rather high. I could only just see your head above it. Am I right?"

"Yeah, it's about five feet high."

"So how in hell did a drunk, with a belly full climb up there?"

"Well I, er..."

The directness of my question dented his confidence a little. But he's got to learn, got to get rid of this cocky attitude.

I turned it up another notch. "I'll tell you how. He didn't. If he'd climbed onto the bridge and hurled himself off, he's likely to have suffered severe fractures to his arms and legs. He hasn't. From that height they don't usually land on their head. If he had, the damage to his skull would have been much more severe. More likely that his cranium would have shattered and his brains spewed out."

McLean chewed on his lower lip.

"And what about those deep indentations to the scalp?"

Andy McLean's usually over-confident style was taking a beating.

He could only stutter, "Er. If it's not impact damage Guv I don't know."

I despaired. "If it's not impact damage McLean? Course it's impact damage, but not from jumping off a bridge. They've been caused by heavy blows from behind." I stuck the knife in, "How are we so far *Detective* McLean?"

In a subdued voice McLean answered, "Learning boss. I'm learning."

"Good. The lesson isn't over yet. Did you take a look underneath the body?"

"No sir."

"It's always good practice. When SOCO has finished it's your baby. So check it all out. Especially those parts you can't see."

"Why's that boss?"

"You don't want to look a prat at the post mortem when the doc pulls a poker or a bloody great kitchen knife out of the dead guy's guts do you? Like I did with one of my first murders." I chuckled at the distant recollection. I don't think McLean believed me. He needed some encouragement and a bit of guidance. I said to him, "Remember what we've discussed and look at the body again."

McLean down on his haunches reached out and pulled the body towards him.

He started as the deceased gurgled through exhaled gases being forced from him.

"Get on with it, he won't bother you. Feel around. Is there anything you've missed?"

McLean ran his hands over the outer clothing. The raincoat was bundled up tightly around the shoulders. He would be able to feel the cold firmness of the body where an old woollen jumper and well-worn shirt had ridden up, revealing scratches and scrapes to the bare back.

"No Guv. No weapons or serious wounds that I can see. And definitely no poker."

I had to smile to myself. Definitely no poker! I liked that. It told me something about the lad.

Constable McLean rolled the body back and started to rise.

"Stay there. What does the rain coat tell you?"

I could see that he was finding this in-house training a little different to that he'd no doubt experienced at the bank. But that was three years down the line. He's got to move on if he wants to get into CID. He took a long time before he came up with anything, probably searching for something positive to tell me.

I was surprised when he gave a shrug of his shoulders and said, "Nothing boss. It tells me nothing."

I was disappointed. I'd thought we were getting somewhere but he'd surrendered without a fight. I didn't exactly respond by talking to myself but the decibels were at the lower end of the scale.

I spoke quietly as if trying to reassure that broken body crumpled in front of me that we were still on the job, out for a result.

"Nothing, it tells him nothing. And he wants to become a detective? The most valuable tool available to a detective, apart from good informants, is the ability to observe and deduce from those observations." I couldn't keep it up. Eyeballing McLean I increased the tempo and volume. "The rain coat is screaming out to you. Murder! Murder! Murder! Can't you hear it? If you can't it's back to the blue suit and pointed helmet."

McLean stood up, surprisingly for him at a loss for words. I wasn't and continued with the practical training.

I asked, "Why is the raincoat bunched up at the shoulders and neck? Why is the shirt and jumper half way up the man's back? Why the scratches and grazing? According to you he's jumped off a bridge and his leg's been lopped off by a train. So are you now saying he's got hold of himself by the scruff of the neck and frog hopped himself along the lines?"

McLean's mouth fell open. Before he could answer, though I suspect he had nothing really to contribute to his defence, I demanded, "What did you notice about the man's outer clothing?"

116

McLean said cautiously, "It was wet through Guv?"

"Wet through. All of it?"

It was a simple enough question. But for a moment constable McLean looked for all the world as though he was a victim strapped beneath the hovering blade of Madame Guillotine.

He stuttered, "All of it? Er ...just a moment."

Dropping to one knee McLean felt the raincoat facing him. Reaching under the body he rummaged around before standing up.

"Well?"

"Erm. No Guv, not all of it. The top of the raincoat is but underneath it is still quite dry."

"Well?"

"Well what Sir?"

In the manner of a patient pedagogue I deliberated on McLean's findings.

"The condition of the clothing, wet on top, dry underneath tells us the weather condition at the time the body was left. Clearly it became wet on top whilst it lay in the rain at the side of the railway line. Don't you think that is an important clue Mr. McLean?"

It wasn't exactly rocket science but he appeared as excited as if he'd found the secret of life.

"Yeah Guv. It gives a clue to the time of the attack."

With an exaggerated sense of relief I breathed out, "Thank you Mr. McLean. Where does that take us then?"

Suddenly he was pumped up, confidence soaring, he answered chirpily, "He'd leave some pub in town at closing time. If he came straight here it would take him about half an hour to stumble to the bridge. There he was attacked. He could have been dragged down that bank, which would be dry, because he's dry underneath, then to the lines where his leg was cut off. The screwed up clothing and grazes to his back support his being dragged."

"Simple isn't it?" I said, "Just remember to try and put yourself in the offender's shoes. Think like him, act like him and you'll nail him." I let that free advice sink in and continued, "It started to rain last night just after twelve. The mail train, regular as clockwork, passed through shortly afterwards. So we're looking at a time roughly between half eleven and midnight. He was certainly killed before the rain started. He was killed on the bridge. Bundled down that slope and dragged by his feet to the lines. He was dead when the mail train hit him."

McLean seemed unimpressed by my reasoning. He snapped back impulsively, "How do you know that then Guv?"

I ignored his impetuous outburst putting it down to his cockiness and inexperience. Instead I responded casually and said, "No heavy bleeding. That's because his heart wasn't pumping when the train hit him. He was already dead. Murdered! Not suicide as the killer intended us to believe. Let's go and get the show on the road."

TWELVE

I loosened my tie and took some deep breaths followed by a couple of big gulps. That was my regular routine before I went into the butchery department. That's how I saw the mortuary; nothing more than a glorified butcher's shop. And I never got used to the smell. It permeated everything, nostrils, clothing, hair, even the skin, that sickly, unavoidable odour of disinfectant. Even then it couldn't disguise the stench of death, of leaking, putrefying human tissue and escaping body gases that seemed to cling to everything. That awful smell never seemed to be far away.

"Thirteen hundred hours, Monday ninth of August nineteen eighty two; the Mortuary, Mansfield General Hospital. I am examining the body of a white male, aged about sixty. Auburn hair, powerfully built, fourteen stones four pounds, five feet eleven inches. The major part of the cranium has suffered massive trauma. The left leg has been severed nine inches above the knee..."

I stood on the opposite side of the slab watching and listening to Professor Alan Gordon. The Home Office Pathologist always reminded me of a florid faced, modern day Mister Pickwick in green rubber apron and matching wellies. He was speaking into a hand-held tape recorder. The Professor's assistant fussed about double-checking the

119

screw-top bottles, jars and miscellaneous containers he'd lined up on a nearby temporarily unoccupied slab. I could guarantee that by the end of the post mortem examination most of them, if not all, would contain body parts and tissue suspended in formaldehyde ready for forensic examination.

I've lost count of the number of autopsies I've attended. I don't like having to witness them but it's an important part of a senior investigator's job. I take my deep breaths, gulp and get on with it. Apart from the smell it's that first slicing incision to the upper chest, laying open pink flesh and creamy fat that brings on the nausea and makes you want to turn away. I could see McLean was sweating. He gulped and looked towards the floor and his shuffling feet.

He was gradually edging away from the action. I smiled. He's not so cocky now. Taking hold of his arm I stopped his progress and drew him back to the slab.

I whispered to him, "You'll have to get used to coming in here if you want to make it on CID Andy my boy. It's all part of the job. If you can't hack it, get out of the butchery department, there are always plenty waiting to take your place."

McLean didn't reply; he was too busy trying to hang onto his breakfast.

Casting my eyes along the length of the body lying on the slab, for a cruel moment it made me think of Angie and what she'd been put through. Behind my back I squeezed my hands together until they hurt.

Pushing the painful realism aside I said quietly to McLean, "Never get used to it do you?"

McLean swallowed hard, retched and whispered from behind his hand, "It's my first one Guv."

I was surprised and made a mental note to ensure that

post mortems were included on subsequent CID training courses.

"When I started," I said, "all County coppers were Coroner's officers. We dealt with sudden deaths from start to finish. Remember Professor?"

"Good old days eh Inspector? In the sixties I often paid the duty bobby half a crown to sew up the bodies when I'd finished."

"That was a bit before my time Doc but it's not like that now. Some coppers go their whole service without attending an autopsy."

Doc Gordon didn't answer, he was busy telling his assistant what photographs he wanted during the examination. Next he checked the arsenal of terrifying weaponry that he would wield with such enthusiastic efficiency during the post mortem. As I looked at the scalpels, hand saws, mallets, chisels and other tools spread out alongside the containers on the other slab, I couldn't help thinking, cynically, that even Jack the Ripper or Sweeney Todd would have been impressed.

Taking advantage of the moment I said quietly to McLean, "You'll get used to it. The secret is to remember it's no longer a human being. Whatever you believe, the life force has left the body. It's simply an inert mass, a lump of meat. If you don't come from that direction you'll go mad."

McLean nodded and said, "Thanks boss. I'll try and get my head round that."

I'd always got on with the pathologist, knew him well before he accepted the chair as Professor of Forensic Pathology at a local University; and still called him Doc. He seemed to prefer that down-to-earth, hands-on title.

I said to him, "Doc, can you explain things as you go along? It'll help us get a clearer picture."

121

Professor Gordon peered over his bifocals and nodded. He knew what was being asked of him, knew I'd had been present at many of his post mortems and knew exactly what was going on.

"Right Inspector, I'll try and make it as interesting as I can."

I took a deep breath and prepared myself. It was that time again, pink flesh, creamy fat and nausea. I'd seen it many times during my police career but never got used to those first precise slicing cuts skimming into unresisting flesh. In the upper chest close to both shoulders the pathologist sliced two measured incisions meeting at the bottom of the breastbone. From that point the scalpel continued in one cut down the middle of the body to the pubis. The result was the classic "Y" shaped portal which would give him access to the dead man's organs and the examination to follow.

Then the job took over, the professional detective. I watched as, with practiced ease, the Doc teased the yielding flesh aside to expose the rib cage and breastbone which protect the heart, lungs and other organs. Like a flensed whale they protruded, obscene in their curved nakedness.

The sternum and rib cage grated as the pathologist sawed through them. McLean gulped and turned away as the Doc snapped them off with a forceful wrench, revealing the contents of the thorax. McLean flinched.

"Well calcified," the pathologist explained, laying the severed breast plate to one side.

By this time McLean appeared to have settled down. Maybe my advice had helped. He still turned his head away occasionally and gulped a couple of times but he became absorbed in the systematic dissection carried out by the pathologist. True to his word he made the post mortem interesting. The expert manner in which he routinely sliced up the lungs, heart and liver as efficiently as any chef seemed to fascinate McLean.

The Doc gave a running commentary of his actions, pausing now and then to record his findings on tape.

At one point he scraped the scalpel along an opened length of coronary artery laid out on the slab. It grated like two pieces of sandpaper in conflict.

"Hear that?" he said. "Calcified hardening of the arteries." He concluded, "In poor condition."

The lower sections of the lungs had lost their soft flexibility, reduced to a hard, useless mass. As he scraped mucus from the sliced organs the Professor declared sadly, "A heavy smoker."

He flicked the slime like deposit from his scalpel onto the mortuary slab. The liver appeared to have fared no better from a lifetime of alcohol abuse. By now that sickening smell was heavy about the body. It became worse when the Doc removed and opened the stomach. The smell was overpowering. The partially digested contents of the organ looked like a mash of over-ripe fruit, mingled with meat and cheese that had gone way past their sell by date. The unsightly mess swilling about in stale beer combined together to create this enveloping, gagging choking gas. You could taste it and seeing the stomach's glutinous contents did nothing to ease the ultimate discomfort of that sickening cloud that seemed to hang about for ever. I felt sorry for McLean. He retched. But I'll give him his due, he stuck it out. But he suffered.

The pathologist reported, "The deceased had consumed a fair amount of alcohol prior to death. And heart, lungs

123

and liver show a gross appearance of a more than healthy appetite. He didn't have too long left."

That was important information. I pursued it. "So you're saying their poor condition hasn't contributed to his death?"

"Yes Inspector, that's what I'm saying. When we have closely examined the cranium we shall no doubt see the cause of the unfortunate man's demise."

As he spoke the pathologist ran his scalpel from ear to ear across the top of the deceased's smashed head. McLean grimaced. I leaned over the victim, absorbed in the search for evidence as the doctor peeled the front scalp forward to cover the silent face beneath. As he drew the remainder down the back of head, I saw more clearly the damage to the exposed skull, which always reminded me of a moist, pink, ostrich egg. It was clear that blows had rained down on the victim with savage intent.

"See here, here, here and here." Professor Gordon indicated with a bloodied, rubber-gloved finger. "Four distinct blows with a blunt instrument. Note the overlaying of the injuries which have shattered the skull, suggesting a determined and pitiless attack." He paused, "Let's lift the lid and look inside."

The dull whirr of the hand held Desouter circular saw, as it rapidly cut through the circumference of the skull, made McLean grind his teeth. He wasn't alone. The numbing vibration jagged into the nerve ends of my ivories. It always did. And the smell of heated bone was sickly. But it was absorbed almost instantly into that invisible smell drifting about in the mortuary, adding to its unpleasantness. I gulped. Job done, the pathologist prised off the bony dome with the chisel ended elevator bar.

"Just like topping a boiled egg," I mused.

"Aaagh Guv! Shan't eat another boiled egg." McLean had taken on a shade of greeny, bluey, yellow.

"The cerebrum is extensively damaged," Professor Gordon recorded. "Bone splinters are evident, the result of violent trauma. In my opinion death would be almost instantaneous."

I continued to look at the mashed grey and pale pink matter and the embedded pieces of fractured skull. I asked, "Can you say which blow caused death Professor?"

"Yes, each injury standing alone would have caused death, and so the very first of the four blows killed your man. The following three were to make sure. There's your intent I suggest."

"That's certainly persuasive evidence for malice aforethought Professor. So we can rule out accident and self inflicted injury?"

"In my opinion Mr. Stirling, yes. The fatal blow satisfies your definition of expressed malice as I understand it, the intention to cause death at the outset."

I nodded in agreement. "On the face of it, the killer doesn't appear to have a defence to murder, though no doubt a brief will think something up."

"That's rather a cynical swipe at the legal profession Inspector."

"You know I'm right Doc. We've both taken hammer in the box on many occasions from some smart-alec barrister, pushing for an acquittal against the evidence."

The pathologist gave a non committal shrug then said, "Maybe so, maybe so."

I returned to reviewing the evidence currently at hand.

"To attack a drunken old man from behind and smash in his skull was a deliberate act. In my book that's premeditated murder." I leaned closer to the body scrutinising the shattered skull and asked, "Can you indicate what type of weapon was used Doc?"

Without hesitation Professor Gordon said, "An object some eighteen inches in length, smooth and round in section."

"Such as a length of lead pipe, a metal bar?"

"Yes, or even a length of broom handle," he paused, "or a police truncheon." He laughed.

Throughout our legal deliberations McLean had remained silent. He appeared to be alone with his own thoughts, as if something was on his mind. I could see he was champing at the bit eager to get out of the mortuary. He was clearly relieved when Doc Gordon removed his bloodied gloves and washed up. I arranged for his official report, including photographs, to be forwarded to me as soon as possible. McLean didn't need any telling. Quickly hurrying past the mortuary attendant busily rinsing the pathologist's instruments and hosing down the white slab, he headed for the door. It was noticeable that he turned his head away as dilute blood swilled around the body, swirling and twisting like pink smoke, to be devoured by the chrome-throated drain awaiting it. And the Doc's assistant had been kept busy. He had finished his Lord Lichfield routine and set out the newly labelled screw top jars and bottles on that other slab. They looked like a selection of jams and pickled veg on a WVS stall. Except it was some unfortunate John Doe on display. And he wasn't for public consumption.

*

126

Driving back to the incident room set up at Mansfield police station I spoke to McLean.

"How did you find your first post mortem Andy?"

"A satisfying experience overall Guv, very satisfying."

"Satisfying? A satisfying experience?" I exclaimed, "What's satisfying in seeing a fellow human being butchered on a mortuary slab?"

McLean's reply was measured, with a sense of finality to it. "Satisfying that I faced my own demons during the PM, and overcame them, and satisfying in the knowledge that the system works and in the end murderers get their just deserts."

Not too sure of the logic of the reply I reminded him, "We haven't caught the victim's killer yet," adding, "and yes, sometimes the system works. Not always in the interest of truth mind you, that tends to go out of the window when it falls into the hands of lawyers. "

"You aren't a great supporter of the legal profession then Guv?"

"There are some good lawyers, but they're like a lot of others, out to turn over a few quid. They've got to pay for the big house, flash car, golf club, Masonic and kids' school fees. Truth isn't part of their remit. They never talk about seeking the truth. It's the justice bandwagon they tie their souls to."

"Nothing wrong with that is there Guv? Isn't that's what it's all about. Justice?"

"Justice is what it should be about Andy, seeking justness, a fairness, but in the real world, man's world, it's an imperfect system."

"Are you saying that our justice system isn't fair?"

"I think its imperfect. It's been said that the first victim

127

of war is the truth. And it's often a casualty during a trial. If it's not in the lawyers' interest they'll try to get it slung out in closed session before a jury ever get the chance of hearing it. Without truth there can't be justice. Truth, fairness and justice, should go hand in hand. Protecting the innocent, convicting the guilty."

"I haven't been on the job very long Guv and I haven't got your experience, but I understood the trial to be the process which examines the facts and determines the truth. Surely that's justice."

"If only that were true Andy. Unfortunately the adversarial system has become a game for lawyers. Many see justice as seeking the acquittal of their client, innocent or guilty, within a framework of rules. And don't forget it isn't the man on the Clapham omnibus or you or me that's made those rules, it's lawyers. Then the whole lot's rubber-stamped by politicians, many from the same chambers or lodge and pissing in the same pot. And when it suits them, truth doesn't come into their equation. And the legal aid bills get bigger."

"Are you saying that lawyers are dishonest Guv?"

"No. Not all lawyers. But what can't speak can't lie. Look in the jails, you'll find bent lawyers, just the same as bent coppers, politicians, doctors, academics, accountants, bankers. Criminals come from all backgrounds. Most cons are there because their objective has been an overwhelming desire for power, money, sex or revenge. Often the whole shebang. Lawyers aren't excluded."

McLean didn't answer. He just sat there. Something was on his mind. But on reflection I suppose it was a natural reaction. He'd spent all morning involved with violent, unnatural death, breathed in its odour and been sickened by it in the butchery department as he witnessed the mutilation of human remains.

For all but the most hardened individual it would have been traumatic. McLean needed a bit of space and time to reflect

As we drove into the police station yard, in an effort to be supportive, I said, "You've had a good day. Keep it up."

"Thanks Guv," he said, "I'm working on my next objective. Getting in CID."

McLean's chirpy reply, with no hint of stress or unease at his experience, took me by surprise and set me on my heels for a moment. It seemed the butchery department had been assailed, defeated and locked away. He was dealing with it quite well. Maybe I'd misread Police Constable Andy McLean. Perhaps he was harder than I thought or maybe he had other things on his mind.

*

We joined the CID teams designated for the enquiry assembled in the conference room at Mansfield Police Station. They were an assorted bunch. Men and women of varying ages and service brought in from their respective divisions. I knew most of them from previous investigations. A number were already under my command. Others I'd lectured at detective training centre at varying stages of their CID careers. All were experienced investigators, professional detectives, street wise and dedicated, knew their way around, especially within the criminal community.

The general buzz of conversation was brought abruptly to an end as I called out, "All stand."

To the sound of scuffing chairs and the odd throaty cough, the assembled officers stood respectfully as the Senior Investigating Officer entered.

He acknowledged the gesture and said, "Thank you. Please be seated ladies and gentlemen."

The chairs scraped and clattered for a few moments as the officers settled. Detective Superintendent Peter Davey took the floor. He was a no-nonsense detective of the old school. With his neatly trimmed greying hair, moustache and dark, heavy-framed glasses he didn't look like a policeman. In his heyday he had been tough as old boots. Now nearing retirement he had mellowed. But he was a good boss and a good detective.

He addressed the assembled officers. "Afternoon ladies and gentlemen. You'll notice I didn't say good afternoon because no afternoon is good when murder's involved." He paused, "You have already been briefed so I won't go over old ground. The purpose of this enquiry is to name the deceased and obtain evidence to identify, arrest and charge to successful conviction, the murderer of this unfortunate man. You're all experienced detectives. I don't have to tell you to get out there and turn the place upside down, I know you will. You're all specially selected for the job."

He went on, "The main questions to be asked are, who is the victim and why was he murdered? Having answered those questions we should then be on the way to finding out who had opportunity and the means to kill a penniless, homeless, old man. Any questions?"

From the back of the room a voice queried, "Is this guy a big fella, thin sandy hair, sharp moustache sir?"

Mr Davey queried, "Have you got somebody in mind Charlie?"

Detective Constable Charlie Baker was a good undercover detective. He lounged in his chair, stretching out long legs. With his mane of mousey blonde hair and

130

faded denim jacket and jeans he reminded me of an escapee from a heavy rock band.

He replied, "Yeh boss."

The room was silent, all eyes on the detective, awaiting a follow up. It didn't come. I was impatient to see what he knew and said sharply, "This isn't a bloody quiz game Charlie get on with it."

DC Baker rubbed his nose, sniffled and said, "Could be a guy called Tom, Guv. An old fighter. Sleeps rough in the railway carriages most nights. Uses the Black Boy and all the other tasty boozers in town. You name it he's been barred from it."

"Tom who?" asked the Super.

In his casual laid back style DC Baker replied, "Can't tell you boss. Only know him as Tom or Kelly. That's the name he used to fight under in the late thirties early forties. A good 'un by all accounts till the wine took over."

I could swear I saw the SIO's eyes twinkle. This is what he wanted. That's why these detectives had been selected. Street wise, knew what was going off. Without cracking his face it was clear he was happy with that information.

"Charlie, thanks for that. Are you on DI Stirling's team?"

"Don't know yet Guv."

"You are now. DI Stirling is tasked with identifying the deceased."

Turning to me he said, "That could be a good lead Jim. What I want from you is a positive ident. Then a complete, I mean complete, history of this man and his life. From the day he was born to the day he died. I want to know about his family, love life, friends, enemies, especially his enemies, pastimes, sporting activities. I want you to concentrate on him and report back to me. Alright?"

I nodded and replied, "Right Sir."

He continued, "In the meantime if you identify him positively I want informing pronto. Right Inspector that's you sorted."

I knew where I was going and gathered my team together. McLean was part of it. I'd asked for him so that he could continue to learn under my supervision. We moved off to an office that had been set up for us. There wasn't much in it apart from a few tables and chairs and a blackboard and easel out front. We didn't need much anyway, we weren't expected to be in the nick too long. Our job was out on the streets gathering information.

When everybody had settled I said, "Right folks listen up. I'm not going to repeat what the SIO has already said but I want this bastard. He's still out there and could strike again. He may have a penchant for homeless old men, may see himself as a Don Quixote, a man with a mission, if that's it we've got to stop him before he kills again. On the other hand it may be a one off and he may disappear like a shadow, melt away into the wicked world where he'll gloat over his evil deed, pick up his old age pension and die in absolute anonymity. So what's the motive? Why was such force used on this homeless old man? Does that violence give us a clue to the reason for his death? Is there a background to it? Excessive gratuitous violence is often associated with anger and hatred. And don't forget revenge and jealousy. Keep sight of those classic triggers for brutal homicide throughout your enquiries." Turning to McLean, I said, "Your first job will be to collect actions for the team. I've already supplied the incident room with details."

I continued with the briefing, "So I want you out there, turning over all the dossers in the carriages, railway staff, boozers, your contacts on the streets, day centres, spikes, soup kitchens, church organisations and the like. I want a name for our victim. Bear in mind this old fighter, Tom or Kelly, he fits the description of the deceased."

I said to DC Baker, "Charlie get down to the mortuary and see if you recognise our man."

"OK boss," he replied and left the briefing room.

I was joined then by a smartly dressed guy wearing a conventional dark suit with collar and tie. He was an imposing figure of a man. A head turner. At over six feet tall he was built like the proverbial brick outhouse.

I took the opportunity to introduce him. "Many of you will know Detective Sergeant Johnson; he's my deputy for the duration of this job and he'll accompany me on various enquiries. When I'm not available he's in charge."

The powerfully built Detective Sergeant stepped forward raising a hand in acknowledgement. The guy looked as tough as his reputation. He liked to blame his distinct shortage of hair on the many scrapes we'd been in over the years but I always put it down to his "bad genes".

I continued with the introduction. "For those of you who don't know, Sergeant Johnson is known affectionately to his few friends and many enemies as 'Styx' Johnson." I waited expectantly but nothing winged back from the team. No one was going to be the one who asked. I enlightened the uninformed. "He's called Styx after the river in Greek mythology. Cross him and you're a departed soul."

The introduction went down well, general laughter, an under-current of chatter and glances in Sergeant Johnson's direction. The big man wasn't fazed by my comments but then that was to be expected. Not too many chanced crossing him.

McLean returned with a bundle of action sheets. DS Johnson took them from him. Leafing through the documents he asked, "Whose actioning Tom or Kelly Sir, there's no sheet here?"

"That's my enquiry Sarge. Charlie Baker's actioned to view the body and see if it's this Tom or Kelly. My first stop, Central Library and the microfiche records. I'm going to go through the old local newspapers covering the late nineteen thirties and early forties. Might tell me something about a fighter called Tom or Kelly. It's a long shot but it's worth a try. Be back for debrief at nine o'clock."

After finalising a few administrative matters I left the incident room with McLean. As we walked I rubbed at a dark stain smudged on my overcoat lapel.

"Problem Guv?"

I continued rubbing and scraping with my thumbnail, not looking at McLean.

"Get's everywhere, you can't clean it off. "

"What is it?"

"Blood, a smattering of brain. It goes with the territory. Costs a fortune in dry-cleaning. Good source of evidence though. Remember that, transference of particles through contact. Detective training school will cover it." Engrossed once more with the stain I added provocatively, "If you manage to get there."

A shout from down the corridor cut short any retaliatory defiance from McLean.

"Sir!" Detective Sergeant Johnson hurried towards us. It was obviously important.

"Charlie's just rung. It's your man. He identifies the deceased as the guy he knows as Tom or Kelly. I've marked off the action."

"Now we're getting somewhere. Thanks Sarge. Keep Charlie at it and we'll see you later."

THIRTEEN

McLean parked up in the Central Library car park. The drive from the incident room had been in silence. If the killer was a man on a mission so was I. If I'd been a time bomb you'd have heard me ticking. I love this side of the job, the chase, the hunt. I relate to that age-old instinct of man the hunter, the adrenaline rushes, fight or flight. And I've never fled from anything in my life, least of all a cold-blooded killer, and I've engaged in many a fight.

Then I suddenly thought of Angie. I'd fled from her, when she needed me most, when depression and stress were bearing down, black and suffocating; I failed her. The pain, or was it guilt, of finding her like that in the garage still weighs heavily on me.

I was suddenly wrenched away from the dark thoughts by McLean enquiring, "Are you alright boss? We shan't have much time if we don't get in there now"

I took a deep breath and said, "Yep. Let's go. There's work to be done."

The Head Librarian was a gem. She provided me with a visual display unit and all the canisters of microfiche needed for a trawl through the nineteen twenties and beyond. Before she left for the day the librarian set us up with coffee and a key to lock up after we'd finished.

It was a fascinating exercise. Headlines leapt onto the

135

screen transporting me back through time as if I'd been aboard the *Tardis*.

SEPTEMBER 23RD 1925, SESQUICENTENNIAL STADIUM PHILADELPHIA. THE MANASSA MAULER LOSES HIS TITLE.

Sensation at the Stadium. World heavy weight champion Jack Dempsey beaten by Gene Tunney in ten stormy rounds.

WALL STREET CRASH. DOLLAR IN FREE FALL.

Billions wiped off the stock markets. Huge financial losses. Germany hit by hyperinflation.

All the world's great historic events flashed before my eyes in cramped and faded print captured for posterity on those timeless, ink-pressed papers. And local matters weren't ignored. Indeed they were the lifeblood of the local rag. The *Advertiser* told of miners' galas, agricultural shows, ploughing competitions, tragic colliery deaths, and brass band successes. It highlighted murder, rape and robbery and reported the trials of poachers and other acts of violence in the mining communities where drink, dogs, gambling and sport appeared to be the top priorities. Gossip and scandal were written about with relish. No soul appeared inviolate. And then I came upon my first important clue.

NOTTS AND DERBY ADVERTISER. JUNE 22ND 1940.

ANOTHER STRAIGHT WIN FOR
LANGWITH WHITE HOPE

"A packed house was treated to a feast of fighting, during the short time it lasted. Tom 'Kelly' Oakley knocked out Gunner Walsh in two rounds at the Langwith Miners' Institute last night. This young fighter is a rare talent who has endeared himself to the fans who clamour at the Saturday night fights. With more than a dozen straight wins it is surprising he has not yet won a title, but that cannot be too far away now. What Tommy has won is a reputation. This good-looking young fighter and all round sportsman has earned the sobriquet 'White Hope.' A throw back to the glory days of the controversial black world heavyweight champion, Jack Johnson, the Galveston Giant, who white boxing fans had longed to see defeated by a white hope such as Tommy Oakley. But with a knockout punch in both fists his whirlwind knockabout style is more reminiscent of that other great former world champion Jack Dempsey, the Manassa Mauler. Like him he fights from a crouch and we are reliably informed that like Dempsey he will fight anyone put before him and that is not always in the ring. His father, local pitman Big John Oakley, and his manager local bookmaker Albert Ridgeway, believe their man will be a champion if he continues to dominate his division. His brothers, Jack and Ted, both well known local sportsmen, who train him and act as seconds, are certain 'It'll take the best there is to beat our Tom.' The support for this fine young fighter is surprising. Wherever he appears the venues are sell-outs. This young man is one to be watched ..."

"Got him!" I punched the air.

"Got who boss?"

"Our man. Tommy 'Kelly' Oakley."

137

McLean's dark eyebrows knitted in a frown, "Are you sure it's him boss?"

"Believe me Andy. I'm sure. Nineteen-forties. A fighter. A good 'un it appears. Local man. Charlie Baker said Tom or Kelly. This is our victim. Now let's get into him. Find out all about him and catch the wicked bugger that's done him in."

From that moment I knew I'd found my man. Sitting in front of the VDU I read page after page of the local newspapers taking me back to the heart of the community that had been Tommy Oakley's. The more I read, the more was revealed of the life and times of the man whose battered body I had lain down with in the pouring rain on Mansfield sidings, and whose life blood I carried in an unsightly smear on my coat. Having dispatched a thoughtful McLean to report my findings to the SIO, my fingers dashed about the keyboard. I followed every jot and line thrown up on the monitor as I became immersed in my research.

The written records were invaluable. They allowed me to became almost an omniscient presence as unfolding before me I saw the life of the Oakley family and the community in which they lived.

I'd needed to know more about the corpse in the sidings and the reason for his brutal killing. If it was Tommy Oakley then this was a damn good start.

So that's it. I sat back and stared at the blank screen in front of me. Though I'd been able to share so much of the life and times of the Oakley family whilst trawling through reams of old newspaper print, that part of the journey was finally over. And do you know what? I seem to have lost a lot of old friends. It had been an absorbing journey into the past and a lot of what wasn't written I was able to read between those lines of printers' ink. Maybe my intuition and instincts are way off line but I don't think so. I've had to rely on good old fashioned gut reaction too many times during my life to give up on it now. At this very moment it's telling me that not all the characters I read about in the mining community of thirties and forties Langwith were the kind you'd like to call friends; and I'll go along with that. Some were right devious bastards.

One tragic event of the day that made the national news was the murder of local Police Constable Rodney Jarvis. Photographs of the dead man and the senior detective in the case were spread all over the front pages. Alongside, police mug shots of the villainous looking killers, gypsy Baden Durnley and his sidekick Calver Wilson. They were powerful black and white images. Anyone seeing the pictures of the two poachers glaring out from the popular tabloid newspapers of the day must have been assured of their guilt. It showed in Durnley's hateful stare and Wilson's sullen look. I was reminded of the police photographs of Myra Hindley and Ian Brady, the notorious Moors Murderers of the nineteen-sixties. The television and news papers brought those arrogant scowling faces into everyone's front room and as with Durnley and Wilson the public could see they were guilty.

I tried to visualise Durnley on the day of his execution. Hooded, with arms strapped behind him, defiant to the end. Calling to his family, helpless outside the prison gate, as the trap rasped open sending him crashing into the darkness, neck broken, turning just one half turn. A nice clean job, the hangman pleased. Justice satisfied.

And my heart went out to Durnley's wife and family. The press reported her suicide and the tragic deaths of her children. A whole family wiped out and for what?

And I thought I had problems. Just then Angie came into my mind. A prickling coldness washed over me and I shivered and broke out in an uncontrollable sweat. I hope she hadn't suffered.

"What's that Guv?"

I hadn't heard McLean return. He'd been browsing through the rich resources of the library whilst I wandered through the lives of those Langwith villagers. I must have been thinking aloud again.

I said, "I've found what I wanted, a few loose ends but they'll get sorted."

"Did you find anything out about Tom?" asked McLean.

"That session's given me a better picture of him and his family. Still a long way to go but we'll get there."

"Any clues to his killer?"

"Not really. Tom seems to have drifted out of village life after the war. We'll have to visit his old haunts. Then there's the Bembridge angle."

"Bembridge Guv?"

"Yes. You won't know about it but it's to do with a fixed boxing match in the forties. You'll hear about it later. How are we for time?"

"Three a.m. boss. Bit late for the nine o'clock briefing."

TUESDAY MORNING
10th August

Back home I tried to catch up with some sleep. I was crashed out in my old easy chair next to the fire place and must have succumbed to the heavy warmth of weariness. Sleep didn't come easy though. It was restless and disturbed. I kept waking up twitching and grumbling;

and Mitzi didn't help. My legs slipped off the foot stool dislodging the old cat from my lap.

In the semi darkness of the long sitting room I finally drifted into troubled sleep. Dark, confused images stirred within my deep subconscious. I became more restless. Within a waterfall's mellow cascade I saw a movement of bells and heard their hollow peal. The turning wheels and their ropes faded as darkness descended in a storm of anger. Floating high in the hateful night I found myself besides a blackened gibbet set at a crossroads. Suspended from its deadly beam slowly swinging and gyrating in the endless purple gloom I saw a carrion-picked body. The corpse reached out towards me as if in supplication. Then I saw the stretched skin on Death's grinning skull as it reeled away to be replaced by Angie, pale and awful. I reached towards her with outstretched arms. She stared at me through lifeless, sunken eyes, turned one half turn and was gone into the terrible night.

I awoke from the bad dream and poured myself a tot of Pusser's rum.

TUESDAY AFTERNOON

The heavily built old man with a nose splattered across battered features like a lump of knocked back putty, yelled in frustration in answer to my question.

"Remember it? I canna forget it. This is what I won that naight."

I watched as he gripped the arms of his wheelchair and shook them with large hands crippled through arthritis. That nose flared as he relived the awful moment nearly forty years earlier. And that's all he could do. All he was left with in his warden aided council flat were his useless limbs and disturbing memories.

I suppose that in different circumstances I would have had some sympathy for this shell of a man that I sat down with. But now I knew something of his past and so sympathy wasn't on today's agenda. Even then I could visualise him in his heyday. He must have been a fearsome creature and it said something of the man who had faced him all those years ago in the loneliest place in the world, the square ring.

I'd already taken in the pictures hanging on the wall above the tiled fireplace where a cosy glow radiated from the gas fire.

I nodded towards the framed photographs. "But you're still interested in boxing then, Mr. Bembridge?"

"Got nowt else in life me lad. Can't blame the fight game for this." He banged a screwed up hand against an unresponsive thigh.

"What do you blame?"

I watched the old fighter as he sat back in the wheelchair, a sad incomplete figure.

"Not what I blame me lad, it's who I blame."

This was getting interesting, more like what I wanted to hear. I said, "Alright, who do you blame?"

Seaman Bembridge remained silent for a few moments then rubbed a gnarled hand across his mangled ruin of a nose and said, "Me brother Chick, God rest his soul. I blame him and them as put him up to it."

I was disappointed. It wasn't the answer I wanted or anticipated, but this business was always full of surprises, unexpected twists and turns. That's what made getting up in the morning so worth while. You never knew what to expect.

I persevered. "So what happened?"

The old man shuffled in the chair easing himself into a more comfortable position.

"It were a big naight for me and Tommy ya know. Area title fight. No telling how far winner could've gone. Raight tut top wi' out a doubt." He paused in thought. "Tommy were a good un ya know. Could hit with both hands. Cagey. A southpaw, fighting from a crouch. Yeah he were a good 'un. I weren't fraightened on 'im though but I knew I were in for a scrap that naight." The old man paused again, forcing his crippled fingers into fists before throwing short, lightweight punches. "He didn't end up like me but they done for him just the same; as if they'd shot him like a mad dog. They had a lot to answer for."

"Who are you talking about Mr. Bembridge?"

The old battler leaned forward in his wheelchair. It was a struggle but from beneath the heavily scarred tissue of his eyebrows his eyes seemed to be searching my face as though he was seeking reassurance for what he was about to tell me.

He must have seen something, maybe he found some affinity with my bent nose, at any rate he said, "Them as was hung for murdering that bobby."

McLean lounging patiently on the sofa suddenly sat up.

He snapped, "What bobby was that Mr. Bembridge?"

I couldn't believe it. He was at it again. I turned on him immediately and said sharply, "Please don't interrupt when I'm speaking Mr. McLean. It's not good practice. Do I make myself clear?"

He appeared to realise that he'd spoken out of turn and apologised. "Sorry Guv. Got carried away."

I wasn't too happy. It was beginning to become a habit with him. He's got to learn when to keep his mouth shut and when not to, otherwise he and I will have a fall out.

I accepted his apology this time and said, "Just remember in future." I turned again to Bembridge. "Constable Jarvis? Is that the bobby you're referring to?"

"Yeah. That's the one. Couldn't remember his name, such a long time ago. But it were headlines in papers and ont' newsreel at pictures."

"Did you know Baden Durnley and Calver Wilson?"

"Everybody knowed 'em. They was poachers. They were at all the faights and racetracks. Anywhere that they could make easy money."

"Did you know that Chick had fixed the fight?"

The old fighter, tired and spent, slumped in the wheelchair.

"Not till he'd done it then it were too late." Bembridge was silent and then as if he had been waiting a lifetime to assuage the red-hot coals searing into his tortured mind he yelled, "It's a lie. I've been lying for years. 'Course I knew. I was scared of Tommy. He hurt me, every time he hit me. He would have killed me. Chick told me what he were doing and I took me chance. I could have been a champion. A hero but all I got were this."

I watched the broken old man racked with sobbing as he slowly pounded the arms of the wheelchair with his crippled fists. I nodded to McLean and we left the distraught figure struggling with the demons that had burst from their confinement to indict him. It was clear my business wasn't with Seaman Bembridge.

FOURTEEN

tyx Johnson was doing a double check on the officers parading for duty. He'd worked with me long enough to know my methods and that I insisted on punctuality. I'd been in since seven in the morning going through the action sheets, keeping abreast of the enquiry. Johnson knew that the daily nine o'clock briefing was an important part of a major investigation. It often seemed that if we got off to a good start the rest of the day appeared to take the hint. I sipped tea from a large mug with its big OXO motif. Angie bought it for me from Skeggy years ago, during our better times. I smiled to myself. It was a bit of a joke, she knew I hated OXO.

When I could see that Sergeant Johnson was ready I asked, "Everybody here Sarge?"

The big man replied, "Yes sir. All correct. A couple of extra DCs have been brought in from Divisions. I've brought them up to scratch."

I said, "OK. Good morning everybody and welcome to the new members of the team. See if you can't bring us a bit of good luck. First of all the enquiry is ongoing. Nothing dramatic has turned up during our initial enquiries, unless somebody out there is holding back on me." Nobody took

145

up the challenge. I continued, "I'll take this opportunity to apologise for not being here at last night's debrief but McLean and I were tied up."

I realised as soon as I'd said it that I'd made a balls up. And I knew that before I could explain some smart arse comment would come winging in from the floor. I didn't have to wait too long.

"Tied up boss? What with? Perfumed silken cord from Marrakech or a piece of tarred rope from the railway?"

I had to take it on the chin. I'd asked for it and I got it. These guys weren't the sort of company that you left yourself open to. So you just smile and roll with the punch. I smiled and made an exaggerated show of pulling my shirt cuffs down over my wrists as if covering something up.

"You'll never know," I said. "McLean's sworn to secrecy but I can tell you there are no discernible marks."

The light banter seemed to go down well with the team. It helped now and then to prevent any unwanted tension building up. Some of the work out there on the streets is ball aching, not all action and gung ho! It's no fun trudging the streets at all hours in all weathers door knocking just hoping the next one's the one you're looking for. Invariably it isn't but it's out there and you've got to find it. Who knows? It could be your day, your moment of glory waiting behind the next door that you knock on. And sure you've got to have discipline and leadership, but most of the discipline at this level of service is self-discipline. If it's not there then you shouldn't be in the CID. But it's not all regimentation and spit and polish, we have to let go now and then. Those moments are appreciated by the guys who have to get out there and do the business. I know because I've been doing it all my service. I like a laugh with the best of them, at the right time. But when there's serious

146

work to be done then I expect everybody to buckle down and pull their weight. And I think the streetwise detectives who've worked with me before know I don't expect them to do something I haven't done or wouldn't do myself. I've always tried to lead from the front. Earned my spurs the hard way and bled the claret on many occasions. I've had my share of problems but I'm still here, at the helm, and still smiling.

Having got everyone's attention I continued with the briefing.

"You'll be aware by now that we may have identified our John Doe. It isn't a positive ID yet but we are working on it. I'm almost certain that he's Tom 'Kelly' Oakley from Langwith and we'll be following up a number of interesting leads that have been thrown up surrounding him. That's why I'm off to Langwith shortly and leaving you in the capable hands of Sergeant Johnson."

"What sort of leads are we talking about boss?" someone asked.

"During our research we found that as a young man Tom Oakley was friendly with a local police officer, Constable Rod Jarvis. He was murdered some thirty five years ago…"

McLean suddenly interjected cutting me off in mid sentence.

"Brutally murdered. Battered to death. The killer was responsible for the deaths of seven innocent people. Justice …."

"McLean!" I snapped, cutting him off in full flow. "I've told you before. Don't interrupt when I'm speaking. It's a lesson to be learned and remembered. I shan't tell you again. In this company I dispense justice."

The mood of the meeting changed in those few dramatic moments.

Mouthy had got up my nose again. I ordered, "Go and do something useful. Sort out the latest action sheets that have come in."

He left the room, followed by stares and head shakes from the group. I watched him leave and thought, "When is he going to learn?"

No self discipline. No self control. That big mouth is going to get him into trouble one of these days."

One of the new batch of DCs tried his hand at what he believed was more light humour.

"That piece of rope you were on about boss. Might have been better round McLean's neck. Shut his mouth up. Solve all his problems." To emphasis his funny he lolled his head to one side, stuck out his tongue and held a clenched fist above his head, mimicking a hanging.

His intended witticism didn't hit the mark. It backfired on him. But he wasn't to know. I didn't appreciate what he'd said, it was too close to home and I could tell from the reaction of the team that they weren't too happy either. They knew the score. The anticipated laughter never came. A silence descended like a fog. The telling glares they gave the joker caused him to fidget uneasily in his seat no doubt pondering on what he'd said. The lads were looking to me. There were a lot of hard stares checking me out, seeing how I was reacting, a lot of genuine concern from the guys. But I let it lie. No good telling the whole station how I felt, revealing my Achilles heel to all and sundry. Most of them knew anyway. Sticks and stones may break bones but even if I try not to show it I can tell you that words can hurt just as much. I called a ten minute break. Styx Johnson came over. He didn't mention the joker or his witticism. I appreciated that. I told him to carry on with briefing and after the break

I'd go to Langwith and chase up a few background enquires that I needed to pursue. I arranged to see him and the team later. He understood.

*

With Stirling out of earshot DS Johnson turned upon the unsuspecting joker.

"We've got enough with McLean opening his trap at the wrong time. While you're on this team learn to keep your mouth shut unless you've got something to say worth saying. Ok?"

The newcomer, at a loss pleaded, "What have I said wrong Sarge?"

Johnson snapped back, "Wrong! What have you said fucking wrong? Joking about putting a rope around his neck, solving his problems. If you don't know you're the only fucker in the nick who doesn't. His wife hanged herself in their garage and he blames himself for her death. And you've reopened the wound."

*

The morning incident passed into history. I stood in front of the old stone inn looking up at the heavy wooden sign hanging from black wrought iron fittings.

I found myself reading aloud, "The Net and Ferret Inn."

I moved closer to make out the writing on the black board displayed above the lintel of the imposing stone doorway. The white lettering loomed large and the hair at the back of my neck tingled as I read, "Proprietor Amos Jimson. Licensed to sell wines, beers, spirits and porter, on and off the premises."

149

The tingle became an ice cold finger running down my spine.

"Well, well! Still here after all these years. Amos Jimson". This could be just what I was looking for. A link to Tom's past. Jimson's name featured prominently in Tom's story and the trial of Durnley and Wilson. I'd come across it many times during my trawl through the old newsprint but I hadn't expected him to still be around. I stepped back a couple of paces taking in the atmosphere of the place. The inn looked out through a myriad of tiny uneven window panes across the village green to the River Poulter. Now it's just a pleasant stream splashing and tumbling over moss swept pebbles and stones that had lain in that watercourse for an aeon.

I was impressed. It looked just like a picture postcard. And it all seemed so familiar.

A double decker bus, destination Mansfield, crossed the small humped back bridge to my right.

As I stood there, a heavily built man in well worn tweeds wearing polished brown leather gaiters and heavy brogues walked towards me. He was ram-rod straight and though no longer young he walked with a confident swagger. In his hand he carried a cudgel formed from a stout piece of twisted rose wood. It was an evil looking device but it didn't look out of place in the man's hand. He nodded and touched the brim of a battered trilby with the cudgel, adding with an air of authority, "Mornin'."

I managed a quick, "And Good morning to you Sir," as the stranger made his way up a couple of well trodden old stone steps into the hostelry.

I followed. Bending low beneath blackened oak beams I entered The Poachers' Bar. As soon as I passed through the low doorway I could feel it all about me. The presence of the poacher gang, Durnley, Wilson, Fallows. On a wall the heads of a fox and badger snarled down at me. Other relics of the poacher's trade were displayed about the walls. Among them the gaping steel jaws of wicked animal and man traps, Badger tongs and a plethora of cruel devices, tools and nets. Stuffed ferrets, game birds, old shotguns and braces of pistols were arrayed about the room. Sepia photographs of armed gamekeepers, or perhaps poachers, posed in moleskin breeches, waist coats, neckerchiefs and battered trilby hats. The centre piece of it all was the large open fireplace with its iron dogs and smouldering logs. It truly was a poacher's bar.

The sturdy old man in tweeds nodded from his seat near the fireplace.

Speaking through a twisted mouth set below a nose spread like punched bread dough he said, "You're a stranger here mister?" The voice was nasal and grated as if it were forcing its way through gravel.

"Yes." I replied and indicating the chair alongside him I asked, "May I?"

"Ya may that lad. It's a free world an' the chair don't belong to nobody except landlord. Though I 'spect I paid for it a hundred times all these years."

As I settled, a short man, ponderous amidst rolls of gross flesh, with heavy belly preceding him, came over, wiping his sweating, florid face on a not too hygienic-looking piece of towel.

The tiny effeminate voice squeezing out of that enormous body seemed out of place.

It took me by surprise. "Mornin' sir. Amos Jimson at your service. And I've no objection to you using the chair. What'll it be?"

I looked at him. So this was Jimson. The mountain of fat

151

continued to leak sweat into that horrid piece of towel.

"Thanks Amos. I'll have a pint of bitter."

"Right sir. Not seen you here before?"

That voice, surely it couldn't be real. Maybe he's not real. Maybe he's a big blubbery blow up doll and the squeaky sound only comes on when somebody squeezes him. No he's real alright you couldn't reproduce the amount of sweat he's exuding or the sour body odour that's hanging about him. Amos Jimson hey? First impression? Unfavourable. But then I don't have to squeeze him, love him or live with him, just drink his beer and keep upwind of him.

Like the good landlord he surely was and eager for some lunchtime gossip he set about wiping down the table, my order apparently on the back burner. The concentric sweeps with the damp cloth grew smaller, the action slower.

He chanced a further glance in my direction. "But you do look familiar," he squeaked.

Delivering a few heavy breaths onto the surface of the table he rubbed at some imaginary mark before forcing his ponderous bulk upright and wiping his hands. Replacing the cloth back in his belt, which struggled to prevent itself being overwhelmed beneath tyres of rolling blubber, the landlord waited for me to respond.

"Just visiting. Trying to locate a few people if they're still about," I said casually.

Tweed suit asked, "Family?"

"Not really. Just a journey into the past."

"Who are you looking for sir? If I don't know 'em odds on Jess will."

For the second time in as many minutes the hair at the back of my neck tingled. I said incredulously, "Jess? Jess Fallows?"

Tweed suit stopped drinking as if turned to stone. He

stared at me through narrowed eyes across the top of the pint pot, frozen against his lower lip.

The landlord rubbed his hands on the towel at his waist. I'd thrown something into the ring and raised his blood pressure. He wasn't sure what it was but he was eager to find out. In that sparrow-like voice he twittered, "Ya know Jess then?"

"Not exactly," I said. "But I've heard a lot about him."

A newspaper headline from my earlier research flashed into my mind.

MEMBERS OF POACHER GANG TURN KING'S EVIDENCE DURING MURDER TRIAL.

I had to be careful. Didn't want to reveal too much at this early stage.

Now, arms folded, body language spelling vigilance, the old poacher drilled into me through screwed up eyes.

He growled, "What do you want to see me about mister?"

Ignoring the question, I addressed mine host, reminding him curtly, "It was bitter I ordered wasn't it?"

With a glare the landlord reluctantly returned to the bar wiping his hands for the umpteenth time on that grimy towel,

"I'll ask thee agen lad. What do you want to see me about?"

This time there was urgency in the question and not a little underlying threat.

I hung onto the moment and waited for my drink.

The landlord placed the beer on the table making a show of wiping it down once more with that filthy rag. But I didn't want him around at that moment.

"Thank you landlord. That'll be all for the time being."

Scowling, he wiped his sweating brow on the towel. I watched and thought, "Remind me not to eat here."

Not yet finished, as he wiped the lintel around the fireplace, the landlord squeaked, "Like something to eat sir? We do a nice game pie or a delicious home made soup of the day. I prepare all the ingredients myself."

I couldn't take my eyes off the greasy towel grasped in Amos Jimson's pork sausage-like fingers.

"No thanks. I'm not a big eater. I'll let you know if I want anything."

Jess Fallows just sat there staring at me. I could feel those screwed up poacher's eyes giving me the once over.

He spoke. "By the look on yer ya could do wi' a good meal. You'll soon be all skin and bone lad. I can vouch for the game pie, cetched 'em me sen on his Lordship's estate."

He peered into my eyes and seemed to be watching for my reaction. The old felon was in for a disappointment. He didn't get what he expected. I've been round the block too many times to be drawn that easily.

"His Lordship's estate? What's that about?" I asked.

Fallows leaned across the table attempting to intimidate me with those hooded eyes. "You saying you're not from town looking for prime birds or venison mester?"

The 'mester' leant forward, confronting the intended threat eye to eye and replied cagily, "Should I be?"

Jess Fallows tapped his splodge of a nose and laughed. A deep gut rolling laugh, and sat back.

"Can't be too careful me lad. Game birds and venison fetch big money these days and I can't afford to lose more'n me quota. Don't want too many questions to be asked now do we?" That laugh again as he spat into the glowing ashes of the log fire. It spat back at him, hot grey ash flirting and crackling before it settled.

"Are you in the market then for such commodities Mr. Fallows?" I asked.

"In the market for his Lordships game? Don't ya know lad I'm his head game keeper."

So that was it! Again the headline flashed into my mind. "POACHER TURNS KING'S EVIDENCE." For a moment my resentment for the man facing me overrode my professional instincts. I retorted, "That was your reward then Fallows?"

The poacher turned gamekeeper screwed his eyes even tighter. It seemed he was confused and didn't know what to make of the question.

The landlord stopped wiping his hands and watched.

Fallows asked tentatively, "Reward? Reward for what?"

I snapped back, "Turning King's evidence against your friends."

I'd turned over a stone and neither man liked being confronted with what had lain hidden beneath it for so long. The landlord gasped. And with an agility belying his age Fallows jumped up from his chair knocking it backwards into the hearth. In the same movement he raised his gnarled rosewood club and brought it crashing down towards me. Amidst the confusion of shattered glass and spewing beer it smashed into the oak tabletop.

I'd had the measure of Fallows and I'd expected some violent response from him but this exceeded my expectation. Though the old countryman had moved quickly, thankfully my anticipation and footwork were quicker. Otherwise if that shillelagh had caught me it was likely that I'd have been reduced to minced meat. Sweeney Todd style, savoury filling for some of Amos's meat pies? As it was I was already standing back from the table calmly taking in the brutal frustration of his Lordship's Head Game Keeper and the wittering panic of the landlord.

I said, advisedly, "Now, now Gentlemen, this is no way to treat a paying guest. And you, Fallows, owe me a pint of best bitter."

With chest heaving and sickly pale beneath his weather beaten countenance, the old poacher recovered his fallen chair. He slumped back onto it. The table was awash with Mansfield bitter and littered with broken glass. Snatching up my attacker's battered trilby I swept the beer and glass from the table top, on my side at any rate, and sat down again. With that evil-looking cloth mine host hurriedly made to wipe away the debris littering the table. I threw the beer-soaked hat down and waved him away.

"I'm likely to contract some unpronounceable disease if you continue to use that germ incubator. Just bring us a drink whilst I have a word with the maniac here."

The landlord waddled off to oblige, no doubt pleased to be out of the combat zone.

It took a few minutes for the gamekeeper to recover from his burst of violent activity. In the meantime Amos returned with two pints.

I took one and nodding towards Fallows directed, "Put them on the maniac's slate. And charge him for the breakages and labour while you're at it."

More composed now, "the maniac" finally wheezed, "I've no more to say to you mister. Get your drink down yer and be on your way. Newspaper men isn't welcome round 'ere."

I took a pull on the pint and wiped my mouth. I said, "I'm not a newspaper man."

Fallows slowly shook his head and took a huge swig of beer before declaring forcefully, "Don't gi' me any a that bull mester I can smell 'em a mile away."

"Take it or leave it but I'm not a newspaper man. I'm here to ask about an old friend of yours. That's all."

"What old friend?" he asked suspiciously.

"Tommy Oakley."

The landlord and Fallows looked at one another in surprise. They answered simultaneously.

"Tommy Oakley?"

The ensuing attempt to pursue two conversations at the same time became lost in a jumble of confused rhetoric.

Fallows bellowed, "Shut up Amos!"

The landlord reacted immediately. Performing a credible impersonation of a ballooned-up Uriah Heep, he shuffled backwards from the room, rubbing his hands on that infested rag.

The mouse within the mountain squeaked, "Yes, …er yes gentlemen I'll leave you to your, er, deliberations. Just call if you need anything." And he was gone.

Jess Fallows wanted to know more. "What's your interest in Tommy?" he demanded.

"I'm told he was quite a character in his day."

"Character? Tommy Oakley in his day could've whipped any two men wi' his hands tied a'backon 'im. Finest faighter this country even seen. Could 'ave been world champion. World champion. And he were my friend."

"That was the problem wasn't it? He was everybody's friend?"

"There ya go agen. As soon as we start gerrin' on ya put

157

ya locker int' wheel. Everybody were proud to know Our Tom. It weren't just faightin either. Cricket, football wi' his brothers. Gi' anybody his last shilling. Ask anybody they'll all have a good word for Tommy."

"Do you know what happened to him?"

"What, after they took his licence ofn' him? The bastards. Weren't his fault. He just sorted them lot out that doped him. They ought to have give him a medal as big as a dustbin lid. Yeh! A dustbin lid. That's how big his heart is. Bless 'im."

"Had no enemies then that you knew of?"

"Enemies? Naw! Tommy'd got no enemies. Everybody thought world on 'im. Even them as done 'im down. They only done it for the money. They still admired him."

"Where did Tommy go when he left here?"

"Last I heard on 'im he were livin' Mansfield way. I seen him one naight int' Drum at Shirebrook a couple of years back. He were dishin' out some fist to some brothers from Mansfield Wood'us. Thought they could do 'im. They ended up in hospital."

This was getting interesting. I said, "Who were the brothers?"

Fallows didn't answer immediately as he cast his mind back to the incident.

"Let me see. There were Frank and Ray Northbridge that naight. But allt' six brothers threatened to do 'im after. Now come to think on it they did. Set on him one naight and battered Tommy wi' one of them iron road ponches. Ya know for ramming tar down ont' road. They couldn't do it wi' their fists."

"So they took their revenge?"

"Ya mighta' thought so. Tommy had sixteen stitches above his eye. That 'ud be enough for any man."

"That ended the feud?"

"No! Not in a thousand years. Tommy hunted 'em down one by one and thrashed 'em. Man to man. That were his way. He din't need no help. Tommy carried answer in his own two fists."

"That's interesting, the Northbridge brothers. So they may have held a long standing grudge against Tommy?" I was talking to myself again. I'll have to watch it. It could be dangerous. Say the wrong thing in the wrong company.

"What's that mister?"

"I was just asking myself if there's anyone else about who'll remember Tommy?"

The gamekeeper sat for a moment shaking his head before suddenly slapping a large gnarled hand on the table.

"What am I thinking on? Course there is. Edith, Tommy's sister, still lives in Big John's house up Portland Road."

I didn't believe what I was hearing. I felt the excitement, a tingle in my belly. Bembridge, Fallows, Jimson, Edith, these are real people, not newspaper characters, real flesh and blood, I could sense that the answer to Tommy Oakley's murder lay here.

I was really up for it now. I saw off my pint, stood up and asked Fallows, "How do I get there? Can I walk it?"

"It's quarter an hour. Left at bridge, up hill, past green wooden butchers shop on't right. That row a terraces. If you gu down't side you'll look along backs and see t' green porch Big John built, years agu." As an afterthought the gamekeeper added, "Give me regards to Edith. Tell her I'll drop a couple of brace off int' next few days."

It seemed the dismissal was complete. Jess Fallows leaned back in his chair and appeared to doze off. His cudgel with beer soaked hat atop lay across his thighs.

Ducking under the oak beam at the door, I spotted Amos

wiping glasses behind the bar. I cringed when I realised it was *that* cloth.

"Amos I'm leaving my car out front, I'll pick it up later. And get yourself and Jess a pint. By the way have you thought about getting an automatic glass washer? You might end up with more survivors."

As he held the five pound note up to the light, from somewhere within his rolling jowls, Jimsons's falsetto queried, "Survivors sir? Don't you mean customers?"

"That's it. Exactly right Amos. Customers that survive. Good day."

*

I was eager to meet Edith and set off at pace walking on the path running alongside the cut where it bubbled and swirled amidst the stones and boulders. Half a dozen ducks and drakes paddled and bobbed in the calm pool beneath the old stone bridge, completing the idyllic rural scene. Turning left I made my way up the hill passing some very desirable residences set back off the road, almost hidden amongst the trees on the right. On the opposite side bushes crowded over a rickety wooden fence. It was a pleasant day and an enjoyable walk. I strode on beneath a wide splash of blue sky, which faded towards the Lowry-like rooftops and chimneys silhouetted against the distant skyline. Reaching the bend at the top of the hill the green wooden butcher's shop and row of terraces on the far side came into view. I stopped to catch my breath and take in the scene. Very quickly I was left in no doubt that I was in a pit village. Even though I couldn't see the headstocks and towering pit chimneys there was no escaping the nagging bite of stale sulphur grating in my throat. The pit had been closed for some time now but just like the "butchery department" it had its own distinctive, nose-gripping stench.

I thought, "Colliery terraces and pit fumes. Smells mucky and looks mucky."

The blue quarry tiled footpath at the rear of Portland Road led me to the Oakley family home.

I had a suspicion of what she would look like before she answered my knock on the green porch door. I wasn't disappointed.

"Miss Edith Oakley?"I asked.

She didn't answer; but through wire rimmed glasses, busy blue eyes looked me over. I returned the compliment taking in the short auburn hair, greying but thick and wavy. She reminded me of an old school mistress. Yes just like an old school ma'am. But then I knew she would.

The woman didn't speak but continued to stare, weighing me up.

I broke the silence and said, "I take it then that you are Edith?"

She replied sharply, "Yes."

I said, "Thank you Edith. I've come to talk to you. You don't know me but I think we need to talk."

Straight backed, arms now folded across her spotless pinny she replied, "Don't know you you say? Mmmm, but you look sort of familiar though. You'd best come in." The bespectacled eyes watched my every move.

My first step into that tiny conservatory was a step back in time. It wasn't the stool, the copper jardinière or the polished miner's lamp hanging from the roof beam, but the atmosphere that wrapped itself about me, warm and familiar. Momentarily I seemed to be floating, not walking, sort of

161

drifting through into the living room. It was so familiar; the cheery coal fire burning in the large, black leaded double fireplace, the rocking chair and large central table with its brown plush cover and tasselled fringe. I took in the Austrian regulator wall clock, reflecting its cosy glow from the brass pendulum, moving in time to its mellow "tick, tock." What was missing to make the moment real, to fill that room with vibrant life once more, were the performers, Big John, and his family. I half expected them to make their entrance onto the set. But of course they didn't. Perhaps Edith could resurrect them, fill in the missing gaps and maybe give me some pointer to the killer of her brother.

"I suppose you'd like a cup of tea. Most men do."

It wasn't a question, more a directive. I nodded like an appreciative schoolboy.

"Thanks," I said.

I stood before the mahogany sideboard. It took up nearly one wall of the living room. Pride of place was taken by a well-thumbed copy of a King James Bible. Set out in front of the large ornate mirror and on small shelves either side supported on turned and crafted Doric columns with carved finials, were a series of photographs in silver frames. I didn't have to be told who they were. There was Tom, taped hands, silk shorts and boxing boots, crouching in a fighting pose. Unbelievable to imagine that this magnificent specimen of manhood was that battered corpse, abandoned in the rain at the sidings, and that mutilated carcass on the mortuary slab whose life blood I carry in an unsightly stain on my overcoat. I felt a pang of sadness standing in the dead man's family home, in the presence of his sister and so many memories.

Then there was the beaming, moustached face of what I took to be Edith's father Big John and a frail looking lady most likely his wife. The pictures of two fine looking young men in uniform, one wearing a sailor's square rig the other an army tunic bearing the commando insignia and dagger. They were probably her brothers. A most attractive young woman cuddling up to a man in football gear appeared on another photograph. A very young Edith posed with a couple of toddlers whilst in the final frame she appeared with her parents and a pony and trap.

"Fine collection of photographs," I commented.

Edith, pouring boiling water from the kettle, into a brown Denby teapot on the fireplace hob, didn't look up.

"Yes they are aren't they? There's my Dad John and Mother Polly, my brothers Jack, Tom and Ted and my beautiful sister Rita. They keep me company. I talk to them a lot."

"Do they answer?" I asked cynically.

As she stirred the pot the homely old lady said, "Oh yes. They always answer. No point in speaking to them if they don't speak back."

That was a good lead in. I took advantage and said, "Do you speak to Tom?"

As though surprised by the question Edith said, "Yes. Especially Tom, but I love them all."

"When did you last speak to Tom?"

Edith didn't answer immediately as she concentrated on pouring tea into two Denby ware cups with matching saucers.

Placing the woollen cosy, with its fluffy bobble, carefully over the teapot she finally said, "Last night. I spoke to our Tom last night."

"You mean you spoke to the photograph of Tom?"

She looked at me in an old fashioned way; the message

was clear. She said sharply, "I'm not simple or deranged Mister, whatever your name is."

"Stirling. Jim Stirling," I offered.

"Mister Jim Stirling," she said pointedly. "Of course it was the photograph. Tom's no longer here."

"When did you last see him?" I asked?

"Oh good gracious. It's months. No! More like a year now. Drifted in and out of trouble and he's been too ashamed to see me."

"What sort of trouble?"

"The usual. Drinking, fighting, brawling. Never the same since we lost Mam and Dad."

"Oh! I am sorry I didn't know. What happened?"

She turned away from me and poked the coal fire with a brass poker. It was clear that Edith was uncomfortable on the road I was taking her. Perhaps it was a road she had not intended to revisit, an unhappy road with more unhappy memories. But I intended to take her along it and put more questions to her. I sensed that beneath her benign image was a steely determination and that she wasn't keen to help me. She was going into her protective shell. I had to winkle her out. Laying the poker down in the hearth she settled in an old rocking chair and rocked to and fro slowly. Edith appeared to be gathering her thoughts. Then she started her defensive attack.

"You're from the police aren't you Mister Stirling?"

I'd known something was coming but I wasn't prepared for that question. I pulled my warrant card from an inside pocket and produced it to her. I said, "Detective Inspector Jim Stirling from Mansfield Division."

"I had an idea it was you. He said you'd be calling."

That was her first googly. I tried not to look too confused but at that moment I was.

Amidst the confusion I asked, "And he said I'd be calling? When did he say that?"

Without hesitation the old lady replied, "Yesterday, he rang yesterday. Said you'd be coming to see me and be asking questions about our Tom."

She'd bowled me a Chinaman. Nearly lost my middle stump. This couldn't be right. It didn't make sense. It was only this morning at the briefing I'd told anyone I was coming to Langwith. Even then it was a casual throw-away thing. On the spur of the moment, an escape mechanism coming into play after that hanging comment. And I'd only learned of Edith's whereabouts today. So who was this phantom caller with so much to say? I meant to find out.

"Who rang you, Edith?"

Taking a sip of tea she looked at me for a moment. "Didn't give his name. Told me to be careful what I said to you because you were a cunning devil."

My mind was on red alert. What's going on here? Who's this unidentified caller? Is it the killer?

I tried to draw more information from Edith. "Did this person tell you where he was ringing from?"

Edith replied quietly, "No. But he told me our Tom was dead." She closed her eyes tightly but tears squeezed through. "Found on the railway at Mansfield he said. And I'd be wanted later for identification. That's all. He sounded quite official. Like a lawyer or a something. Just said don't tell him too much. It wouldn't be in Tom's interest."

I was hooked. Well and truly hooked. I'd suspected it all along. This little pit village holds the key to Tom's murder and I'm not about to let go.

I plugged on. "What is there that you can tell me Edith that wouldn't be in Tom's interest?"

She snapped back, "Family matters are private matters. Not for gossips and the likes of you. Everybody knows about him and they either love him or hate him. I happen to love him so there's nothing I'd say against him."

I wasn't about to be denied. "So the caller is right? He knows there's something, and he's worried."

Edith responded sharply, "Worried? Why should he be worried?"

"Yes he's worried. Why? Because I suspect he's involved in Tom's death and is afraid you'll point the finger at him."

The cup rattled in its saucer as Edith clattered them onto the table.

"What do you mean something to do with his death? He said it was an accident. Had too much to drink and fell off a bridge."

I stared hard at the woman. This was an important link in the chain of circumstances that could eventually shackle the killer. I kept at her staring hard into those cold blue eyes

"Edith. Just hear me out. This is important. Tom was murdered, battered to death. It was no accident." I didn't allow her eyes to move from mine. I held her in my gaze and kept up the momentum and demanded, "Do you know the caller?"

Edith, with great difficulty, closed her eyes, seemingly breaking the contact between us as surely as if she had severed an umbilical cord. Raising herself up she poked at the fire, then quietly, in a tired voice quivering with emotion she answered. "No Inspector. I can't say I do. Now I'll ask you to leave."

I drew back. I wasn't convinced, but knew this was the moment to leave. I needed to see her again. It wouldn't do to alienate her. Before I left I thanked her for her hospitality and told her that she would be contacted to arrange a statement and formal identification, adding, "Edith. If you do recollect anything and want to talk about it, I'd appreciate it if you give me a ring. Alright?"

The old lady gave one of those old fashioned looks but replied, "All right Inspector."

As a parting shot I handed her my calling card and said, "If he gets in touch with you again, try and get a contact number, but don't tell him of our arrangement. Will you do that?"

Edith didn't respond immediately. My visit appeared to have disturbed her. She suddenly looked her age, staring at the card but appearing not to see it. It was as if she didn't want to see it; as if it was an inconvenience, a distraction that had found its way, uninvited and unwanted, into her world. It was clear that she would have preferred it and me out of her life forever. But even then she extended me the courtesy of acknowledging my request with a polite nod. But I wasn't too convinced and made my way back to my car at the Net and Ferret.

As I reached the bend just past the green butchers shop I looked back. I could see Edith standing at the front door, obviously watching until I was out of sight. I waved. She didn't respond and I turned the corner.

The going was all downhill and I made good progress. As I walked my mind went back to Edith. I could visualise her taking up the Bible I had noticed on the sideboard and running her fingers over the family photographs, probably lingering for a moment with Tom. In my minds eye I imagined her clutching the book to her as she sat in the rocking chair and pondered upon my visit.

Without a doubt I should be seeing her again. There were many questions I needed answering.

FIFTEEN

WEDNESDAY AFTERNOON

There's nothing I hate more than shopping. I always feel uncomfortable, out of place, even here in Marks and Sparks. It always seems that someone's watching. There's an uneasy feeling of guilt walking the store with me. It's even worse if I don't buy anything. Going through the checkout I feel suspect, half expecting to be nicked by a store detective leaping out from behind a pile of cardboard boxes or a pyramid of tinned tomato soup. I can't relax until I've walked half way down the street. As I said I never liked shopping. I suppose a shrink would tell me it was something to do with my childhood. In our house Angie always did the shopping. She was quite content to let me drive her to the shops while I waited in the car. She liked to take her time with things. Have a good look round. Check the prices and the brands. She was a dab hand at finding the bargains. But she seemed to take so long over things. I could write up a whole report while she shopped.

But it's got to be done. There's no Angie now to do it. And so here I am, an alien wandering about the store. Enormous coloured signs direct me up and down alley ways lined with shelves stacked with everything from pickled walnuts to ladies' knickers. And at every twist and turn I am beleaguered by more bewildering displays and notices and signs. Finally, I've emerged from the maze at the Gents' Outfitters department. Now comes the difficult part, buying something. I'm really missing Angie now. I wish she were here, I'd even go to the lingerie department with her, but as usual I can't make up my mind.

"Can I help you sir?"

I heard the question but didn't look up, too busy weighing the two cellophane wrapped packets one against the other in either hand.

"Can't make my mind up which colour."

The helpful voice suggested, "You won't solve your problem by flopping them about like that sir."

I stopped flopping them about and looked at the young woman offering me advice. Her face was as pleasant as her voice, framed in mousey blonde, shoulder length hair, the sort that they swish around in slow motion on the TV ads. I'd guess mid forties, not beautiful. Pretty? No, handsome. A handsome woman in her smart company uniform, and she was helpful.

"Is it the right size sir?" she queried.

"Sixteen and a half. Angie always got me a size sixteen and a half," I said.

Helpful assistant eyed my neck with professional aplomb.

"If you look at me like that for much longer I'll suspect you're a vampire," I quipped.

"Sorry sir but I'm not happy that you are sixteen and a half. More a sixteen."

"Sixteen? Not been a sixteen for years. I'm a bull necked sixteen and a half. Give me your hand. Just feel. Sixteen and a half."

I put the two packets down on the counter took hold of Helpful's hands and placed them about my neck. I shivered to her touch. It didn't go unnoticed.

"Let me measure you," she said.

169

Helpful looked me full in the eye. I melted. The small tape encircled my neck for a brief moment then rattled into its case to be swiftly returned to a uniform pocket.

"Sixteen sir. Try the satin cream. That's a neutral colour. Go well with anything."

"Er. Thank you miss," I looked at the name tag on her breast pocket. "Miss Downey. Thank you."

"A pleasure sir I assure you. Is there anything else?"

"Erm, no thank you, I'll have two of the satin cream shirts."

I took in her trim figure as she turned away to process my order. For the first time in many months I felt a twinge of pleasure through being near a woman. I picked up the shirts and headed for the exit.

"Just a minute sir!"

The insistent call was followed almost immediately by firm pressure to my right shoulder causing me to gasp with embarrassment, "Bloody hell! I'm nicked."

It was no good doing a runner. I turned back immediately, almost knocking Miss Downey over.

"I'm sorry. It's a mistake. I forgot to pay but I'll settle up now," I said hopefully, reaching for my wallet.

Miss Downey smiled. An understanding smile.

"Nothing to worry about Mister Stirling, you left half way through the transaction. You seemed to have something on your mind. Here's your cheque book and card."

Slightly embarrassed I took them from her and mumbled, "Er thank you miss."

"No problem sir. Have a good day. Do call again."

*

I parked up at Mansfield Divisional HQ and headed for the incident room. The morning events drifted about inside my

170

head, woolly and blurred. They were soon overtaken and pushed to the back of my mind by more pressing matters. At the cutting edge of my thought processes I had a murder to think about. There was still a brutal killer on the loose somewhere out there. Who knows – I may just have driven past him. He could be on the doorstep or a thousand miles away by now. But he's out there, taking me on, trying to outwit me, beat me at my game. And maybe he thinks he can. Others have tried and failed, maybe he'll be the one to draw it across me. But it's early days yet. The clock's still ticking. Let's wait and see who has the last laugh with this one.

As I had done on many occasions in recent years I made for the front entrance to the nick. It didn't change. It was still the same dreary grey Victorian building where I'd joined up. It wasn't the most architecturally satisfying, nor aesthetically pleasing, but it fulfilled a purpose sitting there in the middle of town. I saw the police station as an island fortress constantly invaded by human flotsam and jetsam which ebbed and flowed in and around it. Not always violent but demanding. Demanding that one commodity so valuable to a policeman, time. Over the years I'd seen increased demands upon police time which has led to unacceptable pressures. I wasn't happy with the way the job, unlike the building, had changed. Years ago it had been more personal, dealing with people on the ground, resolving issues, solving problems, clearing crime. Yes, more personal, more time for people but the Panda car culture has changed that. Politicians created the myth that the police in their Panda cars would be at the scene of an incident within minutes, reassuring, solving, resolving, meting out Justice. What a con, what a lie. The public swallowed it. The complaints have flown in thick and fast ever since. Because their expectations haven't materialised. As far as I'm concerned the end product in attempting to satisfy the public expectancy of immediate response is inefficiency. Fire brigade policing, with numerous incidents attended but fewer dealt with properly. So I'm not a fan of the Panda car culture

I walked through reception and let myself in through a security door. As soon as it closed I was wrapped in that familiar dank smell and surrounded by the dowdy unimaginative décor. Dark green gloss paint everywhere. Must have been a bulk order of out of stock, unwanted, un-saleable crap that the Police Authority had got years ago for next to nothing. And then there are the inhabitants of this place. Its people, dashing here, dashing there, people dashing to God knows where. They clatter along passageways, in and out of offices, reception areas, cell block. People, people in a hurry, the end of the world is nigh, Armageddon. It never stops. Hustle and bustle, it's worse during a major incident. More bodies drafted in, Scenes of Crime, Special Operations, Force Intelligence, typists and communication buffs. And Senior Officers not involved in the enquiry getting under everybody's feet during the first couple of days. It was always the same. Weaker individuals had cracked up years ago under the tension, the constant stress, but I hadn't succumbed, yet! As I'd once told Angie, "I've been inoculated against it."

But she hadn't.

In the ops room I quickly got up to speed leafing through the action sheets and updated information. Things were moving along but no breakthrough yet.

Superintendent Davey joined me. "Some interesting lines you've fed in Jim. A thorough background research, at least we know our man now."

"I wouldn't say that yet Sir. We know a lot about him

172

but I suspect there are some important pieces missing."

"Such as?"

"Tom's lifestyle for one. Everybody's pal 'til the booze kicked in. Then it was knuckle pie and barney time. Left a few with a bad taste in the mouth. Mostly their own blood and a few missing teeth."

"So you think it could lie with the roughs and toughs he brawled with?"

"A possibility Sir. They'll want fetching in. And I want to try and locate his sister Rita and any of the old local Bobbies that may still be around."

"I don't know if that's a good idea Jim. I can't see how going back into the past that deeply will help. Let's concentrate on the present."

"I can't agree with you there Sir. Tom's past and the present are inextricably linked. I've already come up with a couple of leads in that direction."

The Super peered over his specs. "Yes, I've read your report. Fallows and Jimson isn't it?"

I had to smile, got a lot of time for the governor. The good old boy never missed a trick.

"Yes sir and Tom's sister Edith. It's early days yet, they've all got to be opened up but my gut feeling is that the past holds the key to the present."

The Superintendent thought for a moment and as he turned to leave he said, "You maybe right Inspector. I'm a dinosaur in my own time."

"Aren't we all Guv?"

I was still beavering through the paperwork when the team came in for the nine o'clock de brief. Sergeant Johnson brought them to order.

"Right folks. Calm down."

McLean took the opportunity to speak. "Guv I'd like to apologise about this morning …"

I cut him short. "No need for that McLean. Thanks for the gesture but remember what John Wayne said."

McLean screwed up his eyes and queried, "John Wayne boss?"

"Yeh," I said, "John Wayne. The Duke. He famously advised, 'Never Ay-pologise. It's a sign a weakness Kinkade.'"

The team burst into laughter, the room suddenly full of bandy kneed cowboys and quick draw gunmen. Even McLean smiled. All was forgiven.

We got down to serious business. I updated them and asked for comments.

"Are you thinking there's something in Tom's past that has finally caught up with him Sir?"

"It's just a gut feeling at the moment. Maybe the answer lies in the pubs around town, but we've got to cover all eventualities. Maybe someone has been carrying a grudge against him for a long time, and it's only now, as he's become older, that he's become more vulnerable."

Charlie Baker from the floor added, "If we're thinking of all those who Tommy's upset by his brawling boss we've got a lot of ground to cover."

"Why's that Charlie?" I queried.

"Tom's been barred from most of the pubs in town for fighting. In or out of ale he was too good for anyone around here. He was like Jesse James. Every body wanted a pop at him. Wanted his notches on their gun. They learned the hard way that Tommy didn't give 'em up lightly."

Leaning back in my chair I closed my eyes. I was alone in the self-imposed darkness and thinking aloud, mulling over what Charlie had said.

"So they couldn't take him face to face. Had to wait their opportunity. Come from behind and smash him to the ground. Make sure he stayed down. Didn't want him to get up and turn on them. That would account for the extreme violence." I thought for a moment. "Or maybe the killer knew Tom. Had his confidence."

I sat up quickly and opened my eyes. "What's the latest on Tom's movements for that night?" I enquired.

Sergeant Johnson leafed through the actions.

"A regular routine boss. When he was in town he started early doors at the Black Boy. Did the market pubs, Dial, Tavern and Crown. Ended up at the Black Swan, the Mucky Duck, till closing time then made his way back to the railway carriages for the night."

"Who did he see in those pubs? Did he have any problems? Any violence? Threats? "

"DC Barlow did the enquiry Sir, he can fill you in." He called, "DC Barlow."

The Detective Constable stood up and said, "Right boss. Like Sergeant Johnson says it was a regular routine, regular as clockwork. Never changed."

I was disappointed. This wasn't what I wanted to hear.

"Mister Barlow. Are you telling me that he met exactly the same people in exactly the same place at exactly the same time every night?" I asked cynically.

Barlow had been caught out and he knew it. He'd not got the right answers. He stalled for a moment. "Er. Well no sir I'm not saying that."

"No you're not Mister Barlow. What you're saying is that you're generalising. What usually happens has become what did happen. That's not good enough. That's where evidence is lost, where confusion enters the equation. I want you out there eliciting facts, specifics, double-checking and confirming. I don't want crap. I expect better from you. Alright?"

"Alright Sir. I didn't mean to let you down I'll get onto it straight away."

I nodded. He's learned a lesson. Won't make the same mistake again.

I made my feelings clear to Sergeant Johnson. "I want every alibi statement analysed and double-checked. I want no generalisations. Specifics, facts. Nothing less. If we don't get it right at this stage we're in for a long haul. Remember our role is to find out everything we can about the victim. The other teams will be concentrating on their particular aspect of the enquiry so it should all come together like a jigsaw. Make sure our pieces all fit. I don't want any missed or forced into wrong places. OK?"

"OK boss. Leave it with me."

As the office wound down for the evening and the late turn went about their duties I dragged Styx Johnson next door to the Loco. He didn't offer much resistance.

I like the Locomotive Inn. Its solid, square, stone structure breathes age and Industrial Revolution. You can almost smell the smoke and steam and hear the clank of heavy engines, the rattle of chains and the hiss of steam and screech of whistles. If only it could talk it would surely tell some riveting stories. Nowadays it's handy for the police station. Coppers are regular customers, rubbing shoulders with the good, the bad and the downright undesirable. Inside there are just three poky little rooms open to a bar area. They call that the main bar. It's the only bar. Half a dozen tables and chairs in the snug fill it to capacity. There's more space in a police cell, as some of The Loco's clientele could testify. But I like it. Its beamed ceiling and old fashioned interior give a feeling of intimacy.

An atmosphere, a warmth, that the new up and coming so called "fun pubs" don't have. This is where the CID come to relax. A place to air our grievances. Let off a bit of steam. Have a go at the top brass, before we drift out onto the front line again, onto those unpredictable, often dangerous streets.

We went into the snug just off the main bar and sat down at the table next to the little cast iron fireplace. McLean had joined us. He was at the bar getting the drinks in. He wasn't a regular like the rest of us but Styx had obviously been training him up. He got his order in and squeezed past some of the off duty detectives and other punters crammed into the main bar.

He was chuntering away. I heard him say, "The place is bleeding filthy."

He'd got a point but to my mind the "well lived in" look added to the character of the place.

McLean navigated with difficulty and a lot of luck through the crush of bodies and tables and chairs that had seen better days. With a sigh of relief he placed two pints of Mansfield bitter and a tot of Captain Morgan onto our wobbly table. Styx pushed a folded piece of beer mat under a leg to stabilise it.

I picked up my tot and said, "Cheers Andy. Welcome to the club house."

McLean raised his glass gave an awkward smile and returned the toast. "Cheers boss."

I glanced around. "Not many locals in tonight Sarge."

"Keeping their heads down boss. They'll be back."

"Has anything come from the pub enquiry Guv?" McLean asked.

"Not yet Andy. It's early days but we need a break soon or it's going to be a long, hard, slog."

Sergeant Johnson advised solemnly from somewhere

within his pint pot, "That's when the fun and games begin. Top corridor will want all the credit for a result but they won't like paying for it."

"There's a lot of truth in that," I said. "Another nine day wonder in the ivory tower, then it interferes with all the Home Office initiatives that the force wastes so much time and money on."

"Too many do gooders boss who know fuck all about catching thieves," declared Johnson.

I should have expected it but I was surprised when McLean joined in.

He said, "Sooner do gooders than incompetence and corruption sarge."

"What do you mean by that McLean?" queried the sergeant.

"It means just what I said."

"And I said what the fuck does that mean?"

"Meaning they're not doing the job they're sworn to do."

"Sworn to do? Give over. Have you looked in the cell block lately? "

"There's more to modern policing than just locking people up and throwing away the key."

"You what? Enlighten me then Supercop."

"No need to take the piss Sarge."

"Like they say. Can't take the piss out of the brown stuff lad."

I could see the sabre-rattling building up to full fledged conflict.

I said, "Let's calm it. Pull your claws in and show some respect for one another's point of view."

Johnson looked hard at McLean who returned his glare and said, "He hasn't got a point of view Guv. Doesn't follow the rules. Does just what he likes. That's my point. It's these outdated attitudes that need scrapping. The sooner the better."

Johnson snapped back, "What Utopia have you been swanning about in? On the street if you go by the rules you're in for a kicking. That's when the bad guys shaft the good guys."

McLean wasn't persuaded. "If the police don't stick to the rules where does that put prevention of crime, protection of life and property, the maintenance of order and the prosecution of offenders against the Peace? "

Styx Johnson spat back, "Ten out of ten for your Training School definitions McLean. But this is shit street mister. The garbage bin, the real fucking world, not some cosy classroom where you can sit playing with yourself waiting for the dinner bell to ring."

Things were hotting up. Getting personal now, a sure sign that logic and common sense were heading for the pan. I wasn't about to pull the chain just yet. I was interested in seeing where this meeting of the minds would end up. I'd just remind them I was still here. I sat and rolled the glass of rum slowly between my hands and gave McLean and Johnson one of my best withering looks.

I said, "Now, now, let's not get 'em in a twist. We're on the same side you know." I could see that Styx Johnson wasn't too happy with my assessment.

He confirmed my suspicion when he said, "Not too sure about that boss. I'd have to think twice about him backing me up."

McLean immediately returned to the attack. "There's no need to worry about me Sergeant, I'll do the job I'm paid to do and do it properly."

"What the fuck are you getting at McLean? What's eating you? If you've got something to say spit it out now. Let's all hear it."

McLean didn't answer. He just looked at Sergeant Johnson.

But the DS wasn't letting up. "Come on then genius let's hear your gripe. Or are you posh talking 'suvveners all wind and piss?"

McLean came back at him, his voice deliberate, cold. "No Sergeant I'm not all wind and piss. I leave that privilege to you lot north of Watford Gap. But it seems to me that if you spent less time in the boozers and more time on the streets you'd catch some real criminals."

"Real criminals McLean? I don't think you'd recognise Reggie Kray if they stuck the fucker in your cot with you."

"The truth disturbs you then does it Sarge?"

"No, but the crap you spout does."

"It's not crap if the past is anything to go by."

"I don't know what the past has got to do with it mister but let me ask you a simple question. Where do you go to find villains in this town?"

"That's why I'm on this CID attachment. To learn that sort of thing."

"Well let's start the learning right here. I'll tell you first where you won't find 'em. Vicars' garden parties, afternoon tea dances, Girl Guide jamborees or the local Women's Institute. OK?"

McLean nodded. The learning curve was shaping.

"Now I'll tell you where you will find 'em." The Sergeant took a deep swig of beer before counting off on his fingers, "Night clubs, casinos, boozers, race tracks, restaurants, cafes, brothels, shabeens. And you don't drink slim line tonics with the low lives plotting and performing in those dives." Styx Johnson was living the reality of experience. He was in full flow. "And who rubs shoulders with the scum?" With

180

determined jabs he ticked off his fingers again. "Clubbers, gamblers, piss artists, taxi drivers, dealers, barrow boys, landlords, totties, pimps, druggies, receivers." He paused before making his final point, prodding his chest forcefully, "and plain clothes coppers like me, the CID. To catch the bastards we have to go down to their level, wade in their slime and shit. It's not a pleasant job but it's got to be done. And if it means bending the rules you bend 'em. So if you're not up to it McLean, hand your fuckin' badge in." Detective Sergeant Styx Johnson rested his case and sat back.

Applause rippled around the group of detectives who had moved closer to listen to the heated debate. It was clear to me where their sympathies lay, and it wasn't south of the Trent. I passed Johnson a five pound note, "Get 'em in Styx. You'll need one after that lot."

"It's my shout boss, I'll see to 'em."

The Sergeant pushed his way through the detectives crowding about the bar, exchanging banter with them and giving knowing glances in McLean's direction.

McLean just sat there fiddling with his drink.

I said, "What was that all about Andy?"

"I was just trying to make a point, that's all Guv. Sergeant Johnson didn't like what I had to say but that doesn't bother me. Only to be expected. One of the old school. Hidebound, stuck in a rut. And there are lots more like him."

"Old school? Yeah. Stuck in a rut? No. You're wrong about that and you've got the wrong impression about Sergeant Johnson. He's one to have in your boat, not firing salvoes at you from the other side."

"If you say so Guv; but the police have a lot to answer for."

"Do they now? Tell me about it."

"You hear about it all the time. Prisoners released from jail after serving years for a crime they didn't commit. They didn't volunteer for the experience. Bent coppers and lawyers put them there. That's what I'm on about."

The penny suddenly dropped. I knew what he was on about. "Bent coppers and crooked lawyers! Right Andy, now I see where you're coming from."

"I'm glad you do. Sergeant Johnson obviously doesn't"

"He might if you explained what you were getting at. We all know they're out there, a small group of rotten apples in a very large barrel."

"That's my point. Everybody knows about it. It's been going on for decades and nobody does anything about it."

"You're very misinformed Andy. But just remember who pulls out the rotten apples and locks them up. Coppers! Honest, hard working, hard pressed, dedicated coppers. Like Sergeant Johnson over there, regularly putting their lives on the line."

At that moment Styx Johnson returned to the table and put down the drinks.

"Still at it Guv?" he enquired.

"He's making a fair point. I've tried to put him straight."

"I've been at this game too many years boss, and when villains work nine to five and stay out of the hot spots then I will. In the meantime I go for the baddies anyway I can."

McLean didn't intend to be side tracked or ignored, he said, "That's one of the problems Sergeant. People like you are living in the past. Hide bound. It's time to move on. Accept change. In the new world it's called progress you know."

"Progress, McLean?" Johnson moved towards him aggressively.

That was my cue. It had gone far enough. Like Nelson I

slipped in between the opposing "men o'war"and engaged them more closely. I stood up and took a firm hold on Styx Johnson's shoulder redirecting him back to his seat.

I turned to McLean and said, "Progress hey Andy? I'm in favour of progress if it's going to make life better for Joe Public, but not progress for progress sake. Henry Ford was right when he said 'if it isn't broke don't fix it'"

"That's just my point Guv. The system is broke. Has been for a long time. I realise now that Justice is a smoke screen for dishonesty and corruption. There's got to be change. That's why the Police and Criminal Evidence Bill and a Crown Prosecutions Service are being proposed, to prevent miscarriages of justice in the future. Protect the innocent. Convict the guilty. "

Sergeant Johnson, still seated, was spitting fire. "Fucking charters for toe rags and their mouthpieces that's all they are. More jobs for the boys. More solicitors, bigger Legal Aid bills. Legislation that'll cut the balls off coppers at the sharp end. If you're a glimpse of the future McLean, God help the police force and the public."

It was my turn to comment, my opportunity to put in my half penn'orth. I said, "And if this new CPS takes off and the Pace Act comes into force it'll be even worse. The CPS will be a toothless tiger, and unscrupulous solicitors will have the justice system by the balls. Don't you think?"

"Can't be any worse than it is Guv. Look at the high profile cases that have been splattered all over the media. False evidence, perjury. That means the guilty are still out there. On the streets, free to commit more crimes. And the innocent rot in jail, worse in some cases. If the system doesn't work there's only one alternative for the aggrieved."

He'd certainly got something to say. I asked, "And what's that Andy?"

"Be their own judge, jury and executioner."

Johnson stared at him. "He's fucking bonkers boss. Judge, jury, executioner? Where does he think he is? Alabama? He'll be calling in the Ku Klux Klan next." Addressing me he said, "You won't mind if I go and join the rest of our corrupt team boss?" He nodded towards the detectives grouped around the bar, "If I stay here much longer I'll be covered with all the bullshit that's flying about."

I gave an understanding nod to my right hand man who moved off to join his colleagues whilst McLean glowered after him.

An uneasy silence descended upon the two of us left sitting at the table. After a few heavy moments I broke the impasse. I asked McLean, "Does this revenge theory mean midnight visits by men in balaclavas and flour bag hoods, burning crosses on victims' lawns before they string 'em up from the nearest lamp post?"

He wasn't impressed. He replied, "You don't have to take the piss Guv. Sergeant Johnson does enough of that for everybody. All I'm saying is that the system's failed and the police are at the heart of it. Jacking up evidence. Slip in a verbal here, another there, nudging the truth a bit, tweaking it, a bit of fine tuning." He added cynically, "making sure the system doesn't fail the public. We all know that innocent people have been wrongly convicted. That's what I'm on about. When justice fails. That can't be right Guv can it?"

"You're very cynical Andy but anarchy isn't an option. Nothing justifies taking the law into our own hands."

McLean gave me a long knowing look. Strange really. And then he said, "I wonder if that statement will ever come back to haunt you Guv?"

I couldn't see what he was getting at and I said, "Come back to haunt me? I don't think so Andy. I know where I stand on the issues, I know myself and my beliefs, the question will never arise."

McLean said cynically, "Hope you're right boss."

Sergeant Johnson came over again. With pint pot in hand he leaned his big frame against the dividing screen and said curtly, "Is he still blowing wind boss?"

"Got to give him his due Sarge, if nothing else he's consistent."

Styx Johnson's assessment was more down to earth and direct. "More like constipated boss. It seems to me he's full of crap."

McLean didn't respond. He appeared to have calmed down. He said quietly, "You've made some very cynical observations Guv," adding, "and very depressing."

"Cynical? Depressing? Maybe you're right. At one time we saw the police as *The Job*, now it's *A Job*. But the likes of me and Styx here'll keep the flag flying. God help the job when our generation's gone."

However, Sergeant Johnson had more important duties to perform. He saw off the last of his beer.

"If I'm going to keep the flag flying boss I'd better go and do my bit for Queen and country at the marble shrine in la pissoir." Like the loyal officer he was, the big man strode off to do his duty.

We waited for him in the small passage near the pub entrance. Suddenly a heavily built, unkempt figure lurched in from the street barging into us. By the look of him he was a down and out and half cut. As he attempted to force himself past us I cautioned him, "Hey! Watch it mate."

A slurred voice ground out, "Or?"

185

"Or you'll be out quicker than you came in. I think you've had enough anyway."

Before attempting to bulldoze past us the big man blustered, "Got bugger all to do wi' you mister."

I wasn't having lip from him and took hold of his arm.

At that moment Sergeant Johnson returned. He spoke sharply to the drunk, "What's the problem Duggy?"

The man staggered and leant against the passage wall for support. He peered at Styx. Delayed recognition caused him to mumble apologetically,

"Oh. Sorry Mister Johnson. Didn't see you there. I'm just going."

The down and out peered at McLean through bloodshot eyes. Mumbling something unintelligible he stumbled out into the night. With footwork and body swerves that would have done Georgie Best proud, he adjusted his bearings and with a final backward glance aimed himself in the direction of the railway sidings.

"Friend of yours Styx?"

"Duggy Davis? Been helpful in the past. Bit of a knuckle bosun'. Dosses in the railway carriages. That's where he'll be heading now."

"Does he know Tom Oakley?"

"More than likely Guv. They all piss in the same pot. "

"Ok," I said, "I'm off. See you both in the morning. And don't be late. There's work to be done."

I made my way back to the operations room. The Job was calling.

SIXTEEN

12th AUGUST
THURSDAY MORNING

"Now let me see. Bull necked sixteen and a half?" The mischievous twinkle in her brown eyes brought a tingling shiver to my stomach.

"You've got a good memory Miss Downey."

"Not really Sir. It was only yesterday that you bought the two shirts. Size sixteen wasn't it?"

I laughed. "Alright, so I was mistaken."

With head held slightly to one side the supervisor looked at me as though she was trying to read my mind.

"No you weren't. You were wearing sixteen and a half. You've lost a bit of weight haven't you?"

In the men's wear department of Marks I felt drawn to her. I liked the woman; I was enjoying the simple conversation. I could sense the interest, the compassion within her.

"Yes, I'm eating more sensibly now. Not so many chips or curry," I said.

"Your wife's put you on a diet then?" she asked.

For a moment I didn't reply but fiddled with a couple of cellophane wrapped packages on the counter.

My negative reaction to her question seemed to have confused Miss Downey. "I'm sorry, have I said something wrong?" she queried.

"No. No. Of course you haven't. It's just me. At the moment I'm a little touchy that's all."

She looked at me. Her brown eyes were even softer now.

"If you'd like to go for a coffee or something, I'm due for my break in a few minutes."

That tingling feeling gripped my stomach again.

"That would be nice," I said. "I could do with the company."

THURSDAY MORNING

The telephone rang. It startled Edith. She was black-leading the hearth but struggled to her feet before carefully placing the black lead brush and tin of polish on the hob. Wiping her hands on her pinny she picked up the receiver.

She had a good idea who was calling but enquired cautiously, "Hello?"

After a moment she said, "Yes I'm alright thank you. I thought it might be you."

"Yes just like you said, but he seemed a nice sort of chap to me. Not a bit like you described him."

"That's your opinion and you're entitled to it."

"No I didn't tell him anything. Family business is our business, nothing to do with anyone else."

She responded indignantly, "Of course I'm sure. I'm not a complete fool you know. I've lived with the secret all these years, I'll live with it a few more."

"Of course I know the consequences. What's done can't be undone. God knows I've prayed night after night for nigh-on a life time. It was just beginning to fade and lose its bitterness until you turned up."

188

"No I'm not blaming you. I can't forget what's happened but I do understand. In the end we all have to stand before God on Judgement Day. Even the ones we loved on this earth will have to account before the Throne of God for their sins."

"I know he'll keep coming to see me, but don't worry, I shan't weaken. You just remember what I've said about Judgement Day. That's what you should be worrying about, hell's damnation and the eternal fire."

"Well you should worry."

"Yes. I do think about the family."

"We'll see when all this terrible business is finished with. You might not want to see me then."

"Alright. Goodbye."

With a shaking hand Edith returned the telephone to its cradle. A confusion of feelings coursed through her as she slumped in the rocking chair, drained emotionally. Some time later she reached for her Bible, holding it close. With tears in her eyes she picked up the photograph of Rita, kissed it and said, "Why Rita? Oh Why?"

*

I felt very uncomfortable. No, not uncomfortable, more like apprehensive, sitting in the café with Miss Downey. Just the two of us facing one another across the red formica and chrome metal table. The only thing between us was the red and white spotted plastic cruet set isolated there in the middle. I think we were both a little nervous, I certainly was. It wasn't something I did every day. In fact I hadn't socialised with an attractive woman for a long time. I don't know if having a cuppa in a café counts as socialising. Anyway we weren't alone. There were a couple of other people seated nearby. But they weren't taking any notice of us, they were too engrossed in their toasted tea cakes and cups of tea.

I'd finished my coffee and was feeling a little nervous when I said to her, "How long have you got?"

Miss Downey reached over and took the empty cup and saucer from me and put it on the tray in front of her.

"This is my ten minute coffee break," she said, adding expectantly, "I get three quarters of an hour at half past twelve."

I felt clumsy and tried to make light of her flirtatious comment when I said, "Sounds like a good firm to work for." I followed up with a laugh. It didn't come out as I intended. It rasped like a dry sore throat.

With apparent concern Miss Downey reached over and patted my hand.

She asked, "Are you alright Mister Stirling?"

The tingling started in my stomach again. "Yes, er yes. Just a bit of a frog."

I felt her hand gently caressing mine. An overpowering desire to touch her came over me and I placed my other hand on top of hers. I felt pleasantly warm and said to her quietly, "Jim. It's Jim. Jim Stirling."

She responded by placing her free hand on top of mine and saying in a quiet seductive voice, "Sandra Downey. I'm very pleased to meet you Jim."

I looked down at our intertwined fingers. Sandra's were delicate, long and well manicured. They reflected her femininity. Mine were just the opposite. I'd always had big hands with strong fingers, must have been something to do with my genes, and they could never be described as delicate in a million years. The couple of displaced knuckles would

190

disqualify them from that category in any case. But they were a legacy of the tough professions I'd followed.

I was beginning to relax. Sandra certainly had a way of making me feel comfortable and at ease; I hadn't felt like this for a long time.

"Now we've met formally I'll tell you a bit about myself. Alright?"

I nodded. At that moment, she couldn't do or say anything wrong. She gently changed the position of her hands, realigning them and holding mine in hers.

She looked into my eyes and said, "First of all I'm a Nottingham girl. Divorced, nearly two years now. He's an accountant. It only lasted four years. He turned out to prefer male company to mine. Lives in London, Earls Court; we've no children. I've been working for M and S for over ten years now. Been a supervisor for two. Looking towards management. Live at Ravenshead. A small bungalow. Gotta phone, gotta car, no pool, no pets. A boring non-smoker and that's me. What about you?"

My mind raced. I'd been put on the spot. Where did I start? My life story was a little more complicated than that and I didn't want to put her off. Were things moving too quickly? I made a snap decision and jumped in with both feet.

"There's not much to tell really." I gently squeezed her hands. They were warm and soft. I continued, "I'm a Nottinghamshire man, born at Hucknall I believe. Can't ever remember living there."

Sandra laughed and chided, "Mucky Huckna'?"

I rallied to my birth place's defence with a more selective image of Hucknall Torkard.

"It owes its existence to coal, but it's got a fair share

191

of cultural and historic connections. Lord Byron's buried in the family vault at St. Mary's Church. Eric Coates lived and composed there. Newstead Abbey, the Byron ancestral home, Annesley Hall and Bestwood Hall are a stone's throw away from the town centre. So it's not all muck and coal dust."

Sandra squeezed my hand. "I was only joking. Don't be so serious all the time. Relax a little. Come from behind that defensive barrier you surround yourself with. Try and share your problems. If you don't, they'll destroy you."

I was warming to her but I was still uncomfortable. She was opening herself up to me right from the start. I could feel her caring nature reaching out to me, eager to ease what she probably saw as my burdened mind. She reminded me a lot of Angie and I didn't want her to go the same way.

I made a point of checking my watch. With what I hoped Sandra would take for concern I said, "Look at the time! You don't want to be late back."

Sandra looked at her watch and asked enthusiastically, "Shall I see you at half twelve?"

I felt myself being drawn into an uncontrollable situation. I wanted to see her, wanted to be with her, but the barriers had gone up. Each time I approached them, each time I assaulted them, each time they appeared to be yielding, I stepped back. The barriers were not breached.

Sandra looked at me. She held my hands tightly. She waited expectantly for my answer.

"Not today I'm afraid. Business calls. The Job you know. Maybe I'll see you around."

She tried to hide her disappointment behind a wide smile, which showed off her white teeth and the soft dimples in her cheeks. But I could tell she was upset and I didn't like myself any the more for it. But she didn't intend giving up. Taking a biro out of her uniform pocket she jotted down her telephone number on the back of a coffee mat. She offered it to me holding it in those long slender fingers. I took it.

"You can ring me anytime," Sandra said hopefully.

She stood up, smoothing down her uniform skirt before offering her hand. I held it gently.

"I'm not Royalty, I won't break you know," she said and kissed me lightly on the cheek.

I suppose I didn't respond as she wanted me to. I stood full square behind my barrier. Understandably she flounced off, her shoe heels tapping sharply on the restaurant floor. Their message was clear.

Looking at the coffee mat and then the attractive woman walking away from me I realised I was alone once more. But then I had "The Job."

SEVENTEEN

THURSDAY AFTERNOON

The morning's events hadn't left me feeling too good about myself. My unresponsive attitude towards Sandra didn't seem to have gone down very well with her. She appeared disappointed in the way I had reacted. But I hadn't intended to be so cavalier. She seemed to be a very nice person and I certainly didn't want to do anything to upset her. I liked her a lot but I wanted to go at my speed, pick up the pieces slowly before I committed myself. That didn't seem to be Sandra's way. My impression was that she was a bit of a go-getter. Made her mind up about things and went for it. I wasn't on that track yet. But I wanted to see her again.

In the incident room there was the usual buzz of activity. Everybody hard at it, moving the paper, keeping the monster fed. The card index was growing like Topsy. Even the Superintendent was at the VDU.

I pulled up a chair alongside him. "House to house hasn't thrown up anything then Sir?"

"Not yet Jim. Pubs seem the best bet. We're still analysing that information. What about you?"

"He's left a trail like a bull elephant on the rampage. It's just that last hour or so that's evading us."

The Super pressed a couple of keys and read from the

screen. "Last seen in the Black Swan. That's where the trail goes cold. Haven't found anyone who saw him talking to another punter or leaving the place. That's strange. What's the landlord say?"

Leafing through a wad of action sheets I pulled one out. "Spike Jones, Licensee, former fireman, knew Tom, never had any problems with him. I get the impression that by the time he rolled into the Swan he was too oiled to be any trouble. Remembers serving him a couple of pints. Sat out of the way in the snug. Not too many in that night he recalls. Didn't see him with anybody and didn't see him leave. No lock-in that night. Definitely gone by eleven."

Superintendent Davey thought for a moment before speaking.

"That means he either met up with his killer in the pub and left with him, without attracting attention, or met him en route to the doss."

I nodded in agreement and said, "Either he walked with the killer along the whole or part of the route, rode with him in a vehicle or was followed by him. Someone may have seen something. Do you want my team to look at it?"

"No you've got enough on Jim. Your anonymous caller needs some special attention. Keep plugging away into Tom's background, I feel sure you'll come up with something. I'll get one of the other teams onto this." As he left the room the Superintendent added, "Just keep me updated."

I sat down at the VDU and tickled the keyboard. Sure, I shared the Super's enthusiasm for the computer's future. I'm all in favour of anything that helps nick villains. At the moment though the technology is still in its infancy as far as the Police are concerned, not fully tried and tested. Its worth as a major crime investigation tool has yet to be evaluated.

I'd been brought up by street-wise detectives who swore by their belief that incident rooms don't catch villains, they access the information put in by coppers to help convict them. That's still my position.

Apart from that the incident with the dosser at the Loco had raised questions that I wanted answering. I trawled through the card index system which was rapidly building up into hundreds of documents. It was slow going. Now this is an area where computers could probably make their mark. In the meantime I was stuck with the ball aching task of flicking through masses of card. I wasn't having much success.

I called to Styx Johnson, "Sarge, has your pal Duggy Davis been interviewed?"

"Should've been boss," he replied. "He does the Loco and the other boozers round about and he's been a bad 'un in his time. GBH man. Got to be in the frame."

I shook my head. "No Douglas Davis has been interviewed. Is that his proper name?"

"Yeah boss. I've nicked him a couple of times."

"He's nowhere in the system. Looks as though we've missed him and he's keeping his head down. Why?"

"Maybe he's wanted Guv and done a runner. I'll get McLean to check with Force Intelligence. There might be a warrant out for him."

"And maybe he knows more about this job than meets the eye. We only saw him last night and now he's suddenly done a runner. I want him in, warrant or no warrant. See that he's actioned and circulated."

He replied, "Wilco Guv."

McLean came into the room. He put a cup of coffee on my desk and handed me a large manila envelope.

He said, "This has just arrived for you Sir from Forensic."

I didn't use much finesse in ripping open the envelope but I was eager to read the documents it contained. And they did hold my attention. There was some interesting stuff that could progress the enquiry. A few more pieces of the jigsaw to slot into place. I'd discuss the implications of the Forensics with the Governor, bring him up to speed and enable him to decide what action to take on the labs information. McLean had remained in the office whilst I went through the report. I said to him. "A very interesting report. I'll update the action on this."

McLean reached out for the papers. "I'll do it Sir," he said eagerly.

I appreciated his enthusiasm but I waved him aside and said, "Thanks Andy but the SIO needs to see them. He'll file them in his office."

As he turned away I was surprised to see by his demeanour and the look on his face that the aide was trying hard to hide his obvious disappointment. As he left the office I was left thinking what a complex guy he was. Up one minute down the next. He'd have to take stock of himself if he wanted to get through his CID attachment. I'd have to see what his supervisors thought of him. Then the telephone rang. I answered it. "DI. Right. Thank you. I'll be there in about ten minutes. Thanks again for ringing."

I dropped off the forensic report in the SIO's office, buttoned my overcoat and left the station.

Traffic wasn't too heavy and I arrived at the General Hospital in just under ten minutes. I made my way across the car park, past the laundry block and headed for the single storey building to the left of the main complex. I was very familiar with the place and from reception I walked down a well-lit, pleasantly decorated passageway. It wasn't too long before my nostrils were assailed by the sickly smell of disinfectant, mixed with the sweet aroma of "Country Violets."

I hated it. They can't even disguise that stench with an aerosol spray. I took out my handkerchief as I entered the waiting room. By that time I was snuffling. Then I sneezed.

"Bless you Inspector," a woman's voice said.

Pushing the hanky into my overcoat pocket I looked at the old lady. Once again I was reminded of an old school ma'am as she sat there peering back at me through those John Lennon style glasses. She seemed so tiny, so alone in that large waiting room with its regiment of canvas and tubular metal chairs lined up around the green gloss painted walls. It seemed the NHS used the same painting contractor as the police. The result was just as depressing.

"Hello Edith, nice to see you again. Sorry it has to be here in such unhappy circumstances," I said.

It was clear she had been crying. Fighting to control the emotion in her straining voice she replied, "He's my brother and I love him. I'm the only one left that does. He looked so peaceful lying there. I could see my Dad in him."

Try as she might, the distraught woman was not able to keep her feelings from overflowing. She gave three or four sharp, chest-wracking breaths and wept. I felt for her and sat alongside her. I put my arm about her shoulders in an attempt to offer some comfort. I didn't speak to her, I felt it better to allow her to gain control of her runaway emotions. After a few moments Edith removed her glasses, dabbed her eyes, gave one last chest-heaving sigh and sat back.

In a determined but still strained voice she said, "Sorry about that Inspector but I'm alright now. Where were we?"

I chose my words carefully and said, "You were telling me how peaceful Tom looked. I wanted a few words about him but if you're not up to it I can arrange to see you again."

Giving her eyes one last dab, the proud old lady replaced her glasses, before turning to face me. "No, I'm alright now. Let's finish the talking so that I can go back to Langwith and get on with my life."

I said to her, "OK. Have you received any more calls from our unidentified friend?"

"I've received one or two calls from different people Inspector."

She was being evasive. I plugged on. "Including Mister Anonymous?"

"I didn't say that Inspector."

"And you haven't denied it either."

She didn't reply.

"Did you tell him of our arrangement?" I asked.

"If you knew me well enough Mister Stirling you'd know that I don't easily break a confidence."

"That's reassuring Edith. Does your loyalty extend to helping me find your brother's murderer?"

As a school ma'am lecturing a scholar, politely but firmly she said, "I can't help you catch the so-called murderer. If the Lord is on your side you'll catch him without my help. He'll guide your footsteps if He thinks it's right to do so. But remember Mister Stirling, the Lord our God prefers not to punish men on earth for their sins, but welcomes repentant sinners into His fold. All men must stand before Him on Judgement Day to be weighed in the balance. All I can do is pray for the sinner."

I wasn't about to be submerged beneath her pious uttering and two can play that game.

I pressed on. "I understand that Edith, but God also said that man should honour his Commandments. Exodus 20:13. Thou Shall Not Kill. You're disobeying the spirit of the Lord's Commandments by protecting a possible killer."

Miss Oakley didn't answer immediately. Her reaction told me she didn't like to be preached at and my preaching troubled her. Backed into a corner, she retaliated with her only weapon.

Forcefully she declared, "Vengeance is mine. I will repay saith The Lord. Romans 12:19."

Not to be outdone, I countered quietly, "Exodus 21:23-24. Thou shalt give life for life, eye for eye, tooth for tooth. But let's leave it at that. I'm sure you know more biblical references than I do Edith and there are differing views. In the end it comes down to what's in your heart. What does it tell you to do? And remember, when we support a wicked act our conscience is worthless. I wonder what God would say about that?"

She didn't respond. I suspect Edith Oakley was struggling with her religious beliefs, family responsibilities and public duty. I intended to take advantage of her dilemma.

"Edith. Your brother is lying cold and alone in that tiny chapel next door, his mutilated body beyond all human help. For all his earthly sins, he didn't deserve to be struck down by a cowardly killer. Doesn't your God tell you to pour out your heart in support of your murdered brother? In the cause of truth and justice?"

She didn't reply. Hard as it was, she resisted persuasion. I knew I had problems in enlisting her help but like all good detectives I was prepared to change direction.

"Edith, you told me last time that Tom hadn't been the

same since your mother was killed. Do you want to tell me about it?"

The look the collier's daughter gave me told me she wasn't eager to revive the events surrounding her mother's death. But perhaps she saw it as a better alternative than my earlier unsettling questions because she opened up.

With head bowed she said quietly, "Oh! It was some years ago now. Dad took Mam out in the pony and trap. They were in a collision with a speeding vehicle. Mam was killed outright. The pony had to be shot. Dad was badly injured but being so big and strong he survived. They didn't tell him about Mam at first. When they did he gave up. Dead within a month. Died of a broken heart they said. He couldn't live without her. He'd loved and nursed her all those years and then she was taken from him like that. He didn't want to go on without her you see."

"That's a tragic story Edith. What about the driver? What happened to him?"

"The driver? He pleaded guilty to causing Mam's death by dangerous and drunken driving. Sent to prison for 6 months."

"That was a terrible loss Edith. And he only got 6 months. It doesn't bear thinking about."

"Oh! He did a full life sentence. Never out of trouble, as if he had a death wish. Wanted to be punished for what he'd done. He lived with the pain and anguish all his life. That's God's punishment. Hell on earth."

"What happened to him?"

With only the slightest hint of emotion she said, "He's lying in that tiny chapel next door, cold and alone."

I was totally unprepared for the revelation. I gasped, "Tom?"

He'd got no form for it. It didn't show up on his record. Might have been expunged as a spent conviction; but more likely lost amidst the masses of files and paperwork in Headquarters CID and Force Intelligence.

"Surprised Inspector? My wayward brother had a lot to answer for, but now he's at peace with God. I forgave him his earthly sins years ago, but he never embraced the Lord and so he suffered to the end. It's God's way you see."

"How did the rest of the family take it?"

"Mam and Dad's death? Those that were left got on with their lives. Tom took himself away and kept in touch with me when it suited. And that wasn't too often. I loved him to the end. I still do. I love all my family."

Sad though the Oakley story was, maybe I was still wearing my investigator's hat and here was a sudden chink of light in the darkness. I momentarily glimpsed the elusive something. Here was a motive if ever there was one, a loving mother and father brutally torn from the heart of their caring family. Here was fertile ground for sibling vendetta.

"Jack, where is he now?" I enquired.

Edith showing signs of weariness sighed, "In the churchyard at Langwith with Mam and Dad. The war took its toll and he didn't really get over the tragedy."

It was a bit of a downer, finding that the main subject of my latest theory was no longer in the frame but I hadn't given up on that line of enquiry.

"Children? What about children?"

Edith gave me one of her old fashioned looks, removed her glasses, rubbing them with her handkerchief before replacing them.

In a tired voice she said, "Jack's son and daughter are Canadian citizens now. We exchange cards, birthdays and Christmas, but that's all. The family doesn't exist anymore. Not like it used to."

"And Rita?"

A tight smile hovered about Edith's lips. "Our Rita? Been doing your homework Mister Stirling. Seems you don't really want anything from me."

I didn't intend letting go. "I know a fair bit Edith. All part of the job. But I need you to fill in the missing pieces."

Edith closed her eyes and rocked in the chair.

"Oh Rita!" A tinge of pink lit up her pale face as she remembered distant days and her sister. Tears traced the swell of her glowing cheeks and she sobbed.

I asked quietly, "Painful memories Edith?"

Lifting her glasses she dabbed once more the now angry red swellings around her eyes and said, "And many loving ones."

The old lady was struggling with her emotions so I waited for her to draw on that inner Oakley strength to fortify her fragility before I asked, "Where is Rita?"

Without hesitation the old lady replied, "Dead. She's dead. Another part of the Oakley family tragedy."

"Do you want to tell me about it?"

"Not really but you'll find out anyway. You might as well hear it from me. After she left home, just before the end of the war, she was pregnant. Didn't want the shame to touch the family, but it was too late. Rumours spread like wildfire. You can't keep such things secret in a small pit village. Mam and Dad turned against her and there was never a chance to make it up again. Rita went to Nottingham to have her baby. There were complications and she died. Tom and I buried her at Langwith. She didn't want to come back home. The shame still bothered her. But we brought her back to rest with her family where she belonged."

Edith Oakley stood up, brushed herself down and

added, "And that's all there is. I'm the last of the Oakleys now our Tom's gone."

Before I could reply, the sprightly little figure got up from her chair and walked to the door. There she turned and said dismissively, "I can't say it's been nice seeing you Inspector but it has been good for my soul. I'll bid you good day and thank you for your courtesy."

With that she hurried from the room.

Within the hour I was back in the incident room updating an action sheet, based on the information gleaned from Edith. Andy McLean read it before taking it through to reception for analysis.

"Looks as though the Oakleys have had a rough time over the years Guv." McLean said.

"Just a bit! Only Edith left now. I'd like to leave her alone but until I've bottomed that anonymous caller I can't."

"Is it that important Sir? After all it's only a phone call. Could be a nutter."

"No it's more than that. Edith isn't playing ball for some reason. It doesn't appear to be family orientated, because there aren't any close family left. The nearest is in Canada. They'll be checked out but I don't expect anything from that angle."

"From your report sir it looks as though Miss Oakley's a bit of a religious nut. She might just be over the top about the caller."

I was having none of that. I said forcefully, "If that's the impression my report has given, then I'll have to rewrite it. Edith isn't a nutter. Loyal, honest and at ease with her faith, yes! She's far better prepared to deal with the misfortunes of life and death than I am. I have the greatest of respect for the old lady. She could teach us a lot."

McLean took the hint and left the office with my report.

Later, Superintendent Davey called the senior investigators to his office where he addressed us.

"A piece of interesting information has come to light gentlemen. I'll read this statement. It explains everything. It's made by Mister Harry Parker, *'I am a Toilet Attendant at the Town Hall Public Toilets. I have been employed there for eight years. I have known Tom Oakley since his boxing days, I was a fan of his. Tommy has been using these facilities for about four years, on and off. He would arrive in the morning, just before the railway carriages were pulled out of night storage. Tom would have a good wash and shave. He left his washing up kit and few belongings in a holdall in my office. I have produced the holdall and contents to the Police.*

I have been asked if Tom Oakley carried any other possessions with him. It is to my personal knowledge that he always carried a small, brown leather fold over type wallet, with the faded initials 'TKO' embossed in one corner. Though he did not have much in the way of possessions, he valued the wallet most. In it he carried a number of family photographs which he showed to me when the mood took him. To the best of my recollection the photographs were of his parents, brothers and sisters.

I last saw Tommy on Sunday morning 8th August. He had the wallet then. I am aware of Tom's reputation for violence but I can honestly say he never caused me any problems all the time I knew him. I do not know of any one who would have reason to kill him.' There you have it gentlemen. A wallet with family photographs that he always carried with him." The Superintendent paused for a moment, scanning the faces of his officers. "He didn't have it when we searched his body and possessions. So where is it?"

"It isn't likely that we missed it during the finger tip search Sir," one officer said.

"Right! So what if the contents of the wallet are the reason for the murder?"

Now that was interesting. I'd come across some weird reasons for murder in my time, like the guy who kicked his mate to death for pissing in his chair. Then another who beat his girl friend to death with an electric fire because she had more chips than him. And the three armed robbers who battered an old lady to death for a purse and 25p. But I've never heard of anyone being killed for a few family photographs. The contents of the statement raised questions that needed to be addressed.

"If that's the case sir," I said. "Unless he's a serial killer and collects trophies from his victims, and thankfully there's no evidence of that, it's likely he will have removed what was of interest and got shut. But what would be of interest in a few family photographs?"

Detective Superintendent Davey replaced his glasses.

"Thank you Jim. You could be right. But we may strike lucky and find the purse and contents in someone's possession. It could be a vital piece of evidence. It may prove to be nothing more than a red herring, but ensure that the officers on the ground don't lose sight of it during their enquiries. As to the reason for stealing a few family photographs, at this stage of the enquiry I can't tell you. Perhaps there is something incriminating attached to them that the killer wishes to eliminate. Perhaps they hold some personal attachment for him. It maybe that the photographs were not the target for his homicide and that he was expecting to find something else. The missing wallet and contents may have nothing to do with the motive for killing Tom Oakley but the fact is that they are missing and everyone should be aware of that."

There were no more questions regarding the statement so the Superintendent moved the meeting on. He removed a file of papers from a manila envelope. I recognised it immediately.

He said, "Here gentlemen I have the interim forensic report. I shall only cover those points of interest. Firstly, the crime scene is confirmed and the only blood found matches the deceased. Fibres removed from the inside of his trouser legs are of a dark material that is currently subject to further analysis and research. It's likely that they are fibres transferred from the killer's trousers as he stood between the legs of the dead man to drag him along. There's the possibility of a cross transfer of materials from victim to killer and that may include blood. So I remind you to ensure that clothing of suspects is seized and subjected to forensic examination. Use the exhibit officers for that purpose. I don't want any potential evidence contaminated or marginalised."

The meeting went on for another two hours, examining successes, failures and new leads among the hundreds already thrown up. All needed to be investigated. That took time and manpower depriving Divisions of large chunks of staff for long periods and increased the costs in overtime. It was exacerbated when the Force became involved in running more than one major crime enquiry at the same time. Depleting divisional strength meant those remaining shouldering greater workloads and responsibilities. There are no reserves to fall back on. That was a prime cause of broken marriages as I knew to my cost. And there are the growing sickness lists and medical retirements in the force. The whole set up reminds me of an old saying about "a willing horse and a prostitute who works for nothing never being out of work." On reflection I suppose they both end up in the knacker's yard. Perhaps a willing horse is analogous to a Policeman?

After the meeting I updated DS Johnson and ensured the team were out there hard at it. No new leads had been identified, though all the basics were being completed and gradually falling into place. The jigsaw was being set out within a solid framework. Each piece interconnecting, building up, filling out, awaiting those final few pieces that would complete the picture, bringing the enquiry to a satisfactory conclusion. That's the theory of it but I know the reality is different.

EIGHTEEN

13th AUGUST
FRIDAY MORNING

It was a bright summer morning and I walked slowly up the long drive of the cemetery. From the many silver birch and mountain ash I heard the excited chatter of birds. Perhaps they were attempting to encourage the peace and solitude of the garden to burst into life. But their joyous message went unheard. Neither I nor the inhabitants of this urban oasis rejoiced in its living beauty, for it was a place of death.

Reaching the spot I had come to know so well over the past eighteen months, I stood for a moment, head bowed, before looking at the familiar white marble headstone.

I knelt alongside the grassy mound and removed the red and pink roses from the heavy marble pot, replacing them with fresh ones. I drifted a finger slowly along the word cut delicately into the headstone, tracing the name *ANGIE*. The emotion that was always in the background battered at my flimsy resistance but it held fast. I transferred a kiss from my fingers to her name and read aloud the verse from The Rubàiyàt of Omar Khayyàm carved into the marble.

Ah Love! could thou and I with Fate conspire
To grasp this sorry Scheme of Things entire,
Would not we shatter it to bits - and then
Re-mould it nearer to the Hearts Desire.

Finally, I got to my feet and picked up the discarded roses, wrapping them in the fancy paper, and made my way briskly to the nearby car park.

*

FRIDAY AFTERNOON

Back at the nick I quickly assessed the progress of the investigation. It wasn't going as well as I had hoped. I voiced my concern to Sergeant Johnson.

"I want this Duggy Davis. He can't just have disappeared off the face of the earth. He's a dosser, a wino. That limits his choice of hiding places to start with. And why has he gone on the run? Been here for years and then does a runner. There's more to this guy than meets the eye. I want him."

"Couldn't agree more Sir. There aren't any outstanding warrants. He's circulated nationally and I've got a team on it." He added with conviction, "But he'll come."

"We've been at it four days now with no real breaks. So what have we got? Duggy Davis. He's our best bet at the moment. The Northbridge brothers. Had a score to settle with Tom. We've got to fetch them in. The anonymous caller. Got to put a bit of pressure on Edith. She's holding out for some reason. Physical evidence? Post mortem findings speak for themselves. Excessive violence using a blunt instrument. Forensic? Blood, but it's the deceased's.

Could be of value if we find a suspect with a different blood group, with our man's grouping on his clothing. Dark fibres yet to be identified, possibly from the killer. Again of value if we get a good ident and trace them to a suspect. We want the weapon. But he's probably got rid by now. Can't see him keeping it with him. Too incriminating. Same with the missing wallet. Fire backed without doubt."

That was the extent of the evidence to date. Not too much to show for four days effort. I said as much to Sergeant Johnson.

Ever the loyal optimist he replied, "Early days yet boss. We've had worse starts in the past and still come up trumps."

"You're right Styx me lad. There's no telling what the next phone call or witness statement will bring. And we may strike it lucky. He might be a hoarder of criminal trophies and when we spin his drum could find an Aladdin's cave. Won't be the first and won't be the last."

"Yeah! And little pigs might fly boss," said Sergeant Johnson with a wry smile.

McLean interrupted, "Sir, phone call for you. Do you want it at your desk?"

"Yeah, put it through, this could be the big one." I said hopefully.

McLean immediately put the damper on that suggestion, "Don't think so boss. It's Chief Inspector Wonka."

There, he's done it again. Showing disrespect to me and another senior officer at the same time. And whilst inwardly amused I was determined not show it in the interests of discipline.

"I'll pretend I didn't hear that Constable McLean. Which senior officer did you say was calling?"

The CID aide replied, "Sorry Sir. Chief Inspector Wooton."

I left it at that and took the call. "Hello Chief Inspector what can I do for you?"

In a voice declaring he was impaled upon sharp sticks and weighted by responsibility, Chief Inspector Wooton wailed, "There's going to be trouble Inspector, I can see it coming. The Superintendent isn't going to like it when I tell him."

Swinging round in my revolving chair, telephone trapped between chin and left shoulder, I said in a voice inflated with angst, "You don't mean, you don't mean we've used up the month's quota of tea bags already Chief Inspector? Then take my advice. Don't tell him."

Silence followed my jocular retort. A sure sign that I'd unsettled the ranking officer. With a hint of schoolboy mischievousness and exaggerated concern I called down the silent line, "Chief Inspector, Are you still there? Is there a fault on the line? Sir?"

An uncertain, though measured, response finally acknowledged me.

"No Mister Stirling and it's nothing to do with tea bags. It's more serious than that."

As if struggling to protect me, a simple Detective Inspector, from the anxiety and inner complexities of his hard pressed office, whilst realising that duty required him to speak out, with conspiratorial calm and burdened weariness, Chief Inspector Wooton revealed, "One of your CID vehicles is taking up two spaces in the station car park Inspector."

I couldn't believe what I was hearing. What a load of kibosh! That load of old tripe confirmed my suspicion that Wooton was one of the new mirror image candidates promoted above his capabilities. Here we were with a full scale murder enquiry under way and he's prattling on, with,

I might add, monastic fervour, about car parking spaces.

He droned on. The sharp sticks were really prodding. "When spaces are at a premium it is downright irresponsible of you to allow your men to be so cavalier and lax in parking their vehicles. I have a responsibility to ensure that all vehicles are properly parked and I expect you as a senior officer to support me. My job is difficult enough as it is."

If it hadn't been such a pathetic performance from my senior officer I'd have laughed. Instead I used his pathos to turn the complaint upon its head.

"The murder enquiry Chief Inspector? Oh yes! It's progressing well. Thank you for your interest. The team are working long unsociable hours, detrimental to their health and well-being, but they don't mind. It's all in the public interest, as we strive to keep the balance between protecting life and property and ensuring they're not abusing the parking spaces. I'll endeavour to adjust the balance, even add a little extra weight to the worrisome parking problem. How will that suit you Sir?"

"Er. Fine Inspector. Fine. I see we shall be able to work well together."

"Fine, Sir. Fine. Look forward to your cooperation. Incidentally sir I wonder if you could have a word with your Divisional CID for me?"

"Of course Inspector. This dawning of a new age of cooperation between the Divisional staff and the enquiry team bodes well for the future. What can I do for you?"

"If you don't mind, just look out of your office window sir."

"Er, just a moment Inspector." I could hear him shuffling about in his chair. After a slight pause he continued, "Er, yes Inspector, I'm looking out of the window."

"Fine sir. Now I'm sure you'll notice the blue Ford in the car park."

"Yes Inspector, the blue Ford. That's the one I'm complaining about. It's taking up two parking spaces."

"Fine sir. Fine. Got to agree with you it's a disgrace."

"Erm, yes, yes, er good."

"Now I'd like you to tell your Divisional Detective Sergeant, that next time he borrows a vehicle from the enquiry team, he act more responsibly when parking it. Oh! And also to return the key and the completed mileage log book to my admin Sergeant. Tut sweet. Ok Chief Inspector?"

That deathly silence again. Then, "Erm. Tut sweet Inspector. Tut sweet."

As I replaced the telephone I shook my head in disbelief and I had to spit it out, "Bloody Willie Woofter."

McLean must have been hanging about outside. He stuck his head around my open door. He was trying hard to suppress a laugh when he spluttered, "What was that Sir? Willie who?"

In an attempt to be serious I ordered, "Get about your business McLean," and advised, "and be kind to dumb animals."

*

The evening debrief ended at eleven o'clock. There was to be a "four o'clock knock" for the Northbridge brothers the following morning. Coordinated raids had been planned. As the meeting broke up Styx Johnson asked, "Can I buy you a pint boss?"

I wasn't feeling up to socialising and so I declined the invitation.

"Not tonight Styx. Being a bit boring. Going home. Have

a night cap, talk to the cat and get my head down ready for an early start tomorrow."

Sergeant Johnson understood.

*

When I got home the house was in darkness. The place was cold. In the darkened hallway I hung my overcoat on the newel post at the bottom of the stairs. As I turned over the day's events in my mind a plaintive "meow" came from behind me. Mitzi had come in through the cat flap. Purring like a buzz saw she weaved about my ankles. I stooped to stroke the top of her head before ruffling the fur beneath the demanding, outstretched neck.

Picking up the old lady I held her to my chest and said, "Hello Mitz. Pleased to see me then?"

She nuzzled into my neck, marking me with her cheeks, the insistent buzzing louder now. In the kitchen, I spooned Mitzi's food out of the freshly opened tin into her clean bowl as she continued to rub against my ankles. The purring was almost constant now. She hovered around the topped-up bowl as it was placed on the plastic mat, alongside her water and milk. An old lady she might be, but she enjoyed her food. It struck me that I'd not eaten since breakfast. And a dish of muesli really isn't enough to sustain an active growing lad. Kneeling down I confided in the cat, but she was more intent on devouring her meal. As if the bowl was about to be snatched from her.

"Don't really miss the important things in life until they're not there, do we cat?"

I didn't really expect her to answer and of course she didn't. You can't expect a cat to understand Nottinghamshire

215

English now can you? I rubbed her affectionately behind the ears. Unconcerned, she arched her scrawny little back and carried on eating.

"Too involved with the job. That's always been the trouble. Not fair on Angie really. I expected too much. Offloaded the everyday horrors I'd experienced onto her. Grew to expect it I suppose. Took advantage of her loving me and wanting to relieve me of the stress. But who was there for her? Certainly not me. But that wasn't intentional. Selfish? That's what it comes down to, my unintentional selfishness. But surely you can't be selfish unless you are aware of it. I knew and didn't want to admit it. I needed her. She was my daily fix. Admit it Stirling, you were totally selfish about 'The Job' and the way it was affecting your wife. You didn't care. As long as you were alright to get on with it, the effect on Angie never entered your head. Selfish bastard! So you can't run away from it. You're to blame. You're responsible."

I switched on the gas fire. Its imitation logs glowed in the imitation Adams fireplace. Stretched out in my easy chair I poured a tot of rum.

I muttered, "The Queen. God Bless her," followed by, "Sandy bottoms," and sank the fiery liquid in one gulp.

My thoughts turned again to Angie but I refused to take them past the garage door. Another tot and Sandra Downey came to mind.

A twinge of guilt must have crept in. I found myself saying apologetically, "There's nothing in it Angie. Honest. She just seems a nice person that's all. Helped me with my shirts. I've lost some weight since, since you went. Only a sixteen neck now instead of sixteen and a half. I told her you always got me sixteen and a half. She was right though. I have gone down to sixteen. That's not having you here to

216

look after me. But I've got no friends now, only colleagues and acquaintances. No real friends. Sandra Downey wants to be a friend but I'm resisting."

The navy rum gradually worked its Island magic. I felt relaxed and my resistance weakened.

*

SATURDAY MORNING
14TH AUGUST

It was late when I rang. The voice of the woman who answered was barely audible. It was a muffled, "Hello." Clearly a response from a young woman dragged unwillingly from the warm embrace of sleep. It brought a tingle to my belly.

"Have I disturbed you?" I asked.

It was clear that her mind was still numbed by sleep and she was attempting to regain full focus. She muttered, "What's the time? Who is it?"

What's the time? Did it matter? I was wide awake with no sense of time, eager to converse, pleasantly oiled by a couple of tots of Nelson's blood. Without even thinking I may have been imposing myself upon her I responded cheerfully, "It's me. Jim Stirling. I'm not sure about the time. I'll just check. Half past midnight. Mmm. Didn't think it was that time already. How are you Sandra?"

I could visualise her coming out of her sleep and reaching out to snap on a table lamp alongside her bed before resting the telephone between ear and pillow as she lay bathed in the circle of soft light formed by a pink lamp shade.

"Jim? What's wrong? Why are you ringing at this unearthly hour?"

"I just felt like ringing. You told me to ring anytime. So here I am ringing."

She still sounded slightly confused as she remarked, "I meant a time that any reasonable person would ring. I didn't mean gone midnight."

"Oh! I just took you at your word. Anytime you said. If I've acted unreasonably I'm sorry. It's just me, impulsive. Not thinking."

Sandra suggested, "Selfish?"

In the circumstances that was a low blow. Right up to the elbow.

I offered some sort of an explanation. "Funny you should say that. I was only talking earlier to Mitzi about it. Maybe that's what's on my mind. I think that was the trouble. I was too selfish."

Sandra probed suspiciously, "Mitzi? Who's Mitzi? Some French mistress you entertain?"

I chuckled, "I wish. No Mitzi's my old cat. Some people talk to family photographs, consult the runes, ring adult chat lines. I converse with my cat. A few herrings in and she goes along with anything I say. A good listener."

Sandra sounded relieved. "Asked for that didn't I?"

"You weren't to know. It's not everyone that talks to an old moggie."

"Had a hard day Jim?"

"Not really. Frustrating. Couple of irons in the fire but nothing positive."

"Are you having a drink?" she asked.

"Are you inviting?"

The laugh said she was amused. "At this time of night? I was just enquiring if you were drinking at this moment."

"Always carry on the tradition and toast the Queen. God Bless her."

I fancied that Sandra was fully awake now and enjoying the late night banter. With not a little help from the Captain Morgan's, I imagined her snuggling into her pillow, drawing the covers about her, soft and silky as a butterfly as she queried, "What's the Queen got to do with it?"

"It's the Queen's navy. Didn't you know that?"

"I know that but what's it got to do with you, a policeman, toasting the Queen in rum?"

I laughed and warbled in a forced baritone voice that sounded like a strangled bag pipe, "Fifteen men on a dead man's chest, Yo ho ho and a bottle of rum. Drink and the devil will do for the rest. Yo ho ho and a bottle of rum."

"Jim Stirling. You're drunk," Sandra scolded.

"No I'm not. Only had a couple. Used to sink more than that in the Andrew."

"Andrew? Andrew who?"

"The Andrew is slang for the Royal Navy. Supposed to be from the name of a notorious nineteenth century press ganger Andrew Miller. He pressed so many sailors into service he said it was his navy."

"You're enjoying this aren't you Inspector?"

"I'd be enjoying it more if you were here to enjoy it with me."

"You didn't say that in the restaurant. Does it need rum to give you Dutch courage?"

"That was cruel Sandy. Sandy! Sandy bottoms. Seeus offus. Sippers, gulpers, up spirits stand fast the Holy Ghost." I laughed again, as full of the spirit as a gospel choir.

"What on earth are you on about? Sandy bottoms and Holy Ghosts? You're talking double Dutch."

"No. It's not double Dutch that's Jack Speak, the traditional language of the Andrew. I used to be a sailor. Didn't I tell you? No I didn't. Sippers is taking a sip of an 'oppo's tot, gulpers is taking a big gulp, not too big mind, seeus offus is seeing it off, drinking it all at one go, same as sandy bottoms. Like seeing the sand at the bottom of the sea after the water's gone, only it's Pusser's rum."

"You never cease to amaze me Jim Stirling. I only met you a couple of days ago and I'm learning new things all the time. And talking about time. I need my beauty sleep. You need to be bright and breezy. Sailor! I've enjoyed our little chat and we'll continue it over a tot of Pusser's rum, whatever that is, but for the moment I'll love you and leave you. Goodnight sailor."

"Goodnight Sandy. Thanks for being a good listener. I'll take you up on the Pusser's rum."

NINETEEN

14th AUGUST
SATURDAY MORNING

It was still dark when our convoy of four CID vehicles left Mansfield nick. I settled myself in the front passenger seat of the lead car. Styx Johnson drove. The early morning knocks this morning were planned to hit a number of suspects' addresses simultaneously at four o'clock. Some miles down the road the sign post for Mansfield Woodhouse flashed up. This is where we parted company with the others. They dipped their lights and disappeared into the darkness. We drove on in silence. I was thinking about the job at hand.

After a time I voiced my thoughts. "Northbridge shouldn't be much bother Sarge. With two of his brothers dead the others won't be the force they used to be. If Frank cuts up rough I can always push you in first."

Johnson replied wryly, "Thanks boss. I love you too."

No matter what Mclean thought of him I was glad to have Styx Johnson around at times like this. Never know what to expect on these early morning excursions but I don't expect any trouble today. The Northbridge boys are pub brawlers, so Frank wasn't likely to crap on his own living room carpet.

For the rest of the journey we continued to drive in silence, interrupted only by spasmodic routine traffic on the police radio network.

"We're here boss," Sergeant Johnson said quietly and drove slowly down a side street on the council estate.

He gave a running commentary of the target house. "Number 27. On the left. Street light outside. Terrace. Small front garden. No gate. Clear access down the side of the house to the back. No vehicle by the look of things. Everywhere in darkness."

I said quietly, "OK. Pull up past the house. We'll go in on the hour as planned."

"*If you can wait and not be tired by waiting.*" Kipling's words hurried through my head. Waiting wasn't one of my better virtues. I checked my watch again. Each twitch of the luminous second finger appeared as slow motion, struggling uphill to reach the top. I waited impatiently. Finally the slender, glowing marker launched itself toward the appointed hour.

"Ok let's go," I whispered."

We left the car and picked our way along a track trampled through the long grass of the neglected garden in front of the house. I directed Johnson to the back of the premises and signalled twenty seconds. He acknowledged with a thumbs up. I waited at the front door. Time up I pounded on it. Dogs in the neighbourhood set up an opposing racket. As I banged on the door peeling green paint fluttered to the concrete step. The only response from inside was a slight movement of the dirty orange curtain at the front bedroom window. I knew he was in. He'd been put to bed by a surveillance team and hadn't left the house since.

I shouted to the silent watcher, "Police. Open up."

The curtain was hurriedly pulled to. The house stayed silent. As Sergeant Johnson hammered on the back door the hollow sound rolled and reverberated through the kitchen and hall.

I thumped again on the front door shouting, 'Open up. Police. If you don't open it I'll put it in."

My friendly call was ignored. The only response was twitching curtains from neighbouring houses. We battered the doors. Outside it sounded like hell let loose. Inside it must have sounded like a rumble in the jungle. Half the neighbourhood was up now. Lights flashing on all over. Northbridge must be deaf or dead not to respond. Unless! It was unless. A few feet to the right of me the front downstairs bay window was suddenly thrown open. I knew we were in for trouble when the double barrelled shot gun pointed menacingly in my direction and a rasping voice ordered, "Fuck off before ya get both barrels."

Adrenaline rush clicked in, decision time, fight or flight? No contest. I hurled myself low towards the open bay before the gunman could react. Grabbing the protruding cold metal barrels from underneath in one swift movement I forced them up and away from me before ramming the weapon hard back through the window. The crunch of butt on bone and resultant pained grunt told me my risky split-second gamble had paid off. I'd got the weapon and quickly hurled the whole piece of kit into the long grass then scrambled through the open bay. I landed unceremoniously on top of a heavily built man, semiconscious on the sofa beneath the window. The guy was barefoot and bare-chested, dressed only in crumpled dark trousers. Quickly gaining my feet I gave a cursory glance at the moaning figure. He was bleeding from nose and mouth. He wouldn't be offering much resistance in the immediate future. Hurrying towards the back door and Johnson's shouts and banging I passed a terrified woman in a flannel nightdress, cowering on the stairs.

I said sharply, "Police. Tend to Billy the Kid missus. He's got a busted nose."

Backdoor unlocked, I was joined by Styx Johnson. We made our way back to the sparsely furnished front room now illuminated by a solitary electric light bulb hanging from the ceiling. The woman knelt alongside the sofa dabbing at her man with the hem of her nightie.

He snarled at her in that rasping, now nasal voice, "Clear off woman. Leave me alone. It's not first and it won't be last. Where's that fucking copper?"

The big man roused himself pushing the whimpering woman to one side. Blood still ran from his damaged nose mixing with that on his busted lip. He stood up, unsteadily making his way towards us. We watched warily, ready to react in an instant as he approached. In the poorly lit room the man loomed large presenting a formidable physical presence. Beneath the blood and rapidly swelling nose and mouth was a face that had battered its way through life, topped by a shock of greying hair with a memory of tight curls. I could see that even now he would be a daunting opponent in any bar room brawl. It said a lot about Tom Oakley.

Keeping the initiative I cut in sharply, "Frank Northbridge?"

The man stopped. He hadn't fully recovered from nutting the butt of his shot gun. And he was chary of the man who had so painfully and summarily disposed of him. He wiped blood and snot from his injuries with the back of his hand.

"Who's askin'?"

"Detective Inspector Stirling and Detective Sergeant Johnson, and before you say anything else Northbridge get dressed. You're nicked for possessing a firearm with intent to endanger life."

The big man laughed. "Endanger life? I were protecting me wife, mesen and me property from burglars." Pointing to his face he declared, "I'm the victim not the villain. And me brief 'll want some questions answering about this." He felt his bloodied swollen nose and said forcefully, "You've bust it."

Stroking my own nose I said, "Join the club mester and think yourself lucky that's all that's bust."

The woman was still whimpering.

I said to her, "Get him some clothing missus, you know the routine. He'll need some smokes as well. There's none where he's going."

I bet on Frank Northbridge not being a total fool. Spitting out blood from his busted nose and lip must have told him we were old hands at this game. He wasn't going to try anything with us. Whilst his wife fussed around wanting to please her man, Northbridge dressed. Then with hands shackled behind him he was bundled outside into the police car. The shotgun was recovered, unloaded and put in the car boot. Dawn was breaking. The street lights dimming. The woman was still standing in the doorway sobbing as we drove away.

I reported in on the car radio. Control confirmed that the other targets had been picked up without incident. Following my directions they had been detained in different lock ups around the division. That way they would soon be experiencing a sense of isolation and abandonment. And that suited me.

Back at Mansfield Northbridge was taken to my office.

"What about the 'cuffs boss?" queried the prisoner, knocking the restraining devices together behind his back, the clattering metal emphasising his question.

"Unlock the right Sarge, fasten the other to the radiator. I'll fix up a cuppa."

At that time of the morning the main CID office was in darkness. I switched on a couple of lights. The large half lit room with desks and chairs huddled in the shadows seemed strangely silent and cold. On my way to the small kitchen I suddenly heard a scuffle behind me and Johnson shouting, "You devious bastard."

Rushing back I saw Northbridge slumped on the floor. His right hand was free of the handcuff. Johnson had hold of the connecting chain attempting to pull the prisoner to his feet. Blood was again running freely from the prisoner's mouth and Styx had a graze to his lip.

"What's happened?" I snapped.

"I've clipped him on the jaw boss. The devious bastard tried to do a runner as soon as I'd released the 'cuff. Caught me a glancing shot to the mouth so I downed him."

"Are you alright Sarge?"

"Yeh boss. No problem."

"It's getting a bit of a habit with you Northbridge. You're doing yourself no favours. You've got assault on police and attempt to escape from lawful custody on top of the firearms offences. Makes me wonder what there is behind all this. You were only a suspect initially. Now you're facing charges and a bit of bird. Why?"

The big man, fully handcuffed again, sat down and raised his bloodied face toward us.

"Why? 'Cos you're coppers. You're out to do me anyway. You've been on me family's back since we was kids. Me dad alus said do them fost afore they do you. And I've lived by that rule all me life."

"And perhaps Frank you'll die by it. Like your old friend Tommy Oakley,"

"Tommy Oakley? What's he got to do wi' it? He's no friend a mine. The drunken bum."

"Not such a bum when he sorted you and your brothers out Frank."

"Sorted us out? Ya don't know half. We put him in hospital. Bandaged up like Boris Karloff's mummy. He know'd he'd been in a faight with the Northbridge boys that naight."

"Six to one Frank? Good odds for a win I'd say. And you couldn't do it with your fists even then. Had to use a road ponch."

"Lies. That's all lies. I did him on me own. Me brothers just formed a ring and I done Tommy Oakley."

"That's not what the police records show, Frank."

"Police records? Don't give me that bullshit Inspector. Tommy never complained tut police. Not his style. Coppers never got involved. They knew about it but just let us get on wi' it. They couldn't care less about the likes of us faightin among oursens."

"Hated Tommy Oakley then did you Frank?"

"Hate him? In a way I suppose. But you couldn't really hate Tommy. Gi' anybody his last ha'penny. A hard man though, good wi' his fists but a maniac when his dander were up. An' you're raight. I couldn't a done Tommy in a thousand years. Too good. He were a pro. Could've been a champion but he was robbed of chance."

"When they doped him?"

"Oh. You know about that then Inspector? Who've you been talkin' to?"

Looking him straight in the eyes I said, "Fallows."

The anticipated reaction was instantaneous. A look of surprise knocked the semi-permanent sneer from Northbridge's swollen, bloodied face.

"Fallows! Might'a known. The gutless bastard. What's happenin' tut dogs? You're not puttin' 'em down are ya?"

His outburst surprised me. Not too sure where he was heading I played along hoping to hit the right buttons.

"More concerned about the dogs than Mister Fallows then Frank?"

"Dogs is more important than that loudmouth. They're good faighters and earners. Not easy to come by. They've got American blood in 'em ya know. Seems a shame. But it goes wi't territory."

"American pit bulls hey Frank?"

"Yeh. Only the best in this game mister."

"Don't really know a great deal about fighting dogs Frank. It's something I've not come across before. You're considered something of an expert aren't you?"

I knew that by now he'd be gasping for a smoke. So I lit one up and stuck it between his battered lips. The big man gave a nod and puffed at it awkwardly. From the corner of his bloodied mouth the prisoner lisped, "Ta. I suppose I could call me'sen an expert. There's not much I don't know about faightin' dogs."

At that moment, Sergeant Johnson returned with the duty police surgeon.

"Hello Doc. Come to look at the prisoner?" I asked.

"Looks as though he needs it."

He said to Northbridge, "How did this happen?"

The prisoner shrugged his shoulders. I removed the cigarette.

"Bit of bother with a shotgun, nothing I can't handle. No complaints Doc."

Tears came to the prisoner's eyes as the doctor, not too gently, examined the damaged nose and wiped the bloodied face.

"It's broken. You need treatment to have it repaired otherwise you'll carry a broken nose to the grave."

Northbridge shook his head. "Don't worry about it Doc. I can live wi' it and I shan't bother about it when I'm laid out in me pine suit."

I had to smile and stroked my own scarred nose. In Northbridge I recognised an almost extinct animal. One of the remaining throwbacks to that age of bare-fist battlers, dog fighters, badger baiters and other cruel activities associated with violent men in rural and mining communities. He was a man content with his lifestyle and confident in his own physical ability. Another Tom, another Durnley, another Wilson, another Fallows, another Duggy Davis. I don't know why but I felt a grudging admiration for the breed. It seemed I shared an affinity with these hard ruthless men at ease in their violent, often cruel, environment. They stood outside the law but were willing to face the consequences of their chosen lifestyle.

The police surgeon did his bit and left.

"You look a little more human now Frank. First time since we met I haven't viewed you through a mask of blood."

Northbridge grinned. The big slab of a face creased about a swollen nose and sticking plastered lip as he recalled, "You should've seen it after Tommy had done wi' me. A rait mess. Ya win some, ya lose some, it's all part't game in't it Inspector?"

I nodded. Couldn't dislike the man. The term "likeable rogue" flashed into my head. Sergeant Johnson scowled.

Frank Northbridge looked at him. "Sorry about the smack to your chops Sarge. Ya didn't deserve it. I'll understand if ya gi' me back some of me own medicine."

Johnson growled, "Like you say Frank. All part of the game and I had my pound of flesh and blood."

Eager to get on with the enquiry I said, "Is that the end of the mutual adoration session?"

Johnson shrugged.

Northbridge asked, "Can I ay another fag Inspector?"

Johnson lit him up.

I continued, "About the fighting dogs Frank. What's the score?"

"Can't keep 'em on a council estate can ya? Coppers and RSPCA 'ud soon know about 'em. Best place is where dogs is expected ta be. That's where Jess Fallows come in. A gamekeeper wi' proper dog compounds and all them private woodlands belonging tut Duke. Brilliant set up. Worked a treat until now." He pondered the situation for a moment before adding, "shame about dogs. They di'nt know no better. Can't ya save 'em Inspector. Gi' 'um to a good 'ome?"

Seeing that Northbridge was genuinely concerned about his dogs gave me an avenue to exploit.

"Can't guarantee anything Frank, but a few words in the right ears might have some effect. Alright?"

"Thanks Inspector. If ya can do owt, I'll owe ya one."

"I'll hold you to that mister," I said.

"You'll find I'm a man a me word Inspector if I'm good for nowt else."

"What about Tommy Oakley then Frank?"

"What about him Inspector?"

"When did you last see him?"

"Oooh! Some weeks ago now boss. He were drinkin' int' Drum down Shirebrook. Livin' rough by the look a things. Why d'ya ask?"

"Do you know where he is now?"

"Last I heard he were dossin' down Mansfield way, knockin' about wi' Duggy Davis. A right pair they make."

230

"So you've not heard about Tommy then?"

"Heard what Inspector?"

"Tommy's dead."

"Tommy dead? Bloody hell! We din't ger on too well but I wouldn't wish death on him. He's not that much older than me ya know."

"You haven't seen it on telly or read about it then Frank?"

"Naaw! 'ant gorra tele and I don't bother wi' papers. They're all full a lies and rubbish and such. Why what's happened to 'im then?"

I wasn't sure about the man. I stared at him. He attempted to return the gaze, but it was a half hearted attempt and he lowered his head. I answered his question.

The words slipped out. Like a knife sliding into the ribs. "Murdered. He was murdered."

Frank Northbridge sat bolt upright. The handcuffs clattered and his plastered lips opened in shocked disbelief. His words stuttered out.

"Fucking hell chief! Murdered? Tommy? I don't believe it."

"You'd better believe it Frank. What's left of him is stuck in a big fridge at the mortuary. Payback time for Tommy Oakley and you're top of my list as paymaster."

"No! This i'nt right! You've nicked me for dog faightin' an' I'll not argue about that. But I don't know nowt about killin' Tommy Oakley. Faightin' and killin' is two different things. And I don't know of no man that could faight Tommy and kill him. More likely t'other way round."

"Who mentioned fighting Frank?"

"Well wor else wi' Tommy?"

I didn't answer, left him dangling and changed tack. "Out last Sunday Frank?"

Northbridge hadn't sorted his head, confused, unsure

he said, "Sunday? Last Sunday? Oh yeah! I were out with Fallows. Walkin' down't Copse. It's on't Duke's land, there's some badger setts there."

"What time was that?"

"I come outtat wood, cross't fields and gor in't Net and Ferret about nine o'clock. Had a few pints till closing time. Took missus a bottle a stout, and that were it."

"And that was it Frank?"

"Yeh. That were it."

"And who's going to back you up?"

Northbridge thought for a moment. "Jess, Amos, he's landlord at Net, and my missus."

"Did Fallows go to the pub with you?"

Calmer now, Northbridge was thinking. "No Inspector. I left him in't wood. He were makin' his way 'ome. Got some business on he said. And let me tell you this. I wouldn't 'a said nowt if Fallows had kept his trap shut. But he's let rabbit out bag so I don't owe him no favours. Watch him, he's a cagey customer, got a nasty streak and he didn't care for Tommy neither."

"What do you mean by that Frank?"

"There were bad blood between 'em. Guz back tut days of Bade Durnley and that bobby that were killed. I can't say no more'n that."

"You're going to have to mister. If you're landed with this you're facing a lot of bird. We aren't talking about poaching on the Duke's estate we're talking about murder. Murder Frank, nothing less, twenty years at least."

Innocent or guilty, Northbridge for all his swagger and brawnging didn't fancy the thought of being banged up for a score. Never knew which way a jury would jump. He's a country lad. Been sent down a few times over the years. Always did his time hard. Then he was younger. Now he'll find it tougher. At the moment my best friend is the prisoner's mind. In the solitude of a prison cell it could run riot. That's what I want, some way into his mind. I'll leave it at that and bang him up down the cell block

Sergeant Johnson had finalised the notes of the interview.

I spoke to the prisoner, "Right Frank, we'll continue our enquiries and see what we come up with. I'll be looking at the firearm offences and assault on police. Anything else depends on what turns up."

"OK Mister Stirling. But you've got to believe me. I don't know nothin' about Tommy being murdered. But I do know that Fallows knows more about that bobby being killed than he's let on over't years. Get into his ribs. He's nasty but not that much bottle. He'll cough if you get him in a corner." As an after thought he added, "He couldn't do Tommy but he'll know summat about it."

I looked him over. The morning's events had knocked that brash spirit out of him. Sitting there he was a sorry dejected figure. The hard man wasn't so hard now. It was always the same. Once they'd lost control over their situation they weren't so tough. Northbridge wasn't any different. He'd resigned himself to his fate. Prison would be an imposition upon his lifestyle but his main concerns were the dogs.

He pleaded, "Boss, you'll do yer best for the dogs?"

I gave a sympathetic nod and said, "Ok. I'll see what I can do."

As Sergeant Johnson took him down, the prisoner said, "Thanks Inspector. I owe you one."

Styx lit a cigarette and stuck it between the prisoner's battered lips.

TWENTY

Northbridge was out of the picture, getting reacquainted with lumpy porridge and fine dining courtesy of HMP Lincoln. Now it was time to put more pressure on the other suspects in the frame. With Sergeant Johnson driving and McLean as back seat passenger we headed towards Wembourne Hall. At the main entrance to the estate we passed between two impressive stone pillars supporting heavy wrought-iron gates bearing a gilded coat of arms. Conveniently they were open. On the drive red gravel crunched beneath the vehicle's wheels. Now and then a rogue piece flitted like a bullet into the flowing mounds of rhododendrons, shrubs and trees massed up to the edge of the driveway.

Sergeant Johnson slowed the motor down. He indicated an area ahead of us.

"You can just see part of the gable end sir, about fifty yards on the left, off the road in the trees. If we go any closer he'll spot us,"

"I see it. Stop here. I'll do a recce. When you hear the dogs bring the car down and join me."

Johnson nodded. I got out of the vehicle and checked my watch.

"Six o'clock. If he sticks to routine he'll be having his evening meal now."

I wet a finger and stuck it in the air. It indicated that I was heading into a slight breeze. That was good news. It lessened the chances of the dogs locating my scent too soon. Trees and shrubs proliferated, almost hiding the Victorian gatehouse from the driveway. Bending low and peering through the thick undergrowth I could just make out part of the roof with a small turret tower at one corner. A few more paces gave me a clearer view of the red brick cottage. It had originally been built for the guardian of the gate and stood in a grassed area enclosed on three sides by trees. Stacks of logs stored for winter fuel were neatly piled against the wall of the building and beneath the portico leading to the front door. I'd got no view of the rear of the building but had a good idea of its layout. There would be dog kennels with timber and link-wire covered runs. Chicken coops and a couple of pig sties. The ferrets would be housed in wood and wire cages.

The racket started up the instant I stuck my head around the shrubbery to the side of the cottage. The rural calm was ruptured by an urgent outburst of ferocious barking and snarling. I was thankful to hear the steady crunching of gravel and the purr of an engine behind me. That told me Sergeant Johnson and PC McLean had arrived as planned. Leaving the vehicle, the three of us crossed over the neglected sward of grass to the front of the house. The dogs to the rear set up an even mightier commotion. The reason soon became apparent. Appearing from the back of the building to our left, the shirt-sleeved figure of Fallows, cudgel in his right hand. Straining at a heavy chain grasped in the other, a massive black and tan pit bull terrier panted

235

and slobbered with us in its sights. Fallows heaved on the chain, hauling the pit bull's front legs off the ground and preventing the beast from launching itself towards us. The studded choker dug into the thick folds of the animal's neck, causing it to salivate and pant all the more. The keeper peered at us through squinting piggy eyes. None of us took our eyes off that ferocious fighting dog.

Hoping I sounded confident I spoke to Fallows.

"Good day to you Jess. Spirited animal you've got there. A bull terrier?"

He set me with those narrowed eyes. "What do you know about dogs mister? You wouldn't know the difference between a poodle and a piss pot."

"Maybe not Jess but I'd say that's a cross between a bull dog and an old breed that's extinct now, the white English terrier. They're called bull terriers or pit bulls, but yours has got a bit of American in it. Incidentally a piss pot has a handle."

Fallows growled, "For a newspaper man ya got a better nose for dogs than ya 'ave for folk."

The old poacher turned gamekeeper spat onto the grass as he jerked hard on the chain, momentarily choking the straining animal, causing it to wheeze and dribble all the more.

He warned, "Just be careful where ya put that nose mister, it's likely to get bit off. Or worse."

I snapped back, "Like Tom and Frank Northbridge?"

A frown creased Fallows's brow. "Frank? What's it got ta do wi' Frank?"

"Not heard about him either? "

"Frank? He's not dead an all is he?"

"Heard about Tommy then did you?

236

"I hadn't when I seen you, but I heard after. Everybody were talkin' about it."

"That's the problem with something like this Jess. You can't keep it quiet. Everybody gets to know about it. Murder can't be kept secret. Like the old saying, the truth will out."

"What's that got ta do wi' me an' Frank?"

It was clear Fallows wasn't feeling too self-assured about me even on his own ground. Perhaps he was feeling unnerved. Maybe he was wondering what I knew and really wanted.

"Now we've been re-introduced Mister Fallows I suggest you put Uncle Sam back in his cage and then we can continue our talk. OK?"

Fallows ran his tongue over dry lips jerking once more at the leash.

"Wait here," he growled.

Yanking the pit bull round he turned and walked out of sight to the rear of the cottage. The hullabaloo started again. I could hear Fallows's voice raised above the snapping and snarling as he hurled out sharp words of command. The baying hounds were reduced to whimpering submission. I was impressed.

The Gamekeeper reappeared at the front door of the lodge.

"You'd best come in," he directed.

As we made our way towards the covered porch Fallows cocked his head to one side and raised a finger wagging it in the direction of Johnson and McLean. "Just a minute mister. Who's them two?" he demanded.

We kept walking towards him.

"Two colleagues," I said. "Styx Johnson and Andy McLean. All right?"

He glowered at me from beneath heavy eyebrows and

gave a barely discernable nod, signifying acceptance of the explanation. Fallows went back indoors and we followed.

We were pulled up short as he growled, "Wipe yer feet."

The cottage was a disappointment. I'd expected a gamekeeper to be surrounded with the trappings of his trade. But unlike the description of Bade Durnley's poacher cottage, recorded at the time of his arrest, and the tap room of the Net and Ferret, there was neither hide nor hair to be seen. No Badger or Fox heads grinning from the walls. No bewildering collection of nets, traps, woodsman's contraptions and guns, with one exception. Displayed over the front door a beautiful Purdy double barrelled twelve bore shot gun. However, evidence of a woman's influence was apparent, confirmed when Fallows explained, "Missus is out at her sister's. Not be back till tomorrow mornin'."

The neat sitting room with its comfortable three piece suite protected by chintz arm-and headrest-covers was welcoming and cosy. A tartan throw, carefully arranged over a large easy chair, signified the seat of the man of the house. Reflected in the polished surface of a folded table, standing in front of a lace-curtained window, a splash of colour from flowers in a glass vase. Pictures of rural scenes hung on the pleasantly decorated walls. And photographs of stern-faced individuals watched the goings on in the little room.

Jess Fallows sprawled his bulk in the tartan chair and with the air of a robber baron holding court, beckoned the three of us to be seated. At ease now in his castle he addressed me, peering through those searching eyes.

"Now what's it all about mister? An' don't give me no bullshit," he ordered.

If it was an attempt to intimidate me he'd picked the

238

wrong man. I returned his glare. The gamekeeper gave way first and shifted uneasily upon his not so easy chair.

It seemed that I'd gained a psychological advantage and said, "The bullshit won't come from this side Jess, we've got nothing to hide."

"Hide? What have I got to hide?"

"The truth?"

Fallows gnawed on his twisted lower lip and rubbed his broad splodge of a nose as he tried to weigh me up.

Finally he asked, "What is it you want then? What ya lookin' for? Sommat ta do wi' Tommy's death? I can't help you there."

"That's the first lot of bullshit Jess, and like I said, it didn't come from this side."

I sensed that even in his own home, in his den, Jess Fallows felt uncomfortable in our company. Maybe he felt like a trout in his meadow stream that he played on a taut line. He didn't like it. His only option was to go with it or break the line.

"Alright mister. You ask the questions an' I'll try to answer 'em. No bullshit."

"Can't expect anything fairer than that Mister Fallows," I said.

Sergeant Johnson, who had been following the verbal exchanges, was already making notes in his official pocket book. McLean sat as an interested onlooker listening and learning.

"Where were you last Sunday night when Tommy was killed?"

"You think I've done it? Ya must be bloody mental mister. An' you'd better not put owt like that in your newspaper neither, else I'll be suin' ya. Right?"

239

"I shall be keeping an eye on what goes in the newspapers but you know more about the killing than you're letting on."

"What I know and what others know in't for you to know. It's up tut bobbies to find them things out, not newspapers." Having made his position clear he rubbed that broken lump which doubled for a nose and said slyly, "Is there owt in this for me?"

I shrugged my shoulders and said, "That depends."

"On what?"

"How productive you are."

"Productive? Like a bloody pregnant sow?" He slapped his thigh and laughed. "What do you want? Names? Cos if you do I can't gi' any. An' if I could I wouldna."

"First of all answer my question. Where were you last Sunday evening?"

The gamekeeper sat in silence thinking. Suddenly, pointing a finger toward me he said, "Gor it. Sunday I was out wi' Frank Northbridge till late on. He can vouch for that."

"How late?"

"Eleven o'clock I reckon."

"You sure?"

"As near as dammit is to swearing."

"That's not what Frank says."

"Why, a yo seen 'im?" he said in surprise.

"You'd better believe it."

"What's he got to say then?"

"He was with you till nine. Then he went off for a drink. Left you to attend to some business. Was that Tommy Oakley business?

"Wor is this? What ya tryin' to do? Stitch me up? Put words in me mouth? You're worse than bloody coppers."

"Were you settling old scores in Mansfield, Jess?"

With a look of alarm Fallows hauled his bulk out of the chair. I don't think he liked the way things were going. He scanned the room with nervous eyes, whilst silent watchers from their picture frames followed his every move.

"Looking for this Mister Fallows?" Holding up his wicked-looking cudgel I said, "I think I'll be keeping it for a while."

Fallows lunged towards me in a futile attempt to regain the club. He was confronted by Johnson. His physical presence and determined look was enough to stop any thought of violence contemplated by the gamekeeper.

I tried to keep a lid on things and said calmly, "Sit down Mr. Fallows. Let's not do something we're likely to regret. Mrs Fallows wouldn't appreciate any disturbance in her sitting room I'm sure."

Shaking his head, no longer in control, if he ever was, Fallows slumped into his chair. As if acknowledging his deposed authority, the tartan throw slithered down the back of the chair to lie crushed and wrinkled beneath his weight.

He was tiring. Now I intended playing him a little longer before scooping him up into my landing net.

"We'll move on for a moment. How many fighting dogs do you keep?"

It was a sullen response. "None. Only mi working dogs and some terriers I breed."

"Like Uncle Sam out there?"

Fallows didn't answer.

"Frank tells me you fight dogs and bait badgers. It's no secret. But his Lordship might not be too happy if he hears about it."

That was a low blow. It hurt. Jess Fallows was cornered.

241

Pin prick eyes flittered here and there, searching for an escape. There wasn't one. He remained slumped in his chair, a melting snowman, forced to listen to me. I over-dramatised my account of events that he didn't want to hear.

"I can see his Lordship's face when he reads the national headlines. 'Head Gamekeeper on the Wembourne Estate involved in brutal dog fighting and badger baiting. Former poacher, who turned King's Evidence against his friends in the notorious murder of a Police Constable in the nineteen forties; a prime mover in brutal blood sports. Badgers under his protection cruelly torn from their setts to be thrown to packs of savage pit bull terriers.'"

Though he was down he wasn't out. Pulling himself together Fallows took the initiative, fighting back attempting to break the taut line.

Jumping up he shouted, "That's enough. Get outta my house and off this estate, else you'll find out what sort of dogs I've got."

To his surprise we didn't react as he had expected. Instead he found the line holding, drawing him in.

It was time to put him out of his misery.

"You don't seem to understand Mister Fallows. When we leave you'll be leaving with us."

We stood in front of him. Eyeball to eyeball. His darting eyes dashed from one face to another. In desperation he searched each hardened expression, seeking, like Moses, to read something in the stones before him. He saw nothing but stone. I slipped the landing net beneath him.

I said, "Jess Fallows, I am a police officer and am arresting you on suspicion of being involved in the murder of Tommy Oakley." As I cautioned him, the gamekeeper staggered, collapsing back into his chair. The inner eye in

Fallows's pounding head focussed once more upon the memory of a distant nightmare. Of shattered doors and shouting men, of blood and pain, of handcuffs and the sullen glare of shackled prisoners. He recalled the defiance of Durnley and the whimpering of Wilson, of anger and the demand for retribution for the murder of a Police Constable. The nightmare had returned to haunt him.

*

I could see that Fallows wasn't too happy sitting in my office. He'd been here before, the time and faces had changed but it was still the same game. The old villain would be thinking of wheeling and dealing. He knew who held the keys to his shackles, and freedom, and he'd be trying to assess his chances of some sort of deal. But first he had to weigh me up, find out what I knew. More importantly, what I didn't know. He had to decide what he could tell me. Was he in any danger? Where did it put him? He had to be very careful at this stage of the game otherwise he could end up staked out on a proverbial anthill or snared in his own traps.

Fallows opened up the dialogue. "What's the score Inspector? Do I lose these bracelets? Am I stayin'?"

I put him straight. "In that order Jess. One nil to me. No. And yes."

Fallows gave a resigned nod. He understood.

"Your missus has been informed of your arrest and I've arranged for the RSPCA to see to your animals."

"What about his Lordship? Has anybody told him yet?"

"Not yet Jess. That's something for you to think about. You'll be charged and appear before the first available remand court."

Fallows nodded. A grim expression set upon his rugged face. He knew the game had begun.

In the small reception area of the cell block the prisoner was thoroughly searched and booked in. With handcuffs removed he was ushered through the unlocked gate into the drab green cell passageway. The familiar odour of sweating bodies and stale food mingled with the stench from the cell block's lavatories. The warm air was oppressive and rank. It enveloped us as we walked past the row of dark brown cell doors set into those sea green walls. Fallows gagged. It even made me grimace and I was no stranger to the place. Our footsteps rang out fresh and clear on the concrete floor, echoing high above us.

Belts, ties and laces – removed from prisoners to minimise suicide attempts – were set against the passage wall, indicating the occupied cells. Names chalked roughly onto boards identified the occupants. Our echoing footsteps caused a stir behind the locked doors. They presented an opportunity for anonymous men to declare their presence and relieve the unnatural silence imposed upon them. As we passed each cell voices called out. Some questioning, some in despair, the odd one with an air of rebellious bravado. But I knew that's all it was. They craved an audience for their performance. The sound of a different voice. A contact with the outside world. I'd heard it so many times before and thought how quickly men, isolated and alone, re-evaluate their priorities, realising what really were the important things in life. Fags, booze, visits from wives and girlfriends, or both. Not at the same time though, and decent food. The pleas were ignored. They would have to tough it out, learn about discipline and deprivation. They had chosen to go outside the law. None were conscripted into a life of crime.

They were all volunteers, and being banged up was one of the consequences of that choice. Walking down that dreary passage I thought of my early life. How, with many others like me, I'd suffered hardship and deprivation without the luxury of choice.

As a detective I saw detention in police custody as a powerful weapon. What villains feared most was being banged up and the bail lottery. They feared the isolation and being reliant upon coppers and jailers. They feared losing control of their lives. That was pain. Being banged up, "counting bricks," losing sense of time and reality in their solitude didn't help. Wives and lovers loomed large in their thoughts. What were they up to? Whilst the cat's away! Dark images fermenting in the prisoners' heads found no relief within those four stark walls. No relief for throbbing minds stretched to screaming point. No escape from the all-consuming claustrophobia of four walls forever closing in. No place to hide. Illuminated twenty four hours a day by that single lamp set in the cell wall. It stared at them, mocking from behind the armoured glass. No, villains didn't like being banged up.

Fallows looked disturbed. I doubt if he'd ever thought of finding himself in such a situation again. He was scared. That was clear to see. Stopping outside a cell door halfway down the passage I unlocked it and thrust it open with my foot. As it swung back the dim space it guarded unfolded before the prisoner's fearsome stare.

"Here you are Jess, home from home. But you'll get used to the noise and smell. There's your bed, good solid English pine. That's as near as you'll get to the woods. The cell officer'll fix you up with a mattress and blanket. But don't expect him to carry them, and if you want something to read try to amuse yourself from amongst all that crap scrawled on the walls by previous lodgers. Ignore the personal references to me, Jess. You know they aren't true. And I'll see you some time later. Oh! You might just have missed supper. OK?"

Without waiting for a reply I left the prisoner standing in the centre of the cell. He had all night to think about things as he counted bricks. The heavy door crashed to. I double locked it before chalking "FALLOWS J" on the name board, adding and underlining "NO VISITS".

As I left the lock up, from behind cheerless cell doors faceless voices resumed their assault. They were silenced when the passage gate clanged to. I went out onto the street and gulped in some fresh air.

TWENTY-ONE

15TH AUGUST
SUNDAY MORNING

Constable Underwood was dead, died years ago. I was disappointed. But then at the time I suppose he was. I'd hoped that PC Jarvis's old colleague was still around, able to provide information, some vital piece missing from the jigsaw surrounding his murder. But there was nothing I could do about it. He was dead and that was that.

But my disappointment was quickly forgotten when I learned Sergeant Jack Smithurst was very much alive. In his eighties now, a police pensioner, Sergeant Jack could well be a valuable link to the past, another name from that distant ageing newsprint about to be revealed in flesh.

It was a warm, bright Sunday morning when I located the retired policeman. He was seated on a bench outside his allotment shed pouring a drink from a thermos into a plastic cup. Sergeant Jack watched me approaching down the garden path. I passed row upon row of healthy looking vegetables under cultivation and masses of vibrant colour from a variety of flowers mixing and blending like paints on an artist's palette.

And seated in his retreat the old bobby looked exactly as I'd imagined, a portly figure straining against well worn flannel shirt and waistcoat. With a heavy belly constrained by belted brown corduroy trousers tied around the legs with string, wearing heavy working boots and a floppy-rimmed old trilby, I could easily see him as a navvy, posing with a pick or shovel at some Victorian canal or railway construction; captured for posterity in an ancient sepia photograph.

In a voice that had lost none of its authority, the old pensioner enquired of his visitor, "Can I help you my lad?"

I replied respectfully, "I hope so. Am I addressing Sergeant Smithurst?"

"You are that, lad. And who may I be addressing?" he asked.

Holding out my warrant card I replied, "Detective Inspector Stirling, Mansfield Division. May I join you, Sergeant?"

"You may indeed Sir. Take a seat." It was Sergeant Jack's turn now to be respectful and he edged his bulk along the bench, brushing an area alongside with his hand. "It'll be a pleasure. It's a long time since I enjoyed the company of a senior officer. Don't seem to like getting amongst the muck and mire now days. Not like my time. We had to dig for victory." He laughed, his ruddy face brightening to that distant recollection. "Now I grow that many 'taters and beans I can't give 'em away. I've got some nearly ready. Make a nice boiling or two. Are you interested Inspector?"

"Thanks for the offer," I said, as I sat beside him, "I like a few fresh veg. Trouble is getting time to prepare them. I'm on my own now and I'm not the greatest cook in the world."

"Right lad. Sorry. I mean Sir. That was a slip of the tongue. I wasn't intending to be disrespectful. It's just that

248

you get out of the habit when you've been retired as long as I have."

"No problem Sergeant," I said. "You were talking about your 'taters and beans."

The old bobby touched his forehead with his right index finger and said, "Thank you Sir," adding, "You can take a few when you go. And if you want my advice, for what it's worth, find a good woman as'll do your cookin' for you. They say the way to a man's heart is through his stomach and I go along wi' that." He laughed again as he patted his ample girth.

Whilst he screwed the top back onto his thermos flask I could see that Sergeant Smithurst was running the rule over me. He put down the flask and stroked his chin and looked at me as if he was trying to remember something. To satisfy the old bobby's curiosity meant asking the question. And he did.

"Have we met before Inspector?"

I looked closely at the old policeman then shook my head and said, "If we have Sergeant I don't recollect the occasion. Do you?"

"Nooo. But there's summat about you. Can't put me finger on it yet. But it'll come. Sign of old age ya know when ya forget names and faces. Maybe that twisted beak of yours is throwing me." He touched his own nose to emphasise the point and asked, "How did you win it?"

That made me smile. "It's been called a few things in its time but never a twisted beak," I said. "And I certainly didn't win it."

Under the enquiring eye of the old man I felt obliged to explain how I'd come by it. Stroking the scar I said, "Like your digging for victory Jack, it's a distant memory." Then without any reason I found myself reviving distant memories. Words stuttered out dispassionately. "As a youngster I was brought up aboard a Shaftsbury Homes training ship. It was tough. We daren't complain or cry. If we did it was a whack from a rope's end, no Tender Loving Care. We cried alone in our hammocks at night. It all seemed so natural then."

It suddenly dawned on me that I'd been rambling on to a total stranger about a part of my life I didn't too often talk about.

"Sorry Jack I got carried away," I said. "You don't want to hear my life story."

Sergeant Jack brushed my apology to one side with a wave. "No lad, what you've told me is very interesting. I have this effect on people ya know. Folk talk to me. But one or two regretted it when they ended up having porridge for breakfast in Lincoln jail." He chuckled and added, "But finish telling me about ya nose. It might help me to remember where I've seen you before."

"It was nothing really Jack, just an accident. Tripped over a coil of rope on the upper deck, crashed into a block and tackle hanging from the main yard and bust my nose. Blood everywhere. Bo'sun dished out some rope's end and ordered me round the upper deck three times and once over the mast, for being un-seaman like. Missed my supper. I'd been set to holy stoning the deck; scrubbing out the blood. That was the green rub. As growing lads we never got enough to eat."

"Mmmm. A sad tale Inspector. How old were you then?"

"About eleven."

"Well it's done ya no harm. Look at ya now. A Detective Inspector in a fine police force. Your Bo'sun fella would be proud if he could see how you've turned out."

"Maybe so Sergeant Jack, maybe so, but I didn't come here to talk about me or my nose. I came to talk about Tommy Oakley."

"Tommy Oakley! Now that is a name from the past."

"You've heard about Tommy?"

"I have lad. Indeed I have. A sorry business, Tommy was a good 'un, until the drink took over. Filled the 'stute when he was fighting. It's a damn shame. A damn shame. How can I help you?"

"I'm not too sure Jack," I answered. "I'm searching for something but I don't really know what it is. It's just a gut feeling. You know that tingling sensation in your belly and the urgency in your head that drives you on. Like following a light on the darkest night. Seeing it get nearer and nearer only for it to fly off into the distance as you reach for it. And you'll never know what it is until you grasp it in your hands. Capture it. So that's why I'm here. I want to talk to you about Tom. You might just identify that elusive something and crack this case wide open. Capture it, put it in my hands."

Sergeant Smithurst seemed taken aback. "Well Inspector! Times have certainly changed. I've never heard a senior officer talk like that in thirty odd years of bobbying. Frank Rawlings was the best in my day but he didn't talk like you. Kept things close to his chest. That's why they called him The Fox, he was crafty. Would never admit he didn't have answers. Had to have results. That's how it was in them days. And there was respect for the policeman. When he spoke people listened. And the Courts listened. The bobby's word was law. That's how we kept the peace. Respect and a bit of summary justice."

"A clip round the ear and marbles in the finger ends of your gloves Jack? Policing's changed. The law's making it harder to convict criminals. Seems more concerned with so-called miscarriages of justice and prisoners' rights than locking up villains. But that's the system and we're stuck with it."

The old bobby listened in silence and shuffled uneasily on the bench. It was clear he hadn't liked what he heard. I moved away from the controversial issues.

"Was Tommy ever involved in any crime to your knowledge, Jack?"

Sergeant Smithurst wiped his sweating brow before answering.

"Nooo. Tommy Oakley was straight as a die. A bit of poaching here and there, but who didn't? I was a net and ferret man in my youth, don't mind admitting it, but that's the limit of it. Tommy was the same. Mixed with some rogues through his boxing. Him and Ridgeway the bookie made a lot of money in the fairground booths. That was an illegal venture I suppose. Tom were put up as raw local boy. Challenging the booth pro's. But he was a hardened professional himself. That's the most Tommy got involved in. After he lost his licence things went from bad to worse. The family had its setbacks during the war. His sister Rita went off and died in childbirth. When Big John and Polly died after the accident and he came out of jail, the booze really took hold and Tommy went downhill rapidly. What's happened now is the result."

"The result of what Jack? That's the elusive piece in this jigsaw. What happened to Tom isn't new. Lots have fallen by the wayside but they don't end up being murdered. The answer is waiting to be grasped Jack, it's staring me in the face and I can't see it. I get the feeling that I'm not being told everything. That there's a conspiracy to keep that elusive something out of my reach." I looked hard at Jack. "Are you part of that conspiracy Sergeant Smithurst?"

The old bobby avoided my searching eyes. He breathed onto the flask, polishing it with a shirtsleeve before answering.

"I don't know about a conspiracy Inspector. That makes out there's a number of parties suborning the law. I'm not party to anything like that. What's happened is gone and done, and nothing can be gained by resurrecting it. There's nobody left to be hurt by it, and so I don't see as I can pack and parcel it for you."

"What are you referring to Jack? You obviously know something. The same with Edith Oakley and Jess Fallows. There's a conspiracy of silence."

"Edith Oakley and Jess Fallows you say? Have you seen them then?"

"Jess is in custody with Frank Northbridge and I haven't done with Miss Oakley yet."

Sergeant Jack shifted uncomfortably on the garden seat. "Inspector you're digging a double spit. Turning over a lot of ground best left alone. You might be digging a grave."

"A grave for who Jack? Me? Is that a threat or have you read it in the tea leaves?" I said sarcastically.

Jack Smithurst shook his head. "Inspector – it's going too far. Let me just say this and I'll say no more. There's some as aren't here as might have been if truth were known. And some is here as shouldn't be because truth weren't told."

I pondered the riddle. A statement of Sergeant Jack's home-spun philosophy. A naive simplicity lay at the heart of it, but it needed an Oracle to interpret.

The old Sergeant was unhappy with the way matters had quickly got out of hand. I could see that. He'd allowed himself to be drawn into the centre of the whirlpool that threatened to pull him under. Though, as a former policeman, he was respectful toward me I suspect he realised that this "young whipper snapper of an Inspector" with his fancy words, had nearly got the better of him. Sucked him in. Thankfully he had managed to drag himself clear of the vortex, but now it was best to leave it be. Get back to the things that mattered most in his life. The allotment, the beans, the 'taters. They needed his attention more than an undesirable trip nearly four decades down memory lane.

But I was getting used to the half-truths, innuendoes and silk glove brush-offs from the senior citizens of Langwith. They were up to their pension books in something. I'd not yet fathomed out what, but sensed it was to do with the murder of Tommy Oakley. Here among the crumpled support stockings, zimmer frames and Steradent dental tablets, the elusive light waited to be grasped, captured in my eager hands. I didn't intend to be side tracked by these old conspirators drifting comfortably in their twilight years toward their own Fiddler's Green in the sky. Carrying the secret of Tommy Oakley with them. It was time to change tack.

"Sergeant, you've got a duty to the people of Langwith. Many of them are your friends. After thirty years as a bobby and a lifetime living here you can't just pull up stumps and walk away. Your innings isn't over yet. You've got to get your final score up on that board. It's not in your nature to let the village down."

The old man sat there. He didn't respond immediately to my proposition. He sat polishing the thermos, alone with his thoughts. I waited for his reaction.

Finally he explained wearily, "Inspector, you've come to my little oasis and nigh on destroyed it. You've opened that box that I've tried to keep shut all these years and released many hurtful and unhappy memories that will never get put back. I've got to live with them and suffer their torment. But that's no-one's fault but my own. I'd like to thank you for taking the time out to visit me and I know you've got a difficult job to do. I've searched my conscience and though it pains me and I'm ashamed of my decision, I have to say I can't tell you anything. You'll have to capture the light by finding the truth from someone else. I'm sorry and I'll bid you good day."

Forcing his portly figure from the bench, Sergeant Jack, clasping the thermos, made his way into the garden shed and closed the door. He was alone with his demons and disillusionment. I left without a boiling of 'taters and beans.

TWENTY-TWO

15TH AUGUST
SUNDAY AFTERNOON

I t was less than a week since the discovery of Tom's mutilated body. But so much seemed to have happened and time appeared to be moving apace like a runaway train but getting nowhere. Plenty of intelligence was coming in from the various teams but nothing tangible, nothing to get excited about. Even our own enquiries were fraught with frustration. But I'd been on the job long enough to know that it was always like that. The investigation was still at an early stage and there were positive lines being pursued. Duggy Davis was still a top priority, but he was eluding us. Northbridge had turned out to be a disappointment, but Fallows had yet to be opened up. Leaving him to count bricks might have the desired effect. Whatever happened, the unemployed former head gamekeeper, as he would be when his Lordship heard about his arrest, had to face charges of dog fighting and badger baiting. And with the countryside lobby well represented on the bench Fallows could guarantee at least twelve months lumpy porridge for breakfast and the daily task of slopping out at Lincoln Jail.

I intend to play along with Edith Oakley and Jack

Smithurst for the moment. Clearly they know something, but what? That I've yet to discover and the time for me to find out is fast approaching.

Back home the cat and a tot were my lunchtime companions.

Mitzi's ears suddenly stiffened. Alerted by the musical chimes from the front door bell. My thought processes were interrupted. I wasn't expecting anyone. In the oven my Fine Fare Supermarket pre-packed Sunday dinner of sliced roast beef, Yorkshire pudding and two veg sizzled on gas mark 3. There was only enough for one anyway.

I opened the door. It was Sandra. She looked lovely standing there. It made me realise that the best looking things I'd seen during the last couple of days were a dozen rows of 'taters and a mass of runner beans. I felt a surge inside. A boyish excitement. Pleased she was here. That boy meets girl feeling. Nice, soft and gentle. But I felt clumsy, lost for words.

"Er, come in Sandra." I said, "What a nice surprise. Let me take your coat."

She stepped into the hall, turned her shoulders and shrugged off the three-quarter-length pale blue coat into my hands. Her slender figure looked stunning in the matching two piece. Shapely legs were set off by pale blue high heels. The diffused sunlight filtering through the glass in the door played upon her fair hair. It shone like burnished gold. The sun seemed to tease out a delicate fragrance of roses that enveloped her in an irresistible scent. I felt awkward standing there holding her coat and when our eyes met I shivered inside. She spoke to me through those beautiful brown eyes. It's been said that a woman can make a man melt. Now I know what that

257

means. I melted. I hoped I wasn't showing it but I'd gone weak at the knees.

"Something's burning Jim," Sandra warned.

The smell of scorched beef, Yorkshire and two veg, mingled with the odour of aluminium foil nearing its melting point sent me dashing into the kitchen. Opening the oven door I was pushed backwards by a blast of hot air and fumes. I choked on the sickly sweet aroma of burned out Sunday lunch. Then the smoke alarm went off. Sandra had followed me into the kitchen and quickly switched off the oven, pushing the door to before opening the kitchen window. Still coughing and spluttering I hurried through to the hall and turned off the wailing alarm. I was surprised that it was still working. I hadn't checked the batteries for months.

After a quick look at the incinerated remains in the cooker I proclaimed, "That's Sunday lunch fricasseed."

The afternoon took off from there. In the sitting room Sandra giggled and threw her arms about my neck. I drew her to me. Our lips touched, slightly apart, moving very slowly, moist and silky, melting together. Eyes closed we savoured the moment, wrapped in a warm glow of desire. Sandra pressed closer, gently moving her firm rounded belly against me. I shuddered noticeably and pushed back, aroused. Sandra wriggled pressing harder into me as we allowed the heat of passion to consume us. Moist lips met. Tongues darted and probed. Breathing became heavier. Still locked in our heated embrace I guided my excited partner to the large four seater sofa, lowering her gently backwards. Her skirt rode up and I lay on top of her, gripped about my thighs by long stockinged legs. My hand slipped between them tracing a delicate line alongside a suspender. We were writhing and gasping in expectation. I could feel the heat and smell her body beneath delicate French knickers. Sandra thrust her hand inside my straining trousers and grasped me. We moaned together. In a tiny voice she pleaded, "No need to be gentle darling."

On the chair, Mitzi pricked up her ears and glanced disdainfully in our direction. Stretching herself the old cat retrod her bed before curling up with her back towards us; after all it was none of her business.

That evening Sandra and I lay in one another's arms on the sofa. As I dozed contentedly within a warm glow that still consumed me, I glimpsed Sandra looking at me and felt her gently, oh so gently, kiss my cheek, my scarred nose, my chin, my neck, and finally my lips. She seemed so happy and so was I. The barriers were breached. She gave a huge sigh and snuggled closer to me. I responded from within a comforting dream and muttered, "Angie."

Sandra was up in a flash. I stirred and sat up looking through sleepy eyes. She was standing over me.

"You bastard Stirling!" she yelled.

She stomped out of the room in stockinged feet, tucking her blouse into her skirt and zipping that up as she went. I jumped up, still confused, my beautiful evening disintegrating inexplicably in turmoil about me.

"Sandy! What's wrong. What have I done?"

"Done? You've treated me like a cheap pick up off Long Row. It wasn't me you were making love to it was your wife." She spat out the word, "Angie! Well I don't intend to be a temporary substitute for her. The sooner you make it up with her and get her back in your bed, the better it'll be for all of us."

I was confused and fastened up my shirt as I followed the fireball into the hall.

259

"What's Angie got to do with all this?" I wanted to know.

"Do with it? She is it. You were talking to her in your sleep, even when I was loving you. Sort your problems out and get a life," she snapped.

I watched her as she buttoned up her coat and slipped on her high heels.

"Angie's dead." I said quietly, "Died eighteen months ago."

Sandy reacted as though she had taken a punch under the short rib. She staggered momentarily and grasped the banister rail.

She put her hand to her mouth and said emotionally, "Oh Jim! I'm so sorry. I didn't know. Please forgive me. I was jealous."

I'd already opened the door and stood to one side.

"Thanks for coming. If you don't feel like driving I'll call a taxi." My voice sounded hollow and toneless as I spoke to the distraught woman whom only a few short moments ago had been wrapped in my love, sharing the hope of a new life together.

Tears filled her eyes. Dignity and pride forgotten, Sandra Downey gripped my arm as she pleaded, "Shut the door Jim. Please. Don't let it end like this. I made a stupid mistake. I didn't mean it. I didn't know. Please shut the door."

I was hurt and recognised Sandy's pain. I heard her pleas. Wanted to respond but couldn't find the proper emotional button to press. For a moment I was that small boy scrambling barefoot and bloody nosed up the ratlines of the old training ship. Struggling to escape the bite of the rope's end wielded by an avenging Bo'sun. Show no tears. Show no pain. Show no emotion.

"You'd better go Sandra. I've ruined the evening. It's obvious I'm not ready for a relationship yet."

Sandy sobbed. Tear-smudged mascara mingled with her make-up, painting the face of a tragic clown. The distraught woman quickly kissed me on the cheek, released her grip on my arm and ran from the house.

Those moments of passionate love which had promised so much ended at my closed door.

TWENTY-THREE

We parked up opposite the Shire Hall where Jess Fallows was appearing on remand. The building had long been the heart of the County criminal justice system, set amidst the architectural confusion of the Lace Market in the City of Nottingham. The court complex and adjoining police station were built in the Italianate, neo-renaissance style popular during the eighteenth century. But the Industrial Revolution had put paid to its splendid isolation and concertinaed its magnificence between towering nineteenth-century red bricked town houses. They declared the new money and power of the Lace Masters who had dwelled there. But now they were no longer lived in. Weathered and worn, relegated to County Council offices and repositories for a mass of documents that never saw the light of day.

For decades the impressive columns, statues and heavy studded oak doors of the Shire Hall assured the good people of Nottingham that it was a cathedral of justice. To the many malefactors who were unfortunate enough to pass through its portals it warned of dire punishments including transportation and often death.

McLean and I made our way up the wide spread of worn stone steps rising to the impressive Court foyer, guarded by those great oak doors. I pointed out to the aide a square stone block set in an upper step.

"A bit of local history, Andy. That's where supports for the gallows used to stand. The condemned were hanged here. In later years they were executed in the prison yard at the back of the court and buried there."

McLean wasn't impressed. He stared at the gallows-stone and said bitterly, "They say doctors bury their mistakes and it looks as though the police were at it as well."

Should have ignored him but he'd done it again. Drawn me as easily as a rusty nail from rotten timber and I dived straight in.

"What are you on about McLean?" I demanded.

"Get them out of the public gaze. Kill them behind high walls and bury them out of sight. Solves a lot of problems. Stops a lot of awkward questions."

"We're not still on that tack are we?" I said despairingly. "Once again your warped logic is wrong. They stopped public executions here because a number of spectators were killed in a stampede after a particular drop. So to prevent such a tragedy occurring again they moved into the prison yard. All right? So now you know. Either put up or shut up. You're getting to sound like a worn-out record. If you've got something to say put it in writing to the Chief Constable. Just sort yourself and your problems out. Now let's get on with the business we're here for."

He took my advice and shut up.

The old Nisi Prius court room always impressed me, often awe-inspiring, at times even intimidating. Especially when I was giving evidence at Assize or Quarter Sessions. The spaciousness emphasised its awesome majesty. The whole room was set out beneath an ornate rectangular recessed ceiling, enhancing its opulence. The architectural splendour was designed to strike fear into the hearts of miscreants, at the same time demanding respectful obedience from the servile multitudes. This morning a number of observers occupied the public benches. I could feel the ambience of the past's fearful authority. It pervaded the very fabric of the place. Manifest in the toned-down voices and near silent tread of the Court Officials perpetuating the mysterious rites and rituals of the criminal justice system; in the theatre of Justice. Today Jess Fallows's application for bail was being considered. The prisoner was standing in the dock, hands clasped behind him. He presented a lonely and downcast figure.

The Chairman of the bench was seated alongside the Judge's throne. From beneath the carved oak canopy surmounted by the Royal Coat of Arms he delivered the court's directive. His large voice hushed the courtroom.

"Fallows. The Bench have listened with interest to what the Police prosecutor has had to say about you, and we have noted the defence solicitor's pleas on your behalf. Badger baiting and dog fighting are beastly, wholly un-British, activities made all the worse by your privileged position on the Wembourne Estate. If I had my way man you'd be horse whipped."

The defence solicitor gave a resigned shrug of his shoulders as he packed away his papers. He knew he was onto a loser.

The Chairman continued, "Bail is denied. You will be remanded in police custody for three days. Next."

Fallows's shoulders sagged and he was taken down.

We had just witnessed Justice in action.

As we made our way to the cells I said, "Good! That's a result."

All thought of the earlier episode seemed forgotten as McLean replied, "Is three days long enough Sir?"

"If a week's a long time in politics Andy, three days in police custody is bloody eternity."

Our footsteps echoed around the walls in the narrow cell passage which as usual was wrapped in the gagging stench of sweating bodies and stale cooking. The cell block was as depressing today as it was yesterday, and the day before, and the day before that, and would be tomorrow.

We stopped at Fallows's cell. I was already coughing and spluttering as I opened the heavy door. The place always smelled like stale boiled cabbage. You could almost eat it. It was so thick if you had a knife you could have cut a hole in it. Wonder what they'd had for breakfast?

The smell was even worse in the cell. Fallows stood up as we entered. He hadn't appeared too bad in the dock but up close he looked and smelled rough.

I nodded and thought, "Yes. Stale boiled cabbage and sweat."

The prisoner's grey blanket, edged with red stitching, barely covered the stained rubber and foam mattress laid on the wooden bench that served as a bed and seating.

"Had a good night Jess?" I enquired.

He brushed aside my attempt at friendly familiarity.

"I can't take much more of this Mister Stirling," he wailed. "I'm not used to being cooped up like a wild animal. The place stinks. I wouldn't feed me pigs the swill they serve here. I want bail."

His voice had lost its earlier authority. Counting bricks had taken its toll. His Lordship's Head Gamekeeper licked his lips and ran horny fingers through sparse hair.

I knew that he wouldn't like being locked up in this stinking place with only graffiti-covered walls for company, so I put the knife in.

"You've not been with us five minutes Jess and you're moaning already? Thought you were made of sterner stuff. Everything conforms to Home Office recommendation so if you've got any complaints write to your MP about it."

This wasn't the time for platitudes and kind words. I meant to be ruthless. I could see from the way McLean looked at me that he realised too and Fallows certainly did. He was on the verge and I meant to push him over the edge. Smoothing out a corner of the blanket I sat on the bed.

"Sit down Jess. I bet you've been pacing up and down all night."

He was so wound up that he did exactly the opposite. As if he were an automaton programmed to the suggestion he started to pace up and down the cell.

"No. I don't want to sit down I want to go home." He stopped and looked at me. His voice was heavy with barely concealed emotion and he pleaded, "Let me go home Mister Stirling and I'll tell you all you want to know."

I'd got him on that tight line again but I'd got to play him carefully. Couldn't allow him to gain the initiative or slip the hook. This wasn't television or the movies. It was the real thing. I began to reel in my catch. I'll talk about anything but the murder of Tom. Let Fallows think he's in an advantageous position. Isolate him mentally, feel his mind pulsating in my hand. Then strike.

"I hear what you say Jess but I can't guarantee you anything. The court's made its decision and you're with us for three days." I grimaced and looked around the stinking cell with its graffiti-scarred walls. Then I wound the line in a little more. "It'll seem like three years in here." I deliberately held my nose and added, "Sooner you than me mate. The stink's enough to turn your gut over. If your missus gets around to visiting in this doss hole, it'll be the first and last time. She won't visit again."

The implications weren't lost on the prisoner. He looked terrible. Dark folds underlined his lacklustre eyes set deeply into his furrowed face, highlighting the depth of his despair. He continued pacing the cell.

"I've told you Mister Stirling I'll tell you all I know. Whatever you want that'll help you. You know what I mean?"

He stopped and those red piggy eyes peered at me, an unspoken plea for empathy. I returned the look and Fallows cast his gaze downward.

"This all sounds very familiar Jess," I said pointedly, "You've travelled this road before."

McLean sitting now on the edge of the bed, looked confused.

Fallows stuttered, "What do you mean Mister Stirling?" and set off again on his perambulations.

I think McLean wanted to know as well. He was staring at me intently.

I knew the answer to his question before he'd posed it.

"Cast your mind back Jess. Chief Superintendent Rawlings, Sergeant Jack Smithurst. Remember?"

Fallows stopped pacing as suddenly as if he had walked into the wall. A look of panic flashed across his already worried face.

"The Fox? Sergeant Jack? What ya gettin' at Stirling?"

McLean leaned forward eager to hear what I had to say.

I shuffled further onto the bed leaning back against the wall and said coldly, "Forgotten so soon Jess? I'll remind you. You were one of the main witnesses in the trial of Durnley and Wilson for the murder of Constable Jarvis. Remember now?"

Standing there with head bowed the former poacher

looked his age. He was a worried old man. He seemed riveted to the cell floor, avoiding my eyes. I'm not normally a betting man but I wager he couldn't have felt more isolated and in danger if he'd stood alone on the summit of Everest. He couldn't have felt more at bay if he had been a badger dug from its sett waiting to be savaged by his own slavering pit bulls. That's what I was banking on. But Fallows, like the wounded badger, was still a dangerous animal. He wasn't finished yet. The urge to survive was still strong.

"I want to talk to you Mister Stirling." He nodded towards McLean. "Alone."

The Aide started to object, "Sir. "

I interrupted and said, "Andy. I'd like to speak to Mister Fallows on my own. Get yourself a breath of fresh air and ring Sergeant Johnson. Update him, see if he's got anything for us. Then wait for me."

He didn't like that. He wanted to be in on every twist and turn. He had to learn that that wasn't how it works. A detective is only as good as his informants. They are his bread and butter. And there are times when the only person on earth that matters to him is his informant. No one else. It's an unholy alliance but a necessary one when you're in this business. I could hear McLean making his way up the narrow cell passage. Desolate voices behind cell doors responded to his heavy tread. As he reached the passage gate his footsteps stopped. I heard him shout in frustration.

"Bollocks to the lot of you."

His words echoed in the restricted space, bouncing off the walls and high ceiling. The cell block fell silent.

Turning my attention back to Fallows I said, "What's on your mind Jess?"

The old game keeper flopped onto his mattress. He

watched me through wild eyes. No thought now of fight. In a desperate attempt to stave off what he saw as the dogs gathering to drag him down, Fallows was preparing to turn the key, unlocking the door of dark memory.

Almost apologetically he avowed, "They din't do it you know. They were innocent."

"Innocent? Who was innocent?" I queried.

In an almost inaudible voice he whispered, "You know very well. Bade Durnley and Cal Wilson. God help 'em."

Maybe he was already regretting talking to me.

Thinking back to my research and the headline, 'Poacher Turns King's Evidence' I snapped back, "It's nearly forty years too late for that Fallows. You played God and killed them."

"Do ya think I've not lived wi' that all these years?"

"You lived, they didn't. You lived to enjoy your thirty pieces of silver. Even Judas regretted what he'd done and balanced the account."

I didn't normally become emotionally involved during an investigation but I found it hard not to be affected by the Durnley tragedy. Knowing that Baden Durnley was a cruel and calculating criminal didn't prevent me from experiencing feelings of sadness and regret. And then there were the pangs of sympathy for the mother and her innocent children.

I moved the questioning on. "How do you know they were innocent?"

"'Cos they were wi' me that naight. Poachin'."

"On the night of Constable Jarvis's death?"

"Aye."

"You sure?"

"Course I'm sure."

"Did you give evidence to that effect?"

"Ya know I din't."

"Did you tell anybody?"

"Durnley's brief and The Fox."

I thought about what he was telling me trying to relate it to that trial nearly forty years before. If his story had been accepted by the court the two poachers wouldn't have been found guilty. They may have faced charges with Fallows of armed night poaching, a felony in those days. Might even have got a heavy prison sentence but they wouldn't have ended up sharing a scaffold as guests of the hangman.

"So you were called as an alibi witness for Durnley and Wilson?"

"No. I were called by the Prosecution."

"The Prosecution? Why? Your evidence was invaluable to the Defence."

The game keeper mumbled from behind a restless hand, "That were the plan."

"What plan?"

"The Fox said he'd drop any charges agen me if I said Bade and Cal weren't with me that naight. I didn't like doin' it but he said I'd get ten to fifteen year for armed night poachin' if I didn't, might even get me necked stretched with them two."

"So that was it. You struck a deal with Rawlings that helped you hang your two friends and kill a mother and her kids."

Fallows wanted to justify his treachery. He pleaded, "I were only tryin' to help Chief Superintendent Rawlings. It were a case of me scratchin' his back and 'im scratchin' mine."

I said cynically, "A promise of the head gamekeeper's job, a cottage on the estate and a pension? Some back scratching. More like back stabbing. Stuck your pals dead centre on the hangman's trap." I cracked my knuckles to emphasise the point and said sharply, "Snap!"

It struck home. Fallows recoiled in horror. No doubt at the thought of the two hooded and bound men swinging at the end of ropes; necks broken.

He sobbed, "Oh God! Oh God Almighty!"

I was unmoved and angry. "Get hold of yourself. Stop bleating. Face your problems like a man."

After his attempt at redemption Fallows calmed down considerably and sat quietly on the bed. It seemed as if getting over that first hurdle had been like reaching the peak of an insurmountable mountain. Strangely he seemed to look more at peace with himself.

But I wasn't at peace with myself. Certainly not with Fallows, Rawlings, Sergeant Jack or the lawyers if what he was telling me was the truth.

"You said it was the plan for you to be called by the Prosecution. What was the plan?"

Without any hesitation he said, "Defence tried to pull a flanker. They wanted to discredit prosecution's case. It looked strong on paper. But the Fox were too crafty. He turned it round on 'em." I could see what the defence lawyers were up to. They were relying on some subterfuge of their own.

I said, "The defence were offering you to the prosecution making out that you had no evidence of value to their case. In fact if you went along with Rawlings's plan your evidence would help convict them. So what was the defence up to?"

"You've got it in one Mister. When Bade's brief seen me I told him what had gone off with The Fox. I thought he'd a gone spare but he didn't. He told me to go along wi' 'im and say that I hadn't been with Bade and Cal. Then I had to pretend to crack up during't defence cross examination like

271

and admit givin' false evidence 'cos Fox had threatened to charge me."

"The wicked bastards!" I said disdainfully. "The Judge would have to throw the case out. The defence brief would be the hero of the day and the corrupt Rawlings and Smithurst would go down. Brilliant Brief would grab the headlines and villains would be queuing up for him to represent them. Filling his coffers. But he took a big gamble and as they say in the vernacular, 'fucked up' and they say coppers are bent?"

"You've got in one again boss. I were more afraid of Rawlings than Durnley's brief. Foxy told me to stick to me story and I did. No matter how hard they tried I stuck 'em out. I said they weren't wi' me when Jarvis were murdered. There were some panic down on them defence benches I can tell ya, but they'd shot them sens up their own arses and coudnna do owt about it."

My opinion of the legal profession was not enhanced by Fallows's revelations. Lawyers! They stumbled straight from their traps into Rawlings's. No wonder he was called The Fox. He'd got them by the balls. They'd lost the script, topped their own clients.

"So who killed Constable Jarvis? And what's the connection between that and the murder of Tom?" I asked Fallows.

Now he had come in from the dark and revealed his secret to me he seemed more at ease with himself.

The old poacher answered, "It weren't any of our lot mister, I can tell ya that for nowt. It might a been outsiders but I don't know." He reflected for a moment and added, "Bade were a wrong 'un ta cross ya know and I don't think outsiders would 'a risked trouble wi' 'im."

"So who was it Jess?"

"As God's me witness Mister Stirling I 'ant gorra clue. I reckon Sergeant Jack knowed more than he ever let on. He could play 'is cards close to 'is chest raight enough."

Jess Fallows might just have something there. I feel he's not too far off the mark. Ever since that 'taters and beans day I've not been too sure of Mr. Smithurst. Never got to the bottom of him. The rematch isn't too far away.

For a moment as I stood in front of the graffiti-scarred wall I attempted to decipher some of the frustrated outpourings from tormented souls. I spotted an interesting personal recommendation. I read it aloud. "Stirling's a bastard. Tell him nowt." Alongside I read, "Amen to that but he's not a bastard - he's a ruthless bastard."

I nodded towards the biro scratched brickwork, "Not a very good press hey Jess? But don't believe all you read."

Fallows didn't comment. Probably thought it best not to in the circumstances.

I stroked my scarred nose and thought about what he'd told me. Sergeant Jack could be in the frame. Why not? He knew the Durnley gang well and now it's alleged he helped hang two of them. He certainly knew where PC Jarvis would be that night, his exact location, he'd put him there. And who could get closer to the victim than his own Sergeant? He had Jarvis's complete trust and afterwards no one would suspect him of such a crime. And when I spoke to him he wouldn't cooperate though it was clear he knew something. I'm clearly missing an important piece of the jigsaw here. I can't put my finger on it. And what would be his motive for murder? And then there's the riddle. *"There's some as aren't here as might have been, if truth were known, and some is here as shouldn't be because truth weren't told."*

It was a riddle wrapped in a mystery inside an enigma alright. But this time it wasn't anything to do with Churchill or Russia. It was more local, centred on Jack Smithurst and Langwith. In that stinking cell I made myself a promise. "Sergeant Jack we'll meet again. Very soon."

I left Fallows wrestling with his conscience as he came to terms with his contrition. After running the gauntlet of the voices behind cell doors I left the block. McLean was upstairs in the small kitchen used by the cell duty staff.

As I entered he asked eagerly, "Has Fallows told you something, Sir?"

I wasn't going to tell him anything at this stage. It was a real hot potato and it needed some thought. I had to decide on the proper way to deal with the information I had received from the prisoner. I didn't want to discourage McLean's enthusiasm but until the Superintendent had been briefed I wasn't about to reveal anything to him.

So I said cautiously, "Yes Andy. He's given me something to think about. Probably set me on the right track. Can't tell you about it yet. Not until I've discussed it with the Superintendent."

McLean probed. "Does he identify Tom's killer Sir?"

Good question – shows promise – but I'm not going to be drawn.

In an effort not to dampen his enthusiasm I said, "I've a feeling that the trial of Durnley and Wilson didn't hear the truth, the whole truth and nothing but the truth. I don't want to say more at this time."

That brought the questioning to an end, though I had the feeling that my decision to return to the incident room didn't meet with McLean's approval. He turned sharply on his heel and strode off towards the main entrance of the police station, dashing the car keys against his thigh as he went. I followed him out and made a mental note once again about his petulant attitude.

Back at murder control, behind closed doors, I updated Detective Superintendent Davey. As I related the details the Old Bear paced the office, listening intently behind a tight-lipped scowl whilst he beat out a rhythm on the palm of his hand with his spectacles.

I concluded, "And that's it Sir. If what Fallows alleges is true then we've unearthed a massive miscarriage of justice."

Superintendent Davey continued to pace the room, turning over the new information in his head. Now he tapped the spectacles against his dentures. Both were taking a beating. Their ordeal came to an end as the Super put on his glasses and stood alongside me.

He said, "It's very disturbing Jim but we can't turn back the clock. If the press get hold of this latest angle it'll dominate the front pages for days, if not weeks, and it'll side track our own enquiry."

"That's how I see it Sir," I said. "May I suggest that the information be treated as classified, with a very limited circulation that doesn't include the media at this moment?"

Superintendent Davey agreed. "We need the newspapers and rest of the media on board. When the time's right we'll give them the other as a bonus. I'll order a limited distribution of the information and ensure that it's officially recorded and referred back to me periodically. There'll have to be an enquiry later but meantime you can continue your investigation without hindrance."

TWENTY-FOUR

17th AUGUST TUESDAY

Approaching the grave I could see the roses. They still looked colourful and fresh but I'd brought new ones to replace them. Squatting at the graveside I removed the old flowers from the pot shoving them irreverently into a Marks and Spencer's shopping bag together with a plastic bottle used to carry water. With the pot topped up and replacement flowers settled I allowed my hands to wander across the words etched with such care into the headstone.

I said, "I love you Angie," stood up, turned and walked away.

*

That night, dozing in my easy chair with Mitzi on my lap, wrapped in the warm embrace of a tot, Angie came to me. But it was a different Angie. She looked at peace. I felt the corners of my mouth twitch involuntarily; perchance a smile? I adjusted mine and the cat's position and fell into the most contented sleep I'd known for some time.

*

WEDNESDAY 18th AUGUST

I was at the nick early. Sergeant Johnson arrived soon after followed closely by McLean.

"Get the kettle on Serge." I said, "Nothing like a cuppa coffee to start the day off right."

"Already seen to Sir. Mac – do the honours."

Constable McLean did not answer as he left the office but it was obvious he was not happy with his assignment.

I said, "What's wrong with him?"

"Got a monk on boss. Been like it a couple of days now. Something's bothering him but he won't talk about it. You know how close-lipped he can be."

"Mmm. Now you mention it he has been a little touchy lately. Seems to think I should share every aspect of the enquiry with him. Wants to be in on everything. Very keen, shows potential, if he can keep on top of himself. Not got to be too pushy. He's here to learn. I'll have to have a word with him."

"Probably too set in his ways boss. It must be quite a culture shock at his age chucking in a nine-to-five banking routine for coppering. Has he said anything to you about it?"

"No. And I've never asked about his private life, that's his business. We've discussed his future on the job and he's keen to get into CID. So far he's impressed me but I've noticed this confrontational streak, almost a greater than thou attitude towards colleagues, and he can be surly."

"And disrespectful," Styx Johnson added.

"Yeh. I suspect a bit of pressure's getting to him, that's all. I've thrown him in at the deep end and he wants to make an impression on his first murder enquiry. He's very intelligent, enthusiastic and eager to learn. They're the positive elements we've got to develop. Give the negative things time to sort themselves out. If they don't, it'll be arse kicking time."

McLean came in, two cups of coffee held out before him.

Sergeant Johnson took one and had a careful sip. He said, "If nothing else he makes a good cuppa coffee this lad."

The reaction of the aide was unexpected.

"Less of the *lad* Sarge, and if *nothing else* implies I'm failing in my police duties on this CID attachment, I'd like to be told about it. Officially."

I knew how Johnson would react to the outburst. In an attempt to quickly diffuse what had the potential to develop into an ugly scene I waved a raised hand, and shook my head. Sergeant Johnson had been around long enough to read the signs. Seeing off his coffee in a couple of gulps he thrust the empty cup into McLean's hand.

He said dryly, "I'll be going now Sir. Got a number of enquiries to complete about Duggy Davis. I'll keep you updated."

The hard-eyed stare from the Detective Sergeant as he pulled the door to, should have told McLean that he had not made a good impression. But he showed no concern as he retrieved a beer mat from beneath the paper strewn about my desk. Sliding it in front of me he unceremoniously plumped the cup onto it. Coffee slopped over the lip, spilling in an unsightly brown slick down its length before settling in a glutinous semicircle about its base. McLean was preparing himself for my reaction. I took hold of the cup of coffee leaking onto my beer mat, drawing it towards me. The pattern of coffee followed, blurring into a broad brown band and finally, spidery fingers, resembling dry brush marks on canvas.

Still looking at the aide as I sipped from the cup, I demanded, "What's the problem?"

McLean shrugged and said unemotionally, "No problem."

I wasn't too happy with his insolent response. I gave a curt nod indicating my coffee-gunged mat and desk.

"What about that?"

McLean followed my eyes and shrugged once more. "An accident," he said offhandedly.

"I don't think so Mister McLean. It was bloody mindedness. And 'Sorry' wouldn't go amiss."

I had the feeling constable McLean had been prepared for a battle. But I suspect that little Jiminy Cricket sitting on his shoulder whispered in his ear and brought him to his senses. Told him this was one fight he wasn't going to win. He must have taken JC's advice.

In a flat monotonous voice he muttered, "Sorry boss, I was out of order. I'll get another and clear up."

"No need for that," I said. "I'm not a fussy chap, but I expect my officers to have a high degree of self discipline and self respect. That's not the same as self pity and whingeing. If you've got problems you can't resolve yourself come and talk about them. If not to me or Sergeant Johnson see another senior officer. If it's something you feel you can't speak to them about there's the Welfare Officer, the Force Chaplain or your Federation rep. Is that understood?"

He understood alright. If he didn't he was in the mire. His future depended upon it.

He knew where he stood and said apologetically, "Yes Sir. I'm sorry. Just a bit of domestic trouble. Nothing that

I can't handle. Letting it get on top of me. You know what problems families can cause. Shan't let it get to me again. It'll all be resolved soon."

"Alright McLean," I said. But he knew it wasn't. It must have been obvious that I wasn't too happy about his lack of self control and his disrespectful attitude. I did the man management bit. "Do you want to talk about it Andy? We can have a closed door session. No interruptions. Official or informal. It's up to you."

He didn't answer for a moment, appeared to be weighing up the options, then replied, "No. But thanks all the same Sir. If I need to I'll seek advice."

That appeared to be the end of the matter. But I'd have to write it up and at the moment the red ink was overtaking the black. On the plus side I had some sympathy for him. I knew what family problems could do to your head. He had to learn to keep the job and private life separate. I moved away from the incident and asked, "Have you got plenty to do?"

"I have Sir, but if you've got something for me I can sort them out later."

"No you're alright. Get on with what you're doing. I've got a little job to attend to and it's important I see to it now."

"Is it to do with Fallows's information Sir?"

"There you go again Andy. If I'd wanted you to know about it I'd've told you. So what does that tell you?"

"You don't want to tell me about it."

"Spot on! You'll learn that on this job everyone, sometimes, keeps something close to their chest. If there is a need to share it, then everyone will eventually know about it. OK?"

With an unconvincing tight-lipped smile McLean replied, "Yes Sir."

Gathering up the coffee cups he left the office.

I couldn't make my mind up about him. For a moment I stared at the closed door. But I had more important matters to think about. I left the nick and drove to Sherwood Lodge.

*

Later, at Head Quarters, a civilian from the Force Intelligence Bureau escorted me to the long row of single storey buildings alongside the lower car park. It seemed strange being supervised by such a young woman. But it was reassuring to see that procedures I had put into place whilst head of FIB, were still operating. We chatted as we walked.

"Aren't you Rose, worked in Crime Stats?" I asked.

The attractive, neatly dressed young woman fiddled with the bunch of keys she carried, and smiled.

"You've remembered Mister Stirling. I wondered if you would. You interviewed me and set me on. I've been promoted you know. Office Manager. Archives are one of my responsibilities."

"Office Manager? Well done. I'm pleased things worked out for you. Trust the old gut instinct to get it right."

Crossing over the car park we entered the building through a brick-built porch and walked along a narrow corridor flanked with rows of internal office windows and doors

We stopped outside a door at the far end. Rose unlocked it. We went in. The windows had been blacked out and in the gloom hung the musty smell of damp.

"Not used very much hey Rose?"

"Doesn't seem the interest any more Sir. I'll just switch on the light."

Now I could see and wandered along the corridors of grey metal cabinets checking the index cards. Occasionally I pulled out a sliding drawer and walked my fingers through the hanging files inside. I wasn't having much luck. I couldn't find what I was looking for. Rose was at a desk flicking through a ledger.

I called to her, "Rose, are DPP papers filed under the name of the accused or the victim?" I asked.

"Depends what you're looking for Sir. They've all got a Nottingham Criminal Record number. How far are you going back?"

"Nineteen forties?"

"Nineteen forties! Mmm. Don't know about that. There's a policy now of clearing out old files, even the more recent ones, say the last ten years. Preparing for computerisation. The old files took up so much room and needed so much looking after. And as you've seen, not many people are interested in them."

"What a bloody shame! All that information, intelligence, local knowledge down the pan. It can't be replaced Rose. Can't the top corridor see that? Even if it's down here fifty years it doesn't matter. It may just turn up a murderer or a rapist or a child molester. Machines are running the job."

"Ruining the job more like Mister Stirling. The machines on the top corridor are ruining the job."

"Maybe you're right Rose. But how sad if that's our future."

I got back to the present. Let the future look after itself. The file I'm looking for must be two feet thick, the murder of a police officer. It'll be a tragedy if that's been binned. I asked Rose if she could point me in the right direction.

"Murder of a police officer? That shouldn't have been

cleared. There's a special section for murders, and if we haven't got it you can try the Director of Public Prosecutions in London. They keep copies."

She pointed out some bulky bundles piled up behind a row of cabinets. So that was the "special section." They hadn't been filed, just bundled together, tied up and stuck out of the way.

She said, "Hope you have jolly time sorting them out Sir."

I squatted down by the piles of dusty files and set about going through them. It struck me that it might have been a good experience for McLean. Let him get his hands dirty. Should have brought him along. But it's too late now.

For once my luck was in. After moving only three of the weighty bundles I came across what I was looking for. With the discovery came that tingling sensation to the back of my neck. The hefty dog-eared folder was bound vertically and horizontally in pink ribbon that had twisted and turned into narrow knotted strings. I could see names that had become so familiar to me stencilled neatly in two inch high black lettering on the faded pink cover. I read the names aloud. I was excited.

DURNLEY B/ WILSON C
Murder of Police Constable Rodney
Jarvis.
NCR. 815836.

Rose called out, "Found it already Inspector?"

"Yes. This is it," I called back. "If I can manage to lug it outside I'll take it back to the office and go through it."

"Oh! You can't do that Sir," the office manager said in alarm.

"Can't do what?"

"Take it out of the building. It's against the rules."

"Rules? What a stupid rule. One of the enlightened machines on the top corridor again?"

Following an embarrassing silence Rose muttered almost apologetically, "Er, no Sir. One of yours."

"Mine? Are you sure?"

"Yes sir. Been in force since you left. Here look." She turned the ledger towards me.

I went through the motions, glancing at the typed order held by peeling, yellowed sellotape to the inside cover of the book. I knew it was my signature before I saw it.

I picked up the ledger. "That's years ago. I put that in to prevent files disappearing. Hasn't anybody reviewed it since?"

As I spoke I traced a finger down the list of names under the heading, "Details of Officers Accessing Files."

"What's this?" I asked.

"What's what Sir?"

"Oh. I'm just talking to myself Rosie. It's getting to be a habit. But there's a recent entry here. A Detective Sergeant Evans accessing file number NCR. 815836. That's this one. Who is Evans? And what's his interest in the late PC Jarvis?" Thoughts of Edith Oakley's phantom caller rushed into my mind. Now this was interesting and confusing at the same time.

The file was bulky and had some weight. I carried it to the door. "You can lock up now Rose," I said.

With concern rattling her youthful voice she pleaded, "What about the file Mister Stirling? You can't take that with you. And you've got to sign alongside your details in the register." Her finger trembled as she pointed to the open ledger and the order carved in stone. "The rules. It's the rules," she insisted.

The poor girl was concerned. I couldn't leave knowing that I'd caused her upset and distress. After all she was the office manager. I heaved the heavy file onto the top of a cabinet. Rose gave a sigh of relief. I signed the ledger and then with a theatrical gesture ripped out the order, sellotape and all.

"I made the rule," I said. "Rule rescinded. Lock up please Rose."

The shocked look on her pretty face said it all. Settling the bulky package onto my shoulder as if it were a hammock I marched out of the records office whistling "Hearts of Oak." Rose was still standing there when I walked out into the corridor and made my way back to the car and the murder incident room.

*

"No Sir. I don't know a Detective Sergeant Evans. I'll go as far as saying there's no such officer in our force. But I'll check with Personnel to make sure. Could be a transfer on promotion that I haven't heard about." Sergeant Johnson picked up the telephone in anticipation of a nod from me.

"Yeh. That's a good idea Sarge. We'll get a result one way or the other." As I leafed through the file on my desk I said, "Bit of a puzzler this one Styx. I can't understand what another police officer, who doesn't appear to come from our force, wants with it."

As he waited for the phone to be answered Sergeant Johnson cupped his hand over the receiver and replied, "Could have been doing research. Some sort of a project. Crime stats? Complaints? Home Office? Anything but police work." The DS quickly removed his hand from the mouthpiece, "Good afternoon. Personnel? OK. This is DS Johnson from the murder incident room. Do you have anything on a DS Evans? No. Don't have his collar number. No further information I'm afraid. Sure. No problem I'll hang on."

I must have been wearing my worried look as I flicked through the document and statement file in the Jarvis papers. Trawling through them for the third time just made the frown more intense.

Sergeant Johnson read the signs and latched onto my obvious concern. "Problem, boss?" he asked.

"I'm not too sure Sarge but something's not right. The Index shows the Pathologist's report as pages twenty to twenty four of the statement file. It isn't there. I've checked and double-checked. It's not got shoved in with the synopsis, though there is a brief resumé of the evidence." I shuffled through another bunch of papers and confirmed, "It's not in the documentary exhibits file." I sat back and looked at Johnson, "So where is it?"

The Detective Sergeant was back on the telephone

"Right. OK. Thanks for your trouble. Cheers." He put down the phone and said, "The plot thickens boss. As I thought, no such officer in this force. No record since personnel went over to computerisation and they back-referenced ten years. The guy in personnel did an area check covering Derbyshire, Leicestershire, Lincolnshire Northamptonshire and South Yorkshire. No trace. No requests from foreign forces for an officer of that name to visit our police area for research purposes."

"As you say Styx, the plot thickens. Check complaints department, see if there is or has been a complaint running involving this officer or the Jarvis murder. Then I'll update

Mister Davey. There's something not right here."

I went to see the governor in his office. He was sitting down to a cup of tea. I updated him on the new development.

"So you're connecting this mysterious Detective Sergeant Evans to Edith Oakley's unidentified caller?" Detective Superintendent Davey dunked a digestive biscuit into his cup of tea and asked, "Like a digestive, Jim?"

"Er. No thanks sir, I'll get something later on." He might have expected me to join him in his dunking and I didn't really fancy a soggy Mcvities.

"What about Evans?" he queried.

Here was the chance for a humorous riposte, but it was not the right occasion, the mysterious Evans would have to forego the pleasure of a soggy digestive.

"There seems to be no officer of that name in this force Sir and Complaints have no knowledge of such a person."

"So what are you doing about it?"

"I'm having the sheet he signed examined by the lab and fingerprints. They might do something with the handwriting and then run a ninhydrin test for dabs."

"You're suggesting that if it isn't a copper Jim we've one cool customer successfully posing as one. If you're right he's got some bottle to carry out a caper like that in broad daylight at Police Headquarters." After another foray to his tea cup the Super continued, "You're hoping he's on file then? What if he isn't? Handwriting and dabs aren't going to help."

"You're right Sir but we may strike it lucky. He could have form."

"Ever the optimist hey Jim? Let's hope it's a winner at the end of the day."

"It's just a hunch Sir. We've got to try everything."

I continued, "I've spoken again to Rose at HQ FIB. She

287

never saw this Evans but recollects someone of that name ringing in for the archive keys. They were busy that day and left them at reception for him to collect. It never entered her head that he wasn't genuine. He seemed confident and knew what he was doing. Once he'd fixed up the key all he had to do was drive into HQ, leave his motor in the lower car park and walk up to reception. As you know, security at HQ isn't a top priority but after this it'll have to be tightened up. It seems any Tom, Dick or Harry with a bit of bottle and some know-how can come and go as he pleases. There isn't a permanent presence at the gate so our Sgt. Evans only had to wait for his opportunity and he was in. It's not likely any one will have seen him but enquiries are being made. The receptionist in the foyer vaguely remembers a man in civvies collecting the key and signing for it. She didn't recognise him. The log has been checked; he's signed it 'Sgt. Evans'. That was the risky part over. Once he let himself into the archives block it was a doddle. He'd got all the time in the world to go through the file and help himself to anything that interested him. But I can't see why anyone should want the Pathologist's report? Nothing but technical jargon and graphic descriptions of injuries, blood and gore. Not exactly pleasant bedtime reading. What good is it to anyone after all these years?"

"That's what makes our job so interesting Jim. Nothing is straight-forward. Nothing is what it seems. Every day brings its new joys, new problems, mysteries and adventure. Aren't you glad you joined?"

"I'm sure you wouldn't want me to respond to that proposition Sir. In the Andrew you'd have been told "what a load of old bollocks, a real bunch of bastards if you like. Roll on my dozen." But that would be the opinion of uncouth seafarers Sir, not officers and gentlemen like wot we are."

That seemed to amuse Mister Davey. He guffawed, giving his impression of a steam engine chugging away on full throttle. "Ugh. Ugh. Ugh. Like wot we are. You're a droll one Jim," he gurgled. "I can see why they talk about a yard of naval flannel. But keep up the good work. Keep the pressure on. I'll ensure the enquiry is driving forward and keep the top corridor off our necks. We're getting to that unpleasant stage where I'm going to be fighting our corner for finance and manpower, so I'll be relying on you and the other senior detectives to get results. We need results Jim. And keep onto this Sgt. Evans angle, it looks interesting." He walked off towards the control room munching another digestive and chugging on about naval flannel.

As I watched the SIO leave I had a sudden thought. I punched a clenched fist into my open palm and hurried back to my office. The words "injuries, blood and gore" rattled in my head.

I went straight to the bundles of documents set neatly about my desk. Shuffling quickly through them I pulled out the bound books of photographic evidence. Each book was numbered and indexed. Amongst them black and white pictures of the Jarvis crime scene. The footpath and surrounding woods. A folded cape with lamp, helmet, handcuffs and truncheon and PC Jarvis's bicycle. Durnley's cottage and a plethora of supporting pictures as one would expect from such a horrific crime. Then I went through them all again.

I said aloud, "I thought so. It's missing."

As I bundled the books together Sergeant Johnson and McLean came into the room in time to witness my consternation.

"More problems, boss?"

"Word of the day Sarge. Two documents missing from the Jarvis file."

"Two documents? The phantom copper?" Johnson queried.

Constable McLean, interest aroused, obviously wanted to hear more. "Phantom copper boss. What phantom copper?"

"New mysteries and adventures Andy," I said. "Aren't you glad you joined? In addition to the medical report the PC Jarvis post mortem photographs are adrift."

Sergeant Johnson offered an explanation. Though he knew it was gossamer thin. "Maybe they've been lost through careless use or neglect in handling the files over the years."

"Maybe. But I'm not convinced. Too much of a coincidence. The Pathologist's statement covering the post mortem and the photographs of the post mortem are the only documents missing from the file. Your theory would be more acceptable if they'd disappeared from the same part of the file. But they're from different parts of an extremely large bundle of papers, one from the statement file and another from the photographic exhibits file. No, gentlemen! I suspect they have been deliberately removed by someone for a specific reason."

"This phantom copper you've mentioned boss. Any leads on him?"

I was pleased to see McLean taking an interest in the new turn of events. This Sgt. Evans was a cool and calculating guy. Imitating a police officer and walking large as life into police Head Quarters took a lot of bottle. I was going to enjoy hunting him down. This was the best part of the job, reading the signs, following the trails to where ever they led and finally running down the quarry

290

I answered McLean's question. "No Andy, nothing yet. We're working on it. I've a suspicion Edith might help there."

McLean looked surprised. "Edith? Where does she fit in?"

"That gut feeling tells me she fits the lock. She's the key. Action another visit for me to see her tomorrow morning."

"What have you in mind sir," McLean asked.

"Tomorrow, Andy, I intend to turn the key."

TWENTY-FIVE

WEDNESDAY NIGHT

Edith was a creature of habit. She had spent the last hour talking to her family of photographs and reading passages from the scriptures as she did each evening. Now, in her night attire, she prepared for bed. Ensuring the gas and water taps were turned off, windows secured and doors locked was part of the nightly ritual. Turning the key in the back door was the final act. But it was more than simply fastening it, more than securing the premises. It was locking out the world. Locking her into the home where she had been born and lived all her life, wrapped comfortably in the embrace of so many happy memories. After climbing the steep flight of stairs to her room she completed her preparations for bed and switched off the bedside lamp. The house was plunged into darkness. In her time capsule home, her personal cocoon, Edith snuggled up in her warm bed. She felt secure.

*

As Edith's bedroom light was switched off a dark clothed figure carrying a bulky black bag stepped out of the shadows at the bottom of the garden. The watcher had waited patiently for the house to close its eyes for the night, waited for it to become a dead house. Now was the time for action. Bending low in the darkness the intruder moved effortlessly towards Edith's refuge.

*

The first realisation that something was wrong came from a sharp creak on the stair. Edith awoke instantly. The warmth and comfort of her bed dissolved in a moment. In the chill of night the alien sound threatened. A worn tread on the tenth step, it had been like that since she could remember. It was part of the game of hide and seek she had played as a child with her brothers and sisters. Always miss out the tenth step. It creaks and will give you away. At first she was not afraid. That changed as she sat up, drawing the bed clothes tightly to her. She became aware that someone, something, had violated her sanctuary. It was at her door, waiting. Waiting for God knows what. With mind shrieking she watched the door open slowly. A shapeless figure moved into the room. In the dark it took on huge proportions and towered above her. Cowering now, weak and helpless beneath the spectre's overpowering presence, with eiderdown pulled up to her eyes, she prayed to be swallowed up by her bed. With no one to help her and unable to scream she was gripped by fear and held in the glare of the creature's manic eyes, staring at her through slits in the mask distorting its features. She recoiled at the whiteness of the mouth stretched in a mirthless grin as the phantom hissed, "Dead women tell no tales." They were the last words she heard as her night exploded into scarlet silence.

Downstairs, in the darkness, from their never-changing places on the sideboard, her never-changing family listened, and watched, helpless.

Traffic on the road into Langwith crawled along. I chuntered to myself muttering about the best laid plans, not enough hours, cursed the Highways Authority, local council, Chief Constable, learner drivers and the price of Mansfield best bitter. It wasn't until I'd crossed over the small bridge near to the Net and Ferret that I had any inkling of what was causing the problem. Then the urgent wail of a siren behind caused me to automatically steer the car onto the nearside grass verge. A county ambulance, full bank of lights snapping and blinking like a mobile disco, hurtled past making rapid progress up the hill toward the village. Moments later the siren stopped. I slowly broke ranks and resumed my journey. At the top of the hill, just past the green-painted butcher's shop, gawking rubberneckers slowed down the traffic. A uniformed policeman positioned on the pavement waved his arm in irritation as he ordered the drivers to keep moving. I rubbernecked. Staring at an impressive scarlet fire appliance with its network of fat hoses spread across the wet pavements. Manned by firemen bulked up in black and yellow protective clothing it invoked a childish curiosity. Drawn up on the pavement, Gas and Electricity Board vans, amber lights revolving slowly, added to the carnival of confusion.

Pulling up alongside the gesticulating traffic policeman, I identified myself, "DI Stirling, Mansfield CID. What's happened officer?"

The officer took a brief moment to deal with the social niceties of rank and threw off a quick salute. That out of the way he got on with the job at hand, diverting vehicles around my stationary car.

"As you can see Sir there's a bit of problem and I'll have to ask you to move on. You're causing an obstruction."

"Right officer. Thanks. Oh! Is anyone injured?"

"Another ambulance has arrived sir. That's all I can tell you. Too busy trying to prevent traffic snarling up here and hampering the rescue services." He had wasted enough time with me. With an authoritative sweep of his arm, finger indicating the flow of traffic he ordered, "Move on."

I drove up the main road of the village and turned right into Church Street. The long terrace of sad looking pit houses with the communal yards and outside lavatories were mostly deserted. Many boarded up awaiting the demolition man's ball and chain. Parking well away from the traffic I walked back to Portland Road. It crossed my mind that I was following in the footsteps of Big John Oakley. My eyes ranged over the scene taking in more of the overall picture. Traffic was again progressing steadily. The bobby had everything under control. The Gas and Electricity Board vehicles had gone. Firemen working between appliance and rear of the terrace were moving at a less frenetic pace. They were clearing up. Whatever it was they must have been on top of the job. I didn't foresee any problems.

Walking toward the alley leading to the rear of Portland Road, I spotted two smartly dressed men alighting from a dark blue saloon parked on the pavement in front of the houses. It was the local CID. As I crossed the road they eyeballed me. The taller of the two raised a hand in recognition. We met in front of Edith's house. Both the guys had worked for me on various occasions. Dave Plackett had the potential to progress in the Force but seemed content to remain a Detective Sergeant. Like a lot of officers he preferred the cut and thrust of street work, happy being with "the boys" and saw the drawbacks to becoming a senior officer. Alright changing the nappy occasionally but didn't fancy being left holding the baby. Apart from anything else it took the fun out of the job. His mate, Peter Jones, was a plodder. A thorough, determined man. Never gave in. Powerful, rumbled on like a tank, anything that got in his way, look out!

DS Plackett called out to me, "Morning Sir. Slumming it out in the sticks?"

We shook hands and I said, "You might've thought so Dave but I've ended up gobbling stinking smoke and sloshing about in soggy socks."

Dave's colleague, the younger and heavily built Pete Jones, said "Mornin' Sir. Thought you were on the Mansfield murder."

I shook hands and said, "Morning Pete. That's right. I'm not here to get in your way, just seeing a witness in the terrace." I nodded towards the Oakley house.

The detectives followed my nod then looked at one another.

"Number three sir?" queried DS Plackett.

Not too sure about the DS's question, I nodded and asked warily, "Is that a problem?"

"Could be."

"Why's that Sarge?"

"You don't know?" he asked with genuine surprise, "I'll show you. We're going your way, might as well go together."

As we walked down the alleyway to the rear of the terrace I pondered upon the morning's events and its latest twist. An emergency ambulance, the fire appliance, now two local detectives. And what was it I was supposed to know about number three? Dave Plackett needed to provide some answers before very long.

Turning right off the alley onto the terrace's communal path, I could see the activity at the far end. Firemen were disconnecting brass hose branches, making up their hoses, clearing up debris. A Station Officer holding a clip board and making notes was in deep conversation with a colleague. As we drew closer and the angle of perspective along the terrace widened, I was suddenly confronted with the reason for the morning's activity.

My first reaction said it all. "Bloody hell! What's happened?"

And well I might ask. Big John's green painted wooden porch, built by his own hand, was completely destroyed. Reduced to a pile of smouldering timber and shattered glass. The privet hedge was a row of charred stumps sticking out of the ground like blackened clutching fingers. The back door – Edith's final bulwark against the world – had been reduced to two badly burned door frames. Distorted hinges jutted at crazy angles from the blackened remains. Its lock, a mass of melted metal buried amongst smouldering rubble, lay in the floor space beneath burned and heavily scorched joists and collapsed floor boards. The remains of the family's living room. The sash window had fared no better, its shattered frame hacked out by the firemen to be hurled burning and broken into the debris-cluttered yard. Above the now gaping doorway and windows, wide swathes of blackened brick traced the path of smoke that at the height of the conflagration had poured out following burning wood and exploding glass. Beyond the stark remains of the doorway I could see into the fire damaged room. Anything that had survived the impossible heat and flame in Edith's neat little haven had undergone a dramatic metamorphosis, blackened and unrecognisable. The place reeked of smoke.

I surveyed the smoking ruins of John's porch. I recognised a copper jardinière half buried in the soggy muck and the distorted brass bonnet of what had once been John's safety lamp. I felt a personal loss. For a moment I heard Tom and his brothers laughing and skylarking as they jostled through the small porch into the cosy living room, to be greeted by a smiling John and a sickly Polly. I craned my neck around the still smoking door jamb, peering expectantly toward the wall where the sideboard had stood supporting the family photographs. I was relieved to see it was still there. Smoke-blackened, almost obscured, tilting precariously into the yawning floor space. Wounded but still alive.

I'd only been there a short time but it seemed an age. I was still shocked and wanted answers.

Concerned I asked, "What's happened Sergeant Plackett? Where's Edith? Is she alright?"

My flurry of questions and abrupt tone took DS Plackett by surprise. He replied defensively, "Don't know yet what caused the blaze sir." Pointing to the Fire Officer standing nearby he continued, "Fire investigator's been here some time. May have something to tell us. Edith? Sheffield General - Intensive care. Touch and go at the moment Sir. A fireman's been injured as well. Not life threatening. Falling timbers. Ambulance's just taken him to Chesterfield RI."

That was bad news. Especially about Edith. Sorry to hear about her condition but my main concern was what she could tell me. I'd been relying on her to push my investigation along. But the job couldn't stop for Edith.

I said to Plackett, "Right, I'll have a word with the Fire Investigator." After a quick introduction I said, "I can see you're busy Chief but can you give me some idea of what's happened here?"

The fireman said, "I haven't come to a final conclusion yet Inspector but I suspect the fire was started deliberately. An accelerant may have been used in conjunction with an incendiary device."

I jumped in again, "My concern is Edith Oakley. She's a major player in an enquiry into the recent murder of her brother and it maybe that the incidents are connected. I'd like to have a look around if that's OK with you."

"That's alright with me Inspector," he said and began rummaging through a box of miscellaneous kit. He handed each of us a bright yellow safety helmet.

"You won't be in my way. Put these on and I'll be pleased show you the fire scene."

We donned the head gear.

Jonesy quipped, "Very becoming Sarge. You look like a big yellow daffodil."

Sergeant Plackett countered, "And you look like a big fat round daffodil bulb."

I was saved the embarrassment of a comment on my skid lid as we picked our way through the smoking ruins, with the fire investigator in tow. Forensic, police scenes of crime and other fire investigators would examine it in greater detail. With the fire out and the building made reasonably safe this was the opportunity for a cursory look over. I was gratified to see the most severe damage confined to the living room. That was good evidence that the fire brigade had responded very quickly to an emergency call. Their promptness had prevented a more serious outbreak developing. It was noticeable that inner doors had acted as fire barriers containing the inferno about its source. But charring and smoke damage was present in all the downstairs rooms. It was clearly a major fire. If it was arson, as the fire investigator was suggesting, then it was even more serious, attempted murder at least. If Edith died from her injuries murder pure and simple.

"I draw your attention to this, gentlemen."

Balancing with difficulty across scorched and blistered floor joists, we positioned ourselves as best we could to see what the fire officer was showing us.

"This is undoubtedly the seat of the fire," he said indicating an area to the left of the fireplace, where a gaping hole, four feet in diameter, yawned between the skeletal remains of still smouldering floor joists. He continued, "The severe damage to the timbered flooring indicates a concentrated heat source at this location. If you crumble some of the charred remains and sniff it..."

All three of us had pre-empted the fireman. We were already sniffing at the charcoal rubbed between palm and fingers.

"Petrol," I exclaimed.

"Yeh," said Plackett.

"Definitely," said Jonesy, making it a unanimous decision.

"Right gentlemen.Petrol. So unless petrol for some reason was stored at this location, it points to non-accidental cause."

I made a confident prediction. "It's arson chief," I said. "I was here recently and sat in a chair at that spot. There was no petrol. Edith doesn't drive and has never owned a vehicle. She wouldn't know how to operate a petrol pump. It's been brought into the house for a torching."

"Thanks Inspector. That's an important observation. I'll note it."

After quickly scribbling on his pad he pointed into the void beneath our feet.

"If you look carefully amongst the debris you can just make out the badly damaged edge and protective bars of an electric fire."

We stared into the dark hole.

"Yep. Got it. Next to that little whisp of smoke," crowed Jones triumphantly.

"Yes. I see it," I said.

"Me too boss," said Dave Plackett.

"Keep that foremost in your mind gentlemen as we go to the front room."

We followed the FIO making our way precariously to the far side door. It produced a Barnum and Bailey performance. Our troupe, in colourful head-gear, arms outstretched, toes pointing, balanced like high wire walkers picking our way along charred floor joists bridging the gaping spaces beneath us.

Pete Jones could not resist the temptation. He called out to his sergeant, "You look like that tightrope walker guy. Blondie."

The DS cracked back, "You mean Blondin you thicko. And you look like his bloody wheel barrow."

That amusing exchange caused me to falter and I nearly lost my footing.

With a grin still twitching at his lips, the fireman pushed open the front room door. Apart from slight smoke damage to the walls the room was intact. But, like me, Dave Plackett and Pete Jones were twitching their noses as we glanced about us.

"Strong isn't it gentlemen?" said the fireman who had noted our reaction.

We didn't have to answer. It was an obvious statement

that the FIO had made. A sickly, heady smell of petrol fumes hung heavy in the air.

He opened the front door to provide ventilation and commented, "You can see where the arsonist doused the room with accelerant. See the long finger-like stains spread out from the intended source. Classic telltale signs."

I was already down on my hands and knees to the left of the fireplace. Plackett and Jones joined me.

"Evil bastard!" DS Plackett spat out the expletive.

And I wasn't a happy bunny either. "More like murderous bastard Dave. If this had gone up the whole terrace would have been torched. We'd have filled a charnel house. Doesn't bear thinking about."

Jonesy voiced his opinion, "We're dealing with a psycho here boss. This isn't a normal criminal mind at work. This is Rampton, Broadmore material."

"Impressed, hey Inspector?" Not waiting for a reply, which he didn't really expect, the Fire Investigator continued, "Ingenious device isn't it? An electronic timer plugged into the mains, connected to an electric fire that's covered with cloths soaked in accelerant. And that's been set alongside those two large plastic containers. They appear to be full of accelerant, most likely petrol. Smells like it but it needs forensic to clarify that. Simple but effective. Set for the timer to click in at midnight and switch on the electric fire. The place would have gone up like a bomb. It's not activated because of a technical fault." He added as an afterthought, "This little lot 'may well end up in our Black Museum."

My mind was racing. I was aware that my words were coming out in short staccato-like bursts. "It's intact. Our man expected it to be destroyed in the fire. Hopefully it's not been wiped down. Fingerprints may get a crack at it. It looks new. It might be traceable. Could be a breakthrough."

A sudden thought chilled through me and I looked to the ceiling above.

The fireman saw my reaction. "Yes Inspector," he said. "Edith's bedroom. Straight above this lot. This was the main device. Meant to finish the job. Get rid of any evidence." He hesitated before adding, "and Edith."

I'd seen and heard enough. Turning to DS Plackett I ordered, "Get onto control. I want a couple of uniformed men here pronto. Secure the scene. Scenes of crime and forensic here pronto. Arrange for initial door-to-door. We might pick up on something. Get a CID officer over to Edith. If it really is bad we may get a dying declaration. I'll get over to see her as soon as we finish here. I'll arrange for this enquiry to run in tandem with ours. OK Dave? Are you happy with that?"

The DS nodded and replied, "Sure thing boss it'll be nice getting it together again. I'll get things moving."

The Fire Investigation Officer shook our hands as he prepared to leave. He commented that he had enjoyed his brief encounter with the travelling circus adding, "I thought the implications of that device would put some fire in your belly Inspector."

"Right Chief. But I'd prefer to shove a can of petrol up this nutter's arse and set fire to it."

The FIO grinned. He was still grinning as he boarded the fire appliance. Its swirling lights creating an illusion of the big top. I could imagine him visualising the performance of the gyrating pyromaniac, impaled upon my avenging flame.

*

"Do I really have to wear all this gear Sister? I feel like a reject from 'Emergency Ward Ten'"

"Come come Inspector. Don't be a bore. This is reality not a television soap opera. Anyone visiting Intensive Care must be properly attired in the interest of the patients."

I adjusted my face mask and muttered, "If the Fire Chief could see me he'd swear it was 'The Return of the Mummy'."

Eagle ears picked up on the comment. Admonishing me with a reproachful glare and declaring haughtily, "I can assure you he would not Inspector. There is no swearing on my ward."

Suitably rebuked and appropriately attired, I stood in front of the large viewing window, looking at Edith lying motionless on the special trolley-like cot. The word "lifeless" flashed through my mind. An oxygen mask hid her lower face. Bandages swathed her head. She was plugged in, wired up, stuck with tubes, strapped and surrounded by a myriad of devices, ticking, flashing, undulating and recording. All monitoring the patient's struggle to survive. Edith looked what she was. In a bad way.

"What's the prognosis Sister?" I asked, trying not to sound too pessimistic.

In that direct, professional way, peculiar to nursing sisters she intoned, "At the moment she appears to be holding her own but the next few hours are crucial. The doctor is keeping an eye on the head injury. Could be nasty, especially for a woman of her age. Thankfully she has a strong constitution. You won't be able to speak to her until she comes out of the coma. And even then it depends on her condition."

I was talking aloud to myself again, "Head injuries? What head injuries?" I pressed against the glass peering intently at the prone figure. My bent nose became even more misshapen under the pressure. I muttered, "Heavily bandaged about the head. No obvious burns. Injured in a fall?"

I turned to the Sister. She was busy at her desk. I asked, "What exactly is wrong with Edith?"

"Without being too technical Inspector, Edith has a suspected fractured skull, so there is a possibility of brain damage."

"Brain damage. From what?"

"I'm not the detective. That's your department Inspector. Suffice to say there is clear evidence of Edith being struck violently about the head with a blunt instrument." Consulting the notes before her she added, "Though there are no lasting effects from the fire, she is lucky to be alive."

I gave a final glance at the slight figure bound like an Egyptian mummy in the hospital cot and hurried from the place. Seeing Edith like that had really given me something to think about. As I drove back to Mansfield I considered the implications of the events so far. Almost forty years ago, PC Jarvis, a friend of the Oakley family, was battered to death. Two men, who may have been innocent, hanged for the crime. A woman kills her children and commits suicide. And now it's alleged the identity of the true killer has been hidden all these years beneath a conspiracy of silence. Then Tommy Oakley is battered to death with a blunt instrument and an unsuccessful attempt made to cover up the murder. And now another Oakley almost battered to death, again a blunt instrument and an unsuccessful attempt to destroy evidence of the crime by torching the crime scene. Added up, that's more than unusual, more than coincidence, it's a bloody massacre. And a killer is still out there.

TWENTY-SIX

THURSDAY EVENING

Evening debrief had been more wide ranging than usual. My report of developments at Langwith had upped the ante, elevated the enquiry onto a different plane. If Edith died the investigative teams had been left under no illusion that they would be hunting a double murderer. DS Plackett had been given the job of investigating the arson and attack on Edith, concentrating his team's effort in that area as part of the wider enquiry. I would oversee it whilst carrying out my original remit. Copies of the Constable Jarvis file had been made available to murder squad officers and were subject to frequent reference during regular briefings and updates. I'd trawled through it so many times that I almost knew it word perfect.

Without revealing too much to his investigating teams Detective Superintendent Davey highlighted a reassessment of the killer's profile. "You'll learn about it later but I have to tell you that as a result of certain information received, I now lean towards the theory that the murders of PC Jarvis and Tommy Oakley, as well as the attack on Edith Oakley, may well have been committed by the same offender."

A buzz of conversation filled the room. This was unexpected, a real U-turn. Those officers not in the know were keen to learn what brought about this change of attitude.

Mr Davey continued, "Let's calm down and get on with the business. I know what you're thinking but I'm not at liberty to disclose my reason for supporting the theory at this moment. Suffice to say that if the theory is correct, we are looking for a much older suspect than was envisaged. If he was active in the nineteen forties the killer could well be in his late fifties or sixties."

"That rules out this Sergeant Evans at HQ then Guv."

"Yes. At HQ he was able to pass himself off as a Detective Sergeant. That would put him in his late twenties or early thirties. We have no Detective Sergeants in their fifties and any older he would be retired from the force. Whoever this Sergeant Evans is and whatever his interest in the case, he doesn't fit in with this latest theory. He is too young. We are looking for an older man. That doesn't let Evans off the hook, however. Far from it. He maybe a recent accomplice aiding the killer. So we mustn't lose sight of him."

"How much reliance are we placing on this new theory Sir?" a team member asked.

"It's a theory. No more than that but it's one to be borne in mind as you do your door-to-door enquiries. It's not set in stone. So keep an open mind and remember that the next person that answers the door could be the killer. Eighteen or eighty, black or white, male or female. You're the detectives. You're out there. You know that gut feeling. I'm relying on you to get on with the job."

The detectives were still buzzing as they left the debrief room.

I could see that Superintendent Davey was in thoughtful mood as he prepared to discuss the new developments with his team leaders who had remained behind.

He got straight to the point. "Jim's latest information

307

causes me to re-evaluate our strategy gentlemen. Within the confines of this room we'll talk about the murder of PC Jarvis and its implications. And on that understanding I can tell you it's still my intention to hold back on the alleged miscarriage of justice."

Chief Inspector Mick Walsh looked concerned, "Is that wise Sir? If the press get hold of it they'll hang you out to dry. Allege you're suppressing evidence. A police cover up. It could cause a backlash and put you in the firing line. Damage you and the whole investigation."

"I thank you for your concern Mick but I've managed to survive a few below the belt all these years. I'm not so fast on my feet nowadays but I've picked up a bit of ringcraft on the way. This is a conscious decision that will be entered into the Policy Document, accessible to the Reviewing Body on completion of this investigation. I take full responsibility for not going public at this stage, or reporting it to a higher authority. Nothing can be gained and it may well prove counter-productive. That out of the way I'll hand you over to Jim Stirling."

I took a quick look round as Mr Davey took his seat. I could see he had won them all over. But the old battler was taking a big risk in the twilight of his career. If the brown stuff hit the fan his Super's crown and pension may well be splattered in an unsightly mess over more than the walls and ceiling.

I'd set myself up with a tall easel and a flip chart for the debrief. I've always found it helps to see things written down and what I had in mind lent itself to that concept. The governor had got everyone in the mood with his controversial theory spiel. Now it was up to me.

"OK." I said, "We've been looking for a motive for Tom's

murder and we haven't come up with anything concrete yet. So let's go through what we've got and see if we can't pull something out of the hat."

I centralised the chart and flipped to a clean sheet. In black felt tip I wrote in large letters: PC JARVIS.

"You've all had sight of the Jarvis file and have a good knowledge of the crime. I believe he's central to the enquiry."

Underneath I scrawled DURNLEY / WILSON and said, "If Fallows is to be believed they were not responsible for his death. Accepting that premise, who then killed the local bobby?"

There were no takers, plenty of concentrated frowns, studies of Rodin's thinker but no illuminating suggestions.

It was a disappointing response. "Come on lads get the old grey matter churning," I chided. "Who killed Jarvis?"

From the floor someone volunteered, "Other poachers? They seem likely candidates if we're eliminating Durnley and Wilson."

"Okay." I wrote POACHERS. "Anyone else?"

Detective Chief Inspector Mick Walsh, dark haired and dapper, shuffled on his seat. "I'm just throwing this in Jim, being devil's advocate if you like. Don't really believe it but you wanted something so ..."

"Get on with it Mick no need to prevaricate. Spit it out." I stood with pen poised.

"Alright. A policeman. One of those on duty with him."

The DCI's input certainly cranked up the audience. Simultaneous discussions sprang up around the room, some quite heated.

I had to bring them back. "Alright! Settle down, let's get on with it. Thanks Chief Inspector, that's lateral thinking at its best. A policeman. How come?"

Confident now, Walsh developed his theory. "Both Sergeant Smithurst and Constable Underwood had opportunity and means, knew where he was, Jarvis trusted them, wouldn't be suspicious."

"Thanks Mick but why? What's the motive?"

The silence said it all. I added POLICEMAN to the chart.

"No motive?" I asked. "We seem to have come to a dead end so we'll try and move it on." I felt like a caged tiger prowling about in front of the group as I sought to break out of the constraining grip of inertia that the enquiry was currently labouring under. I attempted to widen the scope of debate. Hoping to encourage my colleagues to come up with credible suggestions that would lead to a breakthrough.

"Supposing certain people, maybe poachers, even policemen, knew the killer. Perhaps aided him in some way, and kept quiet about it. What then?"

Pipe-smoking Harold Wilson look-alike Detective Inspector Alan Lacey offered, "They may be considered an accessory. An accessory after the fact to murder. Knowingly and voluntarily aiding the killer after the crime. If convicted they stood to be punished as a principal."

I said, "Thanks for that Al. An accessory after the fact. Possibly even before the fact. An accomplice would be facing a lot of bird. Even a death sentence. In the nineteen forties I suspect that would keep a few mouths shut. Especially if that mouth belonged to a respected member of the local community."

I developed the theme, "How would that affect somebody living in the community, day in day out, year in year out, quite a bit of baggage to lug about."

Superintendent Davey seated on the front row gave one

of his chugging train impersonations. "Ugh! Ugh! Ugh! Bit of a Lord Byron now hey Jim? That last bit rhymes. Ugh! Ugh! Ugh!" He wiped imaginary tears from his eyes and sat back.

After that brief injection of humour at my expense and the Superintendent's impression of The Rocket the debrief continued.

Mick Walsh fastened another link in the chain. "Going back to what you said Jim. I can see that person turning to drink, becoming a heavy drinker."

I nodded and wrote ACCOMPLICE/ACCESSORY/HEAVY DRINKER.

I suggested, "Hiding in the bottle?" and then asked, "You've read the file, who do you know who'd fit the bill?"

Like a choir on tune the whole group chorused, "Tommy Oakley."

"Interesting Gentlemen! Interesting!" TOMMY OAKLEY joined the other names on the chart.

"So if Tommy knew who had killed his friend why didn't he say something?"

Walsh was leading the group, "Fear Jim. Fear of the killer."

I boldly scrawled on the chart FEAR.

"Let's pursue that Mick. It's interesting. Who did Tommy Kelly Oakley, the White Hope, fear?"

No one answered.

"Not one name offered?" Again silence. "There's your answer Mick. Tommy feared no one. Nothing that walked or breathed. Unless his fear was directed somewhere else. What about loyalty?"

There was a consensus of agreement. LOYALTY sat aside the other key words. I drove the discussion on. "Who was Tommy loyal to? Who demanded and expected that loyalty from Tom?"

Alan Lacey came back, "His family, parents, brothers and sisters, loyal with a passion."

I wrote FAMILY LOYALTY.

Now the chart was beginning to look interesting. "So the presumption is that one of Tommy's family was the killer and that meant Tommy keeping his mouth shut. Agreed?"

They agreed. The chart was developing. I added OAKLEY FAMILY MEMBER.

"Let's look at those family members. Potential murderers. John Oakley? Too honest and open. Polly? Too frail. Jack? Away fighting a war. Ted killed in that war. Rita or Edith? No. They couldn't have inflicted such injuries. Who does that leave?"

Superintendent Davey, following each logical step, offered, "Tommy, Tommy himself."

I heard what the governor said but queried, "Tom's motive, Sir, for killing his friend?"

"I don't have one that fits your scenario Jim. But I can come up with one that covers PC Jarvis, Tommy and Edith. Care to hear it?"

"That's why we're hear sir. Brainstorming. You're in the chair."

If I prowled like a tiger, the Super lumbered like a grizzly. With spectacles in hand, head to one side, moustache bristling, he ambled across the floor.

"Let me remind you of verbal evidence brought by the prosecution at Durnley and Wilson's trial." Stopping in front of his audience he jabbed the air with his spectacles and declared vehemently, "Not denied by the defence gentlemen." He ambled on. "When Durnley's gang saw their

312

profits from poaching threatened by extra gamekeepers and police, Durnley suggested a solution. I'll paraphrase what he said, 'Constable Jarvis knows us all. If Jarvis is out there with his constabulary friends then it makes life difficult. We'll have our collars felt quicker'n you can say Jack Robinson. We'll have to box clever. See if we can't minimise the opposition. Get rid of the problem.'" Mister Davey paused in his delivery allowing the words to sink in. He continued, "When asked 'How do we do that Bade?' he replied, 'That's my worry Jess. That's my worry.' But it wasn't his worry gentlemen, as things transpired it was PC Jarvis's. Now! My proposition is this. Jarvis knew all the poachers. He was a tough character well able to give a good account of himself. The poachers for all their bravado weren't up to it. Remember what happened to Wilson in the Net and Ferret? He ended up flat on his arse and in a police cell. So what to do?"

Mr Davey surveyed his audience. We hung onto his every word, "Simple," he asserted. "Bring in someone unknown to the local police. Someone who would do the business for them. I suppose today we'd call him a 'hit man', carrying out a contract."

Now this was thinking outside the box. Radical stuff. I couldn't offer an acceptable alternative at that time but I was sceptical about the scenario he was presenting. A hit man? That was revolutionary in this neck of the woods.

I said, "I'm with you so far Sir but aren't they taking a chance bringing in a stranger? Likely to open his mouth some time, drop them all?"

"Maybe so Jim. But with a noose dangling in front of his nose, the killer had a very good reason for remaining tight-lipped. And let's face it. Whoever did it has kept his trap shut all these years and nobody's grassed him up."

"I'm still with you so far sir. Not too happy about an outsider. But it's interesting."

The Super said, "Fair enough Jim. This is what we want. Stimulate the old brain cells. Throw in some new ideas. Test them and put them under pressure. But for a moment just bear with me if you will."

I had no alternative but to bear with the old trooper. After all he was the boss and he had a track record in crime detection second to none. He got back into his stride.

"Enter The Fox. Detective Chief Superintendent Rawlings. Shrewd, ruthless, uncompromising. He'd clawed his way from the ranks to the top. Nothing allowed to stand in his way. The murder of Rod Jarvis was food and drink for such a character. At the outset his mind focussed on poachers as the killers. Sergeant Jack saw to that. Oblivious to all else he set about tailoring the evidence to convict Durnley, leader of the poacher gang, together with his lieutenant, Wilson. And we now know that Fallows played a key role in the plot. Get rid of the poachers. The scum. And clear up the murder of a policeman in one fell swoop. 'Reynard' Rawlings could end up Assistant Chief Constable. Even receive a knighthood." He paused for a moment's reflection before continuing. "Ah yes. The foul deed done. The convicted killers hanged. Durnley's family swept from the face of the earth. Things could return to normal. Normal? Never!" Superintendent Davey slammed a fist, hammer-like, into the palm of his hand. It was fascinating stuff. "With seven people murdered. And they were gentleman. As surely as if the killer had shot each one in the head, life for the conspirators could never return to normal. Or could it?"

A few raised eyebrows and muted conversations among the team did not go unnoticed by the speaker.

"No it's not a slip of the tongue gentlemen. I said conspirators. Plural. It fits in with the flow chart there." He pointed toward the spindly-legged easel. "The police killer melted away not to be heard of for nigh on forty years. But he was known. Durnley knew him, he recruited him. In my scenario he didn't keep it to himself. He confided in his close ally Wilson who in an act of bravado told Rita Oakley, with whom he was besotted. It was only a matter of time before Edith knew about it and she confided in her brother Tom. Conspirators, gentlemen, one and all. And they all kept their mouths shut. There. The circle is complete. Constable Jarvis, Durnley, Wilson, Rita, Edith, Tom."

Detective Superintendent Davey turned to me and said, "Nearly finished now just got to put the icing on the cake." Back with the group he said, "Motive! What then is the motive for our current spate of violent crime? I'll throw the question out to you."

Sucking on his empty pipe, DI Lacey provided an answer. "The motive? Tom's drunken mouth Sir. Couldn't keep it shut of late. Lost it. Gone over the top. Talking out of turn. And after all those years the hit man saw himself in danger. May have been in conversation with Tom. Learned that Edith also knew. From that moment Tom was a dead man. Edith next on the list. Rita of course didn't come into the equation; she'd been dead years. 'Owzat Sir?"

Mr Davey showed his approval by slowly clapping his hands as he declared, "Spot on! Middle stump Mister Lacey. And there you have it DI Stirling. For what it's worth. You can pick the bones out of it." The Grizzly Bear resumed his seat.

The governor's address had inspired the group. Everyone was engaged in huddled discussions. It was certainly an example of lateral thinking. I didn't want to stultify the team leaders' enthusiasm but I called them to order and addressed the Super.

"Sir, yours is an interesting proposition and Alan's input gives it some credibility. Your theory raises a number of points that I've been wrestling with but I don't feel totally comfortable with it. For example it may explain why Durnley and Wilson at their trial, if they were innocent, didn't throw the hit man to the wolves. Try and save their own necks. But then in the forties such an admission would have seen them convicted as accomplices and probably topped anyway. So they were relying on the defence's sleight of hand with Fallows and the alibi. But that went wrong. They were caught in their own trap."

Alan Lacey came in, "It could also explain Edith's anonymous caller and her being tight-lipped about him. He could be the hit man."

I did my tiger thing and prowled in front of my colleagues as I voiced my thoughts. "There are a number of questions still unanswered. We believe that Rawlings was the main man in the conspiracy which saw Durnley and Wilson hanged, but he's not about any more to answer for his actions. But what was Sergeant Jack's full role and where does Duggy Davis fit into this puzzle? What about the mysterious Sergeant Evans? Why would he want information about the post mortem of PC Jarvis? But the key question after all our surmising remains. Who is the hit man? Who is the killer? Maybe we're looking at more than one. The Super's theory is worthy of consideration, but having said that I still don't have that gut feeling for it."

The session concluded. We'd taken a change of direction and discussed some controversial issues tonight but there was still a lot to be done before we trapped our killer. Maybe that should be plural, killers, but trap him or them we will. The alternative is unacceptable, a likelihood of more horror and more body bags.

TWENTY-SEVEN

20th AUGUST
FRIDAY

Edith was still in a coma. Her Consultant would not commit himself one way or the other about her chances. He would only tell me she had suffered a severe trauma to the head and was lucky to be alive. He said she was a tough old bird and might come through it, then again she might not. Only time would tell. The Medic's indecisiveness frustrated me.

"Doctors and bloody lawyers. Nothing to choose between them. Tell you nothing. Hedge their bets if things aren't loaded in their favour."

The injured woman's condition, apart from anything else, presented me with operational problems. I voiced my frustration as I drove with Sergeant Johnson from the hospital to Langwith.

Time was a valued commodity during any investigation. Not being able to interview Edith in the foreseeable future ate into that precious resource. I was experienced enough to know that the longer the enquiry ran, the chances of a result became less likely. Time was running short, that critical phase fast approaching. We needed a break, some would say luck, but I always believed in making my own luck. In my book there are no free rides. No one gives anything away for nothing, there's always a pay off. That was my experience, my cynical perception of reality in a materialistic world.

As we drove past the old village green with its meandering stream, DS Johnson asked, "What's the next move boss?"

"Meeting Dave Plackett and Pete Jones in the Poachers Bar." I nodded towards the Net and Ferret on the other side of the humped-back bridge.

We pulled in behind the Divisional CID car parked outside and went into the Inn. Ducking under the low beam we made our way into the bar. Amos Jimson waddled over to greet us.

Johnson stared at the ponderous mound approaching. He winced when from perfectly formed cherubic lips, surrounded by heavy jowls, a falsetto voice piped, "Good day to you. And what'll be your poison gents?"

I returned the landlord's greeting. "Afternoon Amos, My friend will have a pint of bitter. I'll have a tot of rum."

DS Plackett and DC Jones, seated at a table in the window alcove, were the only customers in the bar. They raised their pint glasses in greeting. Jimson saw the gesture.

Thrusting a glass under the rum optic he asked, "Now what would a couple of newspaper men want with the local fuzz?"

"Intriguing hey Amos? Freedom of the press and all that. Give you something to think about."

We joined Dave Plackett and Pete Jones and after the initial handshakes I asked, "Any new developments Dave?"

"You'll know about Edith, boss. Just hope she pulls through."

We all nodded sympathetically.

Sergeant Plackett added, "I've arranged for twenty four hour police cover at the hospital just in case the attacker tries to finish the job."

"Good. Keep me updated on that but I can't see him trying anything unless it's certain she's going to make it. And I'm not too optimistic. What else have you got?"

DS Plackett rummaged through a black brief case and pulled out a folder.

"The Fire Investigator's report dropped on my desk this morning. You take the original Sir, I've got a copy."

I took it and flicked through the document. It was the standard layout with photographs, supporting and clarifying what we already knew.I passed the report to Sergeant Johnson. "Precise and to the point. Gives us a few lines to pursue."

DS Plackett pressed on. "I've had the exhibits dusted. The good news is there are marks." He must have seen the gleam in my eyes. He followed up with, "The bad news is they're not good enough for a search."

I shrugged and said, "Should have known better. Building up my hopes. My old bo'sun always said, 'The higher you climb the ratlines the further you're going to fall.' He was spot on. Where were the marks found?"

Plackett leafed through a sheaf of photographs.

"On the timer," he said, "This is a good shot of 'em." He handed it to me. Something I'd said must have flagged up in his mind because with a note of uncertainty in his voice he asked, "What's a ratline boss?"

I was surprised by the question. Not quite sure whether the Detective Sergeant was taking the Mickey.

I said, "A ratline? It's er, it's a rung on a rope ladder. Strung across the shrouds, mostly on sailing ships. For crew going aloft, climbing the rigging."

Dave was satisfied. "You live and learn every day boss," he declared.

I returned to the picture in my hand. I was looking

at a black and white photograph showing the timing device recovered from Edith's house. A partial fingerprint highlighted by black powder stood out against the white of the timer. There were other smudges littering it but this one looked promising.

I examined the print. "Unfortunate it doesn't have sufficient points to prove it. Still it could be helpful if we get somebody in. What about eliminations?"

"Got the firemen's. And when we trace them we'll take some from the shop assistants who sold them."

I stared at the photograph again and flicked it contemptuously. "When you think about it, this dab's worthless. On its own it's not worth fingers in the ink. They're a long shot really, could be anybody's."

Dave Plackett picked up on my pessimism. "This might change your mind Sir."

He handed me a further photograph. It was another black and white shot, this time of a plastic container. The familiar black powder again looped about the smooth surface of the screw cap.

Heeding my old bo'sun's advice I didn't rush to the ratlines, kept my feet firmly on the deck. My response was guarded. "Tell me about it."

"Do you want the good news or the bad news first?"

"You're getting boring Dave. Just give me the facts."

"OK boss. Fingerprints have lifted marks off a container cap. Like the one on the timing device it's not good enough for searching, but they're satisfied there are sufficient points of similarity to suggest they're from the same source."

I was already halfway up the rigging. "Well done fingerprints. Possible marks from the same source on two separate items? With a bit of luck and some more work it could turn up an ident."

I passed the photograph to Styx Johnson and spoke to Plackett.

"How are you getting on with tracing the timer and electric fires Dave?"

"Not there yet boss. We've turned nothing up at Langwith. We're doing Mansfield next. Could take a bit of time. Maybe get lucky if they're a joint purchase."

I nodded. "Will you want any help?"

Dave Plackett shook his head. "Don't think so boss. It's early days yet. I'll let you know if we do."

"Right keep at it. What about the petrol?"

"At the lab sir. They've confirmed it is petrol and not something that smells like it. There's plenty for control samples. They're analysing it then we can try and trace the source for additive comparison. Different petrol companies put different additives in their petrol so we can get a good idea what filling stations to concentrate on. And someone might remember a customer filling up a couple of plastic containers with petrol. It's a bit irregular."

"And the plastic containers? They could tell us a lot."

"In hand, boss."

"Point of entry. Anything there?"

"No chance Sir. Porch, ground floor doors, windows, totally destroyed."

As he spoke Sergeant Plackett was handed more photographs by DC Jones. He glanced at them before handing one to me.

"This is interesting Sir."

I took it from him. It was interesting. I said with some enthusiasm, "Mmm. Shoe impressions."

"Boot actually boss. Sufficient for search. The lab is comparing the photos with their footwear collection. They're quite upbeat about getting a match."

"Where were they found?"

"That one's on the stairs." He shuffled through the photographs. "This one at the bottom of the garden."

I took the picture. I was encouraged. "Casts?"

"Yes sir. Scenes of Crime have taken a couple."

"Good. That's a positive piece of evidence. Keep on top of it."

"Door to door. Anything there?"

Pete Jones took over, his style slow and deliberate.

"Nothing concrete boss," he drawled, "but interesting. Next door neighbour heard a vehicle round about midnight. On the service road. Thought it strange. It's all pot holes. Hardly used at night. Looked out the bedroom window. Saw a vehicle outside Edith's gate. Couldn't make it out. Didn't see anybody. Didn't see the driver." The detective Constable took a pull on his beer.

I waited.

Jonesey, unhurried, continued, "Waited up, kept a lookout just in case. That's when he saw it." He stopped for another pull on his pint.

I was getting impatient. I said, "Go on then. Saw what?"

"A figure. All in black. Slinking down Edith's garden path. Something covering his head and face."

"How did he know that?"

"The figure kept looking back and he saw the white flash around his eyes and mouth. As if he was wearing a mask or a balaclava."

"Don't suppose he knew who it was?"

"No boss. No miracles today. But he watched him go

to the car. Threw what looked like a big bag onto the front passenger seat. Got in and drove off. No lights."

"Did he report it?"

"Not at that time. Didn't think the police would be interested in a prowler. Got nothing to give 'em. No names or vehicle numbers. He'd be well gone before they arrived. Saw it as a waste of time."

"Who reported the fire?"

"The same neighbour boss. A bit later. Heard a bang. Quite loud. Said it was like a shotgun going off. Thought it came from next door. Oakley's."

"Did he go and look?"

"No. He thought about the man in black. Thought he might have returned. He was scared. Opened the window and looked out but couldn't see anything. Then he saw lights flickering on the yard through next door's porch and living room windows. Then another bang. Flames gushed out of the window, up the walls."

"Did he go down then?"

"Yes. Got his missus out of the front door then ran dialled 999 and ran round the back. By that time other neighbours were there but nobody could do anything, the fire was too fierce. Fire brigade were on the ball. Got there pretty quick."

"Yeh. A good all round job from them," I said. "Shame they have to smash everything up. Water, hatchets and big boots aren't exactly conducive to protecting evidence at a crime scene. But then they have different priorities. Anything on the offender's route?"

"We've collected samples from the garden where he appears to have trodden on the soil just off the path. The impression's no good but it's been photographed."

DC Jones handed me another couple of black and white prints. He continued, "Grounds damp at the bottom of the garden where it meets the ash path. Got a few nice shots of sole impressions and a reasonable cast."

"Good. They look like boots. What about the vehicle? Anything there?"

"Just getting round to that boss." More photographs were passed over. "Great shots of tyre tracks. And we've got some excellent casts. Being analysed at the lab. May come up with a make and size, even wheel base dimensions. Could take a stab at the type of vehicle. In any case it'll be good evidence if we come up with a suspect motor."

Throughout the session Amos Jimson had been watching us, his natural curiosity controlled with great difficulty. Finally his resolve broke. Incarcerated somewhere deep within that fleshy mass I suspect the real Amos existed. I guess he's eager to know what the conspirators in his bar were about. Steering his mountainous prison to our table, breathing heavily, his eyes flicking over the documents spread about, he purred, "Everything all right gentlemen?"

"Yes thanks Amos. That'll do for the moment. I'll call if we want you."

The landlord made his way ponderously to the bar reminding me of the enormous male sea elephants I'd seen at South Georgia so many years ago.

Business finished, I ordered, "Get that lot actioned Dave and into the system. Chase up all those loose ends and keep me informed. I'll leave it up to you to keep an eye on Edith and let me know the score."

"Right boss." He stood up. "We've got plenty to do. Haven't got time for another."

Having bid their good-byes they left. Jimson trundled

over. Not overly happy with his diminishing profits. That soon changed.

"Will you join us landlord?" I indicated the empty window seat.

Amos Jimson perked up instantly. "Surely gentlemen," he squeaked, "It'll be a pleasure."

For a man of such bulk he manoeuvred around chairs and between tables with remarkable dexterity. As the landlord plumped himself onto the complaining cushions I was reminded of a deflating barrage balloon.

It was an opportune time to take advantage of the moment and probe a little, test out this man mountain. See if he was going to be easy to open up, talk about the things I was interested in.

"You've heard about Fallows then Amos?" I said.

"Jess? Aye. Him getting locked up as cut off me supply of meat. Costing me a fortune wi' new suppliers. Ya know what I mean?" He winked.

I gave an understanding nod and moved the conversation on. "How did Jess get on with Tommy Oakley? Were they friends?"

"Friends? Oh aye. When they were younger, when we were all younger, they were thick as thieves as ya might say. Tom got on wi' Bade Durnley and Calver Wilson. Went out wi' 'em many a night. Loved't excitement ya know. Weren't bothered about money. Easy come easy go wi' Tommy."

"Interesting. But I've been told that there was bad blood between them?"

Amos thought for a moment then answered, "That come later. Tommy were still faightin.' Had a bit of bust up with Jess. I remember Sergeant Jack were there. It were in this very bar." He pointed towards the large open fireplace. "Just

326

there. In front oft' hearth. Tommy knocked Jess flat with one punch. Straight on his nose. Broke it. Made a right mess on it. Well you've seen it."

So that's how he'd got his. I visualised Fallows's splodge of a nose. "What was that all about?" I asked.

"Didn't have to be much wi' Tommy ya know. No sooner a word than a blow. Anybody as said owt were likely to get flattened."

"So I understand. What was the problem with Jess?"

Amos scratched his head and wiped a podgy hand over his leaking face. He squeaked, "As I recollect it were about Rita, Tom's sister ya know. A bit of alraight. But ya didn't say that while Tom were about. Jess learned that lesson too late. Said he'd sooner be int' woods wi' her than Tommy. Bump. Crash. That were it. All over. Jess come to in't fire grate. Blood everywhere. Sergeant Jack had to drag Tommy off. He'd a killed him."

"And they never got on after that?"

"That's right mester. Never got on no more."

"Why was Sergeant Jack there with the gang?"

"Now that'd be tellin' wun't it?" Amos eased his frame against the complaining seat. He lolled back with arms folded atop of his huge belly, a smug look slopped across his face.

I read his signal. "Would you like a drink Amos? It's very remiss of me not to have invited you before but I'm intrigued with your stories."

"Thanks very much sir. Don't mind if I do. I'll call the gel she'll see to us."

His voice piped across the room. Amos obviously ran a tight ship because "the gel" responded faster than an Admiral's pinnace. Drinks ordered, I probed deeper.

"You were telling me why Sergeant Smithurst was with Durnley's bunch."

"Was I? I don't recall we'd got that far mester. But if yer askin', now you're int' chair I'll be tellin'. Jack were a poacher himsen. Now ya didn't know that did ya? No I can tell by ya face ya dint' but it's true me duck. Jack had been a poacher sin' he were a lad. Wi' Bade and Jess and allt' others." Comfortable now with me as his newly acquired paymaster, Amos was in full flow. He adjusted his position. I waited. "Now don't get me wrong. Jack didn't go out poaching with Durnley while he were bobbying but he let 'em get away wi' murder."

"Murder, Amos?"

"Only a figure of speech like. Nowt to do wi' Constable Jarvis's job. Not like that any how." The big man shuffled uncomfortably in his seat.

I saw the danger. I had to carry out a bit of damage limitation. Amos was beginning to think. That was the last thing I wanted. The mound with his brain switched on.

"Yes I understand Amos. Only a figure of speech. It must have been quite a time for you when PC Jarvis was killed. Going to court. Giving evidence. Talking about your suppliers, customers, your friends."

There was no immediate response to my observation as "the gel" arrived with a tray of drinks. She wasn't so much a "gel" as a sour faced, scrawny woman of indeterminate age, hardly strong enough to carry the orders never mind hand them out.

We needed to keep Amos on board. Things were getting interesting. The old landlord knew more than I had imagined. Had to keep his confidence, unlock his closed mind. It was on occasions like this that I enlisted the wisdom of my old ancient mariner. My old bo'sun often advised, "Don't always steer the expected course, sometimes sailin' three sheets to the wind is wiser than being fully rigged."

This was such an occasion. Heeding the advice I intended sailing three sheets to the wind, acting out the role of village idiot. In the past I'd found that presenting a smiling face and vagueness to the opposition about the subject under discussion, often caused them to adopt an accommodating attitude towards me. My perceived pathos made them feel superior, which was my intention And that often led to their downfall.

Amos had already siphoned three quarters of his pint into that huge silo of a body. It looked like being an expensive afternoon. I returned quickly to the subject of Sergeant Jack Smithurst and said, "So Sergeant Jack gave the poachers an easy ride?"

"Ya might say. S'long as they din't cause no problems in't village and M'lord din't kick up too much"

"Then why were the local constabulary out in the woods the night PC Jarvis was killed?"

"That's it ya see. When His Lordship complained tut Chief Constable Jack had to make a show on it."

"How do you mean, Amos?"

Amos seemed to be enjoying his role, sitting back in the chair, lording it, showing us stupid townies a thing or two.

"Well, Jack tipped 'em off din't 'e? Told Bade when they'd be on duty and where they'd be. Bade'ud make sure they was out of the way. Jack could have a quiet night. No problems and he'd done enough to satisfy Chief Constable and got a few brace in't bargain."

This was new and important information; my heartbeat increased significantly. I could see by the glance from Styx Johnson that he was in the same boat. Having read the Jarvis file from cover to cover on a number of occasions I knew there was nothing in the file about it. Jimson was alleging that

Durnley knew the location of Constable Jarvis on the fateful night. If it were true, that would be compelling evidence to put him in the frame for the murder. Either as the principle or as an accessory in accordance with Superintendent Davey's hit man theory. In any case the defence would strive to keep that evidence from a jury. It flashed across my mind that maybe I'd jumped the gun and that there may not have been a miscarriage of justice after all.

I needed to test the strength of the new information. In village bumpkin mode I said casually, "It's easy to make that assumption Amos, talk's cheap. How do you know Jack Smithurst tipped Bade off?"

Jimson's beady eyes bulged, a fair impression of golf balls plugged in a bunker, and his voice leapt an octave.

"I'm not a liar mester. An I'll thank you not to make me out one."

I'd pressed the right button. "I'm not calling you a liar Amos but you can't go about repeating gossip and rumour as if it's the truth," I said.

"Gossip? Rumour? Who said owt about gossip and rumour? It's God's honest truth." Amos Jimson banged the table to emphasis his point.

I pressed on. "How can you say that? Were you there?"

"Course I was there. One a two was there. Me, Durnley, Wilson, Fallows, Sergeant Jack."

"And Sergeant Jack openly revealed where he and his officers would be on that night?"

Jimson was becoming exasperated. He emptied his glass and looked at me pityingly. "Oh dear mester! Jack weren't nobody's fool. He was a cunning old sod. Still is. He din't want everybody to know his business. He took Bade to one side and told him. Private like."

"If it was 'private like' how did you know about it?"

"It's my pub int it? I know where to be and hear what I want to hear, wi' out causing offence. Alraight?"

"Right Amos. Right. And what did you hear?"

Jimson made a play of draining the dregs from his empty glass before thumping it down upon the table. The demonstrative hint did not go unnoticed.

"Would you like another, Amos?" volunteered Sgt. Johnson.

"That'd be kind of you mester. I'll have same again."

Styx took Jimson's glass and went to the bar. He'd recognised the signs and meant to keep Amos on track. Allow me to get into him without too many distractions.

I continued," What did you say you heard Amos?"

"I din't. Not yet anyhow. An' it's a long time ago. I can't remember all what were said but it sticks in me mind that he told Durnley they'd be out at night in Scarcliffe Park. He'd be down't lake, Mester Jarvis at Spinney and Mester Underwood at Old Mill end."

"Was that on the night of the murder?"

Amos thought for a moment. "No. It were just afore that. But it weren't unusual though, Constabulary had a few night patrols like. They were for show. Sometimes they'd ketch somebody but they were small fry, not Bade's men. Made it look good for Headquarters."

"After such a long time you may be getting the patrols mixed up."

"Gi' me credit for some intelligence mester." Sweat stood out upon Jimson's florid features, his tiny eyes flashed in their fleshy sockets.

"How do I know you're not mistaken?" I chided, "You've never mentioned it before,"

Wiping his brow with a sodden handkerchief he pushed his bulk forward, great belly flopping onto his thighs. With spirited defiance, out of character for the big man, he came back at me.

"I never mentioned it afore 'cos no bugger asked about it. An' I remember it 'cos it were't time after Calver had a run in with Constable Jarvis." He pointed past me, "There," he said. "in front tut fireplace. Same spot as Tommy done Jess. An it were last time Durnley sat wi' his gang afore't Constable were killed. Does that satisfy yer?"

I was satisfied. I'd read about Wilson being arrested by PC Jarvis in the Net and Ferret during my research at the library and it was referred to in the murder trial papers back in my office. The gut feeling was right. Jimson had made his point and gone a long way towards convincing me. Johnson returned and put a glass in front of Amos. We watched as the landlord took a huge swallow from his new pint.

It was a good moment. I caught him off guard. I said pointedly, "Amos. Who killed Constable Jarvis?"

The spluttering, followed by beer spilled over the wobbling gut, told me I'd struck a mark. The beady eyes narrowed. Jimson went on the defensive as he wiped himself down with those stumpy, podgy fingers and his wringing wet handkerchief.

"Wot ya on about? Are ya daft or summat? Everybody knows who killed him."

"Tell me then Amos. You've already told me things I didn't know. Maybe you can keep surprising me."

"Surprise ya? Its no surprise. They were hanged for it." He emptied the remaining contents of his glass and muttered, "an' good riddance I say."

"You surprise me Amos, you really do. I got the feeling

332

that you were big buddies of Bade Durnley and Calver Wilson. Now what brought about the change?"

It was back to the big boy image. Billy Bunter with downcast eyes and sullen expression, Amos Jimson had suddenly run out of steam. Or perhaps I'd delivered a low blow, knocked some of the fight out of him.

He replied sullenly, "Nowt changed me mind."

He was squirming now. I notched up the rack. I took control. "Let's see if I can help you Amos. Bade and his pals were all good payers. Is that right?"

Head down he muttered, "Aye."

"And you had a thriving business thanks to them, even during the bad old thirties, plenty of game, good living."

"Aye."

I stuck in the knife. "So why did you give evidence that helped hang them?

Jimson became agitated. He squeezed and twisted his chubby hands, not daring to look in my direction. He had to get away. The big man made a move to raise his huge frame from the window seat. It had become the hot seat.

I ordered sharply, "Sit down!"

I could see the fear etched into that flab of a face that looked as though it would drown in the rivulets of sweat that rolled down from his forehead. Amos Jimson was a worried man. The village idiot had suddenly become the town Marshall.

I twisted the dagger deeper into Jimson's troubled soul. "Was it to do with, The Fox?" I lingered on the name. Letting it sink in, stirring up distant unwanted memories. "Did he advise you where your future lay? Threaten you?" I emphasised the final words.

Amos kept his head low and did not reply but shifted his ponderous bulk on the seat.

I probed deeper with that ice cold, twisting blade. "He told you that if you didn't go along with him, provide him with information and give evidence at the trial you'd lose your licence, your livelihood."

Still no reply.

"That's it Amos. You're part of the conspiracy, another of the Langwith upright citizens' brigade. All as corrupt as each other. Help hang two innocent men and destroy their families. So you can sit back and enjoy comfy cosy life styles. Living a lie."

That final thrust, the *coup de grace*, brought Amos Jimson down. He flopped forward onto the table, head heavy upon his arms.

He sobbed, "I'm sorry. I'm sorry. But I don't know who killed Mester Jarvis." Then he pleaded, "Believe me."

I stood up and indicated to Sgt. Johnson that we were leaving. I said to Jimson, "Believe you? Why should I believe you? It doesn't end here. You know the truth. I'll be seeing you again Jimson."

I tossed my calling card down onto the blubbering heap. Reading it would be the last straw. The knife striking home, up to the hilt.

The high pitched scream of despair reached us as we went to our vehicle. Jimson had clearly picked up my card. He now knew who had been asking the questions and why.

I gave a nod of satisfaction emphasising my tight-lipped smile and said to Sgt Johnson, "That's put the cat among the pigeons Styx. Might see a bit of movement now."

*

On the drive back to Mansfield no one spoke for some time. An unsuspecting onlooker may have misread the drawn-out silence, but it wasn't unusual. Sgt. Johnson and I were alone with our thoughts. I was pre-occupied with the new developments in the PC Jarvis case. They troubled me.

I broke the silence. "We can't leave it like it is. We've got to do something about it."

Johnson needed no further explanation for my outburst. He understood and said, "It's a long time ago boss. Maybe best to let sleeping dogs lie. We can't turn the clock back."

"That's the easy way out Styx. If what we've been told is true we're duty bound to try and right a terrible wrong."

Johnson, cynical as ever, replied, "Nobody'll thank you for resurrecting it boss. Bent coppers, corrupt lawyers, perjured witnesses. Innocent men hanged. A family destroyed. The press'll make a fucking meal out of it. TV'll do a documentary. You can just see the headlines, 'Public Need to Know' 'Right and Injustice,' when they don't really give a shit. Sales and viewing figures, that's the Holy Grail. Bottom line, pounds shillings and pence, and power."

I couldn't fault his logic. He was dead right. The media and the lawyers would jump on the bandwagon. Delight in pillorying a copper or two. They'd preach about justice and truth. Then when it suited them they'd abuse that power and squeeze the life out of it with a grip of iron. And the shekels would keep rolling in. And it rankled all the more because it was the sort of activity that Constable Andy McLean had been hammering on about. Police corruption and false evidence.

I was in a grip of iron. Something I couldn't explain. Never felt like it before. I felt driven to right a wrong, gripped with the urge to do more than simply offer lip service. I don't see myself as a moralist or do gooder as I slip and slide in the cess pit of degradation that humanity wallows in. But I believe that striving to keep the lid on life's garbage bin earns me the right to speak out.

"Think of that woman and those little kids. Somebody's got to do something, even if it's simply to let them lay together in a consecrated grave."

That was the end of the speeches. Two troubled minds returned to their contemplative silence as we drove to the nick.

*

It wasn't expected but I was pleasantly surprised to see that whilst I'd been away MacLean had dealt with most of my mail. He was up for a few brownie points. He's not a bad organiser, probably due to his bank training. That'll stand him in good stead on the job. He'll need to be an organiser if he's accepted on CID. But he'll have to get rid of the attitude and that chip off his shoulder. If he doesn't he'll end up lugging a bloody great tree trunk on his back. And that could be a distinct disadvantage in the department.

Superintendent Davey had been definitely upbeat over the potential of the forensic evidence. However his spectacles took a bit of a beating as he nibbled on them whilst taking in the new information from Amos Jimson. He listened with professional interest to what I had to say but didn't intend to allow the current murder investigation to be diverted from its set course. The Old Bear was not going to allow any of his officers, including me, to embark on what he saw, as an unnecessary time wasting crusade. There was a time for that in the future.

With chewed up spectacles safely back in place after a

336

final adjustment, and looking once again like a stern old schoolmaster, he said to me, "I've never known you so affected by a case Jim."

"Never known it myself Guv but for some reason it's got to me. It's the tragedy of the woman and those kids."

"You know better than most that at times you have to detach yourself from personal emotions. If you don't you can lose sight of the real priorities. Can be unhealthy, likely to cloud your judgement and result in disaster."

I knew what he was saying and that he was probably right but I wanted to explain my feelings. "I've never been an emotional man Guv, that's what's strange about it. I was brought up to see emotion as weakness, something to be kept under wraps. Not for public viewing. Now it's driving me, broadening the agenda."

But clearly Superintendent Davey could not countenance a broadening of the agenda. He made his position clear to me.

"I'll remind you, Jim, that the object of this enquiry is to identify and arrest the killer of Tommy Oakley. That's our first priority. Then the attacker of Edith, and finally the killer of PC Jarvis, that's the order of priorities. That's the agenda. At the moment alleged miscarriages of justice draw a low priority. Alright?" It was not a question, it was an order.

The old bo'sun had proved right again. It was a long drop to the deck and I'd landed with a thump but if nothing else I was a professional. Catching the killer was top priority, any other business could wait. It had waited for nearly forty years.

"No problem Guv," I said." We'll stick to the agenda."

"Good. I knew we'd see eye to eye. If we're going to assure the public of our impartiality we've got to remain focussed."

As the Detective Superintendent turned to leave he said, "Keep up the good work Jim, I'm relying on you."

I appreciated the support but I had something else on my mind. "Before you go Guv I'd like to have a word about Edith. I'm a bit concerned about her."

*

I had a lot on my mind, what with Edith and the Durnley development. I was a little happier now about Edith but still disturbed by what I'd learned of the manoeuvrings during the Durnley/ Wilson trial. At home, even as I lolled in my favourite chair, glowing in the comfort of a tot of Nelson's blood, with Mitzi nuzzling into my neck, it continued to nag away at me. But visualising the black-haired Megan Durnley and her young children, desperate and alone in the pouring rain, leaping in despair into the swirling depths of that unforgiving river, tightened that iron grip inside. Urging me to do something to help right a wrong. Rolling the tot glass between my hands I took a decision to do something, anything, without jeopardizing the enquiry. It came as no surprise that during restless sleep that night a dream rolled over me. I saw Megan Durnley with a baby clasped to her breast, floating above a long stone bridge with other children clinging to her skirts. For a moment they turned and looked at me through round, featureless eyes before plunging through smoke-like mists to disappear as swiftly as they had appeared. I had to do something.

TWENTY-EIGHT

21st AUGUST
MORNING

I'd brought McLean to the Coroner's Inquest to give him some idea of the procedure and what to expect in the future if he was to make it into CID. The small court room was almost empty. Her Majesty's Coroner for Nottinghamshire pored over the depositions of the few witnesses in attendance. Other Court Officials sat in silence watching and listening to the brief evidence. This morning's court was sitting to establish the identity of the body found on the railway sidings at Mansfield. The chain of evidence proving identity was supplied by the next of kin, police officers and the Home Office Pathologist. With identity established, the Coroner further ordered that the body of Thomas Oakley remain in his custody and control until he authorised its release. The court was then adjourned *sine die*.

McLean was obviously not impressed by the proceedings we had just sat through. He complained, "What a total waste of time boss."

I wasn't impressed either. But I had no complaint about the Coroner or the court proceedings. They had dealt with the issue of identity of the deceased in a proper and respectful manner. No, it was McLean and his attitude. In response to his banal comment I said, "Tell that to the Coroner. He'll bite your balls off."

He came straight back. "What was the point of it? We've not learned anything we didn't know. The deceased is Tom Oakley and the body stays put until the Coroner orders its release."

"What did you expect to learn? " I said sarcastically, "Who killed Tommy?"

"I expected some indication in that direction."

"Did you now? And where's the Coroner going to get hold of such information?"

"I don't really know, but isn't that his function, to decide who killed Tommy?"

"You amaze me at times Andy. Don't they teach you anything at Training School? Didn't you learn the acronym VUS?"

"VUS?"

"Violent, Unnatural or Suspicious."

"Violent, unnatural or suspicious what?"

"Deaths! The Coroner, remember? That's his main function. To hear evidence and decide on a cause of violent, unnatural or suspicious death, not who's responsible. That's for others to resolve though he can make recommendations. Alright? Oh! and he inquires into treasure trove but that doesn't concern us today."

But McLean is McLean and he isn't happy. He intends to have his say. I let him get on with it.

"It still seems a waste of time."

There he goes again. That chip's growing. I gritted my teeth. McLean was getting on my nerves. I intend to have *my* say.

"PC McLean you're a pain in the arse. It's about time you got rid of that chip on your shoulder."

He still hadn't learned. He came straight back at me.

"There's no need to get personal Inspector. I am entitled to my opinion."

I was getting a bit fed up with his whingeing. So I gave him both barrels.

"What you're entitled to do is listen and learn and keep your big mouth shut. You might have been something in the bank but you've decided you want to be a copper and you're right at the bottom of the heap at the moment. And the way you're going that's where you're going to stay. You obviously don't know, but the office of *custos placitorum coronas*, The Keeper of the pleas of the Crown, the Coroner to you and me, has been around since 1194 and it's worked very well since then thank you. Now get off your high horse and let's get some work done. If that's alright with you?"

He didn't respond to my remarks. I stopped outside the Coroner's enquiry office and said brusquely, "I'm going in here. Wait at the car."

Without acknowledging the order he strode off with an undisguised show of pique.

It was some twenty minutes later when I returned to the CID vehicle. McLean stood at the driver's door watching me approach.

I was about to open the passenger door when he said, "Sorry about that Sir. I was out of order. I'll take your advice and think before I speak in future."

I looked across at him, "No need to be sorry. Just loosen up a bit. Relax. Don't be so confrontational." I eased myself into the front passenger seat. "Let's forget it. We're going to Lincoln, a bit of a job there."

As we drove towards Newark picking up the Lincoln road the silence within the vehicle was strained. A different silence to that shared with Styx Johnson. Neither of us wanted to be

341

the first to start a conversation. We had nothing in common to talk about. But I couldn't allow it to go on. Somebody had to be grown up about it. It was my turn to be contrite but I'd do it like Frank Sinatra. My way.

"I want to check out a cemetery in the town and later on another near Langwith," I said.

"To do with the investigation boss?"

I replied, "Yes. The Jarvis murder." McLean had quickly cast off the cloak of petulance. He appeared almost friendly. I can't fathom him out. Up and down like a bloody yo-yo.

He turned his head quickly toward me and said, "Something interesting?"

The strident scream of an oncoming vehicle's horn caused me to grip the seat with both hands as McLean swung the CID car back on line.

I snapped at him, "Keep your eyes on the road or we'll never live to find out."

Cool as you like he replied, "No problem boss. All under control."

It wasn't my intention to explain to McLean why I was showing so much interest in the Jarvis case but after more miles of embarrassing silence I said, "You'll hear soon enough but it seems likely that Durnley and Wilson didn't kill Constable Jarvis."

Once again it was the unexpected. McLean's reaction to the news was to suddenly hit the brake throwing me forward against my seat belt. It was only a momentary inconvenience – a split second thing – and he kept the car under control and eyes on the road as he drove on. But he's so unpredictable.

I made no comment about what appeared to be the driver's involuntary action but said, "So it seems you were right."

McLean appeared unconcerned as he replied, "About what Sir?"

"Corrupt police officers. Remember our heated exchange in the Locomotive?"

"Yes sir."

"It's looking likely that a couple of police officers gave perjured evidence at the trial and two innocent men were hanged."

He didn't answer immediately but when he did a note of sarcasm wrapped in not a little triumphalism tinged his reply.

"Old fashioned justice sir. Hang 'em high mentality. Hang anybody to satisfy the system and the public's bloodlust. Leave the real killer on the loose to kill again. British Justice? It stinks!"

I ran a finger over my scarred nose and said quizzically, "That's a turn up. I recollect that you supported the adversarial system. Lawyers tilting at the lists. Us against Them. Games played under rules created by lawyers. You were wavering on the justice versus truth issue."

"I've been converted Sir. I'm convinced that seeking the truth is paramount in achieving justice, and the Courts must ensure proper punishment of the offender. Anything less is immoral."

"And when that fails?"

"Then the law of the jungle prevails. An eye for an eye. Survival of the fittest."

"Anarchy? Revenge?"

"Call it what you like boss. Call it True Justice."

I wasn't too happy with much of the Constable's diatribe and said, "I don't think we're exactly on the same wave length but I can go along with some of your comments." I moved the conversation on, "Superintendent Davey is suggesting a hit man may have been involved."

With undisguised sarcasm McLean mocked, "A hit man? I like that. Who's he put up, Al Capone, Babe Ruth or Rocky Marciano? They were all big hitters."

The man was making my hackles rise again. He had the innate tendency to ruffle my feathers.

I said, "I don't appreciate such banal comments Mister McLean. I expect considered replies, perhaps debate, from an officer wanting to become a detective, a contribution, not sarcastic rhetoric. Sarcasm is the currency of a bankrupt mind and I don't recommend such a base commodity for CID."

The CID aide replied flippantly, "Is that your last word Sir?"

"No PC McLean. My last word's a piece of advice. See the Police Surgeon. You might need help."

Surprisingly he didn't respond. The rest of the journey continued in uncomfortable silence.

I left McLean with the vehicle in the car park of the cemetery in the Parish of St. Peter. The weather at the start of the day had been bright but now had turned dull, even a threat of rain in the air. I made my way to the older part of the burial ground, passing the more recent graves. They were generally neat and tidy, gold lettering bold and bright on headstones as yet unworried by time and inclement weather. Many were wreathed with bright flowers in cellophane wrappers. Or fading floral beauty drooped in marble pots *in memoriam*. As I wandered between rows of graves I saw time-worn monuments, broken columns and headless angels tilting at cock eyed angles. And there were headstones leaning into broken graves partially submerged like stricken ships plunging into the timeless earth. And once proud tombs collapsed and shattered, open to the ravages of man and beast. Now simply dumps for discarded beer cans, cigarette packets and a mass of other rubbish. The debris of the living, abandoned as surely as the debris of the dead.

It wasn't difficult to locate the stones I sought. The Reaper had conspired to cut down the living and they lay conveniently in date order in his burial ground. I looked down at the two grey square slabs, no larger than a family Bible, pressed flat into the earth, bearing only the initials and year of death of those hidden beneath. I stood in silence looking down at all that remained of a vibrant Romany mother and her children, snatched from the promise of life, to die unfulfilled in the freezing waters of a nearby river. I knew that Megan Durnley had called me to this place. Called me to show how man's knot of Justice had not only hanged Bade Durnley but killed his family. It buried them deep in this un-consecrated plot hidden behind Yew hedges away from living eyes, so as not to offend them. The knot tightened in my belly.

Squatting to scrape away the lichen, creeping wilfully to obliterate the roughly carved barely discernable initials 'MD 1946' I felt the urge to reach down into that inglorious earth. The cipher revealed graphically the anonymity of Megan Durnley and her family in death, as they had been in life. More of life's abandoned dross discarded in the convenience of death. I lingered for a while scraping and scratching at the stones with a piece of broken marble from a nearby ancient grave, cleaning them as best I could. After trying to bring them back from the shadows into the light, I finally left, knowing I would return.

Then the rain came. I hurried through the first sudden

shower, gaining safety in the car as the downpour followed. A thousand tiny fingers drummed on the roof and a thousand rain drops burst and splattered upon the bonnet. The windscreen wipers sweeping from side to side frantically tried to stave off the deluge.

"Just made it boss. Looks like a real cloud burst."

My response was a grunt, neither one thing nor another. At that moment I didn't feel inclined to engage in small talk, or any other talk for that matter, with Constable McLean. It was clear that he was not yet ready for the CID, and with other things on my mind I couldn't be bothered to guess whether I would be talking to Doctor Jekyll McLean or Mister Hyde McLean.

It was the Doctor personality which spoke, "Was your visit productive Sir?"

My response? Another grunt. Jekyll took the hint.

During the drive to Langwith I closed my eyes and leaned back in the seat taking advantage of the silence. Snatches of evidence cascaded into my head, tumbling through my mind. Dave Plackett is on top of his end. Forensic is likely to come up with something. The laboratory will soon be coming back with a result on the fibres found on Tommy's trousers. And then there's Sergeant Jack and Edith. And don't forget Duggy Davis. He's the best bet so far. Not difficult to fit him into the hit man theory. Right age. Right mentality. Close to Tom. Like the old adage, 'keep your friends close, your enemies closer.' Ideal for Davis. Keep close to Tom all these years. Lately hear his moans and groans, realise he was losing it. Hold him closer. The kiss of death? Problem solved. No one'll miss Tommy. But Duggy's proving elusive. That's strange. NFA. A dosser. A drunk. Keeping that one step ahead. Mmmm. Could fit in with the hit man image.

A Jackal-like figure. Able to kill and disappear. No. Don't have that feeling for it. But he'll come. Look at the Durnley angle when it's all over. See about getting his body from that unmarked grave inside the jail. Don't forget Wilson. It's just the same for him. Then Megan and the kids – they'll need to be with Bade. Together again. Help make up for some of the past pain. Unite the family. And at that moment it struck me. I opened my eyes and almost jumped out of my seat. Only the seat belt held me back. I shouted, "Unite the family!"

McLean's own thoughts must have been disrupted by my unexpected outburst. He exclaimed, "What family's that boss?"

My left index finger worked over time massaging my scarred nose. I didn't answer the driver. I was busy walking through my mind.

"Which family are you talking about boss?" McLean asked again impatiently.

I wasn't deliberately ignoring McLean but my mind was in overdrive, switched off from everything except the death of Megan and her three children. Mentally isolated, I was able to recall large chunks of the Coroner's report, which I'd viewed that morning in the Admin office. And as I trawled through it I came up with a vital statistic that I'd missed before.

It was with a sense of triumph that I declared, "That's it!"

McLean not content with being kept in the dark any longer knocked on the door again, "What is Sir?"

Now I was back in the real world. My voice vibrating with excitement I answered the Constable, "Megan Durnley! She died with her three children. That's what the whole enquiry surrounding her death centred on. Three children.

Three children died, the inquest was about three children, three children are buried in that cemetery." I had that gut feeling and turned to McLean. I said, "But she had four kids. Four. One was a baby being breast fed. Found wrapped up near the bridge. What's happened to it? Is it still alive? Is it a boy? A girl? Does it know about its parents, brothers and sisters? This could be our killer. What a motive. Revenge!"

McLean in that cold, offhand manner with which he often surrounded himself showed less enthusiasm. He said, "If the child managed to reach adulthood it's unlikely to know of its origins. The adoption agencies aren't too free with such information. It really is a long shot sir."

I ignored the Constable. I was enthused. I had that feeling twitching at my guts. It wasn't often wrong. I'd hauled myself up the ratlines, navigated the futtock shrouds, over the fighting platform, and I was now shinning up the final twenty feet of Royal mast to the truck, ready to haul myself on top, be the button boy. Top'o the world! I'd cast aside my bo'sun's warning. If I fell it would be an exceedingly long and painful drop. But I had to go with that feeling. If I fell there was always that safety net stretched out below to catch me. But on reflection I realised I was more likely to end up like a spud that had gone through a chipper, than a circus high flyer, bouncing gently in the spotlight to rapturous applause. But whatever, when I get back to Mansfield tracing this fourth child is top priority.

We passed over the humped-back bridge and the watercourse that was still referred to as a river. Through the sheeting rain the Net and Ferret appeared cold and bleak. Its windows like eyes staring out at the miserable weather. I could visualise Amos Jimson sharing their misery, bemoaning his diminished trade as he contemplated my earlier visit. We drove up the hill toward the Lowry skyline, no stranger now to this dark and dreary canvas. Past the butcher's shop and Edith's torched home, on toward Whalley and St. Luke's churchyard. As we drew into the tiny car park the rain eased to a spitting drizzle. McLean remained with the vehicle as I made my way through the now all too familiar landscape. Irregular rows of gravestones, many leaned like drunken sailors or collapsed into unsightly heaps. Memorial pots that seemed to have surrendered to time, lying discarded and neglected atop the graves they once delighted with flowers; so lovingly arranged. I searched among the ranks of headstones. I found the one I wanted on the north side of the church set at the side of the gravel path.

The Oakley family plot was still a splendid-looking edifice. Big John had seen to that. Even though it was no longer tended it had resisted creeping twitch and ground covering weeds, leaving the large, grey gravelled square, edged with marble, free to set off the imposing central memorial; constructed of Portland stone. Eagerly I leaned towards it reading the names cut into the three tiered main plinth which supported a clinging ivy cross monument. They were all remembered; John, Polly, Jack, Ted, and Rita. Hers was the lowest name on the plinth, though she was not the last to be laid to rest in the bosom of the family. I thought on the two remaining Oakleys. One lying upon a mortuary slab, the other struggling to survive in a hospital intensive care unit. If Edith didn't survive what hope was there of the last of the Oakleys finding eternal rest with their kinfolk?

Then I spotted it amidst the grey stone and gravel. A single splash of scarlet, it lay to the side of the name RITA. I reached over and carefully picked it up. It triggered memories of a screen legend that had died in tragic circumstances some years ago and her distraught former husband.

I turned it gently in my fingers and said aloud, "Marilyn Monroe and Joe Di Maggio. A single red rose. A symbol of everlasting love. Who's put that there and why?"

I stood for a moment and thought of the Oakley family, their rise and fall, the happiness and the sorrow. This sombre burial plot was all that remained of their yesterday, what of their tomorrow? Carefully replacing the rose I walked back to the car. I stopped at a large refuse container standing against the church wall. Nearby, water dripped from an old tap onto the slimy green tarmac. A plastic bottle lay alongside. I lifted the container lid and grimaced as the sickly smell of decomposing vegetation rose up to meet me. Still recoiling from the stench I prodded amongst the discarded refuse, flowers and soggy wrapping paper. The abandoned plastic bottle had come in handy. My perseverance paid off. I found something that aroused my interest; a couple of discarded single red roses.

With plenty to think about I got into the car and settled into the passenger seat. PC McLean drove.

I was feeling pleased with the day's work. "I think we're onto something Andy my boy."

McLean didn't reply.

"Got a monk on have we?" I said, "Thought you liked to be kept in the picture. Or have you taken your ball home or something?"

"It seems quite pointless asking you anything. It's clear you don't wish me to know too much. I know I'm only a plod but how am I expected to learn anything unless we can communicate openly? Sir." The Constable deliberately emphasised the last word.

It took a lot of effort not to smile at what I saw as his childish stance but I managed it. I was in a happier frame of mind and could afford to forgive Doctor – er – Constable McLean his misdemeanours and let his petulance go over my head.

"Don't take things so personally, Andy. In life we all get our arses kicked and none of us like it. It's part of the learning process. Just make sure that you learn. Don't keep falling down the same hole. It makes it harder to get out next time."

"Yes Sir." McLean's reply was unconvincing. He attempted to recover lost ground and asked, "So what's making you so chirpy?"

I leaned back in my seat and said, "A single red rose for Rita. Is it a symbol? A reminder of everlasting love? A secret admirer all these years? Lost virginity perhaps? Who knows? That's for us to find out."

*

21st August
AFTERNOON

In the office I took off my wet overcoat and hung it on the back of a chair. Sergeant Johnson knocked and came in. His expression was grim. In anticipation of I didn't know what, I asked tentatively, "Well?"

He came straight out with it, "It's Edith Sir. She's dead."

The stark declaration seemed as tactful as a thump to the head with a sock full of wet sand.

"Oh no!" I exclaimed. "Poor lass. After all she's gone through. What happened?"

McLean came in with a couple of mugs of coffee, one of his less contentious moments. An unkind commentator might have suggested ingratiating.

He showed a keen interest as Johnson replied, "Hospital contacted the Super while you were out. Said Edith had suffered a massive cerebral haemorrhage. Just slipped away. Never recovered consciousness."

"That's the last of the Oakleys gone," I said. "And a lot's gone with her."

McLean said, "Maybe boss, but it takes some of the pressure off you. You can forget about the anonymous phone caller and the arsonist now. Concentrate on more important things."

I gave McLean a withering glare and said disparagingly, "I don't know where you dig up these ideas Andy. Of course we still need to trace them. More than ever now. It's likely they're one and the same and maybe even a triple murderer."

McLean gave that theory short shrift. "But that's only an assumption Sir."

"If you get to know me better, PC McLean, you'll learn that I never assume anything. My old bo'sun always said, 'Never assume. It'll end up making an 'ass' out of 'u' and 'me'. And I make an ass out of myself on enough occasions without enlisting the aid of assumption." I gulped another mouthful of coffee and added, "Facts, evidence and that old reliable gut feeling. That's what a good detective needs in his sea chest."

The telephone rang. Sergeant Johnson answered.

"Murder Incident. DI Stirling's office, Sergeant Johnson speaking." After a brief pause he said, "Right Sir, I'll tell him," and replaced the phone. Addressing me he said, "Chief Inspector Wooton Sir. He's all excited about something. On his way to see you."

"That's all I need. Him to come blathering about car parks or coffee or ..."

The young Chief Inspector hurried into the office, face beaming. He hadn't wasted any time to come down the corridor and see me. He was bursting to tell me something but was trying to control his excitement. After all he was the Divisional Chief Inspector.

"Inspector Stirling, the uniformed branch has not been neglecting their duties you know. The murder enquiry is uppermost in our minds."

He pulled up a chair, took out his pocket book and flipped it open at a block of pages wrapped around by an elastic band. A bright smile still wreathed his lips as he leaned back before announcing, "I have something you may well be interested in Inspector."

"A new car parking plan Chief Inspector?" I suggested. My response was not unexpected by my staff.

But it was by Mister Wooton, who responded as if I had slapped him across the face with a wet towel. The smile was replaced by a schoolboy sulk.

"I thought we had moved on Inspector."

"Moved on Sir? Of course, what can I do for you?"

The Chief Inspector perked up. "It's what I can do for you Inspector."

I waited for the follow up but it didn't come. What did he want? The CID to sweep up the car park or paint the rockery white because he's got a big tin of whitewash for us from Stores?

"Go on Chief Inspector" I urged.

In the driving seat now the Bramshill flier asked, "Evans! Does that name interest you Inspector?"

I have to say I was taken by surprise and said, "You've been reading the crime bulletins Chief Inspector."

My reply didn't register offence but enabled the Chief Inspector to display his bumptiousness. "Of course Inspector. Would you expect anything less? We are on the same job you know."

I didn't take up the challenge I just said, "Erm OK. What've you got for me?"

In that pompous manner which distinguished him from other mere mortals the Chief Inspector said, "The local beat officer has been making enquiries into a series of garage and shed breaks on the Hallfarm council estate. Criminal damage to premises and miscellaneous items stolen. You know the usual. Lawn mowers, assorted tools, that sort of thing." He paused to note the effect on the listeners.

I was listening and urged, "Go on then Chief Inspector but I'm not in the market for a lawn mower."

Unhurried now he was in the chair, Wooton continued, "Garage number 168 is rented to a Mister Evans of 27, Pelham Drive, Mansfield." He sat back pausing for effect.

I waited and thought, "Good God. Here sits a future Chief Constable. Mister Dynamite himself." I said, "Good Sir, Good. Is his name Taff by any chance?"

Chief Inspector Wooton with serious head screwed tightly into place flicked through the pages and replied, "Sorry. Can't help you there Inspector. We've only got his surname, Evans. But the address is bogus and the registration plates on the garaged Datsun Bluebird relate to a Hillman Minx." He closed the notebook with a flourish and concluded, "There! What about that?"

I was already mentally manipulating the new jigsaw pieces, searching for a match. The potential for the information was very interesting.

"Mmm. A ringer hey? It's worth a going over. Good work Sir. Anything else?"

My few words of genuine praise for the information and the obvious work it had entailed in collecting and collating it, brought the beaming smile back to Wooton's face.

"Left the best for last Jim."

For a moment again I was concerned. The Chief Inspector was getting familiar, calling me by my first name. I'd better watch it. He'll want to go out for a drink or something if I'm not careful. I prompted, "You were saying, Sir?"

"I was saying I've saved the best for last. On the back seat, a toolbag containing a black torch and a large Stanley screwdriver. The handles bound with black tape, and there are other bits and pieces. In the boot of the Datsun a pair of dark coloured trousers. Dirty, stained and with a smell of petrol to them."

My belly turned, that gut feeling. This sounded promising. I maybe quick to criticise but I'm just as quick to praise.

"Good work Sir. Good job all round. Hope something comes of it. Could be worth a commendation. What I want now is a uniform presence at the lock ups. Twenty-four hour coverage at the moment. I'll get over there straight away." I turned to Sergeant Johnson. "Arrange for Scenes of Crime to attend. Then we'll get down there. OK?"

*

I knew the Hallfarm council estate well. Some of our best customers hang out there. A post-war housing estate, it had promised so much. Now it had its share of problems. The usual excuses were wheeled out to justify them; unemployment, poor housing and lack of facilities for the youth of the estate. But that didn't prevent some of the residents taking personal responsibility for their lives. They struggled to keep up standards with nicely tended gardens and neat houses, attempting to survive in the encroaching jungle. I stood with Sgt. Johnson before a block of typical council built utility garages, basic and practical. A row of ten units squeezed onto a spare piece of land occupied for years by an abandoned air raid shelter. The oil-stained forecourt was littered with broken building bricks, crushed cola cans, screwed up and driven-over fag packets. There were a few condoms, of varying colours, all obviously second hand, and an abandonment of other junk. How anyone managed to drive in and out of the garages without encountering frequent mishaps surely required a miracle. Perhaps that's why the suspect vehicle was hidden away in that particular block of lock ups, an ideal place to hide it from prying eyes. Just another abandoned wrecker among the graffiti-scarred up-and-over garage doors.

Sergeant Johnson was the first to speak. "This green and pleasant land. What a dump."

I said, "It was alright until people moved in, then it became a dump."

As we picked our way through the rubble I brushed at my still-damp overcoat. It had no effect upon the untidy network of creases that had worked their way into the fabric.

To the amusement of Sergeant Johnson I complained, "A shower of rain and this bloody overcoat looks like a shipping chart of the English Channel."

Johnson smiled at my concern. "You look the part

356

boss. Dressed for the occasion. A dosser at the dump."

I assumed a pained expression. "Cheers Sarge. Very uplifting. I shouldn't be surprised if somebody didn't mistake me for that TV detective. The one with the shabby raincoat, Columbus."

Wearing his serious face Johnson replied, "You mean Columbo? No way boss. He smokes big cigars and likes dogs."

I had to smile at Styx's sense of humour. It was very uplifting, but there was work to be done.

Standing before the vandalised lock ups Johnson observed, "Half the metal doors don't fit. Looks like all the garages have been screwed at one time or another."

I kicked a broken padlock and hasp. It rattled and slithered across the tarmac before colliding with the remnants of a thrown-down wine bottle and a building brick. "Not for the first time judging by the jemmied locks and missing door handles," I said.

"That's ours sir." Johnson pointed. "Fourth along. Just see '168' stencilled in the top right hand corner."

I observed, "I see Kilroy's still active, Willie loves Irene and Nottingham Forest Football Club have deposed the Monarch."

We didn't have to wait long before a Scenes of Crime vehicle drove onto the forecourt. The driver quickly assessed the situation, reversing from the minefield onto an adjacent grass patch. His relief was short lived. He'd reversed into a booby trap. The transit collided with the remains of an abandoned concrete street lamp half hidden in the overgrown green stuff. The resultant crunch from the rear of the vehicle as the back wheels climbed over the obstruction told him the suspension hadn't enjoyed the manoeuvre either. The driver realised too late that he was in a war zone and he'd been well and truly ambushed!

He was not a happy Scenes of Crime Officer but, like the thorough investigator his breed undoubtedly are, he asked the most searching of questions, "Who the fuck put that there?"

Sergeant Johnson was only too pleased to inform him, "You can bet your fingerprint powder against a pinch of shit it's the thieving little toe rags from the estate."

Not keen to lose such an important part of their kit, neither the SOCO nor his partner took up the wager but concentrated on sorting out their parking problem. That done, I conferred with them outside Council garage 168.

"Right lads. I suspect an arsonist and attempted murderer used this Datsun Bluebird. We know an accelerant was used at the fire, possibly petrol, and we understand there may be a bag and various other items in the car. We've not looked yet, left it to you. And then there's the murder of Tommy Oakley. You'll know all about that, so I want you to secure the scene, give the car and garage a thorough going over and see what you can come up with. Take possession of everything of interest. OK?"

"Right boss we'll get on with it," the senior SOCO replied.

They unloaded their equipment and set about their business. Whilst I'd been briefing them Sgt. Johnson had been speaking to two uniformed Constables who had arrived.

I had to smile as I heard the big CID officer telling them, "Team up with SOCO. Keep everybody out of their way and stand no nonsense from the local toe rags. Kick arse. That's all they understand." Blunt and to the point, that's No

Nonsense Johnson. What you see is what you get. A first class sharp end copper.

Johnson and I made a reconnaissance of the area, noting the routes to and from the garages. It was clear that the driver of the suspect vehicle knew his way around otherwise he would never have found his way through the warren of side streets and alleys. He'd selected his lockup well.

Door knocking proved a fruitless exercise. No one had seen or heard anything of value. We'd expected that in a place like Hallfarm. But doing the knocker was an essential part of street policing. Valuable information sometimes came from that initial contact even though nothing was forthcoming on the doorstep. The anonymous phone call, the note through the police station door, the subsequent covert meet, all had their place in the bigger picture.

Back at the garage I had a quick debrief with the senior SOCO who showed me a number of plastic and paper bags containing items recovered from the scene. The officer sniffed at an exhibit bag containing a pair of dark coloured trousers before offering it to me.

"Smell what appears to be petrol Sir? We've put it in a nylon bag."

I took the exhibit and sniffed. There was a distinct odour of petrol.

I passed the bulky object to Sergeant Johnson who sniffed it enthusiastically. As he returned the bulky bag to the SOCO he joked, "If we carry on like this we'll get nicked as trouser sniffing pervs or solvent abusers."

The SOCO was still grinning as he handed to me a couple of small plastic exhibit envelopes.

"These were under the carpet on the driver's side. May get some marks off them. You might even get an ident."

I looked at the items inside the transparent packets. I recognised them immediately. Without speaking I handed them to my DS.

Johnson took the packets and scrutinised them. After a moment he declared, "Looks good boss. Are they Tom's?" He handed the packets back to me.

"I'd say so. Edith's were destroyed in the fire."

Sergeant Johnson asked, "Are we fixing up for obbos on the lock up guv just in case somebody comes back?"

I shook my head, "No sarge. It's pointless. If he's about he'll have seen the police activity and done a runner. But we'll have to have a police presence until the boffins have finished with it. If we don't the local juvenile Mafiosi will trash everything they don't nick. I'll have a word with SOCO."

Having taken photographs, thrown about some finger print powder and packed samples and a variety of exhibits, the Scenes of Crime Officers were preparing to leave. I collared them.

"Thanks for your help lads you've given us a few more lines of enquiry to follow up."

"All in a day's work boss. Anything to oblige."

"Then just oblige me once more and arrange for the vehicle to be taken to HQ for forensic examination. Get the lab involved and Vehicle Examiners. I want this motor going over with a fine toothcomb. And the garage as well. This could be our breakthrough."

That attended to, Sgt. Johnson and I carefully picked our way around the garage. In the time-old tradition favoured by detectives we thrust hands deep into our jacket pockets and carefully perused the vehicle and lock up. With hands safely out of the way, I squatted alongside the front of the black

Datsun Bluebird and cast an eye over the front nearside wheel. It looked like a result. With a sense of satisfaction I said to my colleague, "Similar tyre pattern to the photos from the back lane at Edith's. Could be onto a winner here Styx me boy."

Johnson, examining the rear tyres, was already reaching the same conclusion. "It's starting to come together with a rush boss." adding, "I've got to take my hat off to Mister Wooton and his lads."

"Mister Wooton. That's nice to hear, Styx. I think he's earned our respect over this one. I'll make sure he knows."

*

Back at the police station Chief Inspector Nigel Wooton strutted around with a semi-permanent grin on his youthful countenance. At my request, Detective Superintendent Davey had given him and his officers a pat on the back. An accolade beyond Nigel's wildest dreams. For the first time during his meteoric rise through the ranks, he experienced something he had not encountered before, he felt useful, a contributor, part of the team, a real policeman.

And Davey too was happy. "The jigsaw's coming together Jim. Still a lot to do but it's clicking into place." But the wise Old Bear added a cautionary note, "Unless something comes along and derails us."

But the bits and pieces were rattling into the box at a remarkable rate. No sign of a rail disaster on the horizon. Sergeant Dave Plackett rang with more good news.

"The lab has come up trumps with the petrol from the arson sir. The additives identify Shell as the source. I've chased them up and they've given me a list of outlets around the area. Jonesy and myself have done the rounds and come up with a guy buying two cans of petrol two days before the fire. He paid cash. The till receipts record the sale." He paused for a moment, "And wait for it sir. The firm use one of those security cameras. We're going through it now. Might take a bit of time and it's not a certainty but it's looking good."

Stirling punched the air. Johnson listening in on the extension clenched a fist and yelled into the mouthpiece, "Good on yer Davey lad."

"Alright Styx? Listening in to private calls again? No flies on these kiddoes you know."

Johnson, face creased with delight jested, "No but you can see where they've been. All flyblown."

Sergeant Plackett's swift response in nautical terminology impressed me. His reference to the ro'lock, a device that supports an oar, plural of course, showed the breadth of this man's learning. Well it sounded like ro'locks.

Johnson had additional good news. "The Lab has identified the sole impressions as coming from Doc Marten boots. Identical to batches provided to the military and emergency services in 1975."

"Good! Can they narrow it down for us?"

"It's nigh on impossible. After that length of time, apart from anything else, they'll have been replaced."

I said, "Still it's a bit closer. We know what to be looking for. If we get a suspect we may turn up the boots. What about the containers?"

Plackett had the information at his fingertips. "They're standard containers used commercially for hand cleansing liquids. But the red cap signifies it's a special formula produced exclusively for government and local authority departments, hospitals and the like. So we're chasing that up."

"What about the timers?"

"You know about the partial fingerprints, and enquiries have turned up a sale of two timers and two electric fires in Nottingham. I'm pretty certain they're ours. The assistant has a record of the purchases, again two days before the fire. It was a cash transaction."

"Any description?"

"She remembered the customer because he was a tall, good -looking guy. Might remember him. I'm getting her to look at some mug shots."

"That shows promise Dave. Don't forget to use at least twelve photographs at a time. We don't want crafty mouthpieces having a positive ident thrown out because we haven't complied with the rules."

"Right boss. I'll take her over to Force Intelligence. She can go through the books there."

"Get the actions updated and through to the incident room. I'll brief the Superintendent. Keep me informed as you go along."

The contents of the two small plastic exhibit envelopes recovered from the Datsun Bluebird interested me. Why would anyone take them from the dead man and hide them in the car? Why would they want to kill the old battler in the first place? What was the connection? If I was going to crack the case I needed to know. But then there were lots of things I needed to know before I reached the end game.

*

Fallows had been released on bail. I had kept my promise and not objected when the gamekeeper made his application to the Magistrates. If not a happier man, he was at least relieved to be out of the claustrophobic confinement of the police

363

cells and back in his beloved woods. And I'd bet diamonds that it wouldn't be long before the old poacher was round at the Net and Ferret paying Amos Jimson a visit, trying to suss out what he'd been telling the law. And I was just as sure that the oversized lump of landlord wouldn't reveal a thing. Then neither would Fallows. But life would never be the same for them again. Their cosy lifestyle had been disjointed as surely as Fallows's battered nose. The turmoil of recent days may have caused them to reassess the part played by them in the tragic deaths of so many innocent people. Maybe their consciences would trouble them after so long in denial, perhaps shame them into making serious decisions that could impact upon the rest of their lives. Only time would tell.

I felt that elusive something close at hand and intended to keep the pressure on. Some unhappy players would feel that pressure, and as a consequence seriously consider revealing more long-held secrets. Sergeant Jack Smithurst was a likely candidate for my thumb screw and rack, operated in the most humane manner of course.

I'd put an action sheet in to the incident room outlining my theory regarding the fourth Durnley child. One of the other teams would chase that up. It wouldn't be easy tracing the kid. Even if it was still alive after all these years. But it was another iron in the fire.

After the evening debrief I sat alone on the front row of metal and canvas chairs and stared at the flip chart still set up on the easel. As I revisited the words scrawled across the paper I sensed they held the answer to the question, "Who killed PC Jarvis?" Clear that up and I suspect strongly that we clear up Tommy Oakley's murder. I re-read the entries on the chart, lingering over the names that had become so familiar to me in such a short time. I added the "hit man" to the list.

PC JARVIS
DURNLEY/WILSON
POACHERS
POLICEMAN
ACCOMPLICE/ACCESSORY/HEAVY DRINKER
TOM OAKLEY
FEAR
LOYALTY
FAMILY LOYALTY
OAKLEY FAMILY MEMBER
HIT MAN?

The night Inspector had seen the light on in the debriefing room and stuck his head around the door.

"Alright Jim? Everyone else's gone."

"Yes thanks," I said, "Just burning a little midnight oil. Nothing at home but the cat."

"OK. We'll be brewing later. If you're still here I'll send a cup up for you."

I appreciated the thought and raised a hand in acknowledgement before going back to the chart and my word game. Clearly I was missing something or somebody but what or who? Edith? No, she's a family member. Sergeant Jack? No he's included under Policeman. Fallows? Poacher. Rita? Family. But hang on, Rita was having a baby. I'd missed that off. Alongside OAKLEY FAMILY MEMBER I wrote RITA/BABY. I knew she had died during child birth, but who was responsible for her condition? Who was her mystery lover? I allowed my mind free rein and played about with names on the list. Now let's suppose, I drew a couple of lines connecting RITA to the names PC JARVIS and WILSON. I stepped back to reappraise my handiwork.

I was pleased with my effort, an exercise in thinking outside the box. I hadn't solved the crime but I'd provided myself with some interesting reading and another line of enquiry to pursue. I checked the time. It was half nine. That just gave me enough time to test out the new angle and perhaps apply pressure where it might do the most good.

I was still turning the new development over in my mind as I drove onto Mansfield Road heading towards Nottingham. In a leafy suburb on the outskirts of the city I visited a large detached Victorian house standing in its own extensive grounds. As I walked up the drive, the security light snapped on revealing the imposing building. I was there for about an hour. When I left I was troubled. From a public phone box at the corner of the street I rang Superintendent Davey at his home. The Old Bear listened. Very soon he too was troubled.

*

The house was cold when I got home. I switched on the electric fire and shared my easy chair with the cat and a tot as I pondered on those matters that were causing me and the Super concern. By the time I returned to duty a few hours later I knew what had to be done.

TWENTY-NINE

SUNDAY

The morning briefing had gone well. There was a distinct upbeat atmosphere about the place. More light-hearted banter and smiles breaking out on what had of late become serious faces. The enquiry was still moving apace. A number of positive areas were still to be exploited. Forensic was coming good. Yes, things were definitely upbeat, even McLean seemed to be touched by the spirit, smiling and joking with Sergeant Johnson. But in my office I wasn't part of that upbeat tempo. My face was set in serious mode. This was *noblesse oblige* in action, the Detective Inspector facing up to another of the responsibilities that came with rank. What I was about to do was a calculated well-thought-out action, in everyone's interest.

I called out, "PC McLean."

The officer popped his head around the open door and replied cheerfully, "You called Sir?"

"Yes come in. Close the door."

The effect of those three final words wiped the smile from McLean's face as efficiently as a blackboard rubber removing chalk. Nowadays, closed door sessions with senior officers did not bode well.

"Take a seat Mister McLean," I said.

But his mood had changed. He was on his guard. His eyes had narrowed. His jaw was tense. McLean replied tersely,

"No thank you Sir. I prefer to stand on such occasions."

"Such occasions PC McLean?"

"No need to play games Inspector, I'm a big boy now. I can take the knocks. If you're going to fire bullets get on with it."

I said, "Alright, I won't delay you any longer than necessary, other than to remind you that it is my responsibility to report on your progress during your period of attachment to the CID, and inform you of my decision."

McLean snapped, "You can't do that. My attachment isn't up yet."

I ignored his outburst and continued, "I've decided that you're not likely to become a detective. Another few days or weeks wouldn't alter that decision."

I'd been here before, on many occasions. Every police officer on attachment to CID knew he was on probation, and not every police officer made it. In the main, though disappointed, they took it well and benefited from the experience. After all, not everyone could be a detective. The Job was bigger than that.

I watched McLean clenching and unclenching his fists and grinding his teeth in a display of barely controlled anger. I wasn't impressed.

I continued, "Your attitude and demeanour forces me to conclude that you're not the right material to be a CID Officer. In fact you're not cut out to be a policeman. The problem is that as you're no longer a Probationer you can't be removed unless you breach Police Regulations, and are dismissed by the Chief Constable. I'll be putting my reasons and comments in writing. You'll see them and I'll notify your Divisional Commander. Thank you Constable McLean. You're released to return immediately to uniformed duties."

McLean's faced twitched, eyes wide and wild. Thrusting forward over the desk he stabbed a finger towards my face and yelled, "You'll regret this day Inspector. I'll see the Federation. Demand a hearing with the Chief. Get legal representation. You won't make a fool out of me. I joined to be a CID officer not a plod all my service. I told you I'd set my objectives. And I'll achieve them. I'm not a man to be crossed."

And neither was I. Standing up I brushed his prodding finger to one side and leaned across my desk, eyeballing him, almost rubbing my scarred nose into his face. This was one-to-one, street wise menace versus unbridled anger. It wasn't what I'd intended but I'd been forced into a situation and I responded like for like.

With my voice almost a whisper I said, "Your demeanour has removed any lingering doubts I might have had about my decision McLean. I don't like being threatened. It brings the worst out in me. I've told you nicely to leave. Now go under your own steam. Or I'll throw you out. Alright?"

It was clear that McLean had never confronted such an animal before. With eyes flashing, he wisely chose my first option and left, slamming the door behind him.

Sergeant Johnson was in the office almost immediately.

"Problems with McLean boss?" he queried.

Job done, I had no qualms. I said casually, "Problems? Turning McLean down for CID was no problem. It was a necessity. He's the one with problems. Watch this space."

"You're the boss," Styx said, "and I don't think anybody will disagree with your decision."

"Agree or disagree Sarge, making unpopular decisions goes with the territory and I stand by it."

Sergeant Johnson gathered up a number of completed actions from my out tray and glanced through them before taking them to the incident room. In the meantime I wrote across Police Constable McLean's folder NOT RECOMMENDED and filed it. I had a funny feeling that life in the CID, with or without Andy McLean, was about to take a few surprising twists and turns.

My instinct hadn't been wrong. The first surprise came within half an hour of McLean leaving my office.

I was at my desk when Sergeant Johnson knocked on the door and walked in. It took him all his time to contain himself as he asked, "Have you heard the news Sir?"

I looked up and shook my head. Whatever the buzz, it hadn't reached me.

"He's put his ticket in."

"Who's put his ticket in?"

"McLean. He's just slapped the report on Mister Wooton's desk and walked out. No explanation. Looks like you've done The Job a service boss."

I was on my feet in an instant. "Does Mister Davey know?" I demanded.

The question took Styx Johnson by surprise. "Er... I don't know Sir," he said, "I can find out." He reached for the telephone.

I was impatient and said, "No leave it with me. Wait here. Don't go anywhere until I get back. OK?"

I could see Sergeant Johnson was confused. He wasn't sure what was happening.

"OK boss," he said.

He was talking to himself. I was already halfway to the Bear's lair.

Anyone passing Detective Superintendent Davey's office would have heard the animated conversation behind closed doors and seen the anxious look on my face as I came out.

That look was still with me as I got back to my office where Sergeant Johnson was waiting patiently. My anxiety spilled over into my voice.

I said, "Get your coat Sarge we're going for a walk."

Johnson's look of apprehension would normally have brought a smile to my face, today it didn't.

"What's happening boss? Where are we going?"

As I put on my overcoat I replied, "We're going for a walk in the park. I've got things to discuss and we can do with a breath of fresh air."

Johnson was quick off the mark. Having grabbed his top coat he met me outside my office. He didn't say anything. He knew better than to ask any further questions. I'd leave him to speculate. After a few minutes of brisk walking towards the local park he'd soon give up. He'd no idea what was driving me. But he was patient and knew I'd reveal all in my own good time. As we entered Titchfield Park, a small park and recreation ground not far from the nick, I had a quick look about me. Satisfied that no one was within hearing distance I slowed the pace and stuck my hands deep in my overcoat pockets.

I said to Styx Johnson, "Now we have got a problem. It's McLean."

Johnson casually kicked a pebble and watched it plop into the small brook that cut through the rec. Just as casually he queried, "McLean boss? How's he suddenly become a problem?"

"It's not sudden Styx. I've not been too sure of him for a few days now. That's why I got shut of him. But I hadn't anticipated him packing in the job. That's upset the plan a bit so we've got to get back on course."

"You've lost me boss," The big man said. "The only problem I can see with him is that he'll stir it with the press.

Give away a few tit-bits that might hurt the investigation. We can live with that."

I suddenly stopped. Johnson stopped alongside me. I looked him straight in the eye. I was wearing my serious hat as I said, "It may go deeper than that Styx. I suspect McLean has problems, you know how unpredictable he is. He might do something stupid."

The DS screwed up his eyes, returned my look and asked incredulously, "McLean boss? That gormless toffee-nosed prat? Take what he says with a bucket full of the proverbial. He's talks a load of bollocks. No bottle when it matters."

"I think you're wrong there Sarge," I said. "So I'm taking you to see someone and hear what they've got to say."

"Is the Super in on this guv?" he asked.

"Yes. He's in the picture and he's given me a free hand for the moment. But there are some things I'm not at liberty to divulge at this time so don't ask me. Now you know, and it goes no further. We'll get back to the nick and drive to Nottingham. I'll say no more till we get there."

I set off at a pace. Detective Sergeant Johnson settled into a long stride keeping up with me. His mind would be in overdrive, McLean's name spinning in his head. He'd be scrambling pieces of the jigsaw, re-adjusting them, trying to make sense of it all. The good old boy would be struggling with the emerging picture just as I was.

*

During the drive to Nottingham neither of us spoke. The usual routine, alone with our thoughts, but this time the subject of our deliberations would be the same; McLean.

As we neared the city I peered through the windscreen

and said, "Next left Sarge. Then fifty yards on the left you'll see a big notice board, pull up just past it."

Sergeant Johnson followed my instructions. There was the notice board at the imposing entrance to the grounds of a large Victorian house, one of many in that leafy suburb. It read "Forest Private ..." then we were past it before you could catch the rest of it.

"Pull up at the end of the close," I directed.

We parked up. I scanned the area for any undue activity. "No one about," I said. "But we'll do a quick recce to make sure."

Leaving the car we walked beyond the large house and carried on to the road junction. We stood for a moment and looked about. There was nothing untoward, just plenty of traffic heading into the city.

"OK!" I said. "We'll pay our visit."

As we walked back up the cul-de-sac Styx broke his silence. He asked quizzically, "What's with all the cloak and dagger boss?"

I didn't respond to the question.

We entered the driveway to the big house. Styx suddenly stopped in front of the large notice board. I could see that he was checking out the wording which was now clearly visible, *"Forest Private Clinic and Rehabilitation Home."* He looked at me. I shrugged my shoulders and carried on up the drive. The big guy seemed mystified. We walked in silence to the main entrance of the house.

The Sergeant's puzzled look became more pronounced as the Nun in reception said in her charming Dublin lilt, "Hello Mister Stirling. Everything is satisfactory." She looked questioningly at Styx.

"It's alright Sister Abigail," I said. "This is a colleague of mine. We'd like to see your guest if that's alright."

Her rosy complexion glowed amid the simple black and white of her Order's distinctive apparel.

"To be sure it's alright. Visitors will be a blessing."

We followed her along the passageway, its walls lined with religious pictures, crosses and crucifixes. Our footsteps clip-clopped on the polished floor. I felt ill at ease. Styx didn't look too comfortable either. I wondered if he was feeling the same as me. It seemed as though my very soul was under scrutiny in that holy sanctuary and my quilt of life didn't carry too many pure white patches. But in my favour I could claim many differing hues, though I concede some were of a darker value, none were "wicked black."

Sister Abigail stopped outside a door at the end of the corridor. She put her ear to it and listened for a moment.

Satisfied she whispered, "I'll just see if everything is alright," knocked gently and went into the room. She returned almost immediately. "You can go in. Stay as long as you like. Let me know when you leave. God Bless you both." She smiled sweetly and walked back down the passageway of redemption.

It was a pleasant room; self-contained with a combined bathroom and WC and small sitting area. The pale blue duvet on the single bed beneath the bay window matched the full-length curtains hanging from the pine wood rail. A low pine wood unit with three drawers fitted neatly along the left side of the room. A matching integral door screened a refrigerator in the unit. On top sat a television. A King James Bible lay alongside a number of framed photographs. From cream-painted walls obligatory prints of *The Virgin Mary* and William Holman Hunt's *The Light of the World* looked down on us. There was no one about, the room appeared to be unoccupied, but the sound of a flushing toilet soon dispelled that thought. The cream door marked WC opened.

It was clear from Sergeant Johnson's expression that he had no idea of the identity of the figure standing before him. I'd guess his first impression, like mine when I first saw her in this place, was of frailty. She looked frail. The bandage about her head, the dressing gown and slippers that she wore emphasised that impression. But notwithstanding her physical appearance her bespectacled eyes were keen and sharp, indicating an inner strength that shone through her feebleness. She looked at us and smiled.

I didn't know what Styx was thinking but I could imagine. His thoughts wouldn't be a million miles away from mine. Standing there, vulnerable and frail she could have been another Mother Teresa. Yes! The old girl would make a bloody good Nun. And through sorrowful eyes *The Light of the World* would look down and reprimanded us both for our irreverent thought. And that would be another patch on my quilt, a darker shade of pale? I couldn't speak for Styx's colour coding.

The old lady took a few cautious steps and eased herself into an adjustable easy chair. I helped fluff up the cushion behind her.

"Thank you Inspector," she said quietly. "I've been expecting you. Who is your friend?" She examined Johnson from head to toe.

"This is Detective Sergeant Johnson," I explained. "Close friends call him Styx. We've known one another for many years. Worked together on a number of cases."

"Goodness gracious!" she exclaimed. "Styx! What a heathen-sounding name."

"Spot on ma'am," the Sergeant declared. "They don't

come much more heathen than me. Er in the nicest sense that is."

"Oh! A nice heathen Mister Styx. And here you are in a Christian house. Have you found The Lord?"

"To be honest ma'am I've not been looking too hard. Spend most of my time locking up toe rags and scum bags."

The old lady said sweetly, "I can assure you Mister Styx that I'm not one of your toe bag scrum rags or what ever you call them." She offered her hand, Queen Mother like, and said, "I'm very pleased to meet you Styx Johnson. My name's Edith. Edith Oakley."

I watched for Sergeant Johnson's reaction. He was holding her hand lightly but the shock of the introduction caused him to release it immediately and take an undignified, stumbling, step backwards as if he'd been whacked in the head with that bag of sand. With eyes wide and mouth open, worldly wise Johnson stared at the old lady. Flesh and blood without a doubt. He glanced about the room taking in once again the holy symbols before looking once more at Edith.

In a voice tinged with cynicism he said, "If this is Heaven boss I'm not too impressed. What does your old bo'sun say about this miracle?"

I'd enjoyed the moment and trying hard to repress the humour bubbling inside said seriously, "I'm sure he'd have said, 'Them as die of death seldom recover. But there are exceptions to the rule.'"

Edith was amused. "It seems your old bo'sun person had me in mind Mister Stirling. Apparently my death was official, but I must complain. I never had chance to speak to the Almighty."

Sergeant Johnson was over the initial shock of meeting one of 'the living dead.' Now he wanted explanations.

376

He insisted, "Will somebody tell me what's going on?"

"Don't get them in a twist Sarge," I said. "That's why you're here. Since Edith came out of the coma there's been no holding her."

"Came out of the coma? What about the fractured skull and her dying?"

"It was a suspected fracture but the Super and I decided to upgrade it. Helped make the sudden death report more acceptable. Take the heat off our witness." I said to Edith, "We've come to see how you are and go over a couple of things. There have been developments that are causing me concern. I'd like to run them past you."

"I see," the old lady said thoughtfully. "So you have a problem Inspector?"

I took in the child like expression and innocent eyes before replying to her question.

"You're my problem Edith. After what's happened to you I think it wise to have contingency plans in place to ensure your safety."

"But I'm safe here Inspector. In the bosom of the Lord." She turned to the DS for support. "Don't you think so Styxy?" As she emphasised the epithet the old lady couldn't prevent the mischievous flutter pulling the corner of her lips.

A half-melon smile flashed across the Detective Sergeant's face. He warmed to Edith. Only just met her and already she's calling him by his nickname. And nobody called him Styxy. Not to his face anyway.

"I'm not too sure about that Edi my girl," he said seriously. "Whoever's out there isn't as close as we'd like to have him and The Lord's got a habit of not letting us know what's going to happen till it's too late."

377

She replied, "Well of course that's his privilege. He is after all The Lord God Almighty."

I knew we couldn't win. I moved it on. "During my last visit Edith you told me you had spoken with your family, through their photographs, the ones that survived the fire, and they advised you not to hold back on certain matters. Remember?"

"Yes I remember very well Inspector. I told you about the telephone caller."

Sergeant Johnson glanced at me. I went on, "I'd like you to tell me again." Suppressing a laugh I added, "For the benefit of Styxy here."

She looked sympathetically at the DS, "Of course Inspector. For Styxy here."

The old lady eased herself into a more comfortable position settling amongst the cushions, and then like a benign old school marm spoke to the rugged DS.

"You'll understand Styxy that family business is family business no matter how distasteful. Loyalty is to God and your family. I tried to protect my family but when my house was burned and I was beaten in my own bed, well I was annoyed. I'd lived there with my family all those years and he destroyed it. Now that wasn't nice was it Styxy?"

"Er no Edi. It wasn't nice," he agreed.

"I knew you'd understand." She went on, "Whilst I was in hospital they said I was in a coma. I let them think that, but," She lowered her voice to a whisper. I strained to catch her words. "But I was on a journey to the other side. I saw Dad and Mam and my brothers and Rita and they told me to tell everything. Even our Tom. He looked a picture. They all did. I didn't really want to come back you know. But they'll all be waiting for me when it's my turn." She sat back in the chair and continued her tale. "When Rita left all those years ago I visited her a few times. My dear sister told me who had made her pregnant. I didn't tell Mam or Dad only our Tom. I shouldn't have done really because it upset him so much."

"Who was the father?" urged Johnson.

She cautioned, "Don't be so eager Sergeant, we'll get there in good time. Rita knew she was going to die and made me make a promise on my Bible. I always carry it with me." She reached over and took the King James Version from the unit clasping it to her chest. "I promised that if the baby lived. I'd look after it." She held the Bible closer and rocked slowly in the chair. "My lovely sister died all those miles from home, only me and the baby with her. And I kept my promise."

Styx Johnson was well and truly hooked. I let him get on with it. I'd already heard it all from Edith. Now he was being primed.

He leaned closer to her. "Rita Oakley gave birth to a baby? Did the child survive?" he queried.

She didn't answer immediately but looked towards the photographs on the unit. I saw the woeful look and reached into my inside pocket. I handed her two small plastic envelopes. "Will these help with your story?" I enquired.

The old lady peered closely at the exhibit packets. Her spectacled eyes mirrored surprise. She pressed the envelopes to her lips and cried, "Rita! Oh Rita and the boys. Where did you find them Inspector?"

Sergeant Johnson watched the drama unfolding. I don't think he was quite sure where it was leading.

I had to keep the old lady talking. From experience I knew that emotion could disrupt her delivery. I said quietly, "They're from the suspect's car. Who are the people in the photographs Edith?"

She removed the pictures from the packets lingering over each one as she relived distant memories.

"This one is my dear sister Rita. Isn't she beautiful? Like an eastern princess. Oh I wish she were here." Emotion was flooding in.

"And the man?" I asked.

Her face hardened as she looked at the picture of the man cuddling up to Rita. She attempted to summarily dismiss him, disassociate him from her sister.

"Oh him. He's the cause of all the trouble." She slipped the offending image beneath the other prints. Out of sight, out of mind. She quickly regained her enthusiasm as she gazed at the other familiar photographs. "That's me." She shuffled through them comparing one picture against another. "Not as pretty as our Rita. But then no one was. She was too lovely to live. God wanted her in his garden."

"And the boys?"

"Oh yes. The boys. Handsome little chaps aren't they? I took them both in about the same time. Mam and Dad had relented by then. The boys would be about two years old when the photo was taken. Richard, the one on the left, looks like his mother and Maffi looks like his dad. I loved them both. Broke my heart when they took them away from me. Put them into care. Said I wasn't a fit person to look after them. Said I was too involved with religion. How can you be too involved with God Almighty?"

I could see Johnson was still confused and I wasn't faring much better. He asked, "Am I losing the script boss? Did Rita have two children? Were those boys brothers?"

Edith gazed sympathetically at the Sergeant and answered his query, "No Styxy, Richard was Rita's boy."

"Who was this Maffi kid then?"

"That wasn't his real name. His full name was Mafeking. Isn't that a splendid name? Mafeking! It conjures up the mystery of the Dark Continent, the White man's burden, the British standing alone against the Boers; Empire."

"What's that got to do with a little lad living in a pit village in the Midlands?"

"Pride, National pride Sergeant. The relief of Mafeking. The relief of Ladysmith in the South African War. Great events in our nation's history."

Sergeant Johnson was bemused, "I still don't get it."

"I'm disappointed Sergeant. Didn't they teach you anything at school? The hero of Ladysmith was a great scout, skilled in the arts of woodcraft, hunting and tracking, just like the little boy's father. But they couldn't call the boy 'Ladysmith' now could they?"

"I don't suppose so Edi but they could have called him after this scout bloke."

"Not really. His father was already named after him."

"Who's that then Edi?"

"Maffi's father? He was called after Lord Baden Powell. Baden Powell Durnley."

The photographs had certainly opened Edith up. This was all new stuff to me. I was taking it in and trying to fit it into the jigsaw. To Styx Johnson the resurrection of Edith and the whole shebang was new and it showed. His mouth hung open in surprise and he stuttered, "Bade Durnley?" He clicked his fingers as more of the jigsaw dropped into place, "Of course! The fourth child. The one on the bridge. This is a different ball game boss. Where do we go from here?"

He had the reins. I let him drive and said, "You'd better ask the hundred dollar question Styxy. Then we can decide where we go."

Sergeant Johnson shuffled forward in his chair leaning toward Edith.

"What happened to the two boys Edi?"

The old lady was looking nostalgically at the photographs.

"What happened to the boys? Sadly, like Topsy, they just growed and growed. I lost touch when they went into care. They were just whisked away. Disappeared for ever."

"Haven't you heard from them since?"

"I've never had contact with Maffi for over thirty years. Rita's boy telephoned me about four years ago. It was quite a surprise I can tell you."

"How did he know about you?"

"He'd been adopted by a doctor and his wife. They'd died and he'd found some official documents about the adoption amongst their papers. He made enquiries about the Oakleys and traced me. He wanted to know about his biological parents and arranged to come up."

Edi stroked the bundle of pictures, her eyes warm and soft. The dainty face glowed as if a light were reflecting her inner joy.

But Sergeant Johnson wanted more. He urged the old lady on. "What did he say? What did he look like? What did you think of him?"

"Goodness gracious Sergeant Johnson you're bombarding me with questions. I'll need to catch my breath to think." She smiled demurely as the hard-nosed copper took his foot off the accelerator and sat back in his chair allowing her to continue. "He seemed a nice young man," she said. "I could see Rita in him but he was tall and straight like his father."

Johnson's foot moved quickly toward the accelerator but Edith had anticipated him.

"All in good time Sergeant. All in good time. Everything comes to him who waits you know."

Johnson looked at me and settled back in his chair. I nodded. He waited.

Edith picked it up again and continued, "Richard knew nothing of his background and was terribly upset when I told him about his mother. The boy had no idea."

The DS had waited long enough, "What about his father?"

"Alright Sergeant. I've heard you. I know it's not very Christian of me, but I dislike talking about the man who is responsible in my view for many of the troubles that befell my family. But Constable Jarvis was a disgrace to his uniform."

Sergeant Johnson slumped in his chair as if he'd been knocked back by a solid right cross to the head. What with sand bagging and punching he must have had a hell of a headache. I awaited his reaction to that large piece of jigsaw that had suddenly landed in his lap.

"PC Jarvis! The village bobby. The pillar of the community. Having it off …"

I cut in on him quickly, tactfully, not wishing to offend Edith. "I agree Sarge. Having it off such a reliable source as Edi makes it good evidence. Go on Edi."

She tilted her head slightly, courteously acknowledging me and my clumsy attempt at diplomacy.

"Thank you Inspector." She continued, "When I told Richard about his father's death and the tragic circumstances surrounding it he became inconsolable. Said he'd been robbed of his birth parents and became quite violent. He frightened me."

Sergeant Johnson pressed on. "Did he threaten you Edi?"

But the old lady was flagging. She seemed to deflate, slowly settling amongst the cushions. I went over to offer assistance. She waved me away, flicking her hand in that dismissive manner she had.

"I'm alright Inspector," she said. "Just getting a little tired." She returned to Sergeant Johnson and explained, "No he didn't threaten me then but he was planning murder."

"Murder? Whose murder?" he demanded.

I could see that Edith was suddenly showing signs of stress. I had to go carefully, didn't want to overdo it.

I said calmly, "Won't be long now Edith. Then we'll leave you to get some rest."

Johnson was champing at the bit, eager to get to the finish line but he could see how it was with Edith. He knew the score.

Drawing back he addressed the question to me. "Who was he planning to murder boss?"

Not to be outdone Edith mustered one final effort answering the DS's question. "He tried to murder me. I recognised his voice when he came into my room. But you musn't be too hard on him Sergeant. I've forgiven him and I'm sure the good Lord has too."

With that revelation Edith flopped back in her chair, physically and emotionally drained. I saw it as the opportune moment to end the session. There was a lot more I wanted to know from her but now wasn't the right time. I'd have to be patient. Better to let her rest, we could see her again when she felt better. I pressed the emergency button alongside Edi's bed.

Sister Abigail was there in a moment fussing about her charge. In that way peculiar to nurses she politely but firmly chastised us as she helped the old lady to her bed.

"Gentlemen, Edith needs to rest. It seems you may have caused her some distress and though it was probably unintended I must ask you to leave her in peace."

Supported by her carer, the ailing old lady had the last word, "Thank you for coming to see me gentlemen. I feel better for it. It's all the excitement catching up with me. I hope to see you both again." Offering a pale cheek to Sergeant Johnson she said, "It's been nice meeting you, Styxy. God bless you."

I know he'd deny it but my burly bruiser of a sergeant blushed as he pecked her cheek and said with feeling, "It's been a pleasure ma'am."

And I knew he meant it.

THIRTY

Back at the incident room, I'd just addressed Detective Superintendent Davey and my fellow Senior Investigators. It was clear from the buzz of conversation sparking about the room that my debrief had set off a few firecrackers.

The Senior Investigating Officer spoke, "Calm down gentlemen." He waited for everyone to come to order before continuing, "Now you've heard Jim Stirling's latest update you'll realise miracles can happen. Edith Oakley has risen from the dead. Two prodigal sons discovered, Maffi Durnley and Richard Jarvis. PC Jarvis's son is right in the frame for the attempted murder of Miss Oakley and the arson at her home. He may well be involved in Tom Oakley's killing but we're reserving judgement at the moment. We've nothing yet against young Durnley. He may be involved or able to throw some light on what's happened, so we've got to find them both. Bring them in, get stuck into their ribs."

He ambled over to the easel where he leafed through the large pages. On a clean sheet he wrote in bold lettering EDITH OAKLEY/RICHARD JARVIS.

He turned to face us and said, "These then are our new priorities." The Super paused, allowing us time take in the new strategy. Satisfied, he continued, "Our other enquiries will continue apace but the safety of Edith Oakley and the identification and arrest of Jarvis are our main concerns. If we can trace Maffi Durnley and interview him that'll be a bonus. You'll be aware now from the handouts that forensic and the lab has done a masterly job supporting the detectives on the ground, those doing the hard work door knocking and foot slogging. And I can tell you that Jarvis has been connected to the Datsun Bluebird and its contents, which include photographs probably from Tom Oakley's missing wallet. The tyre impressions found at the rear of Edith Oakley's are from that same vehicle. The trousers are still undergoing examination but there are other possibilities there. The finger marks found on the timing devices, whilst not good enough for court, are being searched. They may unofficially support our current line of enquiry. The film showing a man purchasing petrol in containers at a Shell garage has been sent to a specialist laboratory for enhancement. Whether it'll do the trick I don't know. But modern technology such as security cameras is something crime prevention is researching."

DI Alan Lacey sucking on his empty pipe asked, "Did anything come of the red rose enquiry Guv?"

The Super replied, "Yes Alan. Dave Plackett's located a flower shop in town that looks interesting. He's been told that a guy regularly buys a single red rose, nothing else, just a single red rose. Dave's onto it. He'll keep us informed."

DCI Walsh asked, "Can you run through the evidence again that puts Richard Jarvis in the frame Sir? I may have missed something but at present we don't appear to have any hard evidence against him."

Mister Davey replied, "Fair comment Mike. At this stage in the enquiry we are relying heavily on Edith's identification. One: She will say that the man who attacked her in her bed was Richard Jarvis. She recognised his voice. Two: It follows that the attacker was the person who torched her house. Three: The analysis of the petrol left at the scene of the arson matches up with that on the trousers recovered from the Datsun. That puts the arsonist with the vehicle. Four: We can put the vehicle at the scene through the tyre impressions recovered from the slip road at the rear of the house. Five: Photographs found in the car bear Tom Oakley's finger prints so it's a pound to a pinch of snuff that they are his. One, two, three, four, five, once I caught a fish alive. I believe that Mr. Richard Jarvis is the big fish we are talking about. And the evidence even at this point of time gives us enough to lift him out of his pond on suspicion of attempted murder, arson, endangering life etcetera, etcetera." The Super finished his assessment of the facts by adding his own ending to the old rhyme. "Six, seven, eight, nine, ten and we shall not put him back again."

I was impressed and joined in the appreciative clapping that followed the old boy's effort. He certainly had a way of getting over a point, or two or three etcetera, etcetera.

But Mike Walsh wasn't convinced. He questioned the strength of the alleged evidence. "So what you're saying Guv is that we're relying on a sick old lady, who tells us she's been to heaven and back to confer with her dead relatives, identifying her assailant by his voice? I don't know what a good QC would make of that but I've got a good idea. And the other evidence doesn't put this man Jarvis at the scene. Assuming of course there is such a man. It's only Edith's word that he was her attacker. If there is such a man where has he disappeared to? Taken a vacation to see the Almighty? I'm not too impressed Guv."

Davey took off his glasses and nibbled them before addressing the meeting. "Mister Walsh is right. We haven't got positive evidence gentlemen, but I'll pose the DCI a question." He pointed his specs at Walsh, "Mike. Do you have that feeling about Jarvis?"

The DCI shook his head. "At the moment, no Sir."

The spectacles back in place Superintendent Davey re-addressed the group. "I'm sorry that you're not convinced Mike and that you haven't got the gut feeling, but I have. And that's the best test in the world as far as I'm concerned. A detective's gut feeling. Is there anybody here, apart from Mike, hasn't got it now he's in the picture?"

There was no response from the team. They were persuaded. Mike Walsh appeared to be on his own.

An officer queried, "Do we know where to start looking for Jarvis, Guv?"

"No," The Superintendent said. "He came from the past as silently as a shadow and he's left the present the same way. But he'll come. We've got a description, we've got a name, and we'll put a face to it. Then we'll know who we're looking for. He can't hide for ever."

Alan Lacey, now chewing his pipe stem, asked, "Where does that leave us with Tommy Oakley's murder Sir?"

"I've just told you what our new priorities are Mister Lacey. The murder enquiry will not be marginalised as a result. It will be driven with the same vigour and determination. Alright?"

Lacey sucked at his pipe and nodded. A knock on the door took the SIO's attention. He peered over his glasses at Lacey who was nearest to it.

"See who it is please Alan."

The DI partially opened the door and took a document from the caller. Lacey handed it to the Super who read the note on the front, turned it over and opened it.

A huge smile spread across his face.

"Gentlemen. From the lab," he declared. "The foreign

fibres recovered from Tom Oakley's trousers match those from the trousers in the Datsun. Something else for Mister Jarvis to worry about."

On that upbeat note the meeting closed. But I was left with a feeling of uncertainty, though I had the gut feeling about Richard Jarvis I took on board the concerns of DCI Walsh. I'm not one to run with the hare and hunt with the hounds but I could see the danger in making the evidence fit Jarvis, instead of the evidence slipping easily into place. It seemed the train was thundering down the track to Justice but would it bypass Truth?

*

Now our new priorities had been clearly spelled out I arranged for a section of the Special Operations Unit to provide round the clock security for Edith at the clinic. Just in case Jarvis or anyone else decided to take a pop at her. The old lady, comfortable in her surroundings, was unaware of the special attention.

The next breakthrough came that same evening as I worked at my desk.

"Boss, we've lifted Duggy Davis." Styx Johnson's smile was as wide as a piano keyboard. "Stuck him in a dungeon to count bricks till you're ready for him."

I said, "Well done Sarge. Where did you find him?"

"A little bird belonging to Frank Northbridge sang us a song. Told us Duggy was laying off the pop. Doing casual labouring around Derby. Cash in hand jobs."

"Any bother?"

"Naw. Good as gold. Big rough looking guy though. Could be a handful in any bar room bust up."

"Does he know why he's here?"

"Helping with enquiries boss? He's never asked; I've never told him."

"So Frank Northbridge was as good as his word. I'll have to see if I can return the favour."

Sergeant Johnson accompanied me to the Shire Hall cell complex. Like I've said before it never changes from one day to the next. It still oozed the same boiled cabbage stink, sweated in the same putrid atmosphere and echoed to the same ghostlike voices from faceless prisoners behind the same heavy doors. And Duggy Davis was sitting on the same hard bunk which countless others had shared before him. But he wasn't the man I'd expected to see sitting there and I could see how he'd managed to evade capture. He was unrecognisable as Duggy Davis the dirty, unkempt dosser I'd last seen in the Locomotive. Today the big man was clean and shaven, sensibly dressed in recently washed jeans and open necked shirt, wearing a heavy jacket and brown industrial boots. But true to form he viewed us with suspicion as we entered the cell.

I watched his craggy face for a moment before I spoke. "You've given us a bit of a run around Duggy. What've you been up to?"

The big man shrugged his broad shoulders as if he hadn't a care in the world and said, "A bit 'ere, a bit there, ya know."

"No I don't know. You tell me."

"A bit o' duckin' an' divin', bobbin' an' weavin', ya know, this way an' that."

"Don't piss me about Davis."

"I'm not pissin' ya about boss. You asked me I telled ya."

"Tell me again then. What have you been up to?"

"Like I said, a bit a this, a bit a that, ya know. Duckin', divin'."

391

"You are pissin' me off now Davis," I warned him, "Don't push your luck."

The prisoner sat up, squared his shoulders and wiped the back of a big rough hand across his mouth. He certainly was a cool one.

He said casually, "Have you got a smoke boss? I 'ant 'ad one sin' I were lifted."

Johnson and I didn't use them but we carried cigarettes for such occasions; tools of the trade. Styx flipped one toward the prisoner. He caught it in those pan-sized hands. The DS left another pink scar on the graffiti-covered wall as he rasped a match against it and lit up the ciggie. The prisoner cupped both hands around it as excited as a kid with a lollipop. With head laid back he inhaled deeply before blowing out a stream of smoke.

"Right," I said, "Now you've been seen to let's get down to business. And cut out the crap. Why did you do a runner after we'd seen you in the Loco?"

"I din't do a runner, I just moved on. I weren't going to stay around an' get lifted. I were scared."

"Scared? What have you got to be scared about? A bloke your size and with your reputation. I can't imagine much out there bothering you."

"We all get scared sometime. Don't we mister? And I were scared an' I still am."

"Bit of a psychoanalyst now hey Duggy? You were scared of being caught because of what you'd done to Tommy."

"Done to Tommy? Gi' over man." Davis was feeling more relaxed, even cocky. "What I done to Tommy? I dint do owt to Tommy. We were mates. Been skippering, ya know, sleeping rough for years. There were no trouble between Tommy and me."

392

As I was speaking Sergeant Johnson was delving into Davis's large brown property envelope. He took something out and handed it to me.

Davis, drawing on his cigarette watched us, straining to hear what we were saying in our close head-huddle. Returning to the prisoner I flourished the object from the envelope in front of him. I could almost see the cogs in his head grinding away as he looked at it.

I stuck it straight in front of his nose and said somewhat triumphantly, "Explain this Duggy."

Davis took another long drag and continued to stare at the brown leather wallet in my hand.

He came straight out with it. "It's Tommy's. Got his initials on."

I said sharply, "Ten out of ten. I know whose it is. Why have you got it?"

"Fount it," he snapped.

I'd heard that pathetic explanation a thousand times before. It was answer number two, following close on the heels of answer number one 'It's a fair cop guv' in the Crook's Handbook of Replies to Police Officers. Why can't they be more adventurous with their verbals? Or at least try and make life a little more interesting for me.

"Found it where?" I asked cynically

"On't railway lines."

"When?"

"That naight."

"This is getting a bit like pulling teeth Duggy. Let's get to it. You took it off Tommy after you'd smashed him over the head. When he wasn't capable of defending himself. Cowardly. Like a thief in the night. Some tough guy you are."

The prisoner still possessed some spirit and pride in

his reputation, he didn't like being classed a coward.

"That's a load of bollocks and you know it. That's why I went on't run. Cos I knew you lot 'ud set me up."

"Why should we set you up?"

"Lookin' after yer own. Ya alus do. Like ya doin' now. Likes a me is nowt to you lot. Just another crime number cleared up. Don't matter who done it so long as yer books's straight."

"Interesting Duggy," I said. "Very interesting in the circumstances but it doesn't answer the question. Where and how did you get this wallet? And before you come back with some stupid answer, just think on the fact that it could send you to jail for life. Remember? Murder, life."

Something I'd said must have struck home because he suddenly changed from being the awkward idiot into a compliant defeatist.

He yelled, "Alraight! Alraight! Don't gu on about it. I know when I'm licked. But I din't murder nobody. I'd seen Tommy earlier that naight in't Black Swan down Albert Street. Round't corner from't Loco. I went to meet him later on to walk back tut railway carriages. I missed him so I went off on me own. Then I seen him raight up in front on me an' I were goin' ta shout. But then I seen this bloke. He were like follerin' Tommy. Steppin in and out ut shadders like. So I did't same. Tommy kept stoppin' an' lookin round then he'd be shadder boxin' like he alus dun. He went ovver for a piss int' hedge but afore he could do owt this bloke come out ut shadders and cracked him straight on his nut with this long thing. I heard't crack from where I were. Tommy din't have a chance. He went straight down. And this maniac were still smashing 'is head. It were 'orrible. Tommy never knew wor hit him. He just went down like a sack a taters. The bastard

394

'ad done him. Poor old Tommy. No matter what, he din't deserve to go like that."

Davis was shaking. He drew the last remnants of nicotine from the cigarette end held between thumb and forefinger as if it were the last he would ever take. Styx Johnson lit another and threw it to him. He caught it deftly and took a long pull. I waited until he'd settled.

"What happened then?" I asked.

"This bloke looked round, then pulled Tommy up and dragged him intut hedge and shoved him down't banking. I waited till he were out a sight and went and looked over't hedge. He were stood between Tommy's legs and draggin' him ontut lines. He stopped though and started goin' through his pockets. He took Tommy's wallet out his jacket, looked through it, took summat out and put it in his pocket. Then slung it. He started pullin' Tommy again. He were just gettin' him ont' rails when a train come. He left Tommy and legged it. That were it Mister. 'Onest I had nowt to do wi it. I just went down to look out for Tommy. But it were no good. He were long gone. A bloody mess. And his leg were chopped off an all. It were 'orrible. Tommy din't deserve to die like that."

"And the wallet?"

"I admit I picked that up and kept it. More like a keepsake from my old mate. There were nowt in it. No money nor nowt."

"Any documents, photos, anything like that?"

"No boss. It were empty. All Tommy's photos had gone. I suppose that maniac took 'em. I din't."

"Did you know Tommy's killer?"

Davis hung his head again and drew on his cigarette. He didn't answer.

"I don't want to have to ask again Davis. Did you know the killer?" I demanded.

He mumbled, "I seen him."

"We're back to pulling teeth again. Where did you see him? Do you know him? Do you know his name?"

"I don't know his name but I've seen him before. That's why I done a runner."

"Why did you do a runner?" I asked impatiently.

"Cos I seen 'im." He looked from me to Johnson and back again, not too sure whether to unburden his soul, then he blurted out, "I seen him in't Swan a couple a times when I were wi' Tommy. He just sat on his own, watchin' like. I thought he were a coppers nark. So when he done Tommy I cleared off."

"Why didn't you report what you'd seen Duggy?"

"Do you think I'm that daft boss? Grass up a nark that could smash up Tommy like that? My life wouldn't a been worth a piece a second hand shithouse paper. So I kept off the booze and went on me toes."

So that was that for the moment. Duggy's story had a certain ring of truth about it. The search for the elusive dosser had come to an end. Instead of an offender he'd probably turn out to be a valuable witness. And the investigation ground on. I banged him up for the time being. That would give us time to check out his story and show him some pictures of bad guys. In the meantime he'd have to bum somebody else's smokes, while he counted bricks.

Reflecting upon the changed situation as we left the cellblock I said to Sgt. Johnson, "A day's a long time in police work Styx. Things don't always turn out the way you expect. We build up a case but it's just a sandcastle on the beach. There one minute, gone the next, washed away by the tide.

And all we're left with is nice clean sand waiting for the next new sandcastle."

Johnson, not too sure of my philosophical outpouring, looked at me sceptically and replied, "Sure boss. I'll take a statement off Duggy and exhibit the wallet. And I'll try not to knock over your next sandcastle."

THIRTY-ONE

SUNDAY
LATE EVENING

My telephone rang. I took the call at my desk. It was DS Plackett. He was excited and bursting to tell me about it.

"Boss I think we're in."

"Why Dave. What's happened?"

"The young girl at the florist's rung. They were just closing when a bloke answering Jarvis's description came in and bought a single red rose. We're doing a stake out of the churchyard. Just in case."

"That's good news. Get set for an all night job. I'll fix up a dog man to be on standby. I'll come over with Sergeant Johnson and give you some back up. Any problems?"

"None that I can see boss. We'll see you there." He hung up.

I updated Mr. Davey and made the necessary arrangements.

It was nearly eleven o'clock when Johnson and I clambered over the wall next to the vicarage into the churchyard of St. Luke's at Whalley. We'd left our vehicle at the nearby infants' school. Dave Plackett and Pete Jones were already concealed in the vicinity of the Oakley family grave.

It was a dark night. Low cloud prevented any moonlight

breaking through. We picked our way silently between the gravestones, avoiding pots and overgrown mounds. The black bulk of the church and its finger of a spire reaching up into the eerie darkness reminded me of something out of a Gothic Horror movie. Shapeless shadows appeared to move in and out of the darkness creating uncertainty in my mind. The cold night air moving through outstretched branches of the yew trees whispered and sighed. And all the while the ancient guardians of the churchyard swayed this way and that, distorting the already confused imagery. The muted sounds of the burial ground were all that penetrated the heavy mantle of pitch-black night. As we settled into our watch the clock high in the church tower struck eleven.

I signalled to Styx to take up a position over to the right whilst I watched the front gates leading into the churchyard. I couldn't see Plackett or Jones but knew they were well placed to react in an instant.

A persistent blanket of low cloud obscured the moon's silvered face and the night grew colder. I folded my arms across my chest and hugged myself to keep warm. It didn't help but made me feel better. Suddenly a shadow darker than most, seemingly floating above the ground, glided by the side of the church. I watched it, not sure if it was really there, as it came and went like a phantom. I continued watching as it flitted toward the Oakley grave and Dave Plackett. Moments later the silence was shattered by raised voices and the sound of a struggle.

I was up and running in an instant with Johnson close on my heels. At the graveside a violent fight was taking place. The tall figure dressed in black and wearing a black ski mask was punching, kicking and gouging, causing the two detectives plenty of problems. Cursing and swearing sliced through the night air sharp as razor blades. We piled in. Bodies struggled and rolled about on top of the grave.

Bulldog Pete Jones finally pinned the man to the ground then hauled him to his feet. I reached out to unmask him. Suddenly the restrained man exploded into action once more, taking Jones by surprise and throwing him off. He brushed me aside with ease and escaped into the darkness.

"The bastard's away," yelled Jonesy.

We took off after him. But our shambolic quartet had been outsmarted by the man in black who then proceeded to out-run us. He was loose again. Back to square one. A single red rose crushed into the churned up earth and gravel during the melee was all that remained of the phantom visitor. But we weren't finished yet, not by a long chalk. I had a contingency plan in place. I radioed control and called in our back up. I'd positioned him in the area which was just as well, as it looked as though we were going to need all the help we could get. It was going to be one of those nights. I could feel it in my water and my twisted beak.

With the dog van parked up I briefed the handler who quickly made a cast. Almost immediately his German Shepherd dog, Simba, set off at a pace across the fields towards Scarcliffe Park. He was onto something. Sporting cuts and bruises we jogged behind the enthused handler and his eager canine working on its tracking leash.

As St. Luke's clock struck the three-quarter hour the dog handler called out, "He's raised something. Just up front. Stay back, I'm going to investigate."

In the distance I could hear the distinct sound of something, someone, crashing through the undergrowth in the wood.

"That's him. A pound to a penny," yelled Jonesy and urged us to "Come on."

"He won't outrun old Fido there," panted Sergeant Johnson. "Sooner him than me."

The dog handler shouted back to us, "He's just crossed the railway lines and broken out onto the lane. He's heading for the road. He won't get away. Simba's onto him now."

We forced our way through the wood and scrambled over a rickety fence. Pressing on we crossed a railway line before clambering up a steep bank onto the lane. In darkness the going was tough. Then, as if aware of our plight, the moon slipped its mantle of low cloud bathing the countryside in moonlight. Now I could make out the running figure of the dog handler some way in front. Then I caught sight of a figure ahead of his pursuers. He was still running well but the dog, now free of his leash, was rapidly closing him down. At a bend in the lane the fugitive approached a low wall on the right hand side taking it in his stride like a steeple chaser. His scream was short-lived as the mail train burst out of the tunnel below, speeding through the night smashing into his falling body.

I was knackered and the rest of the team were in a similar state. We were all showing signs of our exertions as we joined the dog handler at the low wall of the railway bridge. With his dog sitting alongside him the officer peered over the edge to the tracks below.

He was taking in great gulps of air. It helped hide his emotions, after all it wasn't every day that a chase ended like this. After a few deep breaths he regained his composure. We were faring no better as we leaned over the bridge, looking down, shocked at what we'd witnessed. Hard-nosed detectives or not this was a shocker.

Along the railway lines converging in the distance I could see orange flashes sparking from the wheels of the engine, grinding and screeching as they responded to the emergency brakes, steel to steel, forcing the resisting beast to an unscheduled stop.

The whole stage on which the drama had been enacted was still moonlit until a scud of dark cloud drifted across the moon's cold face. The rolling shadows swept away the light and brought down the curtain. Darkness closed about our stunned group. I reflected that though it had only been moments since that fateful scream it seemed an age. And down the line, as if warning us of what to expect, the guard lights on the back of the stationary diesel locomotive flashed incessantly; blood red.

I was the first to break the heavy silence. "There's not much to see down there. The mail train's hit him full on. It's going to be a mopping up job. Buckets, not a body bag for this one."

"Can't help you with buckets boss but there's plenty of bin bags in the dog van," said Sergeant Johnson in his usual sensitive way.

I radioed for back up from SOCO and to their credit they arrived in double quick time. Having set up emergency lighting I left them to get on with their job. There was no need for an ambulance in this case. They weren't in the market for transporting body parts to the morgue. That would be left to me and my team. We grabbed a bundle of black plastic bags and scrambled down the railway banking. I thought about the runner. It'd had been a helluva way to die. He must have panicked when he saw the dog on his heels and mistook the bridge for a low wall. I'll bet he was surprised when he found he was running on fresh air and couldn't fly. But then he didn't have much time to think about it. The mail train put a stop to that. In fact it put a stop to everything. And he didn't need a first class stamp for onward delivery to wherever he was going.

It's no secret that I don't like post mortems. And I relish recovering body parts from railway lines in rural locations during the hours of darkness even less. At least the emergency lighting brought to the scene by SOCO helped. But slipping and sliding on blood, brains and guts is bad news anytime. Here in the damp and cold of a railway cutting in the early hours I found it, well not to place too fine a point on it, shit! Pure shit!

Sergeant Johnson didn't see it like that. He'd been given a job by his boss and he set off with a will. This wasn't a good guy he had to scrape up. It wasn't as if it was a kid, a woman or an old fella deserving his sympathy. Whoever it was he'd got a vicious streak, had a go at him in the cemetery. Got the cuts and bruises to show for it, so he had no feelings for him. After SOCO had finished their David Bailey bit, lumps of flesh and splintered bone, miscellaneous mashed up limbs, ripped and bloodied clothing all found their way into Styx Johnson's black plastic bin liners.

After a time he shouted to me, "Only want his head and a few bits and pieces and we'll have the full set boss."

From down the line Pete Jones called back, "Get your arse down here then Sarge. I've found what you're looking for. If it's not his I'll throw it back."

Black humour helped at times like this.

I joined Johnson, Jones and Plackett. We stared at the severed head on the track, its features distorted beneath a tattered, bloodied ski mask. Through the eyeholes it stared back at us wild eyed and terrible. Impaled by the probing shafts of light from our torches the awful face shone China white. Set beneath those intimidating eyes I saw a hideous gaping mouth, the chamber of that final tortured scream, frozen in terror, as if carved from stone. Torn from life the ghastly visage in death made not a sound. I don't know about the others but it was thunderous to my ears. I shivered.

Styx Johnson quickly brought me back to reality. Stating the obvious he held the severed head by the hair and declared, "Fucking hell boss! Not a pretty sight now is he?"

No one answered. It had been quite a shock. There would be plenty of time for discussion and analysis at the later debrief. Like me I guess they'd seen enough of the grisly object. Styx shrugged and dropped it into a bin liner.

"And what about this?" I said as I took a handkerchief from my pocket and carefully unfolded it. I shone my torch onto it. The photograph was creased and bloodied. "This was clutched in his right hand, he must have been holding it all the time he was running."

DS Johnson peered at it and said, "It's Rita Oakley and PC Jarvis." And then offhanded as you like he said, "That's the lot boss. Better get it back to the butcher's department."

I nodded. He threw the plastic bag onto his shoulder like a sailor's kit bag. Jonesy followed suit with his bloody baggage. I carried the head and we set off in Indian file back to the bridge. As we stepped out on the sleepers Styx said dispassionately, "Goodbye and good riddance."

*

Back on the bridge with chest heaving and tongue lolling from the cavernous mouth in his leonine head, the faithful Simba sought his master's pleasure through baleful eyes. The handler ruffled his dog's black mane and said reassuringly, "Good lad. He shouldn't have tried to outrun you."

*

Talk in the incident room, not unnaturally, centred upon the identity and bizarre death of the masked man. Superintendent Davey, in a more than usually sombre tone, addressed the assembled officers.

"You will all be aware by now of the night's events. Some of you were there. Though the night ended tragically, as far as the investigation goes it was a result." He paused for a moment to gather his thoughts. "It's been an unpleasant job attempting to identify the man who died on the railway line. As you can imagine, having been hit full-on by a speeding train there wasn't much to work with. But the lab and fingerprint staff have stuck to the unenviable task and come up with an ID. It is positive and as such will bring our enquiry to a close. But before we pull down the curtain I'd like to express my thanks to you all for your hard work and professionalism and I'll hand you over to DI Stirling for the final debrief."

There hadn't been the usual "end of a successful enquiry" triumphalism in the old detective's delivery, rather the opposite. But that was understandable given the circumstances.

I took my place before the troops and thanked the governor on their behalf for his comments. He'd led us to a good result and now it was wash up time. The last debrief. This was the part I liked. Putting the enquiry to bed. I got straight on with it.

"So now you know, straight from the horse's mouth. It's back to divisions for most of you. But the job isn't finished yet. The loose ends have to be tidied up and you need to know where your enquiries have taken us. How we can be sure we've got the right man. See that we've put all the pieces of the jigsaw together and produced a complete picture, a true picture, the truth. I'll start by asking that question again. Who killed PC Jarvis? The key to the whole case, including the killing of Tom and the attack upon Edith, who for your information is doing well, settled in her retirement home."

I went to the flip chart flicking back to the list. "You'll see a couple of additions since we last looked at it. We now know PC Jarvis was the father of Rita's illegitimate son, Richard Jarvis. We know Sergeant Jack Smithurst told Bade Durnley where the duty patrol would be on the night of the officer's murder. Durnley told his right hand man Wilson, who bragged to Rita about it and she told her sister Edith. She in all innocence told her brother Tom. Later he was driven to a murderous frenzy when his sister died in childbirth. He blamed Constable Jarvis. Knowing where he could find him he drove to the woods on his motor bike, confronted the Constable, and, in the age-old tradition of the village, challenged him to fight. Sportingly, some may feel, he allowed the officer to remove his cape and other cumbersome items before proceeding to beat him to death with his fists. He told his sister Edith what he'd done."

"How do we know all that, Jim?" asked Mike Walsh. He was still a little sceptical and wanted reassurance that we'd got it right.

"OK Mike, Edith's poured her heart out. Told me everything. And in pit villages in those days that's how family honour was upheld. Man to man. No quarter given. But unfortunate for PC Jarvis it was a maniacal Tommy Oakley he was up against. No contest. After that, Tom's decline into the gutter was inevitable. Chief Superintendent Rawlings, Sergeant Smithurst and Jess Fallows set up Durnley and

Wilson for murder knowing they were innocent. The Fox saw the advantage to his career in hanging two well-known poachers, rather than a drunken, broken down ex-fighter. Tom, it seems, was happy to leave matters as they were and kept his mouth shut. Fallows took his pieces of silver and Smithurst took revenge on Durnley and Wilson. He'd never wanted anyone killed, but I suspect because he'd told them where his men would be that night he felt responsible for PC Jarvis's death. To this day he doesn't know that Tommy killed PC Jarvis. Rawlings kept that back from him. He probably believes that Durnley and Wilson brought somebody in to do the job using the information he'd supplied. Bad result. His constable was killed. If he hadn't said anything to the poachers it's likely the whole tragedy wouldn't have occurred. Sergeant Jack has a lot to regret and more to answer for."

Sergeant Johnson asked, "What's going to happen to Smithurst and Fallows Sir?"

"The truth's caught up with them. They'll face charges."

I continued, "Now we come up to date. Richard Jarvis, on the death of his adoptive parents, learns about his biological parents and seeks them out. Tracing his mother's sister Edith, he learns from her of his father PC Jarvis and his death at the hands of Tommy Oakley. Richard Jarvis set out to revenge his father's death. It wasn't difficult for him to locate Tommy and biding his time followed him one night from the Black Swan. With a weapon he brutally smashed in his skull and then made a botched attempt to make the killing appear like suicide. Duggy Davis saw him batter his mate to death. He goes on the run because he's scared."

Mike Walsh quizzed, "Scared of what Jim?"

"Scared he'd get set up. Thought he knew the killer. Seen him in the Mucky Duck a couple of times apparently watching Tommy. Suspected he was a police informant."

A wit quipped, "That rules out Chief Inspector Woofter then boss. He doesn't know where the Mucky Duck is and he wouldn't know a snout if you stuck one in the middle of the car park."

Laughter rippled around the room. There was that end of term feeling about the place, almost a party atmosphere, but that would come later. They'd been involved in a successful enquiry but now the pressure was off, self-discipline drifting. They really wanted to go partying. I knew the signs but they'd have to wait for the end of session bell.

"All right folks, "I said. "Get it together. We've not finished the job yet. Just bear with me a little longer."

The room settled.

"And so finally, fearing that Edith would talk, Richard Jarvis decided to kill her, again an attempt to make murder look like an accident. Again it went wrong and Edith survived to point the finger at him. You may like to know some of the other twists and turns in the saga."

"I'd like to know where the mysterious Sergeant Evans fits in Sir?" an officer said.

"Okay. With such poor security at HQ Jarvis managed to pass himself off as a Sergeant Evans and gain access to the old files store room and the Durnley Wilson file. He went through it and removed various documents. Incidentally, the handwriting at HQ reception and the archives has been analysed by a graphologist at the lab who is satisfied that they are Richard Jarvis's. The missing post mortem photos of his father and the medical report from the file were found in Jarvis's flat with the word 'Revenge' scrawled over them in his own blood. That gives some indication of his cunning and his mental state. The murder weapon, recovered from his home, bore traces of blood of the same group as Tom's and Edith's and his Doc Marten boots match the impressions at Edith's. They also tested positive for blood. The film taken at the Shell garage of the man filling two plastic containers with petrol has been processed and enhanced. The man is identified as Richard Jarvis aka Sergeant Evans. The lady at the flower shop has since identified him by photograph, as has the assistant in the electrical shop where he bought the timers for his incendiary devices. The photographs found in the Datsun and the one recovered from the body are from Tom's wallet. And there you have it ladies and gentlemen. Two for the price of one. Three with Edith's escapade. And so the truth triumphs and justice is not only done but seen to be done. Summarily in Richard Jarvis's case, brought to book by the very train that he had marked out to make Tom's murder look like suicide. Job done! All that remains now is for me to thank you all for your efforts and I'll see you at the next one. Oh! There is just one more thing. A pie and a pint have been laid on at the Loco."

No one moved. The whole team sat looking at me waiting expectantly for the punch line. The one that I didn't deliver. I deliberately withheld it and awaited the outcome as I gathered up my papers. After a moment I looked up. In mock surprise at seeing them all still sitting there I asked, "Still here? Thought you were gagging for a pint or two."

A detective answered, "We are boss, but we want to know who's in the bin bags?"

"I've already told you who's in the bin bags, Richard Jarvis alias David Evans."

"Yeh but they're just names boss. Can't you put a face to the names?"

Sergeant Johnson came up with a suggestion. He kept a straight face as he said, "What about the Pathologist's photo from the post mortem. You know boss from the railway smash? That's a good likeness."

I was already sifting through the photographic evidence. "Here we are. See if that'll help."

The inquisitive detective took the picture eagerly. He looked at the distorted face screaming out from the severed head. In shocked disbelief he gasped, "Fucking hell boss, Andy McLean. What a fucking mess!"

The photograph did the rounds, passed from hand to eager hand. There was no doubt now whose remains were in the bin bag. The late Police Constable Andy McLean aka Richard Jarvis aka David Evans. My little charade was over. To paraphrase Sinatra, now the end was near. The final pieces of the jigsaw were about to be slotted into place.

There was a stunned silence before I responded. "Yes. McLean. Having learned from Edith about the killing of his father PC Jarvis, as well as the hanging of two innocent men wrongly convicted for the crime, he devised a plan to kill Tommy Oakley the man responsible. He resigned his position at the bank. Though we have been referring to him as Richard Jarvis son of PC Jarvis, we now know at adoption he had been provided with a new identity. He became Andrew McLean. He subsequently applied for and was accepted as a probationary constable with the Notts force. With eyes set firmly on murder he bided his time planning each move to that end. It took him some three years during which time he used the system to get onto CID as an Aide. During those years his mind was consumed by an ever-increasing psychotic hatred for his unsuspecting victim. But his plan was coming together, he was in the ideal situation, this was the chosen time for him to execute his plan and kill Tommy Oakley. As an aide in local CID he had calculated that he would be involved, even if in only a minor role, in the investigation which he knew would follow the murder of Tommy Oakley. He believed that would put him in a favourable position, enabling him to track the progress of the enquiry and deflect any suspicion away from him if it ever arose. His evil plan was murder pure and simple. I don't know what he was like working in civvy street but he wasn't a very good copper and an even worse villain. Sure, McLean had a genuine grievance and who knows how any of us would have reacted in similar circumstances. His father was killed by Tommy Oakley and his mother died soon after his birth. He was an orphan. He was also pompous and full of his own importance but in the end he was victim to his own arrogance and sick mind. It was two strikes and out Mister McLean. That's it. Dismiss folks. Have a good evening."

There was an undignified rush for the exit and the Loco.

*

But that wasn't the end of the affair. Back at his allotment Sergeant Jack Smithurst's troubled mind probably thought on what he had told me. *"There's some as aren't here as might have been if truth were known and some is here as shouldn't be because truth weren't told."*

He was found in his allotment shed, a bottle of Paraquat weed killer lying beside him. He had settled the account. The note written on an empty seed packet in Jack's distinctive copperplate said it all.

"Mr. Stirling. You'll capture that elusive something without my help so please forgive me for I know I have sinned."

*

In the meantime, on the Wembourne Estate, Jess Fallows prepared to be evicted from the gamekeeper's cottage. The past few days had taken their toll on the former poacher. His wife had left him and, having wandered around the empty rooms, he went outside and stood before the now-silent kennels. His world had collapsed about him. It was too much. Walking slowly back to the house he took down from above the kitchen door the only friend he had left in the world. Hugging it to him for a brief moment the sad old man kissed both barrels of the trusty 12 bore shotgun. Then in one determined movement pushed them into his mouth pulling the trigger for the last time.

*

The final act in this bloody drama was played out in my office. I opened an envelope addressed to me, marked "Personal." I recognised McLean's writing. Inside was a copy of a birth certificate stapled to an official-looking letter. I read the certificate first.

> *"Mafeking DURNLEY. Born 15th August 1945. Cresswell, Derbyshire. Father: Baden Powell Durnley. Itinerant Dealer. Mother: Megan Durnley. Seasonal Fruit Picker."*

Interested but puzzled I read the covering letter.

> *"Mafeking Durnley aged 2 years, taken into our care 1947. 1956 considered suitable for training aboard school ship 'Arethusa' in preparation for a career at sea. The child was re-named on coming into our care, hitherto he will be known as James STIRLING."*

The letter was signed, *Superintendent, The Shaftsbury Children's Home Society.*

I stared at the letter. I stared at the names Mafeking Durnley, Baden Powell Durnley, Megan Durnley and my own – James Stirling. I thought of the visitations and bad dreams. I remembered those haunted eyes and desolate graves. I remembered those, then unexplained, emotions aroused by the tragic deaths of the family. And I stared at the note scrawled across the bottom of the letter.

"When Justice fails what now; Anarchy and Revenge Inspector?"

McLean was resurrected in the written word and was speaking to me from the grave. He'd known all along.

My head pounded. My mind stretched as taut as a t'gallant in a fierce north westerly. My eyes misted over, smarting. My old bo'sun wouldn't have approved. I was showing emotion, showing pain, I was crying and I rang Sandy.

Acknowledgements

As the author of Murder Pure and Simple a crime novel I take this opportunity to acknowledge the use of verse 73 of 'Rubáiyát of Omar Khayyám translated by Edward Marlborough Fitzgerald (1809-1883) illustrated by Anthony Rado, Printed c 1956 by The Victory Press, Leicester, England, reproduced in Chapter 18 of my book.

I further acknowledge the use of verse 6 of 'The Norman and the Saxon' and a line from 'If', both by Joseph Rudyard Kipling (1865-1936) reproduced in Chapter 2 and 19 of my novel.

I confirm that I have no intention of claiming these works as my own and respect the total ownership of the writers who created and left them for posterity to inspire others.

Carl T. Jackson BA (Hons) MA.

Author's Notes

I am sure the reader will have noted that throughout the novel there is no mention of DNA (deoxyribonucleic acid) or digital fingerprint systems being used by detectives to assist in their investigations. The reason is simple. During those years there were no such facilities avaliable to them. Blood was categoriesd using the ABO blood group and group D of the RH system or one of the minor varieties of the groups. By today's standards they were quite basic. Their evidential value was limited. With the discovery of what we know today as DNA fingerprinting the National DNA Database (NDNAD) was set up in 1987. The use of DNA evidence that same year saw the first criminal caught and subsequently convicted for the double rape and the murder of two young women in Leicestershire. The system is now an integral part of cime investigation worldwide.

The manual fingerprint system used by UK police forces for identification and prosecution in judicial cases was replaced in 1998. LiveScan digital fingerprint units are now standard police equipment. The National Fingerprint Collection (IDENT1) successfully uses automated searching to compare finger marks at crime scenes complemented by expert evaluation.

Carl T. Jackson BA (Hons) MA.